I0744436

ABOUT BROKEN TIES

I was the hero once, until I was betrayed.

Now I'm something else. I am the shadow that haunts the night. I am a hunter, a protector. I am Jonas Castillo.

For years I've existed on the edge of the dark, protecting innocents who can't protect themselves. Until... her. Jessica "JJ" Jones. The bane of my existence. A bright light in the dark. The crack in my armor. A loud, argumentative beautiful crack in my armor.

But first, there's a more immediate concern. JJ is running scared. And to protect her I might have to break the vow I made years ago.

BROKEN TIES

M. MALONE

NANA MALONE

ISBN-13: 978-1-946961-31-0

BROKEN TIES

PART 1

CHAPTER ONE

Jonas

She was lying to me.

I eyed my client, Mira Ashton, carefully. She'd been beaten and abused by her ex-husband for years. She was still cagey around men. But since I was one of the people who'd gotten her away from that asshole, she shouldn't be afraid of me. So why was this whole situation off?

I'd met her at the café just on the edge of the theater district as she'd asked me to. Normally, we would do a site visit at her home but given her history, I didn't think anything was unusual about her asking to meet here. But now I wasn't sure.

Something wasn't right.

"Mira, you sure you're okay?"

Her gaze snapped to mine. "I'm fine. It's just that it's really crowded in here."

"We don't have to stay here. If you would like, I can drive you back to your apartment." She lived about three or four blocks from here.

Her eyes went wide. "No. This is fine."

"Are you sure? Did your husband call? If you're scared or unsure, we can help with that. That's the purpose behind these check-ins. We do this for all our clients. It's no trouble at all for us to look into another matter for you if someone's bothering you."

She shook her head. "It's nothing like that. I just—I just hate that I needed you in the first place. That I got myself into the situation. That's not who I am; that's not me. I don't like how everything turned out, but I'm fine. I just have to learn how to deal."

I nodded. "It's going to take some time. Just know that he can't hurt you. We got him out of the house. And you got a restraining order against him. It's not in his best interest to come near you. If he breaks that restraining order, he goes back to jail. He doesn't want that. So you're safe."

She shifted her gaze away. "Yeah. Safe."

My brow furrowed again. "Can I get you another slice of pie? Something else to eat?"

"No. I think I'm just going to head home."

"Okay, let me give you a ride. I parked just across the street."

For a long moment her gaze lifted and met mine, holding it. It was as if she wanted to tell me something. Wanted me to hear something. But what the hell was she trying to say?

"No, I think I'm just going to walk."

I wanted to argue with that. But she set her jaw, and I'd seen that look before. It was the I'm-not-fucking-around look. It was the look people got when they set their minds about something and had no intention of changing it. "All right. You have a good night now, okay?"

She scooted out of the booth and stood. "I will. Thank you for everything. You don't know—" She cut herself off and sighed deeply before continuing. "You, all of you at Blake Security, you don't know what you have done for me. Thank you."

I waited exactly thirty seconds before following her. I had no idea who the hell Noah had to blow to get special curbside parking access around most of the city, but all of Blake Security's cars were equipped with special plates so we could park anywhere. Farther down the block, she hopped into a taxi.

It took her the few blocks to her apartment. I figured she might not have wanted to deal with the summertime crowds in the theater district, as it was packed.

When she reached her apartment, she climbed out of the cab and stared up at the building for a moment. I parked across the street and watched her intently. And then I saw what she was looking at. Someone passed by the front window. Someone was walking around.

My eyes narrowed. It wasn't so much that she had a guest that had me concerned. It was that I recognized the movement of the guest. The guy was mostly in shadow, but I recognized the way he walked and rolled his shoulders. That was her ex-husband. What the fuck was he doing in her house?

Mira's building didn't have a doorman. Luckily, I had a key. I tried to wait patiently until she was up the elevator before following in the service elevator behind her. It was farther down the hall than her apartment, but I'd be able to observe her. *Stalker much?* Damn it, I just wanted to make sure she was okay.

You need to let this go. She's not Emma.

I shoved away the painful memory of the woman from all those years ago. The one I'd been unable to help. The one that had cost me my career. Probably better if I didn't think about her right now.

I shook it off. Mira wasn't Emma. For starters, I could help Mira. I watched from the shadows as she stuck the key in the lock, but the door opened on its own and she was dragged inside. Just as I was about to head down the hallway, the door to the stairway opened and someone yanked me into the stairwell.

I dislodged the grip in less than a second and had my hands

up, ready to fight. It took a moment longer to realize I knew the asshole who was trying to pick a fight. "Noah? What the fuck?"

"Matthias notified me that your GPS was headed to Mira's place. Did she meet you at the café?"

"Yeah, dumbass, she did." I ran a hand through my hair. "But she was acting cagey and weird. So I wanted to make sure she was okay and got home safe. There's a guy in her apartment right now."

Noah sighed. "I know."

"What do you mean you know?" I glared at him.

"Look, when Matthias came to check in on her last week, I noticed her ex in the doorway. She hugged him. Kissed him. They're back together."

"Son of a bitch."

I tried to yank open the stairwell door, but Noah stopped me. "You need to follow the Disney princess's advice and let it go. Mira made her choice."

No, this wasn't Noah talking. "We got her away from him. He has to have something on her, be scaring her or something."

Noah shook his head. "No. We've tailed her for over a week. She's back with him."

"We have to do something. After everything we did to get her away from him, after everything we went through to keep her safe ..."

"I know. But this is her choice. You can't want something for her she doesn't want for herself. You have to let it go. We can't intervene unless she asks us to."

I shoved him. I had to help her. Problem was, Noah was just as big as I was. Not to mention the guy was good. Assassin good. But that didn't stop me from fighting with him. I had to get to her.

"Look man, you're one of my best friends. I'm happy to fight with you so you can let off some steam, but this is a fight you can't win. Not with me, or with her. She is making her choice. You can't make it for her."

Noah's last words finally sank in. I couldn't make her choices for her. So just like before, all I could do was stand by and watch as someone I cared about set herself on a path for disaster.

I sagged against the wall. "This is bullshit."

Noah clapped me on the shoulder. "I know. But how about we focus on the people we can actually help? We'll be here when she comes back. But for now, let her go."

I knew what he was saying. But I had zero intention of letting this go. Sometimes people needed to be saved from themselves.

———

Jessica

"ALL I'M SAYING IS that he's a pain in the ass. I mean, can you believe that he told me I was being a prima donna? *Me.* A prima donna! I'm the least prima donna person I know."

I spun around on my stool as I watched my best friend style a mannequin for an upcoming fashion show. A quick glance told me what I needed to style the makeup to match.

"Actually, maybe go with the orange belt? I can do a really pretty gold shimmer with that."

Lucia Blake raised an eyebrow. "JJ, I have *no idea* why he would call you a prima donna," she said with a smirk.

I rolled my eyes. "Okay, I like things a certain way. There's nothing wrong with that."

Lucia giggled. "I'm not saying there is. I'm saying I think you and Jonas like to push each other's buttons. Why don't you just give in and say you like him already?"

"I do *not* like him. Matter of fact, I *hate* him."

Never mind that half the time I wanted to pick a fight with

him just because he got my blood pumping. And also, never mind the fact that my lady parts throbbed every time he gave me one of his annoying smirks.

"Just because he thinks he saved my life, it doesn't mean he can say whatever he wants to me. Bigger men than him have tried." Except that wasn't true. Jonas was big, and I actually liked the way he talked to me.

"Honey, he *did* actually save your life," Lucia pointed out oh so helpfully.

I shuddered when I remembered the fire that razed my apartment to ash. It had nearly consumed me, too. I'd been asleep in my bedroom when the fire started.

The memory of choking on smoke made my stomach turn. I hadn't been able to wake up at first, almost like I'd taken a sleeping pill or something. Next thing I knew, Jonas was bursting through my bedroom door even as smoke licked at him from the living area.

Management said it was an electrical fire. The building had been renovated about fifteen years prior, but they said something went wrong with the wiring between the trio of apartments on the corner. My place took the brunt of the damage, so now I was living at Blake Security headquarters. The view at the penthouse was better, but I missed my own space.

"Okay, fine, you have a point. He did save my life, but he's still a caveman. And a jackass. Saving my life does not preclude that."

Lucia snorted. "You may have a point."

The man was just so damned frustrating. I wanted to hit him, *and* I wanted to jump his bones. I knew that wasn't a healthy response. So I was just going to keep that to myself. Besides, my history with men involved picking exactly the wrong kind of guy. And Jonas was the wrong kind of guy. Besides, he hated me just as much as I hated him.

Which isn't very much at all.

I shoved that thought down. So what if I occasionally busted out the battery-operated boyfriend when I was thinking about him in my bed alone at night. So? Lots of women did that. It didn't mean I was a glutton for punishment or that I was ever going to do anything about it.

Yeah, you just keep telling yourself that.

"I mean, just because he and his boys are part of some secret government hit squad doesn't mean he's so cool."

Lucia's eyes bugged, and I stared at her. My best friend was no good at lying or keeping secrets usually. She would never blurt them out, but ask her a direct question and she was toast ... every time.

"Holy shit, are you kidding me right now?"

Lucia flushed. "Given everything you've seen in the last year, you know you need to keep that to yourself, right?"

She didn't have to tell me twice. "I'm not an idiot. Usually the people coming after us have very big guns. So fine. He is part of a secret government hit squad. I mean talk about #squadgoals."

A laugh burst out of my best friend. "You're ridiculous."

I grinned. "Take that Taylor Swift. My squad is hotter than your squad."

Our boss Adriana poked her head into the styling room. "There you are."

We both glanced over. Adriana had the kind of former-model's body that any stylist would be thrilled to dress. Long lean lines, with high cheekbones and a beautifully sculpted face. She was fifty and looked like she was thirty-five. I had no idea how she did that. I figured she must use some seriously expensive European creams.

I grinned up at her. "What's up boss lady? Lucia is just finishing the styling, and I'll have the final makeup color palette for you soon, probably this afternoon."

Lucia nodded. "JJ suggested using the orange belt. I like that one. Or maybe this one that's a little more salmon. JJ, that'll work for you right?"

I nodded. "Yeah, that works too. I have a really pretty peach shimmer I can use that will still work."

Adriana agreed. "Use Lucia as a test model. She has that gorgeous olive skin and we can see how it all works together. But that's not why I'm here, actually."

"What do you need?" I asked.

"This year we're working with a new charity, Hope Springs. It's for domestic violence survivors. I'd love for you to spearhead this. Sit down with the board and help map out the campaign. There are a lot of women who have just managed to leave their situations. A lot of them need some help to get back on their feet. But it's sort of impossible to go back to work when you're covered in bruises and scars.

"We wanted to do a benefit makeup campaign; raise funds, raise awareness, and then train makeup artists on how to help these women put on a brave face. A *survivor's* face. And every woman knows that you always feel a little better with makeup. The best part about this is we're pairing with some lower-cost makeup lines, so we want to do some simple looks that will work to get these women back in the workforce. Some of the work that you did with that homeless teenagers' charity last year was amazing. Some quick, simple, and cheap solutions. I think you're just the person."

As Adriana spoke, my gut curled in on itself. All I could hear were Adriana's words clanging around my head. *Abused women. Domestic violence.* I couldn't do this. There was no way.

I cleared my throat before I spoke. "That sounds like a great cause, but is there any reason *I* need to sit with the board and help them? They can just repurpose what I used for the homeless teenagers. It would be a lot of the same work."

Adriana raised a brow and Lucia slid me a glance. I wished I could explain everything to my best friend, but this was not something I could talk about. And it was certainly not anything I could be involved with. It hit too close to home.

Even though Adriana had her brow raised, she carried on. "You're the best makeup stylist I have. Doing pro bono charity work is really important to the organization. I'll tell them to expect a call from you this afternoon."

Adriana left without another word. And she could do that because, well, she owned the joint. All she had to do was put down an edict, and she should expect her word to become bond. The problem was, this was the last thing on earth I wanted to do. I didn't want to go back to that time in my life. A time when I'd had to cover physical and emotional bruises. I didn't want to think about the girl I'd been.

You can do this. This is your job. This is your dream job. Make it happen. One way or another.

When Adriana left, Lucia studied the two belts, the orange and salmon ones, holding them up to the mannequin. I didn't look over at her, but her tone said it all. "You okay, JJ?"

I forced a smile into my voice. "Of course I am." *I have to be.*

"You don't have to do that with me. But it's not like you to turn down a job Adriana gives you, especially since this is the kind of thing that you love to do. And secondly, why would you say no to something like this? It's a really great cause." Lucia turned to face me. "What's up?"

"I told you. Nothing. And it *is* a great cause. You're right. Of course I am going to do it. It just seems like I'd be repeating work I've already done, ya know?"

The lie sounded clunky to my own ears. I had to get out of there before Lucia saw through the lie for the excuse it was. That was the problem when you worked with your childhood best friend. She could see through anything.

I wished I could tell her. I really did. But there were some things better left in the past. The things I'd been through were some of them. "See you later, okay?" I muttered as I escaped the styling room before Lucia could respond.

Now I'd just have to figure out how the hell to get out of this project.

CHAPTER TWO

Jonas

I had considered taking Noah up on his offer of a fight. Seriously considered it. But there was something about hitting a guy who was truly, deeply happy that sucked all the fun out of it.

I'd started imagining what would happen when we got back to the office, and Noah's wife saw our black eyes and bruised knuckles. We'd have to explain what had happened and then Lucia would fuss over the both of us, caught between her outrage that we were fighting like schoolboys and her compassion for our abused client.

In the end, I'd decided the release of steam wouldn't even be worth it. I chuckled darkly. Damn, we'd all gotten soft as of late. Being around a woman who loved me, albeit one that loved me like a sister, made a man soft.

I decided to take a walk instead.

Noah had offered to keep me company, but that would have just led us back to the aforementioned fight scenario. So I'd taken off alone, making sure to get as far away from Mira's building as possible. I'd been so charged with righteous fury that by the time I looked up again, I'd walked all the way back to the East Village. With a calmer head, I doubled back to get my car. By the time I made it back to the office, it was almost midnight.

I parked in my marked space in the underground garage at Blake Security and sat there in the dark for a minute before getting out, trying to get my head back on straight before I went upstairs and had to see anyone. It shouldn't have hit me so hard, seeing Mira with that asshole. I'd been a cop for a long time and had worked in security ever since my time with the force. It shouldn't surprise me at all that people often made bad decisions under pressure. But in this case, it had been like a boot to the face.

Because you thought you'd saved this one.

I shook off the dark thought as I got out of the car. It was quiet and still on the parking level but I scanned the perimeter of the garage anyway. Always vigilant. Never let your guard down. I stayed on high alert as I crossed to the elevator bank and leaned forward so the retinal scanner could verify my identity. As I rode the elevator up to the top floor, I could only hope that no one was still awake. I just needed to grab my laptop.

Noah had decided that having a certain number of our team living on site was for the best, but I was putting off the communal living deal for a while—at least formally. I liked my space, but the truth was I crashed at the penthouse more often than not.

Surprisingly it wasn't all bad. There was always someone around to shoot the breeze with and my workload seemed lighter since I wasn't spending valuable time in the morning and after-noon commuting. I probably should just move in already.

But it was also exhausting having trained security agents watching your every move and analyzing everything you said. I couldn't just lounge in my pajamas when I felt like shit without having to answer a bunch of questions. They were a nosy bunch, my crew.

I loved them anyway.

The elevator doors slid open and I stepped into the entryway. It was dark and quiet, the only sound coming from the direction of Matthias's room. That kid never slept no matter what time of day it was, but he also didn't ask questions. So I was off the hook.

Then I stepped into the living room and was confronted with a tight, toned ass in skintight leggings.

All the parts that had been asleep fired to life. I sucked in a deep breath as JJ shifted her position at the window, the globes of her ass bouncing slightly with the movement. My dick tried to follow her. It should have been a welcome diversion. Hell, at least I wasn't depressed and feeling the sting of failure anymore. But this was JJ. The woman lived to torment me. So as spectacular as that ass was, it was the last thing I wanted to see in the middle of the night coming off a tough case.

"Why are you still awake?"

It came out harsher than I'd intended, but there was no need to apologize. JJ didn't offend easily, probably because she thrived on insults and could throw out verbal daggers with the best of them. As I'd expected, she merely turned her head slightly to acknowledge my presence before turning back to the night sky, dismissing me.

"Why can't *you* mind your own business?" she asked in a deceptively sweet voice.

Never mind that just a few moments ago, I had wanted nothing more than to climb into bed without having to engage anyone. Now I stepped farther into the room, instinctively drawn to her. There was just something about Jessica Jones that I could not resist. It was sick in a way, but I got off on fighting with her. That smart mouth and those killer curves were the perfect combination to make my dick hard while simultaneously pissing me off.

It was a heady combination.

"What would be the fun in that?" I asked, speaking truthfully.

She turned from whatever it was that was holding her attention outside and eyed me with a sneer. "I would ask if you had a hot date but that's doubtful. Jackasses really aren't in this season."

Now that hurt. "Women love me."

She sniffed and slid me a sidelong glance. "Frankly, I don't see the appeal. But then again there are people who like candy corn and Peeps. There's really no accounting for taste ... or lack thereof."

"Hey! Candy corn is awesome." I might have to rethink my taste in women if she was dogging on candy corn. How could you not enjoy something that was pure high-octane sugar? "You're probably just too bitter to enjoy it."

Her eyes flashed and for a moment there was something behind the look that made me regret my choice of words.

"Too bad for you, you'll never have a taste." Her words carried a hint of hurt with them and I wanted to bite off my tongue.

We snarked at each other and played fast and loose with our words, but I would never actually want to hurt her. It bothered me that I even could. In my mind, JJ was as invincible as her comic book character namesake, and finding a chink in her armor was both disturbing and endearing.

"I'm sorry. I didn't mean anything by that."

"Whatever. You're probably right. I'll leave the sweetness to you. I just happen to like my men a little bit ... stronger with a hint of a bite. Same way I like my whiskey."

When I looked up she was watching me closely.

"What?" I asked.

She shrugged. "Nothing. You just look ... never mind. I was enjoying some peace and quiet, but I think that ship has sailed. Good night."

I watched with a sinking feeling in my chest as she walked over to the couch and collected a blanket and a paperback book from the cushions. She did that frequently, curled up in a corner with a book and got lost in another world. It was one more thing about her that didn't compute with the smart mouth and the fuck-off attitude. I would never have pegged her for a bookworm—more like a party girl every night of the week.

"Night," I called out.

She didn't respond or look back. Which bothered me more than I could say.

———

Jessica

I COULD FEEL his eyes on my ass.

The sensation was visceral, as tactile as a physical touch. It was an ingrained response to be annoyed by Jonas, like swatting a fly or clearing your throat. But lately I'd had a harder time denying that having his eyes on me wasn't exactly ... horrible.

Oh, fine. It was arousing as hell to know that he couldn't stop looking at my ass. But that didn't mean I wanted him to know that.

I clutched my book tighter against my chest. It was such bullshit that he'd come in and ruined my night. It had been a perfectly fine day at work, crazy boss demands aside, but I'd been restless and dissatisfied all week. I'd been looking forward to a quiet night on the couch with a book and the stars. Then he'd come along and ruined it. What the hell was he doing coming in so late looking for a fight anyway?

Before I could question the wisdom of it, I spun on my heel and marched back down the hallway to the living room. I skidded to a stop as Jonas came into view. No longer in the middle of the room, he stood at the window with his forehead pressed to the glass. There was a wealth of pain in his expression, like he'd jump straight out that window and to the pavement below if it were possible.

I shifted uncomfortably, sure he wouldn't want me to see him so unguarded. Despite how much we bickered and how crazy he made me, the sight of him so unmoored brought me no joy. Yes, Jonas was an asshole. But strangely enough, I thought of him as *my* asshole. And no one messed with my friends.

"Do you ever have any regrets?" I asked.

He didn't move in any way, but there was a sudden tension in his shoulders that made me think he hadn't known I was there. That, in and of itself, was telling. Jonas had senses like a cat. I'd never been able to sneak up on him before. And I'd tried.

"Besides meeting you?"

I shook my head. Maybe it had been foolish to try to relate to him on a serious note. Jonas and I just didn't have that kind of relationship and there was no changing the rules now.

"I just thought ... never mind. I'm going to bed. You can be a grumpy ass by yourself."

I turned to go, but before I could make it two steps, strong arms encircled me from behind. I sucked in a breath, caught off guard by how good it felt to be held like this. I turned my head slightly, freezing as my forehead brushed against his chin. He was tall and built, something I'd tried like hell not to notice before. But it was damn near impossible not to feel the rock-hard muscles behind me and around me. Or not to get lost in the warm masculine scent that drew me like a bumblebee to honey.

God, he even smells like testosterone. But in a good, nuzzle-into-his-neck-while-he-fucks-you-senseless-against-a-wall kind of way.

My stomach clenched and there was an answering pull between my thighs. Damn it. I was not getting off on this.

"Let me go." I'd meant for it to come out bitchy as usual but there was a soft, plaintive note to my voice that made *let me go* sound suspiciously like *never let me go.*

"Sorry. I shouldn't have snapped at you like that. It's been a shitty day."

He walked back to the window and I immediately missed the warmth against my skin. I followed at a distance, still clutching my book and blanket.

"You didn't lose a client, did you?" Belatedly I realized it was a terrible thing to ask. If he had, would he really want to talk about it?

But to my surprise, Jonas nodded. "Yeah. Not in the way you meant, but ... yeah. I lost one that I tried damn hard to save."

"I'm so sorry," I whispered, feeling for all the world like a complete waste of space. I'd been here snarking at him, and the whole time he was dealing with something serious.

Yes, my life was a shitstorm at the moment, but that didn't mean I was the only one with problems. When I looked up, Jonas was watching me with shrewd eyes.

"What's wrong with you?"

I shrugged. "Nothing is wrong with me."

As he continued to watch with eyes that saw way too much, I suddenly wished I could tell him everything.

Why not tell Jonas? He works in security, after all. Maybe he can help.

But the same silly part of me had once believed that a restraining order would actually protect you, as well. And I knew from experience that was absolute bullshit. So as much as I wished I could tell him everything, I couldn't.

Not that it wasn't tempting. Jonas was an asshole, but he was also really good at his job. I'd seen him with clients before, on the rare occasions he had to bring someone to the office. The women in particular loved him. He had a quiet sort of protectiveness that made you feel safe, yet heard. I had no doubt that he'd listen to me spill the whole story without judgment and then immediately come up with a plan for how to handle everything.

Maybe he'd even hold me again. It might be worth spilling my guts to feel those muscles wrapped around me again.

But it wouldn't be worth the humiliation. I'd worked so hard and come so far. Nothing from my past would ruin this for me. As hard as it was, I pasted on a smile and shook my head.

"There's nothing wrong with me. But it looks like there's something wrong with you." I pointed downward.

His eyes followed my finger, and he cursed under his breath. I felt like a bitch for pointing it out. After all, I'd had a physical reaction to him too, but my blanket was covering up my goose bumps and hard nipples.

"Anyway, I'm going to bed. Alone. But enjoy your hand tonight."

I turned and left him there alone with his hard-on. I tried to ignore the part of me that wanted to rush back there and give him a hand with it. My past was coming back to haunt me, and I refused to take anyone else down with me.

Until I figured this whole thing out, it would be best if I kept my distance from everyone.

CHAPTER THREE

Jonas

I really shouldn't like kicking ass so much. After all, I'd been a cop once before. But there was something really satisfying about beating the shit out of some stalking asshole. Yeah, maybe it was vigilantism, but the cops would be called in the end. After I was long gone.

Who have you become?

I shoved the question away. I didn't want to think about that right now. And yeah, okay, I might be taking some of my irritation and aggression out on this guy. My mind still ran through the reel of having to watch Mira walk into her apartment, back to her ex. Back to the man who had beaten her so bloody she'd had to practically crawl into Blake Security for help.

And I was just supposed to let that shit go?

Never mind that though. The asshole of the evening was none other than Clint Evans. He'd been stalking a girl named Amber Cole for the last two years. Amber's family had come to Blake Security six months ago to try to resolve the situation. The police didn't have much to go on.

Amber had been smart and kept a diary of all the times she thought she was being watched. The problem was that Clint was also smart. Or the luckiest fucking asshole on earth. He'd managed to stay off police radar and there was no probable cause so the cops couldn't just bust in and go looking through his stuff. All the while, he kept terrorizing that poor girl. Well, now it was time for him to be terrorized.

I advanced on him and the guy tried to crawl backwards. "I told you guys I'd leave her alone."

I cracked my neck. "See, that's the thing. You said you were going to leave her alone last time my boys came to talk to you. But instead of leaving her alone, we found you at her swim meet. You realize the girl is sixteen, right?"

The turd in front of me swallowed hard, his hands splashing into puddles as he scrambled to get away. "Look, she never told me she was sixteen."

"Did she *have* to tell you? After all, you were hanging around a high school when you first laid eyes on her."

"Don't make me sound like some kind of freak. I wasn't there for her. I was picking up my sister. Then I saw her. For all I knew she was eighteen. So what? I've seen her around a few times. It's not a big deal."

I just tsked. "No. No. No. You don't get to pretend like you had no idea. She was fourteen when you started stalking her. I've seen the pictures. She *looked* fourteen. *Real* young. So you don't get to pretend you had no idea how old she was. I mean, you even followed her on family vacations. Do you know what kind of sicko that makes you?" I leaned close as I grabbed the guy by the shirt. "It makes you the kind of sick asshole that the guys in prison are gonna love."

The idiot's eyes widened. "I swear. I never touched her. It was just a coincidence that I went to Key West when her family did."

That's right buddy. Keep painting me a picture. One of the key reasons the police hadn't been able to do much was because they couldn't prove that Clint was everywhere Amber said he was. Because it was always just a feeling. Amber would think she saw him out of the corner of her eye, or swear that he was somewhere. But the bastard was good at hiding. Right now, as he rambled on and on about how being where she was had been just a coincidence, he was giving the police everything they needed.

"I love how you say you never touched her, but you sure terrorized her, all right. And when the cops search your place tonight, they're going to find all kinds of pictures of her. Pictures Photoshopped into suggestive positions. You're a sick bastard."

And because I couldn't help it, I closed my hand into a fist and popped the fucker in the nose.

Goddamn, that felt good. *This isn't about Mira.* Again I shoved away any thoughts of the woman who didn't want my help. Instead, I focused on the guy in front of me who was now trying to run. Damn it, why did they always try to run?

The guy crawled a few feet and then pushed himself up onto his hands and knees, and finally to his feet. I let him think he was going to get away, because really, what was the fun if I didn't get to chase him down?

Why couldn't they ever run when I was wearing tennis shoes? No, instead I was wearing brand new Italian loafers. And the jackass wanted to splash around in fucking puddles.

You didn't have to wear your loafers tonight. Yes, that was a good point. But I liked to look sharp. Not to mention we'd had a client meeting earlier.

My mother had taught me that clothes help you make the best first impression. They didn't make the man, but they sure helped. It was a lesson I'd always carried close to my heart.

I didn't know I'd end up chasing after this asshole tonight, or I would have dressed for the occasion. I had a pair of four-hundred-dollar Nikes that would've gone great with a pair of black jeans and a black hoodie. So what? I liked shoes. *Don't judge me.*

"Dude, you're killing me with this running thing, and the splashing around in the puddles. Do you have any idea how much these shoes cost?"

I snatched the guy by the back of his shirt and dragged him around, slamming him into the brick wall of the alley. My hand covered the recording device in my pocket so it wouldn't pick up my next words as I spoke in a hushed voice.

"Now come on. You must've seen where this was going. First, we have to track you down, and I'll give you credit: you're a slippery motherfucker. Next, we play nice and legal and get a restraining order. But like the *fucking idiot* you are, you still don't listen. One of my boys shows up a few weeks ago and warns you to never go near her again. And I know Oskar; he hates guys like you. You probably got his temper all up, and he hates that. It's not easy to get that guy to show emotion. Then we sent Matthias after you. You're lucky all he did was go after your bank accounts. That motherfucker could have killed you and not even blinked. Word is, Matthias left a lovely paper trail, so when the police come looking for you tonight, they're going to find all the evidence they need to prove you've been stalking Amber."

I removed my hand so whatever he said next would be audible.

"You ... you ... you can't do that. You don't have any proof. I was careful. I follow her, but I don't touch her. It's not illegal to fantasize about hurting someone as long as you never do it."

Thanks asshole, that's just what we needed.

"No. We didn't. Not until just now." I took out the recorder before making a big production of clicking the stop button. "I do appreciate you fessing up to stalking her. It helps. Especially when the cops are gonna find this in your back pocket."

The guy looked around. "I don't see the cops."

"Oh, another few minutes alone with me and you'll be wishing they were here already."

"Look, we can work out a deal. I'll leave town. I'll never come back again." The guy clutched my shirt, and I dipped my head down to glare at his hands.

"I suggest you get your hands off my shirt. That's Brioni. You know that's a three-hundred-dollar shirt right?"

Asshole's brows furrowed. "What?"

"Yeah, you break it, you buy it, so I suggest you loosen your grip."

But the idiot didn't feel like listening. And he clutched tighter. "Look, I'll make you a deal. Whatever you want. It's yours. I cannot go to jail. I'm scared. I'm not gonna make it. I was in juvie once. Do you know the kind of crazy people they have in there?"

"You mean crazy like you? I can't wait until some big dude named Bubba starts stalking you around the yard. Watching your every move, plotting to hurt you. Maybe I'll give him a little nudge and tell him you like little girls."

The guy clutched tighter and tugged. I heard the tear, and then muttered a curse under my breath. "Motherfucker. Are you fucking serious right now?"

I popped the guy in the nose again and his head clanked back against the wall, making him groan. "That was for the fucking shirt." Then I hit him again. "And that's for not listening the first time." I released another fist. "And that's for trying to hurt a little girl." I couldn't stop.

You're getting out of control again. Dial it back. Dial it back now!

But I was too far gone. My mind went completely quiet as I let pure instinct take over. Guys like this didn't deserve to walk the earth.

But then there was a voice in my earpiece. "While this is fun and all, listening to you beat this guy's ass," Matthias said, "I've got

JJ on the move. You're the closest. It looks like she's leaving work, but she's not getting in a cab like she's supposed to. Can you swing by?"

Lucky for the idiot in my hands, Matthias had used the magic word. *JJ.* She needed me a lot more than I needed to keep kicking ass.

"Yeah, I'm on it."

After Matthias disconnected, I glanced down. "Damn it. I love this shirt," I muttered as I dragged Clint's limp body over to a light pole. I grabbed the recording device from my pocket and stuck it in Clint's back pocket after I wiped it down. And then I took a couple of zip ties and tied the douchebag to the pole.

The police would find enough information on Clint's stalking to put him away for a long time. And, in case that wasn't enough, they'd get a search warrant for his house, and find all the pictures of Amber Cole. That should do it. Back in the day, I hadn't liked the idea of being a vigilante.

But you're a long way from back in the day, aren't you?

I wasn't going to go back there. I had a new life now. One that Noah had given me. And with that new life came the mouthy blonde I needed to go rescue from herself.

As I walked back to the car, not only did I have to wrangle the demons of my past, I had to wrangle the sexy blonde demon that ran through my skull. *JJ.* Just the idea of seeing her right now made the blood in my veins run hot.

And like the traitor it was, my goddamn dick twitched in my pants. I needed to get that shit under control. I didn't even like her. She was all mouth and a huge pain in the ass.

But there were times I wanted to shut her up by kissing her. And my mind went a little lust drunk thinking about backing her up against a wall and burying myself inside her until she could only scream my fucking name.

Yeah, you need help.

I knew it. But none of that shit was going to happen. The last thing on earth I was doing was touching Jessica Jones.

Jessica

MY FEET HURT. My back hurt. My neck hurt. Hell, even my brain hurt. With a chuckle, I started to sing the song, "My neck, my back..."

Yeah well, maybe it was better if I didn't think about my pussy and the lack of attention it was seeing these days. My vibrator was getting a lot of airplay right now. With Lucia only back part-time, I was having to pick up some of the slack and take over some styling duties for a couple of the fashion shows Adriana had coming.

My specialty was makeup, but I still had a great eye, and experience doing some styling work. So Adriana was making good use of that.

But all of this extra work would be over soon. Lucia was coming back full-time in just a few weeks. And it wasn't a moment too soon. Adriana was even going to let her bring the baby to work sometimes, which made just about every woman in the office happy. Seriously, Noah and Lucia made a pretty adorable baby.

Warmth spread out through my body when I thought about Isabella. God, I loved that kid. All chubby cheeks and baby belly and cute toes. *One day you'll have one.* Ha. My subconscious thought it was a comedian. I was never keeping a guy long enough to even think about kids.

I had left work heading towards the penthouse and considered getting a cab, but it was a nice night and I needed fresh air before I was locked in.

I loved living there. I loved being mere steps away from my

best friend. But what I didn't love were the constant, watchful eyes. And I understood that after some past events and the attempted kidnapping, it was for my own safety. Apparently having friends like Noah and the boys was a dangerous proposition. So I now lived in a fabulous penthouse rent-free. Unfortunately, that came with a slew of big-brother types. Seriously overprotective big-brother types. And one best friend and the most adorable baby on the planet. So I couldn't really complain about that.

But there were nights when I just needed time alone, for the love of Christ. And even though my feet hurt, I liked walking in the city at night. The hustle and bustle of the day quieted to an excited buzz for the evening.

The local bars were hopping for a Wednesday, filled with people who wanted to catch up with friends over dinner and drinks. As I passed a few, I could see couples sitting close together, heads bent towards each other or holding hands.

Would that ever be me? Not that I cared about any of that stuff. I wasn't interested in holding some guy's hand as we strolled around Central Park. Boring. I wasn't really a family and baby sort of person.

Except, you are.

Okay, fine. I was slightly green with envy whenever I saw Noah and Lucia together. And the baby was the icing on the jealousy cake. It wasn't real jealousy. It was more of a *could-I-ever-have-that-myself* kind of longing. But I knew the answer to that already.

No.

And I wasn't hiding from my past. But every time I got close to someone, the nightmares would start, and I remembered what it was like to trust someone who did nothing but hurt me day after day. I wasn't interested in that any more.

So I'd dated a slew of guys that were never, ever going to go anywhere. Not that a couple of them hadn't tried. Hell, one had actually proposed, and there was one I thought I might care about. But I couldn't love any of them. Every single one left me cold. Well, they left my bed warm for a moment or two, but after that I didn't really want to be with them.

Because none of them gets your blood pumping like Jonas does.

Dammit. I'd promised myself I wasn't going to think about him right now. Although maybe that's just what I needed. A fight with him, and then ten minutes with my battery-operated boyfriend, and I'd be out of my little funk. Actually, that didn't sound like a bad idea.

Yeah, I was pathetic. But I had to take my pleasure somewhere. As I passed an empty boutique with the mannequin lit in the storefront window, the hairs on the back of my neck stood. There was a shadow in the window, but when I turned around to look there was nobody there. Across the street a couple kissed. The guy picked the girl up and she kicked her feet out like a movie picture poster. It was cute.

And not for you.

Still unable to shake my unease, I considered a cab but opted against it. I'd be at the penthouse soon. But I did start walking faster. When I rounded the corner at the next street, I heard footsteps tracking mine, moving at the same fast clip. A shiver ran up my spine.

I looked around again, and there was no one there, but a shadow slipped around the corner behind me. "Listen asshole, you should know I have a Taser. *And* a dick. You're going to be very unhappy if you try to do anything to me."

I reached in my purse for some kind of weapon, but all I came up with was ... Oh, hell. My vibrator. Well, technically Lucia's. Lucia had gotten it as a gag gift a while ago, but been too scared to actually use it. The thing was HUGE! And purple. Honestly, no one's vagina could accommodate that monster.

I'd tossed it in my cavernous purse the day before the fire and had never taken the thing out. Well now it was my weapon, and hey, look at that. It was actually a dick, so that part was true. Maybe I could get Matthias to rig it as some kind of Taser too.

While it might do the trick to get me off—hey, sometimes I needed to take the Jonas edge off—it wouldn't be much help against a would-be attacker.

What was I going to do, orgasm him to death? *La petite mort indeed.* Fuck it, I was ready for this asshole.

But there was no one there.

Jesus, I was losing it. I turned back to head to the penthouse, and stopped short, even as the knot of fear lodged in my throat. A car had pulled up on the corner across the street, and I was pretty sure I knew who was driving it. This meant trouble. I only had one choice: run faster.

CHAPTER FOUR

Jonas

She wanted to give me a heart attack.

As I raced through the streets, my eyes went back to my phone again and again to follow the tracker Matthias had sent. A blinking red dot that represented the one woman who could crawl under my skin.

I turned at the next street and gunned the engine. Luckily I'd been close, so the crazy woman hadn't been walking alone for too long. She was determined to send us all into heart failure. What the hell was she thinking walking home this late by herself?

An open parking space ahead beckoned and I almost took out a part of the curb as I swung into it. I jumped out and slammed the door behind me, locking the vehicle with my key fob. I'd deliberately aimed for a street ahead of her so I could intercept her. Not that she'd appreciate my forethought at all. No. I fully expected to get an earful and a sassy string of expletives from the always delightful Jessica Jones.

I didn't have to wait long. She was about ten feet away and still hadn't noticed me, another thing I'd be sure to spank her ass for later. Hadn't I taught her the importance of being aware of your surroundings? But JJ was in a world of her own, her hips swinging as she strode down the street. It was only as she got closer and I saw her face that I realized this wasn't just JJ flouting the rules for fun. Her eyes were wild and darted around her frantically. She was clutching her bag to her side, not so much like she was afraid someone would steal it, but like she just needed to hold on to something.

She wasn't breaking the rules. She was scared. Something had sent her running, and I needed to know what it was.

I didn't move so she almost crashed into me.

"Watch it, asshole!"

I grabbed her arm and we struggled for a moment. "JJ, calm down. It's me."

Her eyes locked onto me, and for a moment she looked so vulnerable that it broke my heart. "Baby girl, it's me. Matthias sent me your coordinates when he saw you leave work without an escort."

She nodded frantically then glanced behind her. "I had to go. I just needed to get out of there."

"Okay, well, we can go wherever you need to."

My words, meant to calm, seemed to enrage her. She pointed her finger at me, getting annoyingly close to my eyes.

"I know I can go where I need to. That's what I'm doing. I don't need a man to tell me where I can go. Nobody controls me!"

I threw up my hands. "No one said you couldn't. I'm trying to help you. Do you know how reckless this was, walking out alone? Anything could have happened to you, crazy woman!"

JJ clutched her bag tighter. "I've walked home plenty of times by myself before."

"I don't think you need me to tell you that things are different now."

The words took the wind out of her sails. JJ sagged a little, her eyes meeting mine directly.

"Yeah. I know."

I fell into step beside her, happy when she followed me back to where I had parked the car. Our usual routine was for one of the guys to escort her home from the office. If she needed to stay late, like she had tonight, she would call them when she was ready to go and someone would pick her up. Ever since everything had gone down last year, when her best friend had been stalked, JJ had seemed to understand how serious this all was and had cooperated with our efforts to keep her protected.

What had happened tonight to change that? I wasn't sure what was going on but there had to have been something to send her fleeing into the night looking as haunted as she had earlier.

I held the door open for her and waited as she climbed up into the vehicle. She settled her bag on her lap and then turned to grab the seatbelt. When she saw me still standing in the doorway to the car, she hesitated. "Is everything okay?"

"Do I look okay to you?" When she recoiled at my harsh tone, I took a deep breath. "Sorry. No. I'm not okay. Not at all."

I didn't offer any other explanation, just shut the door and walked around to the driver's side. Let her stew on that. Maybe then she'd see what it felt like to be left out in the dark, wondering what the hell was going on.

Right before I reached the driver's side door, I stopped. I was angry. Not just annoyed or peeved, but truly angry. Because whatever had scared her badly enough to have her running out without a word to her security was something that she hadn't come to me about. That didn't feel right at all. As much as we bickered, did she really not know that I'd drop whatever I was doing to help her?

I took a deep breath before opening the door and getting

behind the wheel. She looked over at me. What I was feeling must have been broadcast on my face because she groaned.

"I don't want to hear the lecture right now, okay? I was busy at work and just felt like going home without calling out the cavalry, okay?"

I shook my head, unbelievably disappointed. Not just because she wasn't taking her own safety seriously but also at the bold-faced lie. Did she really think I was that unobservant? It was an insult to me, not just as a security agent but as a man. I saw everything about her. She loved Lucia like a sister and put up with her best friend's fussing, even though she hated to be hovered over. She liked to watch Oskar lifting weights, much to my annoyance and jealousy.

I knew that she had a serious love affair with vodka. She had a hate affair with men and always chose badly. Including the dipshits she dated who didn't even bother to pick her up at home.

So why would she think I wouldn't see through such an obvious lie?

"I'm not going to give you a lecture, JJ. Just a reminder. If shit goes bad, we can't help you if we don't know where you are."

I had expected her to have a scathing response or to tell me where to stick it. But what she did next was the absolute last thing I'd ever expected. She turned to me with big blue eyes.

And burst into tears.

Jessica

I HAD BEEN ONLY seven when I first discovered the power of tears.

I'd gotten caught by my father sneaking a cookie. My dad was a stickler for the no-sweets-before-dinner rule. Sneaking a cookie without asking was grounds for losing my television privileges. The moment my eyes had filled with tears, my father had started to shift on his feet. I'd added a sniffle and before I knew it, he was shoving a cookie at me.

I'd learned it applied to men in general when I'd tried it on my first boyfriend at the age of sixteen, Sal Morini. Sal had tried to break up with me before the homecoming dance so he could go out with a girl who'd put out. Namely Vicki Dematto. As soon as I'd turned on the tears, he'd backtracked. Of course at the dance I'd ditched him to party with Lucia and her friends, then told Vicki what he'd said. No girl had gone out with Sal the rest of the year.

Those early experiences had been eye-opening and led to an epiphany for me. Ever since, I'd never had an issue using my big blue eyes to get me out of trouble.

But this time, I wasn't pulling a sympathy card or being manipulative at all. I was honestly just overwhelmed.

And furious that Jonas was the one to witness it.

But, he didn't seem to be enjoying it any more than I was. He stared at me in shock before swinging his eyes back to the road.

"Oh God, I'm sorry. I wasn't trying to yell at you."

Hearing him backtrack somehow only made it worse. I was a strong, independent woman and I didn't need to be pandered to. It was humiliating that I was crying right now when all I wanted to do was rage, but after being so sure that someone was following me, my emotions were raw and right at the surface.

"I'm not crying about that. Damn it, why am I crying at all?" I swiped at my cheeks and glared at him, as if the tears were his fault.

Although maybe they were partially his fault. I'd been holding it together while walking on my own. Then Jonas had to show up looking all kinds of edible and reminding me how much my safety meant to everyone else.

Of course I'd broken down! What woman wouldn't, after a guilt trip like that?

Never mind that what he'd said wasn't even that bad. I needed someone to blame just then, and Jonas was readily available.

"You show up talking about Lucia and my safety. I thought someone was following me, so I told him I had a Taser and a dick, but really, all I had was the dick and I was scared, because even if that dick is huge, it's still not as good as a real weapon."

Jonas glanced at me from the corner of his eye, and then mouthed the word *dick* slowly. Under any other circumstances I would have laughed. He had the cautious expression you use when talking to someone who is completely batshit crazy.

Maybe I had lost it. I reached into my purse and pulled it out. "See, I have a legitimate dick."

His eyes went wide. "Damn, I think that thing is setting some unrealistic expectations."

I rolled my eyes. "It's not for me to use, asshole. It was a gag gift that Lucia gave back. And it was all I had as a weapon."

He worked hard to wipe the smirk off his face. "Jessica, I apologize if I made you feel like I was coming down hard on you. I just want you to know that your safety is our top priority."

He made another turn that had me shifting slightly, almost falling into the door. Part of me wanted to give him shit for his driving, but I couldn't even muster the energy. I'd been running on pure adrenaline before, but now that I was tucked into the safe confines of the car with Jonas, the fear from before came back full force.

What the hell had that been about? I'd heard something; there was no way I'd imagined that. And if I'd heard something, and someone had been there, why hadn't they answered when I called out? Why would anyone want to scare me?

I ignored the voice in the back of my head. *You know who might.*

No. That was my old life. Things were different now. *Are you sure? Because maybe the fire wasn't an accident.*

I couldn't go down that spiral again. I had a brand new life now.

We pulled into the underground garage in the Blake Security building. I had been so deep in my thoughts that I hadn't even realized we were home.

Home. The place you were supposed to feel safe.

I hadn't felt like that about any place in a long time. But I could honestly acknowledge that I'd felt like that the past few months living with Lucia and her crew. My living arrangements had seemed like a gross overreaction to my friend's security issues the prior year, but I'd soon come to love it. Surrounded by muscular, hot men all the time and living rent-free. Not a bad deal at all.

But now I could see that I'd allowed it to lull me into a false sense of security. Sure I was safer living with the Blake Security team, but I must never let myself think I was truly safe. No matter where I went, I would never be safe.

I looked over to see that Jonas had cut the car off and turned in his seat so he could watch me. Suddenly self-conscious, I pushed my hair behind my ear.

"You know you can come to me with anything, right?" he asked.

"Sure. I mean, it's your job."

"No. Not just because it's my job."

Awareness blossomed and I flushed. His eyes didn't leave mine. I fidgeted with the strap of my bag, unsure how to handle this side of him. It was weird to have him looking at me like this and being nice to me. Angry and argumentative Jonas? I could handle him with one hand tied behind my back. But tender, sex-on-a-stick Jonas? Well, I didn't have the first clue as to how to act. What if I admitted that I'd wanted to call him earlier? What if I told him that I thought of him when I was alone in my bed at night and he laughed?

I'd die instantly.

"Well, I'm fine," I protested weakly. "I don't need anyone's help."

"Maybe not, but I do."

"You need my help," I replied, deliberately misunderstanding him.

I could tell by the flare of heat in his eyes that he was gearing up for one of our knock down, drag out wars of words. My body responded in kind. For the first time, I catalogued the symptoms like an outsider. Increased heart rate and breathing. Flushed skin and a sense of anticipation.

God. It was so obvious looking back on it now. The whole time we'd been fighting we'd been engaging in foreplay. I could only wonder if it was as obvious to everyone else in the house. Probably. Which was just great. How was I supposed to look the others in the eye now?

"I need you to want my help. I need to help you. Because the idea of anyone fucking with you makes me crazy."

The idea that Jonas would unleash his rage on someone just because they'd bothered me pleased me greatly. I clamped down on the response. It was far too close to a "girlfriend" type of thing, and way too possessive for my taste. I'd had more than enough of possessive men who thought they owned me.

"What did I just say? Something just made the light go out of your eyes."

I shook my head. "Nothing. But I don't want anyone getting hurt because of me. I just want to be left alone."

"Who isn't allowing you to be left alone?"

Damn him for being so smart. The only way to keep from giving him all the clues he needed was to distract him. Luckily, I knew the perfect way to do that.

"Right now the only one annoying me is you. So I guess I'll say thanks for the ride and good night."

Before he could react, I reached over the console and grabbed the front of his shirt. He let me tug him until he was close enough for me to smell the scent of his cologne. Our eyes met, and suddenly Jonas smiled. The impact of it, especially so close, made me feel like I was flying. And suddenly this wasn't about distracting him anymore. It was about doing what I'd wanted to do for ages.

Kiss him.

His lips softened under mine and he let out a soft groan that ricocheted through the still interior of the car. It was incredibly intimate, secluded there with just the two of us and the rapidly increasing sound of our breathing. For those moments, we weren't Jonas and JJ, mortal enemies.

We were two people who connected like lightning, taking each other in like we wanted to merge into one being.

I gasped and a moan slipped loose. Jonas took that opportunity to slip his hand into my hair, anchor my head, and deepen the kiss, his tongue sliding over mine expertly.

I hooked my arm around his neck, holding him still, and he opened his mouth wider like he was trying to swallow me whole. If the console hadn't been between us, I likely would have climbed into his lap, but instead I just sucked on his lower lip until he moaned into my mouth, the sound finally bringing me back to reality.

We stayed for a beat staring at each other before I pulled back and opened the door. The rush of cool air coming in cleared my head, and I wondered if it had finally happened. After years of pretending to be okay, if maybe I'd finally had a mental breakdown.

"JJ, what just—"

"Good night, Jonas." I closed the door and walked quickly to the elevator.

For the first time that day, luck was on my side, because after I leaned forward for the retinal scan, the doors opened immediately.

The doors closed just as Jonas rushed up. I heard his muffled curse get fainter as the elevator ascended.

"Good night, indeed." I touched my mouth.

CHAPTER FIVE

Jonas

Of all the mistakes I'd ever made in my life that had to be the dumbest one. Kissing Jessica Jones. Because now there was no way I was ever getting the taste of her out of my system. I followed behind JJ, watching her ass sashay back and forth as she headed straight for her room. Aching all over, I went straight for the conference room. I'd left my laptop and needed to collect a few things before I headed home.

What had I been thinking? The problem was that now that I'd tasted her, it was all I could think about. Even before the sweet, scorching slide of her lips over mine, I'd already been a little too obsessed with her. Because while she might seem innocuous, she was sly, working her way under my skin for the sheer pleasure of torturing me to death.

Fuck, I was losing it. I needed to get my shit and then to put some distance between the two of us. I just had to put her out of my mind. It would be fine. I was a master of control.

Not with her you're not.

Under penalty of death, I would never admit just how often I thought about JJ. That would only stroke her ego ... amongst other things. My perverted mind had all kinds of ideas about what the hell else of hers I could stroke.

No. Not gonna go there.

I'd lost count of how many times I'd had a little shower workout just thinking about her lips. Or that sexy smile, or the way her ass filled out her jeans.

I shook my head. Why did I do it?

You really want to answer that?

I ignored that thought. I didn't even like her. She was bossy, irritating, loud ... Fuck, was she loud.

Well, lucky for me, I now have a way to shut her up.

And did I ever. I just kept thinking of the way she'd stared at me. Lips parted on a gasp, looking soft and mussed, right before I'd slipped my hand in her hair, anchored her head, and then deepened the kiss. Now her taste haunted me as it followed me around like a wraith.

Shit.

This wasn't helping. Because, what do you know, I was getting a boner. Fan-fucking-tastic. I stormed into the conference room and tried to slam the door behind me, even though the door didn't exactly slam since it was on soft hinges.

I dropped my ass into one of the cushioned seats and scowled at my laptop. I quickly checked my emails while I willed my dick to lay down.

Damn it.

She was not supposed to affect me like this. Where was some of that infamous control?

Oh yeah? That control you displayed with Mira the other night? How about the control you displayed with Clint?

Shit. Lately it was like I was walking on a tightrope and any little thing would set me on edge. Send me over.

Kissing JJ certainly had me teetering and clamoring to get myself back on steady footing.

We could forget this. Pretend it never happened. Pretend that she didn't taste like sin and sex and temptation all rolled into one. I could forget. It was fine. Everything was just fucking fine. All I had to do was completely forget that soft moaning sound she made when I slid my tongue into her mouth. It was easy.

My dick, *still hard.* "Little note, asshole, you are not doing me any favors right now," I mumbled to my dick. The damn thing didn't care. It just continued to twitch in my pants as if to say, "I know she's over here somewhere; why don't we go finish that kiss?"

The hell I was going to do that. I was never touching her again.

"So, how was it?"

I snapped my head up and met gazes with Oskar Mueller. After Matthias, Oskar was the most senior member of Blake Security. The German was one of the best forensic accountants in the business. And also a general badass with a penchant for knocking skulls.

My first thought was to say 'fucking incredible. She tastes like you think she would taste.' But no, I wasn't an idiot. Oskar liked to gossip more than any high school girl I had ever seen.

So instead, I frowned and asked for clarification. "What do you mean?"

Oskar shrugged. "Blondie rolled in on a tear. Obviously she's pissed about something. Gotta tell you, I'm sorry I missed that fight. You two bickering is often the highlight of my day."

"You're an asshole."

He shook his head. "What the hell was she doing walking on her own anyway?"

I buried the flare of anger at what could have happened to her. "I have no idea why that woman does anything. She's a complete mystery. She makes no flipping sense. Makes her even more infuriating."

"Tell me about it. If I didn't know better, I'd swear she does some of the stuff she does so we'll notice and come along and save her. But that also doesn't jive because she doesn't have a martyr complex. That chick is tough as nails and scares me a little."

I snorted. "As she should. You never know what arsenal of weapons she's hiding." Except now I sort of had an idea. Her lips needed to be classified as certified lethal weapons. And I had a feeling that sooner or later, she'd be using them to take me out.

———

Jessica

THE FIRST STOP I made was the nursery, because I knew that's exactly where I would find Lucia. And after the crazy that had just happened in the car with Jonas, I needed my best friend, pronto.

Lucia looked up with a smile. "Hey, I was just feeding the baby. Wanna hold her when I'm done?"

I nodded absently and sank down into the soft lounger that had been placed in the corner of the nursery, and Lucia raised a brow. "What's the matter?"

How was I supposed to answer that exactly?

Jonas Castillo just made my toes curl with a simple kiss?

That was the core of what was bothering me. It wasn't like he busted out any magic tricks or anything like that. It had been a simple kiss, but it had rocked me to my core.

My whole damn body felt like it was vibrating. This was Jonas. I didn't like Jonas. Moreover, Jonas didn't like me.

So why did that kiss just rock my world?

I groaned and covered my face with my hands. "So, you know

how sometimes we make a stupid choice, and then have to pay the consequences?"

Lucia laughed. "Did you accidentally set Jonas's closet on fire?" Lucia used the word accidentally with air quotes.

"No. I didn't. But I should've. Now you're giving me ideas."

My friend laughed. "Oh no. Just don't tell him I gave you that one. You know how that man is about his clothes and shoes."

"You know, I can't even get excited about that right now I'm so upset."

Lucia sat forward. "What's wrong? Do we need to get —"

I held up a hand. I knew exactly what Lucia was going to say. Get Noah in here; get the whole squad to go beat down whoever the hell had pissed me off. While I did like having an ass-kicking team behind me, they were very unlikely to kick the ass of one of their own. "No. This doesn't need to involve Noah or anyone else for that matter."

My bestie frowned. "What's going on?"

"What's going on is Jonas kissed me." I sat back and waited for Lucia to process that bombshell.

But nothing.

My best friend didn't even raise a brow, purse a lip, or let her mouth hang open. None of that.

"Did you not hear me? Jonas kissed me. I mean, yes I kissed him first but that was just to shut him up. I wasn't expecting him to kiss me back."

"Well, it's about time. My only concern is somehow you don't look at all happy about it, or satisfied." She leaned forward. "Oh my God, is he bad at it?"

I just blinked at her. "Are you serious right now? I'm telling you this catastrophic event happened and you're sitting there like you expected it to?"

Lucia shrugged. "Yeah. Because you two have been snapping

at each other for ages. It's time you guys finally got the ball rolling. So if it wasn't bad, then what's your problem?"

"This is Jonas. My nemesis, remember."

Lucia giggled. "He's hardly your nemesis. He just likes to push your buttons and vice versa." Isabella stopped nursing and whacked her breast with a tiny fist to let her know that she was done. When Lucia adjusted her clothing, she held the little tiny bundle out to me. "You want to hold her?"

That was hardly fair. Lucia was plying me with adorable baby mojo. Still though, I rose and took my little niece. "Hi, Angel. Maybe you'll be appropriately horrified by the fact that Jonas and I kissed."

But apparently Isabella was just as big a traitor as her mother was. She just gave me a happy baby smile and burped.

"Well, fat lot of good you are for advice."

Lucia laughed. "What did you expect? She's a baby. Okay, let me get my bestie hat on." Lucia took several deep breaths and closed her eyes, and when she opened them again she slapped her cheeks. "Oh my God, you and Jonas kissed? What happened?"

I couldn't help the smile that tugged at my lips. "Now that is the appropriate reaction." I eased down on the couch, holding Isabella as she started to fall asleep. "Okay, so I was leaving work and I decided I wanted to walk."

Already Lucia was frowning. I rushed to explain. "I know. I should've just taken a taxi. But you know, I've been feeling like I've been locked up in this penthouse. I just needed a night, hell, even like thirty minutes, to myself. Is that so wrong? And before you answer that, just think about how you would feel if you were me."

Lucia opened her mouth to say something, but then snapped it shut. I continued. "I don't know how he found out, but before I knew it, Jonas was there, yelling at me, insisting I get in the car. Can you imagine? I'm a grown woman. I can walk if I want to."

"But it's not safe, JJ," Lucia said.

"Sometimes don't you think the security protocols are a little too much? You, of all people, should understand that."

She sighed. "Okay, you have a point. So what happened then?"

"So, we're doing the usual thing, you know, fighting. Me threatening to relieve him of his balls."

"Yeah, pretty much like any other day."

I had gone over that span of five minutes in the car a dozen times already. Like a reel in my head over, and over, and over again, I could pinpoint when something had changed, when the need shifted.

That moment when all I could concentrate on was the feel of Jonas's firm lips on mine, his tongue sliding into my mouth. The way his hand fisted in my hair, and the way he moaned when I whimpered. Like I was the best tasting ice cream on a hot summer's day.

"I don't know what happened. But once again I was shouting at him and explaining to him how I could take care of myself. The next thing I know we're kissing. And the worst thing is, it was like a toe-curling, slap-your-last-boyfriend-for-kissing-you-shitty kind of kiss. I mean, the man knows what he's doing. If you ever tell him that, I will kill you."

Baby Isabella just gurgled and kicked her feet, and then sighed before promptly closing her eyes. Oh yeah. Real helpful.

She shook her head. "That doesn't even sound like Jonas. I mean, were you goading him?"

I laughed. "This is me. I'm always goading him. So how was this time any different from any other time?"

"Maybe it was the straw that broke the camel's back. We've been circling each other forever. Maybe he snapped."

"Maybe. What does this mean? Because as quickly as it started, it was over all too soon. I mean, how is the man gonna just give me a taste? It's like he knows it's been too long since I've been laid, and he's devised a new way to torture me. I don't know what to do. Help me."

"You're asking me, but you're not going to like my answer," Lucia said. "But maybe you just talk to him. For once, try not to snap at each other. For once, just acknowledge that you two have the hots and move from there."

I frowned. "You're right. I don't like that answer."

Lucia laughed. "So what are you going to do? It's not like you can avoid him. It's not like you can pretend this didn't happen. Or that you didn't like it."

And therein lay the rub. I had liked it. A lot. Matter-of-fact, I liked it so much I wanted to rub my whole body all over him. Hell, I had arched into that kiss, practically begging him to keep touching me. And I had no idea what I was going to do about that.

Because no way in hell could I do it again.

CHAPTER SIX

Jonas

I held out a hand to assist my client out of the car. Normally I enjoyed these out of town jobs but not today. I glanced around us, edgy as fuck and not sure exactly why. My assignment was to keep Lindsey Meyers and her son safe and out of sight while Noah dealt with her ex-husband. This was nothing I hadn't done before.

"Thank you," Lindsey whispered, clutching her duffel bag to her chest as she climbed down. Immediately, she moved to the back of the car to get her son, Henry, out of his booster seat.

Lindsey had been living in Atlanta for the past year after divorcing her husband. Too bad the asshole hadn't gotten the point.

I sighed. Goddamn I was tired. I would never make fun of Ryan for dodging these types of cases again. Domestic calls were so draining. It was exhausting trying to help people who weren't ready to help themselves.

"Okay, so I've booked us into two rooms here under a false name. No one will find you here. Our rooms have an adjoining door. Please leave it unlocked so I can get to you quickly if you should need me."

Lindsey nodded that she understood. "Thank you. I feel bad that you have to be away from home just to babysit me."

I smiled, trying to put her at ease. That was one of the most common things we heard from our female clients. Women who'd been so conditioned not to make waves that they apologized constantly for trouble that wasn't of their own making.

"There's no reason for you to feel bad. It's my job. Also, I'm pretty sure Noah is going to enjoy intimidating your ex-husband while we're here. So put on a movie, get comfortable. If you want to order takeout, let me know and I'll have them bring it to my room first."

"Okay. I can do that." Lindsey pushed her hair behind her ear nervously, but she looked slightly less scared than when we arrived.

Henry held tight to her hand, peering up at me suspiciously. I'd never spent much time around kids this age, but I supposed I would have been suspicious too if some guy I'd never seen was driving me around.

I led them to the front desk where I picked up the keys to our rooms. Matthias had checked us in remotely, so after retrieving the key, we took the elevator up to the tenth floor.

"Do you have a girlfriend?" Lindsey asked curiously.

I froze. "No time for that. Love is too much work."

The elevator stopped at our floor, and I wasted no time escorting them off. It wasn't unusual for clients to ask about my personal life. Spending so much time with someone, often having your life literally in their hands, forged bonds that felt intimate. Most people wanted to know more about the person protecting them.

Only I'd found that when the clients doing the asking were

young, attractive women, it could lead to uncomfortable situations and misunderstandings. So I tried to remain a mystery.

"Here we go. Room 1014." I swiped the key and we were in. "Wait here."

Lindsey waited by the door obediently, clutching Henry's hand tightly while I checked out every inch of the suite. The door to my room next door was standing open, as I'd requested. That room was empty, too. I came back to find them still standing next to the front door.

"It's okay. You can go ahead and relax now. I'll check in with the team and keep you updated."

Lindsey's sigh of relief was the best thank you I could have received.

She smiled at me. "You're really good at this."

"I hope so. I'm not much good at anything else."

My joke made her smile.

"You're a nice guy. I hope you do find time for love one day, and that you don't let all the bad relationships you see scare you away. Love isn't supposed to be hard. It took me a long time to see that."

I nodded politely and then walked through the connecting door into my room. I'd already dropped my own overnight bag on the bed, but I wouldn't be sleeping. Noah would be calling with an update soon, and I needed to be ready.

With so much time to fill, my brain inevitably went to the one thing I'd been trying to ignore all day. *JJ.*

I sat on the edge of the bed and scrubbed my hands over my face. I'd been trying not to think of her. But trying not to think of her was like trying not to breathe. She was in me, deep, completely entwined with my every thought and function. That kiss, that fucking kiss, replayed over and over on a loop in the back of my mind constantly.

What the hell had I been thinking?

Not that I would take all the blame. Oh no, part of the responsibility for this clusterfuck rested solidly on JJ's shoulders. She'd pulled me in, knowing what her tempting mouth did to me. I shook my head. She'd just been playing around like we always did. She'd kissed me on the cheek before. When she did it I was always worried she'd follow through on the threat in her eyes and bite a hole in my cheek.

But this time the crafty little vixen had gotten a little more than she'd expected. I grunted, thinking of the shocked, furious, and aroused look on her face once she'd finally pulled back. It was a miracle she hadn't slugged me. Honestly, I wasn't sure if she even understood why she hadn't. But I knew all too well what this kind of desire led to. It was dangerous and all-consuming, the kind that made smart men make stupid decisions.

A knock on the door drew me from my thoughts. I sprang up just as Lindsey stuck her head in.

"Everything okay?" I asked.

She held up the room service menu. "Yeah, but Henry will be hungry soon. I figured we'd better put our order in now. Should I order something for you, too?"

I accepted the menu she held out, and then pointed to the only thing on there that looked like a burger.

"Use my phone," I instructed and then moved back so she could reach it. I wasn't even hungry, just grateful for the interruption. Lindsey was a reminder of all the reasons I had to stay away from JJ. Relationships were a minefield, even when the two parties started off on solid ground.

With a past like mine, I wasn't the right guy for anyone to bet on. But it didn't mean that I couldn't look out for her.

I would do what I did best: take care of her from afar.

———

Jessica

I CAUGHT myself twisting the hem of my loose top and clenched my fingers into a fist. It was a little after seven o'clock, and I should have been well on my way home by now. Instead I was reviewing some last minute layouts for a magazine spread and waiting to meet one of the volunteers from Hope Springs.

I gulped. This was really happening.

It shouldn't be that big of a deal, really. This was no different than any of the other charity events I'd worked on.

Bullshit.

I ignored the uneasy feeling that crept up the back of my neck. There was no use pretending this wasn't a big deal. Very soon a woman was going to walk in here with a story that was all too familiar. Someone who understood, just as I did, how important appearances were to rebuilding your life. Wasn't that part of why I had been attracted to makeup? I'd always loved how transforming my appearance could give me a confidence boost. It was only later that I'd learned how transforming my appearance could hide the evidence of my private hell.

A whisper from the hall drew my attention.

"It's okay, you can come right in!" I called.

I frantically tried to clear my desk, pulling all the papers and magazines into a neat pile on the right side. There was always someone staying late at the office. Adriana liked to work her people to the bone and there was never any shortage of things to do, especially as we drew closer to fashion week. But despite how busy the office always was, I knew how intimidating it could be to ask anyone for help or directions.

I stood and stepped over the box of sample clothing on the floor. Damn, I needed to clean this place up. My cubicle was the size of a shoebox anyway, so it really couldn't stand any clutter.

Once clear of the debris on the floor, I stuck my head around the doorjamb and into the hallway.

The empty hallway.

Puzzled, I glanced both ways. I'd definitely heard someone out here. Behind me, the phone on my desk rang. I walked back over to my desk and snatched the receiver.

"Hello?"

There was nothing but silence but I could hear that the line was open. A hush, like someone trying not to breathe too hard.

"Hello? Who is this?" I demanded, creeped out and beyond angry about it. The skin on my arms prickled and I shivered, and I was suddenly feeling very exposed and alone, being in the office so late.

I hung up the phone and rubbed the goose bumps standing up on my arms. My space was bordered by windows on one side, and when I'd first gotten the job, that had seemed like a perk. But now, standing there alone, I felt like I was inside a fishbowl, on display to anyone who might be watching from one of the surrounding buildings.

A knock startled me, and I spun around. The young woman in the doorway took a hesitant step back at my no-doubt feral expression.

"Sorry! I'm here from Hope Springs. The guy at the front said I could come straight back."

"Of course. Come right in." I swallowed the rush of embarrassment at being caught freaking myself out in the middle of an empty office. What the hell was wrong with me?

Luckily the young woman, a studious type named Alison, didn't seem to mind my distraction. I dragged over a chair from the next cubicle so she could sit. Before long, despite my earlier hesitation, I found myself completely immersed in the young woman's description of the new job program.

"This is going to help so many women," Alison concluded.

"Thank you for agreeing to help. Some people don't understand the confidence boost that just looking better can give you. Especially when you've been made to feel that dressing up is flirting. That was always a trigger for my ex. Any time I wore makeup, he assumed I was using it to flirt with other men."

My hand clenched, crumpling the paper I was holding. "Everything becomes your fault. Until finally, you're afraid of your own shadow and can barely look anyone in the eye."

"Yes. That's it exactly." Alison smiled at me sadly. "Sounds like you understand all too well."

That jarred me out of my languid state. I'd been so caught up in Alison's descriptions of the program and all the great things they were doing that I'd forgotten where I was and who I was talking to. It was alarming that I could forget so easily. Especially when I'd spent years burying that part of my life so deep that no one could ever find out.

"Well, I can't even imagine what you've been through. But I want to help however I can." I stood and held out my hand, hoping that would signal that the meeting was over without being rude.

Alison shook my hand with a knowing look. "I'll be in touch about the dates for the makeup seminars. Also, we'll send a volunteer over to pick up the clothes Adriana agreed to donate next week."

I hoped I was nodding in the right places and saying the right things. My head spun a little as a sudden wave of dizziness hit me.

No, I did not have time for this nonsense. I refused to get a migraine right now.

But as my panic increased, so did the throbbing behind my eyes. *Oh, God no, not right now,* I thought. Migraines loved to sneak up on me whenever possible, but I didn't have my medication with me. I closed my eyes briefly and took a deep breath. It was all this stress with no outlet. Of course it was building up. Stress was a huge migraine trigger for me and always had been.

I hated it. Hated the weakness of it and how it rendered me completely vulnerable. For years, I'd taken increasingly stronger medication, hoping to find something that could cure me, but it turned out my migraines were something that had to be managed. By avoiding stress, eating well, exercising, and avoiding triggers.

I sighed in relief as Alison finally walked out. I rubbed at my temples with the pads of my fingers. That was it. Looked like I'd be spending the night under the covers trying not to move. As I gathered my things to leave, the phone on my desk rang again. When I picked it up and heard nothing but silence, I wondered how I was supposed to manage my stress when the world around me was determined to throw my past in my face?

CHAPTER SEVEN

Jonas

I was exhausted. After the last several days with Lindsey Myers, I was ready to get back to New York. But the work we were doing was important. And I was glad to see Lindsey settled in.

At first I hadn't wanted to come down to Atlanta to get her set up. The client was great, a sweet woman. But I internalized too much of this shit, especially when there were kids involved. I remembered people trying to help my mother. But truth be told, this little trip was a good excuse to get the hell away from New York. To get the hell away from JJ. My mind was still rattling with everything that had happened right before I left.

Go on, say it. You fucked up by kissing her.

And yes, I'd kissed her back because my temper was up. And my curiosity had flared. And because she was driving me fucking insane. But still, I knew better. I knew that was a line that I couldn't uncross. But I'd gone ahead and crossed it anyway. What the hell was wrong with me? I shook my head to clear it and dragged my attention back to the matter at hand.

I turned to Lindsey with a smile. "Okay, so let's go over the panel one more time."

She grinned at me. "I swear you're hovering over me like a mother hen. I have the code. It's the reverse of Henry's birthday and my birthday. I won't forget those dates."

"I know. But humor me. It'll help to know that you know exactly what to do."

Though she rolled her eyes, she went straight to the panel hidden behind the painting, moved the painting aside, plugged in the code and a star. The star meant all was safe. If she plugged in the code and hit pound, that was an alert to the security company that even though she was punching in the code, she was doing it under duress. That way they would send the police with a quiet presence, no sirens, no lights.

I would rather not think about what would happen in that scenario. Because that scenario would mean that her ex-husband had found her and their son Henry. It would mean that I had failed her.

Noah and Dylan had tracked the guy down, and lo and behold, he'd had drugs on him, which was a violation of his parole. So it was back to prison. But the jackhole had friends. Too many low-life friends.

Which is why we had to get her as far away from him as possible. She'd left without any money and just the clothes on her back. Noah had a slush fund for such occasions, as well as safe houses in several cities across the country. Blake Security had rented her the house for next to nothing and she could stay as long as she wanted. The only caveat was that if we had someone we needed to hide in a hurry, she put them up in the spare room until we could move whoever it was safely.

We'd also gotten her a job. A decent-paying one that would allow her to afford to send Henry to a good school. All this so she would be safe.

I nodded my approval. "Good. I'm glad you remember."

"I told you I would. Now, do you want me to get your last slice of pie before you have to head back to New York?"

"I think you already know the answer to that." I followed her into the kitchen. I liked her. And I hoped she would be able to stay safe. Unlike the last woman I'd tried to help.

———

I MADE it to the airport and caught the last flight back from Atlanta, crammed into one of those tiny airline seats. I headed back to my apartment around seven o'clock, and the last thing I wanted to do was ever leave again. All I wanted was to grab a shower and crash. But my damn phone rang the moment I stepped foot into my place.

I scowled at it hoping that it wasn't Noah. I simply did not have the energy for some team emergency at the moment. The name on the caller ID however, was unexpected.

"Mira, what's wrong? Are you okay?"

"Yes, I'm fine. I'm so sorry to call so late. But do you think that maybe we can meet for a moment? Back at the coffee shop?"

I didn't even think. All I did was walk faster to deposit my weekender bag on my bed and change out my jacket for something that would conceal my holster. "I'm on my way."

Ten minutes later, I found her at the exact same table where we'd sat the last time. When she looked up, she gave me a weak smile, and I went to join her.

"Mira, I was worried. Are you okay?"

"I'm so sorry I worried you."

When I just stared down at her, inspecting her for any outward bruising, she shifted uncomfortably. "Honestly, I'm fine. Can you please have a seat? I wanted to say something."

I slid into the seat next to her. "Well, you look okay. He hasn't hurt you, has he?"

She didn't even look surprised that I knew about her being back with her ex. But color did tint her cheeks. "I think you were right."

My brows snapped down. "I would rather not be right about all the things I'm thinking. Elaborate. Has he hurt you again?"

She shook her head. But her hands shook. "No. Not yet. But," she hesitated for a moment, "I can see it. The anger in him, the rage. There are flashes of it, and at the end of the day I'm still living the exact same way I was. Afraid. Afraid to do anything, afraid to talk, afraid to move, afraid to not have dinner on the table. He tells me that I don't need to do that. That the anger management worked or whatever, but I don't believe him. And so I'm afraid."

I nodded sagely. "Do you want me and Noah to clear him out? We could grab the guys and swing on by to make sure he stays far away from you."

She shook her head. "I can do this on my own."

"No one can do this on their own." I licked my lips and wondered if I should tell her how I ended up here. Sitting across from a woman like her, one that so desperately needed help but refused to take it. And then the words were spilling out before I could even stop them.

"My mother. She was the most beautiful woman I have ever seen in my life. You know when they say people have a light that shines through them? She was one of those people."

Mira frowned, as if not quite certain why I was telling her the story. But she stayed quiet.

"My father, on the other hand ... Pure asshole through and through. Believed that he walked on water and everyone else should bow before him. And boy oh boy, did he have a shitty temper. It didn't even take much to set him off. A good morning not said the right way, and you'd get a quick knock across your head. He used to pick her up and haul her to the floor for not having dinner ready. You can probably imagine."

Mira nodded. "Oh, too well."

"And then there's me. He wanted me to be the best. To brag to everyone about how I was the best. And God help me if I didn't perform. He would take it out on my mother. Never me. I would beg for him to take it out on me. But always her. And she stayed. It didn't matter how many times I begged her to go; she stayed. Eventually he killed her. I don't want something like that to happen to you, Mira."

Her eyes filled with tears. And she blinked them rapidly away. "I don't want that to be me either. I thought he'd changed. I thought the anger management was working. But I think I'm still the same person. I've still been conditioned to be afraid of him. And he's still the same person. He tries to control his anger, but he's not very good at it. I think I'm going to bear the brunt of that soon enough if I'm not careful."

"What do you need? Do you need a place to stay? We have safe houses all over the city. New Jersey, Philly. We can get you relocated. If you need money, we have a slush fund for these things. Hell, I was just making good use of it today. Let us help you. I don't want you going back to that house. Because he will tell you all about how he's changed and how he'll never do it again, and I'm terrified for you."

She shook her head. "No. I don't need any of that stuff. You and your team did plenty for me, and I didn't listen. I didn't take any of that advice. But I'm taking it now. My bag is in the car. I applied for a job months ago when I was first leaving him. I interviewed, but I didn't hear back so I didn't think anything of it.

"But they called today, and I knew if I told him I wanted to take the job it was not going to end well. And maybe I'm not the same person, but I couldn't stand the idea of him beating me over something I was so excited and happy about. I knew I had to go. I just wanted to say thank you and good-bye before I left. I'm going to use the drive down to reflect on my life and what I really want from it."

Some of the weight that pressed down on my chest the moment I'd met Mira Ashton eased up. "You don't have to say thank you."

"Yes, I do. I know I owe you my life. And you don't have to worry about me. I still have the papers the British guy on your team made me for my new identity. I don't have any family anyway. So I get to vanish. I just wanted you to know. And then to ask you to say thank you to Noah and the rest of your team."

I nodded my acceptance and we both stood. But before she could turn and walk away, I grabbed her hand gently. "I mean it. Mira. You need anything, anything at all, call us. You know the number by heart. We will help you. It doesn't matter what it is."

I could only stand back and watch as she left, and I prayed that this time, this time, I was actually able to save one of them.

———

Jessica

I BALANCED the phone to my ear even as I held two cups of coffee, had a shoulder bag containing several samples on my arm, and teetered on four-inch heels. Adriana had sent me out for a samples run, and of course, I stopped to get myself a reward coffee.

After a week of working with the Hope Springs charity, my nerves were frayed. And my heart was broken. In so many ways, I'd come a million miles from where I'd been. I was no longer that young girl who was too scared to say anything, too concerned about what everyone would think, so worried about my life and those around me. But in other ways, I was still in the exact same spot. I wore my outer shell of bravado every morning like a set of clothes. It was my Teflon suit.

Nothing fazed me; nothing bothered me. I was a poor facsimile of the person I wanted to be. The person I knew I wasn't. So every morning when I woke up, I knew I was telling everyone a lie. Worse yet, I needed the suit. I needed it to survive on a daily basis. Working with Hope Springs just reminded me of who I'd been, of who I was, deep down inside. If that wasn't good enough to fray the nerves on a daily basis, then I didn't know what was.

And certainly, caffeine isn't going to help.

Yeah, maybe not, but coffee was one of life's little heaven-sent pleasures. So I was going to have my coffee, and then I was going to stick my nose back to the grindstone and just power through this whole thing. I wanted to help these women. I wanted to get them to freedom. I wanted to get them safe and away from harm.

The springtime breeze with the blare of taxicabs' horns all around made me almost able to forget. With the flow of pedestrian traffic going mostly against me, I could practically get lost in the sea of faces. I made a right turn at the corner to head back toward the office and stopped short. Across the street in Longwinds boutique, clear as day, I saw a familiar face.

My heart rate sped up and my breathing hitched. *No. It can't be him.* I'd already convinced myself I'd hallucinated his car at the curb the other day. My feet were rooted to the concrete as I stared for a long moment. Passersby jostled me backwards and forwards as they hurried past on the way to wherever they were going.

But still I stared. No, this couldn't be happening. This was not my life. I didn't want this; I didn't need this. I was done with this part of my life wasn't I?

You'll never be done.

Oh, fuck that. I wasn't going to stand here. I didn't want to be afraid anymore. I had to be sure.

I darted out into the traffic between the taxicabs and horns blaring at me. But I didn't care. It's not like they were going anywhere anyway. The traffic was at a near standstill. My heels made a clip-clop sound as I skipped over the pavement and straight to the boutique.

By the time I made it across the street, past the white wood and glass doors, I didn't see anyone. There were a couple of shoppers and one saleswoman helping someone out. What the hell? No, I hadn't imagined that. I'd seen him. He'd been here.

Or is your mind playing tricks on you? You're being forced to examine who you are. Who you've been. And the person who made you that way.

No, no, no. He couldn't be here. I hadn't seen him in so many years. Seven now? It couldn't be. I headed back for the dressing rooms, shoving aside every single curtain. Luckily there was no one back there.

Stacking my two coffees one on top of the other, I opened the staff only doors and peered in. There was no one there. How could I have made that mistake?

"Hey, you can't be back here."

The sales girl had come around to see what I was up to. "I'm so sorry. I was looking for someone. I saw him in the mirror outside. Tall, over six feet. Dark hair."

The sales girl shook her head. "I'm sorry. There was no one who fits that description back here."

I shook my head. "No. I saw him. It was him. Are you sure? I'm not crazy. It was him."

The sales girl's brows lifted, and she backed away a step. "I'm sorry, but I'm going to have to ask you to leave. If you don't, I will call the police."

The police. I would welcome them coming. Except, what was I going to tell them? *I saw my psycho ex. The one I never filed charges against or got a restraining order against. That ex. He was in the store. I need him found.*

No. Likely all they would do was arrest me for trespassing or something. "I'm sorry. I'll go. Are you sure—?"

The sales girl shook her head. "There is no one here except my customers."

I nodded. *Shit.* Maybe my mind was playing tricks on me. It was understandable, considering everything I'd been dealing with over the last week. I was seeing ghosts where there weren't any. Coffees back in hand, I stepped back out of the boutique just as my phone rang.

Again I stacked the cups while I hunted the phone out of my pocket. "Hello?"

"You always did look good in red."

I whirled around, searching for any familiar faces in the crowd. On the turn though, my heel caught, and my coffees tipped, fell over, and splashed everywhere. Pedestrians jumped out of the way of the scalding hot dark liquid. But I didn't care. I'd find him.

"How'd you get my number?"

"I've *always* had your number." The low rumbling laugh on the phone was cold and icy. All too familiar. After all these years.

He'd found me.

CHAPTER EIGHT

Jonas

I knew the moment I heard her voice that something was wrong.

I had just finished a session of lifting weights and was about to grab a shower. I'd had a shitty morning and early afternoon. I figured that if I could get some gym time in, at least I'd have done something productive that day. If it were anyone else, I wouldn't have even answered the phone. But as soon as JJ's picture flashed on the screen, I dropped the weights I was putting away right where I stood.

"Hey, JJ. Everything okay?"

"Jonas! Oh my God."

Her voice came through the phone like a shriek, and the shrill sound froze me in my tracks. I'd heard her sound like a lot of things—pissed off, happy, playful and exhausted—but never terrified. My girl was tough as nails. Which made the palpable fear in her voice even more alarming.

"JJ, what's going on? Where are you right now?"

There was only harsh breathing followed by a soft sob. I gripped the phone so hard it was a miracle it didn't shatter in my hand. In the span of ten seconds every terrible thing I'd ever seen in my nightmares raced through my mind.

"So help me ... JJ, tell me where you are."

"I'm on the street. Outside of Longwinds." Another sob.

I was already moving. "Are you alone?"

"No ... I don't know. *I need you.*"

I could barely breathe as everything inside me clenched and my blood turned to ice. It had to be bad for her to ask for my help. Fuck. I was on the parking level now and my steps quickened as I approached my Jeep.

"JJ, I need you to keep talking to me. Let me know you're okay."

After the world's longest pause, one in which I died a thousand times over, she finally spoke. "I'm here. I'm okay. But I know there was someone."

Her voice was shaky. She was probably in shock.

If anyone had hurt her ... Why the hell hadn't I insisted on accompanying her everywhere? Considering how thoroughly she'd bewitched me, it was hardly a stretch to imagine that other men felt the same way. I'd seen what some men did to the women they claimed to love. Despite how much she hated having a security detail, I should have put my foot down and insisted. Why hadn't I taken care of her?

Noah hadn't spared any expense or left any stone unturned when it came to ensuring Lucia's safety. Why hadn't I done the same?

But Lucia and Noah are together. JJ isn't yours, the rational part of my brain argued.

The hell she isn't, I thought bitterly. She might not know it yet but she was mine just as surely as I was hers. Every breath I took belonged to her.

"I'm almost there, JJ. Just hang on, okay?"

I was probably going to end up in some police chase, considering how crazy I was driving but I didn't bother slowing down. Let them chase me. As long as I got to JJ and made sure she was safe, they could put me in handcuffs. It was nothing that hadn't been done before.

The dark thought accompanied me as I raced through the streets and finally pulled up in front of Longwinds. I knew the boutique only because it was one of Lucia and JJ's favorite stores. My eyes sifted through the crowds walking on the sidewalk in front of the store until I locked onto a small shape a few yards away from the door. JJ was sitting on the hard concrete, her arms curled around her knees, her blond hair falling over her face like a shield.

I parked illegally and jumped out. JJ didn't notice me until I was right in front of her. She raised her head and stared through me, her big blue eyes glassy with unshed tears.

"I want to go home," she confessed in a small voice.

I felt my heart break wide open right then and there.

"Come on, baby. Let's get you off the ground."

The sense of wrongness amplified when she didn't fight me, instead wrapping her arms trustingly around my neck and allowing me to lift her. I noted the spilled coffee a few feet away and the dark stains on her frilly red skirt. Without another word, I carried her to the passenger side of the SUV and belted her in. She allowed me to do it for her, moving her arms and legs like a docile child. It was terrifying, seeing this broken-down version of JJ, like whatever she'd seen had scared her so badly she didn't have the will to fight anymore.

"I want to go home," she whispered again. "My place. I don't want to be around people right now. Please."

It was the please that got me. She was so used to fighting her way through life that I knew what it cost her to ask me for anything. Despite that, I couldn't allow her to put herself in danger. Her apartment wasn't the safest place after the fire, even after all the renovations they'd done. The security there was nonexistent. Before she moved back in, Matthias was planning to wire the place up so tight even a cockroach couldn't sneak in undetected. And in this city, that was saying something.

"We can't do that but I know where we can go." I shut the door before she could protest or hit me with another one of those killer, big-blue gazes that made me feel like I was suffocating.

By the time I climbed into the driver's seat, JJ was quiet again, looking forlornly out the window. Her eyes were trained on the front of the Longwinds store. Had something happened while she was shopping? Had someone hurt her or scared her in one of the dressing rooms? This was New York; anything was possible.

Then she turned and our eyes met, and I shivered at the bone deep pain in her gaze. No, this wasn't just about something that happened today. JJ was running from something bigger than that.

We didn't talk as I navigated the streets, not even when I let out a curse as a group of teenagers ran right in front of the Jeep, forcing me to slam on the brakes. I pulled into an underground garage and glanced over at JJ, wondering if she'd figured out where we were going yet. Not that she'd ever seen my place. Before she'd moved in with the rest of the crew at Blake Security headquarters, we hadn't exactly been friendly enough for her to come over and hang out.

Once I got out, I came around the vehicle to open her door. JJ looked around the dark garage nervously but she unbuckled her seatbelt. "Where are we?"

"My place." I quirked an eyebrow at her surprised stare. "You said you didn't want to see anyone else. My place fits the bill."

She shrugged and then followed me to the elevator bank.

My place didn't have the advanced security we had at the Blake Security building but it was definitely a step up from most places. I swiped my card to access the elevator and then pushed the button for the tenth floor. When the elevator arrived on my floor, JJ stepped out first and then looked around curiously.

"This is a pretty nice building."

I chuckled at her surprise. "I saved my money over the years. It's not like I had much else to spend it on."

Once I opened the door, JJ gave me a small smile and elbowed past me to get inside. I let out a sigh of relief at the small show of attitude. I gave her shit about fighting with me all the time but I hadn't known how much I would miss that saucy mouth of hers. I wasn't living if I couldn't verbally banter with JJ.

"It's so clean." She swiped a finger over one of the tables in the living room and inspected her finger. I know this isn't your doing."

"Actually I can be a bit of a neat freak. But I have a maid service that comes once a week."

"Even though you're not here much?"

I shrugged. "Doesn't mean they should lose a client. And I'm not exactly paying rent at the penthouse."

She grinned. "That's what I said too. The no-rent situation almost makes up for my place being torched." Her smile fell then. "I thought it meant that my bad luck was over."

I opened my mouth to ask what she meant by that but the closed expression on her face changed my mind. It was more important that she feel safe right now. She'd talk when she was ready.

JJ moved from the table to the bookshelves, tilting her head slightly to examine the names on the spines. Her fingers danced over the picture frames arranged on the shelves, tapping lightly on a picture of me with my mother. Then she saw the object right next to it and her mouth fell open.

"You were a cop?"

She picked up the badge resting on the shelf and cradled it in the palm of her hand.

I shivered, wishing now that I'd had time to put a few things away before I brought her here. No one ever came over, so I wasn't used to having to explain things or hide.

"I was. A long time ago."

Her eyes caught and held mine. "You don't have to tell me."

There was a wealth of understanding in her voice. I could drop the subject and she'd never ask again. Something in her eyes promised that she understood not wanting to open certain boxes. She understood wanting to lock them and throw away the key forever. The idea of never opening parts of JJ made me ache. I wanted to wander around and poke through every part of her until there was no door or room in her mind that I hadn't explored.

But how could I ask that of her when I wasn't willing to open up myself?

"Being on the force was all I'd ever wanted. Lots of little boys want to be police officers when they grow up, but most don't know why. Maybe they like the blue uniform or Officer Friendly at their school. But I always knew why I wanted to go into law enforcement. I wanted to protect people who couldn't protect themselves. People like my mom."

JJ's eyes softened immediately. She turned to the picture on the shelf. "This is your mother? She's so beautiful."

The pain welled immediately, swelling, filling every crack and crevice until I thought I'd burst with frustration and impotent rage.

"She was beautiful. The most beautiful woman I'd ever seen."

"Was," JJ echoed sadly. "I'm so sorry."

"She died when I was in high school." I paused and took a deep breath. "She was murdered."

Jessica

I COULDN'T HELP IT. I gasped.

He flinched at the sound. It was such a brief reaction, and if I hadn't been looking at him I might have missed it. But before I knew what I was doing, I was across the room and in his arms. I squeezed him tight, resting my head in the curve of his shoulder.

I wasn't sure what I'd been expecting to hear when I started asking questions. Jonas was such a smartass most of the time that I'd just assumed he'd always gone through life with a happy-go-lucky kind of nonchalance. It was a revelation to discover that his jovial demeanor was masking some seriously painful stuff.

You aren't the only one with ghosts.

Jonas finally shifted, and I pulled back slightly so I could see his face. His forehead was pinched, like he was agitated or maybe even embarrassed.

He cleared his throat. "I'm not telling you this to ... Hell, I don't know why I'm telling you this. Maybe it's so you'll understand. The day I graduated from the police academy I felt like I'd done something for her. Something to help other women like her."

Women like me.

I shivered and wrapped my arms around myself to stop the shaking. If I'd been strong enough to ask for help back then, Jonas might have been one of the police officers who helped me. We could have met all those years ago.

"Your mom would be so proud of the man you've become."

His harsh laughter sounded cruel in the quiet of the room. I pulled back, surprised at the sound after such a serious moment.

"She wouldn't be proud of me. I was naive. You can't change a system that doesn't want to be changed. Instead of helping women, I got pulled into a fucked-up situation and got kicked off the force. Not exactly how I expected things to turn out."

I shivered again, this time by the unexpected conflicting feelings I was experiencing. It was second nature to needle Jonas and try to get a response out of him, but this was different. This was real. The thought that he might not know how much he'd helped people, including me, was incomprehensible.

"Jonas, you saved my life."

He shook his head. "If I hadn't gotten you out of the fire, the firefighters would have. They were right behind me."

I shook my head again, the words I wanted so badly to say getting stuck in my throat. How could I tell him that I hadn't even been referring to the fire? It was all so messed up, and he had no idea that he was saving my life right here and now by staying with me when I felt so unstable.

"You've helped a lot of people. I know how seriously you take every single one of your cases. I normally wouldn't tell you this, but you're one of the good ones, Jonas Castillo."

His head lifted slowly, and our eyes met. This close, there was an undeniable intimacy to the position. My mouth fell open as I was hit with a strong surge of desire that made my belly clench and my mouth water. My eyes drifted closed, lulled by the sense of utter safety I felt in his arms. I nuzzled his cheek with my nose, enjoying the slight rasp of his facial hair against my skin.

My hands lifted to rest on his shoulders, pressing against the muscles underneath the thin T-shirt he was wearing. It was no protection from my determined grip. Soon, I was kneading his shoulders while burrowing my nose deeper into the curve of his neck, trying to get farther into the safety net he created around us.

"JJ, baby, what are you doing?"

I ignored his soft whisper as my tongue snaked out to taste his skin. His neck was slightly salty and the taste was like a drug. I swallowed and then bit him gently on the throat. His answering groan raced through me, igniting all my nerve endings and settling like a hot ball of fire between my thighs.

Yes, this was what I needed. To be held and protected by a man who would never hurt me, only comfort and pleasure me. I hooked my arm around his neck and pulled him into a kiss. Our lips collided in a hard, passionate kiss but then Jonas pulled back.

"We shouldn't—"

"Jonas, please. I need you." I didn't wait for his answer, just moved back slightly so I could unbutton my top. His eyes followed my every movement and when I parted the material to reveal my black bra, he swallowed audibly. The strain on his face was evident.

He might not be sure about this, but he couldn't deny that he wanted me too. The knowledge gave me a rush of power. It was a heady thing to be able to command a man's attention like this, especially someone like Jonas who was practically a magnet for women. When I hooked my fingers in the sides of my skirt and inched it down, his fingers clenched like he had to restrain himself from reaching out and touching my skin.

"No, touch me," I encouraged. "I want to touch you, too."

I pressed against him, and without the fabric between us, my breasts pillowed against the hard planes of muscle. He groaned low and deep at the sensation and one hand lifted to caress one of the heavy weights. By the time we broke the kiss, we were both breathing hard and Jonas looked like he was hanging on to the reins of his control by a mere thread.

"You are so beautiful, Jessica."

His use of my first name startled me, and I was caught off guard by how much I liked hearing it on his lips. It made me feel as beautiful as he'd claimed I was, but even more than that, it made me feel like he saw me. Not just any beautiful woman but *me*. Thinking about how long we'd known each other and the things we'd been through was overwhelming, and I tightened my arms around him.

"Please Jonas," I repeated. "I don't want to think about him. Make me forget."

His brow furrowed for a moment, but I didn't want to wait

any longer. I jumped into his arms, and Jonas caught me. I braced my hands on his shoulders as I kissed all over his face. It took a few minutes before I realized he wasn't kissing me back. I stilled.

Jonas set me on my feet carefully and then knelt to get my clothes. He slipped the blouse over each of my arms and then buttoned me up with shaky fingers. Then he held out my skirt and I stepped into it on instinct.

"What is it? Why are we stopping?"

He took a deep breath. "This isn't the right time. You've just been through something that really has you spooked, and I would never take advantage of you."

Annoyed, especially because everything he said made sense, I pulled my skirt up roughly and turned my back to him as I righted my clothes.

When I was almost done, I felt him right behind me.

"You said 'I don't want to think about *him*.' Who were you talking about?"

I froze. Had I said that? I thought back frantically, all the blood draining from my face when I realized what I'd admitted aloud. "It was nothing. I was just babbling."

"*Bullshit*." Jonas moved so he was standing right in front of me and I couldn't avoid his eyes anymore. "Did someone try to hurt you today?"

Somehow his genuine concern was more mortifying than when he was turning me down for sex. My eyes filled with tears, and I gave him my back again. He could dig into my business, follow me around, and apparently make me so hot that I forgot where I was and who I was with. But he wasn't entitled to every thought in my head or to explanations I wasn't ready to give. No one was entitled to those parts of my past. It had taken me years to learn that hard lesson.

"Take me back to the penthouse. Now."

CHAPTER NINE

Jonas

Something was wrong. Something was very, very wrong with her. First of all, JJ barely tolerated me on most days. Next thing I knew, she was jumping my bones?

And you liked it.

Well, hell yeah. Because the moment her lips slid over mine, every synapse in my body had lit up like a Christmas tree. I wanted her. I'd *always* wanted her.

So why don't you take advantage of that?

Because something was wrong. She wasn't acting like JJ. Yeah, under normal circumstances JJ was impetuous, loud, a little foolhardy, and said the first thing that came to her mind. But she wasn't entirely reckless. And she'd never been desperate. Not once, not ever. That kiss, her trying to climb me like a tree, that had been pure desperation. It hadn't been about me at all.

When we arrived at the penthouse, I parked in the basement, in one of the designated spots right next to the door. The whole ride up in the elevator she said nothing to me, resolutely ignoring me with her face turned away.

Oh, so we were going to play this game. "JJ. You gotta talk to me."

"No. I don't. That's the joy of this little arrangement. I don't have to talk to you at all. Not ever."

Once the doors to the penthouse opened, she stormed out with me hot on her heels. Matthias came out of the kitchen holding a tub of rocky road. "Hey, Jonas. I was thinking we could —"

JJ interrupted his flow of conversation by bumping his shoulder as she stormed by him.

She mumbled a brief apology but kept right on marching to her bedroom. Matthias looked to me. "What happened?"

"I have no fucking idea. But I'm sure as hell going to find out."

As I followed her, I heard Matthias whisper, "Maybe that's not the best idea you've ever had?"

I ignored him. What the hell did he know?

What the hell do you know is a better question.

What I knew was that JJ tasted fucking incredible. That's what I knew. I also knew that something was eating at her, burrowing deep inside her, and she was gonna blow. What I didn't know was why it was so important to me that she not self-destruct. Whatever was bothering her was better out than in. I wanted to help her.

Why, because you're Captain freaking America? No. Because despite our constant fighting, I cared about her. I was worried.

Something was wrong. I didn't bother to knock; I just barged into her bedroom.

"Knock much?" She whirled on me, her movements quick and angry as she rolled her shoulders.

"Well, I knew you wouldn't say come in, and something is clearly up with you." I closed the door and locked it.

Her gaze widened and pinned to the lock. *What the hell?*

That wasn't the anger I was used to seeing, that was cold fear.

I frowned and unlocked the door, and then stepped away from it about three feet, giving her clear access if she wanted to get out.

"See, I'm not trying to keep you in here. I just want to talk to you. Something is going on. You haven't been acting like yourself for weeks. Now you're mad at me because I wasn't an asshole?"

"Yes you were."

I crossed arms. "Explain to me *how* I was an asshole. A woman who most of the time is screaming at me, or calling me names, or trying to throw things at me, suddenly decides that she wants to jump my bones. Wraps herself around me, tasting like sugar and sin and everything I could want. But she's not acting like herself. So, instead of backing her up against the wall and sinking inside her so deep that neither one of us can remember our names, I back off because I want to know what's wrong with her. Oh, and I also want her to want me for *me*. Not because she's pissed off or upset, or scared. And somehow that makes me an asshole?"

JJ blinked. "Wow, that's the most words I've heard you use in a row ever."

"I talk plenty."

"Not to me you don't."

"Yeah well. You don't talk to me much either. You shout."

"That's because you needle me."

"I'm not here to fight." I held up my hands. "What I am here to do is find out what's going on. Because you haven't been acting like yourself and I am fucking worried. So out with it."

When her eyes welled with tears, my blood froze in my veins. *Fuck.* I hated tears. "I want you to be okay. Yeah, we needle each other. But I do care about what happens to you. And you're sexy. But then again, you know that already. But more than I want you, more than I want sex, I want you to be okay. And you're clearly not."

She swiped a tear with the back of her hand. "You really are a good guy, aren't you?"

Her voice was soft; there was no edge to it. No edge to her. Her shoulders slumped forward and I saw that she was defeated. What the hell did she mean by that?

"I am. Mostly. Fuck, not always. But if you need help, or are in trouble, or something is wrong, then I'm your guy."

I just prayed to God she started talking because I didn't have the strength to turn her down again if she wound her body around mine.

———

Jessica

I WASN'T EVEN sure what made me start talking to him. Maybe it was something in his eyes. Maybe it was the gentleness of his tone. But either way, all I wanted to do was curl up into a ball and get a really good hug.

Jonas moved forward slowly then took my hand. "Gotta talk to someone sometime, JJ. How about me?"

I nodded and then eased down onto my bed and waited for Jonas to sit next to me. This was not exactly the kind of action I'd planned with him.

Did you really plan that at all? Or were you operating on fear? Okay, I wasn't going to examine that right now. I was too raw. There was too much going on inside.

"I've had really bad luck with guys. The worst kind."

"Maybe just haven't found the right one."

I shook my head. "When I say bad luck, I don't mean that a guy insisted I pay for everything, even though I have had one of those, or that he lived with his parents, although I've had one of those, too. I've had the kind of people that shouldn't be with anyone, the kind of guys that made me feel bad about myself."

His voice was low and hushed when he spoke. There was also

a hint of an edge to it. As if he was starting to see what I was talking about. "You deserve so much more."

I nodded. "I'm sorry. I'm blabbering on. It's just this project at work is making me feel like I'm back in that place again. Where I've been hurt by someone so deeply but have no one to talk to."

He was silent for a long moment then asked softly, "What about Lucia?"

I sniffed away the tears. "Lucia is the best friend a girl could ever ask for. But when her brother died, she was broken. Really, *really* broken for a long time. It was that kind of visceral pain and loss. Even now, knowing that everything worked out for her, I can still see the look of pain in her eyes at the funeral. I can *still* feel her grief. I wasn't going to burden her with my shit. None of that would be fair. So while she was hurting in her own way, I was hurting in another. I never told her because, you know Lucia. She would feel guilty and there was nothing for her to feel guilty about. She'd lost her brother. She was entitled to crumble."

"I don't know. If you sat down and talked to her now she'd probably understand why you didn't tell her, and wish that she could have been there for you. Maybe it would help to talk to her now?"

I shook my head. "No. Her life is finally the way that it should be. Rafe is back. She has Noah and that beautiful baby." Last year had been one hell of a roller coaster ride. Even if I'd been inclined to share all my deep dark and scaries with my bestie, we'd all had a few things to deal with.

Things like someone trying to kill Lucia. Lucia discovering her brother had been alive all that time. Somehow my past problems hadn't made the top of the list.

"Lucia's your friend. She would want to help."

"I'm not bringing her into any of this." Lucia didn't deserve that.

"You're still not going to tell me what's going on?" Jonas asked.

I shook my head. "Enough. It's just been a long day. I freaked out over ... It's okay. I think I just need someone to distract me right now. Do you think you can do that?"

CHAPTER TEN

Jonas

Shit, I wanted her. I had never felt more pressure to make a kiss perfect. But this was JJ and she needed me. It was about so much more than desire.

Looking down at her face, I took in the details that had teased me for so long. The blond hair that always seemed tousled and messy. The blue eyes that should have looked innocent but always had a twinkle of mischief. The peaches-and-cream skin that taunted me to take a bite. She was so beautiful.

"What are you waiting for?" JJ teased. "Do it already."

I groaned. My dick responded to the words *do it* as if she'd been speaking straight to him directly.

"Always busting my balls, aren't you?"

She grinned. "That's what I live for."

"Maybe I need to give that smart mouth something else to do."

Before she could respond to that, I pulled her up slightly so I could fit my lips over hers. It was so perfect, the way we notched together like puzzle pieces. It was a little scary how well we fit, like we'd been made for each other but were just getting around to discovering that. It probably wasn't the smartest thing, starting something with JJ while she was obviously confused and a little scared about what was happening.

She needed to feel safe and secure, and I would never want to pressure her into anything. The mature thing to do would be to end this, whatever it was, then ask her out for a drink after it was resolved.

I pulled back and looked down at the wide blue eyes watching me like I was a savior and a sinner all in one. She made a little whimper in the back of her throat, a hoarse, needy sound that instantly threw me from foreplay into full-scale need. What was it about this woman that made me lose all control? Around JJ, I was nothing but instinct and sensation, years of experience and finesse going right out the window.

"You really have me all twisted up, you know?"

The statement wasn't exactly a compliment, but JJ beamed. I should have known the little troublemaker would love the idea of throwing me off my game. Not that it mattered. Whatever she wanted I was happy to give. Just the thought of JJ needing something and not coming to me for it gave me a deep sense of dissatisfaction. It would have sounded ridiculous just a few months ago, but I was starting to understand exactly why Noah looked happier than ever but also way more stressed. Worrying about someone else constantly took its toll.

Despite how badly I wanted to strip her naked and do all the things I'd dreamed of doing to that luscious body, I felt obligated to at least try to be the voice of reason.

"Are you sure about this, baby? We don't have to do anything. I can just hold you if you want."

JJ scowled. "Jesus, what does a girl have to do to get a little satisfaction?"

She squealed when I suddenly leaped on her, burying my face in her neck.

"That's it. Now you're in for it," I growled against her skin, noting how she shivered as the words brushed over her skin.

Experimentally, I trailed the tip of my tongue up the soft skin of her neck until I reached her ear. She sighed when I took the lobe between my teeth gently.

"That feels so good," she purred. Her hands moved over my shoulders gently, clutching at them when my tongue dipped into the shell of her ear. "I've dreamed about this so many times."

Surprised, I lifted my head. "You dreamed about me?"

She bit her lip, looking slightly bashful. "I used to fight with you and then sneak in here and imagine that you followed me. That you wanted me the same way I wanted you. Like it was so intense you could barely breathe."

"That's exactly how I want you, JJ. You make me lose my head completely. With you, I feel like I have no control."

One of her hands lifted, tentatively to my face. "So let go then. Just do whatever you feel."

I groaned. That kind of freedom was dangerous. There were so many things I wanted to do and feel with her that I didn't know where to start. Then her fingers brushed over my lips and instinctively I opened, nipping at her fingers gently. Her sudden intake of breath sent a stab of desire bolting down my spine. It was suddenly, desperately urgent that I taste her again. Everywhere.

I leaned down and covered her mouth with mine. JJ was right there with me, a willing participant, sucking and licking and biting. God, those sounds she made and the way her fingers clenched in my hair. I couldn't get enough of her.

Hands tugged at her clothing and then mine, frantic to get skin to skin. The next few moments were a blur as we tussled to get free without breaking the kiss. I didn't want to separate from her for even a minute. Maybe a part of me was afraid that if I let this moment go, it would disappear.

JJ didn't seem to have any hesitation about undressing, either.

The sight of the lacy white panties she wore only cranked my desire higher. Not wasting any time, I yanked her closer and buried my face between her legs. Her soft cries egged me on as I tasted her. I didn't even bother to take the panties off, just pulled them to the side. Something about not waiting made it even hotter.

JJ purred and cried with every lash of my tongue. I felt like a man possessed as I licked and sucked until she screamed her release. Panting, JJ didn't even get a chance to catch her breath before I was on her, nuzzling between her soft breasts. Her arms wrapped around me languidly with a satisfied laziness that made me very happy.

"Damn," she said finally. That one word carried a world of meaning.

"Yeah. The best you've ever had, huh?" As I'd hoped, the cocky words made her smile.

"Actually it was. You're amazing."

It was so unexpected to hear her compliment me when I'd been expecting the usual snarky reply. Pleasure curled through me and made me feel like I was lit from within.

"It was for me, too. Everything with you is amazing. I hope you know that, Jessica Jones."

The sudden flush on her cheeks told me that I'd pleased her, and the thought made me happy, too. What the hell was happening? I'd never cared this much about a woman's approval before. Before I had time to examine it too closely, JJ arched her back, pressing her body against mine, wiping all rational thought from my brain.

Then she reached into my boxers and wrapped delicate fingers around my hard cock. I bit the inside of my cheek to keep from blowing my load like a teenager.

"It seems I'm the only one who's had my fun," JJ teased. "You've been keeping this from me."

"Not anymore," I groaned. I reached for my wallet for a

condom and had it on in record time. Under different circumstances I'd have spent more time getting her ready, but if JJ felt what I did, any more ready would cause a heart attack.

I settled between her legs and we both cried out at the pressure. I rocked against her, sliding through her slick heat. JJ whimpered and her nails dug into my back.

"You ready, baby?" I swiveled my hips again.

"Hurry up or I'll kill you!"

I chuckled, but the laugh died in my throat when she canted her hips forward and I slipped inside. I wasn't ready for the intense pressure and sense of rightness being enveloped in her heat. Then JJ wrapped her arms around my shoulders and pulled me down for another kiss, and the sense of rightness just magnified. This was where I was meant to be and who I was meant to be with.

"Oh my God, so good," JJ cried, her eyes on mine, wide and trusting.

Her pussy clamped down, and we groaned together. For a moment, I was suspended in time, and I wondered if I'd actually died and gone to heaven. If this was how I went, clutched in the tightest, hottest pussy I'd ever encountered, I figured it was a risk worth taking.

"Fuck, you're so tight."

JJ mewled and wrapped her long legs around my waist, holding me against her. It was like being enclosed in heat, the action spurring me to take her harder. Soon I was lost in the sound of her cries and the firm grasp of her muscles squeezing my cock as she came continuously.

Jessica

I WAS IN TROUBLE. So much trouble.

After what felt like having ten orgasms in a row, I could barely catch my breath. But Jonas was still hard. The man had just fucked me to within an inch of losing consciousness and he wasn't done yet.

So much fucking trouble.

He swiveled his hips, as if to remind me that he was still there. Like I could forget. I snorted softly at my own joke.

"Am I amusing you, Miss Jones?" There was an erotic threat in the soft timbre of his voice that made me shiver.

I peeked up at him through lowered lashes. I was used to being snarky and argumentative with him. It was Jonas after all, my favorite target when I was feeling bitchy. But now I would never be able to look at him the same way again. The man was a marathoner in the bedroom and hung like a stallion.

How the hell could I argue with him knowing what he was packing beneath his clothes now?

"I wasn't laughing at you. Definitely not," I finally muttered.

His eyes heated and he thrust again, making me gasp softly. "Good, because I'm not done with you yet. You ready for more?"

I was going to be sore, but I didn't care. "Yes, please."

It was his turn to chuckle, but he didn't make me wait. He pulled me down by hooking his arms under my knees. Once I was in a better position, he brushed his thumb over my clit. My mouth fell open as I tried to gain control of my breathing. I'd just come and was already on the edge again.

"Look at me," Jonas rasped. His deep voice would forever be a part of my erotic dreams.

When I finally met his eyes, he let loose a deep growl that instantly made me wetter. Suddenly it was all too much. This was Jonas, my friend and sometimes enemy, and I was right on the brink of losing myself in him. Trusting a man with everything hadn't worked out so well in the past.

As if he could sense my fear, Jonas cupped my cheeks. "I've got you, sweetheart. It's okay. I just want to make you feel good."

The simple words meant so much more than he could ever know.

"You do. You feel so good."

I clutched at his arms, overwhelmed at not only the physical sensations of taking him deep inside, but the sense of closeness. I'd never felt this close to anyone, not even the one man who'd taught me never to trust again. But I couldn't think about that now, not when I'd come so far and felt safe for the first time in a long time.

That was how Jonas made me feel. Safe and protected and ... loved.

Jonas's fingers tightened under my shoulders, holding me captive as he slid deeper. His harsh breaths in my ear increased, and to me it was the most erotic sound in the world. This was all so new to me, and I was a little scared to examine it too closely, but there was no denying our physical connection. I'd never had this reaction to a man before, like I could completely let go and be safe and secure in his arms with no judgment. Only Jonas had ever made me feel this free. I loved it and reveled in the erotic power I held over him.

Experimentally, I tightened my muscles around him. His groan was the sexiest thing I'd ever heard.

"Fuck! Your pussy just clamped down on me."

I looked him in the eye, holding his gaze as I deliberately tightened my muscles again. His jaw clenched and he closed his eyes in an expression that was a cross between agony and ecstasy.

"You are fucking perfect, you know that?"

His low sexy growl in my ear sent me flying and everything splintered into fragments of light and color.

CHAPTER ELEVEN

Matthias

I could see the bloody writing on the wall. The way Jonas and JJ were going, things were hitting a fucking tipping point. And the way Jonas had gone in that room after her, followed by silence and then, well yeah, I'd had to put on my noise canceling headphones once the moaning started.

Granted, the two of them had been circling each other for God knew how long now. It was bound to happen. I just prayed that they wouldn't be nearly as disgusting as Noah and Lucia. Those two could barely keep their hands off each other. Even when she was pregnant.

You thought she looked gorgeous pregnant. All glowy skin and tits to—

I shoved the thought aside. For the most part, I managed to keep the wayward Lucia thoughts to myself ...deep down, hidden in the dark. But sometimes I couldn't help it. We had a much more appropriate relationship now. Not that we'd had any kind of *inappropriate* relationship.

Oh bollocks. I had much more appropriate feelings about her

now. But every now and again, I would wish for someone like her for myself.

As if that was ever going to happen. *What normal girl was going to want a twenty-five year old virgin with a pierced dick?* Yeah. There was that.

No, I'd just stick to my computers for now and try and ignore the people coupling off around me. At the very least, I had the rest of the guys.

An alarm chimed, alerting me that someone was accessing my restricted files. I frowned and immediately opened up the server access window. I kept the personnel files in a separate server, hidden under lock and key, under a mountain of shit. They were completely encrypted, and even if someone was able to decrypt the files, everything was in code. So what the hell? Who was in there?

I peeled off one of the headphones only to hear a distant moan again. Damn it. The two of them were going to become a problem. But I had bigger fish to fry right now. I pulled out my phone and quickly tapped out a message to Noah.

This was too urgent to fuck with our usual clandestine methodology. In seconds my phone was ringing.

"What's the problem?"

Noah was at Lucia's grandmother's house. They'd taken Isabella over there for a family dinner. Usually Nonna came to the penthouse and cooked for everyone, but the family needed some alone time.

"Someone just tried to access personnel files."

There was a beat of silence. "What do you mean *someone?*"

"Not sure exactly. Access codes were attempted. But I've closed off whatever opening they tried to use. I didn't know if it was deliberate though. I was hoping it was you trying to get in and that you just forgot to let me know first."

"Fuck."

"I might be wrong." It was unlikely that he was. "Might've been a system error or something. But I don't like to fuck around with that kind of stuff. So figured I'd call and check. You're the only other one who has access."

"Not me. Lock it down if it's a system glitch. But what is your gut telling you?"

My gut said all hell was about to break loose. But I wasn't telling Noah that right now. The guy was with his wife, trying to have some much needed family time. "Gut tells me trouble. But I've got an eye on it; the data is locked down and nearly impossible to read. If it is someone trying to break in, they'll have to try again. And I'll be waiting."

"With a machete and a hacksaw?"

I smirked. "Too bloody right." In my field days, when I'd been an agent for ORUS, my weapons of choice had been knives. Knives were personal. Knives conveyed a message.

But you're not that person anymore.

No, no I wasn't. Now I didn't kill people because someone told me to. And that was a balm to my soul. But if I did have trouble, I would fight like the devil to protect my newfound soul. And to protect my family. The family I'd made for myself.

Next time someone came knocking, they were going to get a nasty surprise.

———

Jessica

THE NEXT NIGHT, I pushed aside the heavy glass door and stepped out into the balmy spring evening. I knew the rules. Get directly into a cab and go straight home. I'd gotten an earful from Noah after the last time. And Matthias. Even Oskar had found a way to tell me that I needed to be more careful. I was just about to hop into a cab when I saw the black SUV parked at the curb and recognized the driver.

Unable to help the smile, I slowly strolled over to Jonas, making sure to emphasize the sway in my hips. When he rolled the window down and leaned over, my heart caught just a little. *You should not be feeling this way. You are going to get hurt. This is dangerous. Don't you understand that?*

I did understand. But the knowledge didn't stop me from feeling. When he leaned over, his smile was rakish. "You should get in the car with me."

"My mother warned me about guys like you. You're going to drag me off somewhere and do all sorts of debauched things to me."

He raised a brow. "Is that an invitation?"

I shook my head and giggled. "Possibly."

"Get in. We're going to go eat."

"I love how you just dictate these things."

Jonas shrugged and said, "So you're not hungry for a home-cooked, classic Mexican meal?" My stomach rumbled and he chuckled low. "Your stomach knows what's up. Get in."

Like I was really going to say no to a home-cooked meal. From what I'd heard, he was an amazing cook. I would eat pretty much anything the man put in front of me right now. I was starving.

"You know, you didn't have to come pick me up. I was going to behave and take a cab."

"I know. I wanted to."

As I climbed into the car, his slow perusal of my body told me everything I needed to know. He was thinking about the other night. Of us in bed. Of the way he'd made me scream with just a few simple touches. The way he'd made my heart race. He was thinking about every touch, every movement, every breath. I knew that because that's exactly what I was thinking about. Just being next to him, my skin hummed with anticipation and awareness.

I cleared my throat. "So, Mr. Castillo. Tell me, where did you learn to cook authentic Mexican food?"

"My mom was from Mexico. And I'm an only child. So there was really no one else to pass her secrets on to."

"So you became the daughter she never had?"

Jonas grumbled that sexy, low laugh, just as I'd hoped he would. "Something like that. I'm glad she taught me. Now I use the skill to impress beautiful women."

I shook my head and grinned even though I tried not to. "Seriously. I do appreciate the ride."

"You're welcome. But you know it's nothing. If you call any one of us, we'll come get you."

When we passed the boutique where I'd gotten the blast from the past, I couldn't help the small shiver that came over me. "I know. And I should use it more. I get caught up in being independent, you know? I had a spook the other day. It reminded me that with everything we've had going on in the last year or so, maybe I should take advantage of the big burly security team I have at my disposal. One guy in particular."

Jonas gave me a knowing smile. When we reached his apartment, I noticed a couple of little changes and additions. He'd added a purse hook right next to the door. That hadn't been there the last time I'd been here. And when he turned on the lights, they immediately went dim and were far more subdued than I remembered. Music started to play faintly, a low and sexy sound that sounded like Trip Hop or something.

"Mr. Castillo, something tells me that you planned all of this."

He shrugged out of his jacket and then hung his holster next to it. "Who, me?"

"Yes, you. This looks like mood lighting."

"That's because it *is* mood lighting," he said with a laugh before leading me into the kitchen. "Here, you chop the onions."

"Oh man, how come I get the dirty job?"

He chuckled low and throaty, a familiar sound to me now. He made that sound when he was happy, truly happy and relaxed.

Yeah, like when he's inside you.

"No one eats for free. All the jobs are dirty if they're done right. And that's the way we like it," he said with a wink.

For the next hour, we worked side by side to make what he promised would be the best fajitas I'd ever tasted. He made me laugh. He danced with me a little and regaled me with the happier memories of his mother.

I told him about the places I wanted to visit, the things I wanted to see. My last trip to Europe as well. It turned out we knew a lot of the same people in the fashion industry. How he knew people in the fashion industry confused me though.

"Let me guess, you dated a model or two?"

He grinned. "A gentleman never tells."

"Come on. If you have dated a bona fide model, I'll be disgusted, and then I will also be insanely jealous."

"How would you feel knowing that I'd walked a runway or two myself when I was on holiday visiting my grandmother?"

Oh, I believed him all right. He had the looks, the body. Lord help me, the face. And he was just crazy enough to do something like that on a whim. This also explained his ridiculous love of clothing.

"Of course you were a model."

He rolled his eyes. "Like you couldn't be yourself."

I snorted. "Come on. I'm just Jessica Jones from Queens. Not a model."

"But you easily could've been. You're not super tall, but the face ... and I will attest to the magnificent body."

A flush crept up my neck, and I ducked my head as I stirred the sauce. "Jonas Castillo, flattery will get you everywhere."

"Right now, I'll settle for flattery getting me a kiss."

He wrapped an arm around my waist and slid his hand along

my arm, gently caressing until we were stirring the pot of sauce together. And then he kissed my neck.

For a moment, I couldn't believe that this was my life. It was all so wonderfully *normal*. Like Jonas Castillo was just this hot guy that I was interested in. And we were just standing here stirring sauce like any other normal couple would do.

You can't have this. Because even though this is great for now, your past will ruin it.

I couldn't let myself get too close. Because if I did, I was going to get my heart ripped out.

CHAPTER TWELVE

Jessica

It took about an hour to finish cooking and I had never had so much fun making a meal. It was strange because I'd never been much of a cook, but being with Jonas made everything fun. For the next hour I decided to put away all my worries and just live in the moment. After all, what was life if I couldn't enjoy a good meal with a handsome man?

"This looks delicious," I said.

We worked together bringing dishes over to the small dining room table. I looked around curiously. It was a nice apartment, altogether too fancy for a single man living alone. I remembered the tarnished police badge on the bookshelf. There was so much I didn't know about him. Was it so hard to believe that perhaps he'd had a family in another life? Maybe he hadn't always lived here alone.

Jonas shrugged. "My mom taught me to enjoy good food. So I try to keep up my skills. She's looking down on me. Got to make her proud."

There was something about the way he said it that made me

pause. After the day he'd confided about his mother's murder, I'd tried hard not to pry. I enjoyed giving Jonas a hard time because he was pompous, annoying, and way too sexy. But I never would have guessed he had so much going on underneath the surface. The badass exterior was deceptive. He was really a sweet guy.

"Why would you think she isn't proud?" I asked. From everything that I'd seen, Jonas was a perfect son, the kind that any mother would be proud of.

"I'm sure she is," he replied. But he wouldn't meet my eyes. "Can you grab the wine?"

Jonas kept his eyes down as he set the table. Okay then. That was a clear sign he didn't want to talk about it. *Noted.*

I went back to the kitchen to grab the bottle of wine we'd started working on earlier. The fragrant scent of seasoned chicken, vegetables, and cheese filled the air.

My stomach growled. "I can't wait to dig in."

And just like that Jonas's smile was back. "That's what I love to see. A woman with an appetite."

"Well if that's what you like, get ready for a treat. I don't miss meals." I picked up a plate with a big smile. "I'm sure my ass tells the true story."

"Your ass torments me, that's what it does," Jonas muttered.

I paused in the act of loading the corn tortilla on my plate with meat. I bit my lip and glanced over at Jonas. He held my gaze, not backing down. *Oh Jesus.* Blood rushed to my face and I hurriedly threw toppings on my plate, not even looking at what I was getting.

"That's right, eat up. You'll need your energy later." Jonas grinned as I added another tortilla to join the two I already had. If the man was going to make erotic promises like that, I wasn't going to discourage him.

For a moment, all was quiet as we enjoyed our food, but it was a comfortable silence. I tried not to stare at him but it was hard.

He was handsome, yes, but more than that, he was kind. I'd never thought I could have this sort of easy, comfortable routine with a man, where I was completely fine just hanging out doing nothing.

For so long, I'd thought of men as always having an agenda. The thought of trusting any man had been incomprehensible. No man would have ever been able to get that close anyway.

But somehow Jonas had snuck past every single one of my defenses and become an essential part of my everyday life. With me living at the penthouse and him over so often, he'd quickly become an integral part of my life.

I couldn't imagine waking up in the morning without seeing him in his workout clothes, sweaty from a long run in the penthouse gym. And now it was even harder to imagine my evenings without him. Who would I talk to or rant to about the crazy stuff that happened at work? Who could I call that would drop everything just because I felt uneasy and needed to hear a familiar voice?

Lucia would drop everything for you. You know she would.

I felt an unmistakable rush of sadness at the thought. Because even though it was true, Lucia had a family now that had to take precedence over anything else. Including my friendship. And that was the way it should be. The circle of life. The bubbly girl I'd grown up with was now a wife and mother.

I had no part of that. Lucia had created a new family and I was only on the outskirts looking in.

I'm jealous, I realized. Not in a bad way, I was thrilled that my best friend had found the love she deserved. But there was no denying that I missed my place in Lucia's life and longed to find that kind of love for myself.

"You're quiet. Whenever you're quiet it's either because something bad happened that you don't want me to find out about or because you're plotting something you don't want me to find out about."

I smiled at his attempt to cheer me up. "Neither this time. I was just thinking about work."

He narrowed his eyes. "What's going on at work? Has anything else strange happened?"

Now I felt bad. I'd just been trying to throw him off the scent of my melancholy feelings about my best friend, not worry him.

"Nothing like that. It's actually about this charity event I'm working on. It's to benefit victims of domestic violence. Working with them has been intense. Brings up a lot of old memories."

That actually wasn't a lie, I conceded. It had been intense planning the makeup seminars that we'd finally decided to do once a week. When I thought back to how reluctant I'd been to get involved in the beginning, I was ashamed.

It had brought up some bad memories, of course, but it had also been cathartic in a way. When Alison described some of the women I was currently working with, I recognized myself in their stories. I understood their fear, their hesitation to take a chance and trust someone to help them.

It was incredibly daunting but also humbling. Maybe they weren't the only ones in need of healing.

"Old memories?" Jonas's mouth flattened into a thin line and I knew the moment he got it. "Someone hurt you."

I swallowed, my throat suddenly dry as dust. "It was a long time ago. It doesn't matter now."

"It matters," Jonas rasped, his jaw working furiously. "Everything about you matters to me."

It was such a simple statement, but it meant the world to me. I closed my eyes and willed the damnable tears back. My emotions had been dangerously close to the surface lately, but that was a line I couldn't cross. I'd already screwed up and cried in front of him once before.

"I was really young. Really insecure. And he made me feel special. Even when things escalated, when he hit me or threatened to kill me, he always made it seem like he did those things because he was so desperate to keep me. Because I drove him to it. It was overwhelming for a teenage girl."

His hand covered his mouth. "You were that young?"

I shrugged. "It was right after Rafe died. Lucia was a mess and I was, too. I'd never known anyone who died before. I had no idea how to process it. Then I met D—then I met a guy."

He didn't say anything for a long time, and suddenly I was slammed with a sense of foreboding. Why had I told him any of that? It never went well when guys found out about my past. They either went into hero mode and felt like they needed to save me from my damaged past or they were overwhelmed and got distant. The thought of Jonas distancing himself from me hurt.

"Never mind. I don't know why I'm telling you all of this."

He reached across the table and took my hand gently in his. I was so shocked that I jolted. I relaxed slightly when I saw no judgment in his eyes.

"I want you to tell me anything you want to. I want to know you, Jessica Jones. Inside and out."

———

JONAS SCOOTED his chair over to my side of the table so he was mere inches away from me. He didn't move at all, as if afraid to distract me from talking.

"I'm sure it seems stupid to you that I didn't just kick him to the curb."

"No, it doesn't seem stupid at all."

My head tilted slightly at his statement. Suddenly, Jonas pulled me closer. I went still as a board at first but then slowly relaxed, resting my head on his chest with a sigh.

"When I was a little boy, I didn't understand that my family was different."

I looked up, my attention drawn by the soft, vulnerable tone of his voice. I didn't dare interrupt, though. Even though he'd told me his mother had been murdered the first time he'd taken me to his apartment, he'd never mentioned it again. It wasn't the kind of thing I'd ever ask about, either. Jonas was such a closed book sometimes, but I'd always sensed there was a reason he was so closed off.

"My father was well liked in our neighborhood. He was good with cars, and anything with an engine actually, so he was always helping everyone out with repairs. Everyone thought he was a great guy."

He was quiet for so long that I thought he wasn't going to continue. Tears stung my eyes.

His mother was murdered. Oh God.

"He wasn't a great guy, was he?" I murmured. "Not to you and your mother."

"No, he wasn't. It was a hard lesson to learn so young. That people can be so charming in public and then be a monster behind closed doors. But I learned."

My arms tightened around his waist. "I'm so sorry, Jonas. And here I am telling you about my situation when you've lived through so much worse."

"I'm glad you told me. Pain isn't a competition. I just wanted you to know that I'm not going to ever judge you for the decisions you've made. Because I understand how hard it is to walk away from someone you care about, even when they're hurting you."

"That's just it. I wasn't strong enough to walk away. He left me. Just vanished. I still don't know exactly why. Maybe I have a guardian angel out there or something."

Jonas pulled me forward and kissed my hair. "Thank God for that. My mother never had that. If she had, maybe things would have been different. I wonder about that every day."

"She would be so proud of you. You help people all the time,

All those women who come to Blake Security for protection, you make them feel safe."

Jonas shook his head sadly. "The one thing I couldn't do for her."

I had no idea what to say to that, so I pulled him close for a hug. After a moment of hesitation, Jonas grabbed me and buried his face in my neck. We stayed like that for a long time, until Jonas suddenly coughed and wiped under his eyes discreetly.

I took a sip of wine to give him a moment of privacy. Finally, he let out a deep sigh.

"Thank you. I needed to say that. I haven't talked about her in so long. For years it was just too difficult, and then I thought it was better to focus on the future instead of the past. But I don't want to forget her. I won't let him take that from me, too."

I could understand that. Even though I wasn't as close to my family as I'd like, I couldn't imagine life without my mother to hover over me or my dad's gruff encouragement. They were very different people and hadn't understood my flighty, artistic ways, but they'd loved me the best they could.

"Tell me about your mother. What was she like?"

Jonas smiled and the sight of it took me off guard. He looked so young and carefree when he smiled. I was filled with a deep longing to see that look on his face every day.

"She liked to cook. And to embroider pillows. She was always making something. They didn't always come out the way she wanted, but she didn't care. I think she just enjoyed the process of creating something beautiful from nothing."

"That's how I feel about fashion," I commented. "My parents never really understood where my love for it came from. But I love the idea that you can find beauty all around. Color can make people happy so easily. But I think my parents wished I was more practical. You know, responsible."

"You are responsible," Jonas said.

"I am. But I meant in a more general sense. My parents wanted a child more like you. Someone using their life to be an advocate for people in need. Doing things to make the world a better place."

I shook my head bashfully at Jonas's intense look. I definitely didn't want to rehash all the ways I'd been a disappointment to my parents.

CHAPTER THIRTEEN

Jonas

I studied JJ. "Do you have any idea how strong you are? I know you don't feel it, but I see that strength in you every day."

"Sometimes I just need a reminder that I'm not that girl anymore."

I pulled her closer and lifted the wine glass out of her hands. "Let me take that. And I'll remind you that you are sexy, sassy, and can bring a man to his knees."

"Wait, I'm not finished ye—"

"Don't worry. You can sip it off of me later."

Her lips formed an O. I tugged her into the bedroom, closing the door behind us. "You all right with this? We can stop at any time if you're not."

"Y-yeah." She licked her lips.

I set the wine glass on the bedside table. When I turned to pull her toward me, my hands shook a little. What the hell was wrong with me? I'd already been with her once. Were my hands freaking shaking? Like I was a rookie or something?

Because this time you know what's going to happen. You know how explosive this can be.

Stepping in front of her, I let my hands span her waist, bringing her flush against me. She gasped, and her eyes snapped to mine. The thundering of my heartbeat was all I could hear as I focused on her parted lips.

I dipped my head, kissing her softly. Immediately, she sighed into my mouth and wound her hands into the hair at the nape of my neck. She sucked my tongue into her hot, wet mouth, and I forgot for a moment that I was supposed to be taking things slow. Focusing on drawing this out. I only wanted to keep tasting her.

While she tried to wrestle control of the kiss from me, my hands fisted in the material of her skirt, and I tugged it up. Her sudden shocked intake of breath was all I needed to take control again. I lifted her up until she wrapped her legs around me, but I didn't deposit her on the bed. Instead, I turned us to the door and braced her against it. "Just relax. I'm going to take care of you, JJ."

She used my shoulders as leverage and arched her body so that her slick heat met the bulge in my slacks. She worked her hips in a figure eight, and my eyes crossed. She knew how to move her body. Knew how to work me over.

"Jessica." Her name was more grunt than English, but lust chased desire along my nerve endings, and the part of my brain that focused on the finer points of language had long overheated.

I had to find a way to gain control again.

I reluctantly removed her hands from the nape of my neck and lifted them above her head. I licked at her lips, and very deliberately, slid my cock against the satin undies that blocked my path to bliss.

She hissed. "Jonas. Hurry, please."

No. I was not rushing this. Tonight I wanted to take my time. "Look at me, JJ."

Her lids fluttered open, and her pupils were dilated. As I kissed her again, my body rocked against hers, and she met every movement of my hips with her own. "You want me to take you like this? Hard and fast and up against the wall?" Fuck, the idea made my skin burn.

"At this point I could give two shits how you take me just as long as you're inside me. I'm not going to be picky."

"Hmm." I nuzzled her neck as I slipped my hand under her blouse. When my palm closed over the full globe, we both moaned. Her breasts were so full and firm. So soft and responsive.

"Jonas, please."

I kissed her again deeply, savoring the flavor of the wine on her tongue and sucking on it until she moaned and her body started to rock into me in a steady rhythm.

Slowly, I backed away from the kiss. Releasing her hands, I steadied her by the waist and set her feet back on the floor. Her eyes went wide with questions, but she didn't say anything. She merely followed my silent command, and I turned her around. Skimming my hands over the flesh of her arms, I positioned her palms against the door. I took my time, caressing her. When my hands reached the buttons on her blouse, she stiffened.

Slowly, I popped each button from its tiny loop. With each one I released, she puffed out a small breath, then finally exhaled completely when I had her blouse fully open. I peeled the fine silk off her shoulder, kissed the soft skin of her back as the material fell away. Her skin was satin smooth; I could do nothing but touch it and never get bored.

"Jonas, what are you doing?"

"I'm taking care of you."

When I unhooked her bra, she groaned. I didn't let her bring down her hands so I couldn't remove it. Instead, I skimmed my hands up her torso, palming her softly, then gently massaging. Her legs started to quiver when the massage turned from relief to sensual tease. Gently, I plucked the pebbled tips, and she dropped her forehead against the wall.

"You'll have to forgive me, but I've had a mild obsession with your breasts since I first saw you. I have no doubt spent countless hours thinking about how they would taste, what the weight of them would be like in my palms, how sensitive they were, if you would mind me using my teeth."

Her breath came out ragged and sharp. "Jonas. I can't. You're killing me."

I plucked the tight buds again. "If you want me to stop, all you have to do is say so."

I continued to trail hot, open-mouthed kisses across her shoulders and the back of her neck as I played.

When she started to rotate her hips back against me, I swore and gritted my teeth at the red haze of lust clouding my vision. Dropping my hands to her hips, I stopped them. "Just relax, sweetheart." I'd always known it would be like this between us. A fight for control. And I didn't mind it. But tonight, I wanted her to know that she could trust me. That if she gave just a little I would never hurt her.

"This is torture."

"Tell me about it," I mumbled.

I helped her step out of the skirt. Smoothing my hands over her slender calves and skimming over the backs of her thighs, I hooked my fingers into her panties and tugged them down over the expanse of her honey-brown legs. She shuddered when I kissed the backs of her thighs. "Can you part your legs for me, sweetheart?"

She parted her legs a little.

"Wider." It came out as a harsh command.

She sucked in a breath and planted her feet about shoulder width apart.

I trailed kisses up the backs of her legs, pausing only to nip at the backs of her knees. When I reached the top of her thighs, I ground out, "Lean forward for me."

It took her several moments to do as I instructed. When she did, I rewarded her with a soft kiss on her slick lips, and she shivered. Kneeling, I lapped at her and savored the unique flavor that was JJ. With a hand on her firm ass, I massaged the skin as I teased her by sliding a finger inside her slick channel.

She cursed softly, but I continued my licking, and stroking, working my tongue over her clit while I slid two fingers inside her. Kissing her inner thighs, I encouraged her. "Come on, JJ, come for me. You're safe. It's okay to let go. I'll catch you."

But she held on. She writhed against the door, and her slender hands balled into fists as she fought orgasm. She tensed as if she tried to fight one off, but then she went limp, and tossed her head back. I continued to lick and stroke her until her whole body shook.

With a whisper of my name in the moonlight, she finally let go.

———

Jessica

I SHOOK as Jonas picked me up and laid me on the bed. Orgasm aftershocks rolled through my body, leaving me languid and foggy. What was he doing to me? And could I take more? If I wasn't careful, I was going to fall in love with him. Then where would I be?

He shed his clothes as if he was in no hurry at all, carefully unfastening his cuff links, then slowly unbuttoning his shirt. His slacks and boxer briefs came next. All the while, he kept his burning gaze on mine. Unable to take the intensity of his stare, I let my eyes drift closed.

His voice was soft, but authoritative. "Jessica, look at me."

I shook my head.

His touch was soft on my cheek. "Shh, look at me."

I peeled my lids open to look up at him. "Jonas, I—"

"I'm not going anywhere. I'm right here with you. All you have to do is keep your eyes open to see it." He slid into bed beside me, and I had to scoot over to make room for him. "You with me?" He asked as he drew me close.

I nodded against his chest as I inhaled. Sandalwood. I sighed and immediately relaxed. I loved that smell.

Jonas pressed feather-light kisses along my temple, forehead, jaw line, and the tip of my nose. When he reached my lips, he barely skimmed them with his own, and I whimpered. He angled his head and deepened the kiss and anchored my face in his hands as he devoured my lips. Desire spiked again as his expert tongue licked at the roof of my mouth, and he teased my tongue to follow into his hot mouth.

As I kissed him, I writhed against him, brushing my nipples against his chest, turning them into hardened peaks. His muffled moan made his chest rumble, and the friction against the sensitive peaks of my breasts sent a pull of desire straight to my core.

The length of his erection pressed into my thigh insistently, and I reached down to wrap my hand around the rigid length of it. Massaging.

"Jesus, Jessica."

With sure fingers, I continued stroking him, running my hand over his cock, my palm over the sensitive tip. When I did this twice, Jonas's hips jerked, and a drop of moisture escaped his erection to lubricate my palm.

"Jonas. I want you again. I-I need you." Fear settled into my bones at that moment. If I needed him it would be a recipe for disaster, because at some point he would let me down.

"One of these days, you're going to have to learn to be patient."

A smile tugged at my lips. "It's not one of my virtues."

He growled low and kissed me deep. "I might have noticed."

His fingers dipped between my thighs, and I shivered. When he slipped one impossibly long finger inside my slick heat, I moaned, parting my thighs to allow him better access.

"You are so wet. So ready."

"Mmm, Jonas." Lust rocked my body, and need chased the lust.

Jonas trailed kisses along my throat to my collarbone, moving to my breast. With his mouth poised over a distended peak, he paused. His breath tickled my skin, and I writhed.

"Jonas, please."

"Please what?" His warm breath was a tease.

"Please kiss me."

He placed a kiss right above my breast. "Right there?"

I arched my back in frustration. "No. On my breast."

Jonas kissed the underside of my breast. "Oh, you mean here?"

"Damn it, Jonas." I threaded my hands through his hair. "Stop teasing me."

He kissed the underside of my other breast. "I like teasing you." He kissed me again and hovered over the tip of my breast again. "*You* like it when I tease you." Jonas used his thumb to circle my clit as he slid first one finger into me, then two. *Stroke, retreat, stroke, retreat.*

He kept the pace nice and easy, no matter how much I angled my hips, moving against his fingers. Finally, he withdrew his fingers and shifted position, brushing his lips over my nipple. "Jonas!"

"Yeah, baby?"

He settled his lips around my nipple, and a pull of lust pierced my core. Jonas suckled deep, his cheeks hollowing as he drew me into his mouth. Blood rushed in my head, and all I could think about was him. His lips. His fingers. Like everything else in the world had vanished and all that mattered now was this moment, this time with him.

"I need you to fuck me. Please. I can't—"

"Who's in charge?" He grazed my nipple with his teeth.

"Oh, God. I—"

Jonas's fingers stopped penetrating my core. "Maybe I should ask you again. Who's in charge?"

"Jonas. Please. I—"

He removed his fingers from my heated skin and rolled his big body over mine, bracing himself over me. His erection nudged my cleft, and he swore. "You're so hot, JJ."

I rotated my hips, sliding my cleft along the length of him. "Jonas, please don't make me wait. I need you."

Jonas dropped his forehead to mine and kissed me softly. "All you have to do is relinquish control for a little while. I promise I'll give it back."

I chewed my bottom lip. The fear gnawed at me. The uncertainty eating me. He was too close. Could make me feel too much. He left me feeling open and vulnerable. He also left me feeling like I'd grabbed hold of a live wire. Like I could fly. Like I was beautiful. Like I was special. Worthy.

I dragged in a breath and exhaled. "You're in charge. I'm yours."

He kissed me softly before rolling away and pulling open the bedside drawer. Sheathing himself in a condom, he re-settled back between my thighs.

"Do you know how long I've waited to hear that...that you're mine?" His tongue licked at my bottom lip before he nipped. "I'm not letting you go."

His erection slid against my slit before fully sliding into me.

We both gasped. I met his gaze; his eyes pierced my soul. In that moment, I knew I would never be the same.

I met Jonas thrust for thrust. He kept his eyes on mine, never breaking the intimate connection as my orgasm coursed through me. I bucked as the pleasure rolled through my body. Jonas wrapped his arms around me and held on tight as his body shook.

CHAPTER FOURTEEN

Jessica

We rested quietly together for a long time. I blinked sleepily, torn between wanting to drift into sleep with the thump of Jonas's heart beneath my ear and wanting to stay awake so I wouldn't miss a thing. Normally this was when I'd be looking for exit strategies. I'd always believed that keeping distance between me and the men I dated was best. Don't get too close or too attached. Strong emotion was too dangerous.

But this was different. Jonas was different. I couldn't have left him behind even if I tried. Not that I wanted to. This was bliss. Nothing had ever felt so good as losing all control in Jonas's arms.

"I want to take you out."

His voice came as a shock in the stillness, and I lifted my head slightly so I could see his eyes. There was a peace over him that made him look relaxed and glowing. Was that what I looked like too? Completely sated and happy? It was too much to hope for. I didn't want to examine my current state of happiness too closely for fear it would disappear in a puff of smoke.

"Take me out? Like, on a date?"

He grinned, his amusement obvious. "Yes on a date. Is that so hard to believe?"

I laughed. "Kind of. I'm so used to bickering with you and hanging out that it seems odd to go on a regular date."

Jonas's expression changed then, getting serious. "That was a mistake on my part. I've gone about this the wrong way. I want to take you out, Jessica Jones. You deserve that. I want to treat you the way a man treats his lady."

I shivered, inordinately pleased by the statement. He was looking at me like I was the most precious thing in the world. That was how he made me feel, too. Like I was this delicate thing that he wanted to protect and care for. I'd worked so hard to be independent and stand on my own two feet, that I'd never wanted a man to try to take care of me.

What good did it do to look for that kind of treatment when most of those men only wanted one thing? Why get used to being taken care of when they weren't going to stick around for long anyway?

But with Jonas, for the first time I had no fear that he wouldn't come through. It was amazing how quickly he'd broken down my walls, but I did trust him, I realized with a shock. I absolutely trusted that Jonas was someone I could count on.

"What was that thought?" He brushed a knuckle over my cheek and it took all my power not to curl into the embrace like a kitten looking for a stroke.

"Just thinking about what a good man you are," I whispered. "You are so good to me. Even when I was giving you hell about everything."

His eyes lit up. "I hope you'll continue to give me hell. A man needs a woman who can keep him on his toes."

I giggled at that. He was deliberately being silly, but I found I liked it. He was always serious and it was wonderful to be the one who could bring out this lighter side of him.

"So does that mean you'll go out with me?"

I pretended to think about it. "Hmm, now that you mention it, I don't actually recall you asking me."

Jonas turned us over in one quick motion, making me shriek in surprise. "Okay brat. Here it is. Jessica Jones, will you do me the extreme honor of going out on a date with me?"

I curled an arm around his neck and pulled him down for a kiss. "Yes, I will. I would love to go on a date with you."

"Awesome! Let's go."

I raised an eyebrow. "Right now? Is this date clothing-optional?"

When I raised my hips slightly, Jonas groaned at the brush of my heat against his belly. "Now that you mention it, there are quite a few things I could show you right here in this bed first."

With a sigh, I sank back into the pillows as his lips took a detour down the side of my neck. His hands plumped my breasts, squeezing the soft globes gently. "I like that idea. But don't think you're getting out of taking me on a real date, mister."

"I wouldn't dream of it," he muttered. His voice was muffled since his lips were busy tormenting the skin of my stomach. After one last nip, he scooted lower, propping my legs on his shoulders. He groaned when his lips made contact with my core. I bit my lip to hold back a cry at the first brush of his tongue on the super sensitive skin that was still recovering from the last few orgasms.

"Actually, maybe we can do the date thing tomorrow. I think we have a lot more work to do right here."

Matthias

WAITING HAD BECOME MORE DIFFICULT.

After getting the call, I had changed clothes and then taken the scenic route to the meet, making sure I wasn't followed. It was easy to see if there was anyone tailing me at this time of night. Evasive maneuvers were as common to me as breathing. When you came from the streets, watching your back was second nature. Or at least it used to be.

I kicked the dirt under my feet. I was restless. Or maybe just out of practice. I thought of the warm, spacious room I used back at Blake Security. The kitchen where there was always plenty of food and the common room where there was always someone to talk to. I'd gotten soft and complacent after years of being comfortable. If the Matthias of ten years ago could see me now, he'd probably wonder who the slightly posh, slightly out-of-practice guy was. I wouldn't go soft though. I was never *that* comfortable.

Noah and the crew didn't mess around. The gym at the penthouse was state of the art, and I could lift more than ever with Oskar acting as my coach. It was just unusual to have weight on me after years of being so lean.

You didn't have a choice about being lean back then, I thought. Food had been a luxury I often couldn't afford.

A soft rustle told me I wasn't alone. I didn't bother to turn around. Sudden movements were never a wise choice in the circles I came from.

"You look different."

The voice was soft and the type that was hard to identify. I knew that was deliberate. ORUS agents were trained to be as unidentifiable as possible. It had once been a point of pride for me that I could blend in, become invisible. It was only after I'd gotten a glimpse of what it could be like living as a free man that I'd known the desire to be seen. I'd gotten spoiled, living with people who treated me like I was different. Special.

The first time Lucia had looked at me with those trusting eyes, it made me believe that more might be possible for me.

Thoughts of her were always a problem, so I shook them off. I needed to keep my head in the game. You couldn't let down your guard around another ORUS agent. Not even one you called a friend. It was a good way to end up with a knife in your back.

"Hello to you, too. And what do you mean I look different? Do these pants make my arse look big? I thought black was supposed to be slimming."

"I'm not here to tell you any differently." The other voice held a hint of amusement now.

It was as good an opening as any. "So why are we here? It's not like you to call out of the blue."

"Someone has been digging."

I cursed. "There's nothing for them to find."

A heartbeat of silence. We both knew that no matter how well you scrubbed information, there would always be something you missed. It was the nature of the beast. I had always known that my past would rise up one day to haunt me. I'd just always assumed I'd have more time.

"Thanks for the warning, but I can handle myself."

"Yeah, I heard you took on Libra and lived to tell the tale."

Fucking hell. Noah wouldn't be happy about that. News about Rafe's miraculous return from the dead would surface eventually, but the rumor mill was working even faster than usual.

"Where did you hear that?"

There was a whisper of fabric. Shoulders shrugging? I chanced a glance to my left. My old friend was wearing all black and his head was covered with a baseball cap pulled low over his eyes. *Nothing to see here.*

"I hear things. Word on the street is that you're coming back."

"The street can think whatever it wants," I replied.

"Orion said you were coming back into the fold."

Now that was interesting. Was Ian really that delusional? Or maybe his newfound power was going to his head.

"He heard wrong."

I turned to walk away but stopped at the sound of my old friend's voice.

"Watch your back. Shit has been weird lately."

I nodded and then sped up my steps, eager to leave all remnants of my old life behind. I was never going back to that. I didn't care what the new Orion had up his sleeve.

CHAPTER FIFTEEN

Jessica

Okay, so maybe I was giddy. Several weeks of good sex could do that for you.

So far by silent agreement, we hadn't told anyone. I was so sure any second now, we were going to get busted. It was amazing that Lucia hadn't figured it out yet.

I wanted to tell her. Desperately. But I was also afraid of what would happen when the happy bubble burst. Would I revert to my old ways and run for the hills? Shit would get complicated if everyone knew.

Regardless of keeping that secret, I had a smile on my face and a spring in my step, but that was no reason for all the guys in the office to stare at me like I had two heads. Even the baby was looking at me funny. *No, she's not.*

But I couldn't help it. I was in a terrific mood. And yes, that was Jonas's fault. Not that I was complaining in the least. I usually wasn't one for people knowing my business, but this time I really didn't care. Besides, it was completely unavoidable.

And for a super spy undercover type Jonas was shit at hiding any of what was going on. We'd talked about it. About keeping the PDA to a minimum. About being careful. But it didn't stop him from staring at me. Or looking me up and down as if he wanted to lick me like a Popsicle.

Ooh a Popsicle. Yes please.

I really had to stop. But I couldn't help it. I'd insisted that we come in at different times this morning. Not like I wanted everyone knowing where I was last night. Or the last several nights really. I'd snuck in to my own room at three in the morning. And instead of him just coming in with me, he'd turned up at five, his usual time to use the gym. But instead of using the gym, he'd woken me up again with his mouth and *then* gone to work out. Devious man.

Over the breakfast table, Lucia eyed me suspiciously. And when Jonas walked by and pulled out my stool for me, Lucia's eyebrows popped. The moment Jonas was out of the kitchen, Lucia leaned forward. "You have some explaining to do."

"What?" First of all, I was a shitty liar. I'd never acquired the skill. Besides, this was Lucia. So lying directly to her face was nearly impossible. Lies of omission were simpler to pull off, but that required not seeing my best friend, which was kind of impossible since we lived together. "I don't know what you're talking about."

Lucia grinned, the smile going so wide she would probably split her lip soon. "For starters, you and Jonas are doing it. But where the hell are my details and gossip?"

"Would you keep it down?"

"Really? You two think you're hiding it? Everyone in this office has been watching the two of you fight like alley cats for ages. All of a sudden he's pulling out your chair and looking at you like you're his favorite chocolate dessert and he doesn't want to miss an ounce."

"Look it's just—"

Lucia crossed her arms. "Follow me."

I gave Isabella a kiss on the cheek before handing her over to Noah in the living room. The baby cooed and clapped her little chubby hands together the moment she was in her father's arms. Noah grinned at his daughter as she proceeded to smack him in the nose with her little palm.

I snorted. I'd wanted to do that very same thing before. As I chuckled, I followed Lucia to her and Noah's bedroom, and then my best friend whirled on me.

"Spill. Start talking right the hell now."

I rocked back on my heels. "Um—"

"Don't bother lying; you're bad at it. Tell me everything. Best friend code right now."

"Fine. It's just I don't really know what's going on."

Lucia snorted. "I know what's going on. You and Jonas are boning. First of all, how is it? Second of all, please tell me it was everything. You two have been dancing around the last two years, so it had better be really, really good. Third of all, when? Fourth of all, how many times? Fifth of all, was this the reason you weren't home last night or most of this week and come to think of it last week? And the reason he's at the office extra early most mornings?"

I couldn't help but laugh. "Okay—yes it happened a couple of weeks ago when everyone was freaking out because I decided to walk. I don't know. I've been feeling cooped up, I guess. I'm used to just doing whatever the hell I want, when I want. I mean the place is palatial, and I have everything I could ever need. I don't pay rent, and I don't pay for groceries, and I live in a fabulous penthouse, and my bedroom has a view of Central Park ... So it's heaven, right? But it's still a gilded prison."

Lucia nodded. "Yeah. I know. I hear you. Sometimes it can feel like that. But remember everyone is only worried about your safety. We've had a lot happen to the team, and I couldn't bear it if something happened to you."

I took her hand and then sat on the edge of the bed. "I know. And I am grateful. I mean damn it, I had a fire in my apartment and you guys have been generous enough to let me stay. I do not mean to complain at all, I swear. It's just, I'm not used to having roommates, so it's an adjustment. So anyway, I wanted to walk home and get some fresh air. Jonas found me of course—he was being Jonas."

Lucia chuckled. "Yes, of course, he was being Jonas."

I left out the part about thinking someone was following me. "So he pulled up, and of course he was shouting at me. And I don't know what happened. Well, I do know actually. We kissed. That was the first time."

"Yeah, you told me that part. So what happened next? How did it progress? I feel like I need popcorn for this."

I rolled my eyes. "I don't know. Something spooked me one day when I was running errands for the office. Like you said, a lot has happened in the last year, and I swear I was seeing things. Then, I don't know, I was really freaked out. I called Jonas for pickup and he came and got me. He took me to his place because I didn't want to come back here and have to explain to everyone how I was freaking out over nothing. And everything was fine, and I just wanted to take a minute to breathe. Then the next thing I know, I'm jumping his bones."

Lucia's mouth dropped open. "You *jumped* him?"

"Please don't remind me. It was humiliating enough at the moment."

"Wait, he turned you down?"

I nodded. "Yep, #turnedallofthisdown."

Lucia scowled despite my attempt to be humorous. "He's a moron."

"Yes, I'd have to agree. I was pissed." Again, I left out the nitty-gritty details of the humiliation. And I left out the part about my desperation move. The need to try and block out the unpleasant memories with sex. Lucia didn't need to know all that.

"So, we came home, and I was in a mood. Irritated, ticked off, horny. And he followed me, and of course we were fighting as usual. And then he pretty much asked me if I was okay because he said I wasn't acting like myself. Which was bullshit." *Liar.*

"Aww, Jonas can care sometimes. He can really be very sweet."

"Weren't you just calling him an idiot a second ago?"

Lucia shrugged. "He's just like his best friend. One moment in my good graces, the next moment I want to slap him."

"I know this feeling well," I laughed. "So anyway, he's being all extra sweet, and then I'm losing it because I feel rejected and then like a crazy person he kisses me. And then we, uh, and then we boned."

Lucia whooped. "Fantastic. Wait, where the hell were we? Somehow everyone seems to know when Noah and I are having sex."

"You guys were out. And I'm pretty sure Matthias knows. I'm not exactly quiet. But then I also didn't want a big deal made. You know me. Next week I could run. So we've been keeping it quiet ... sort of."

Lucia clutched her belly and giggled. "Man, that poor kid. We are traumatizing him for life. Do you know how many times he's walked in on me and Noah?"

I held up a hand. "I don't want to know."

"No, you don't."

"Yeah, so that's it."

"No, that is not it. Because sex is one thing, but then what happened after that?"

"Not much. I mean we still had to work. So in the middle of the night, he left my bed, grabbed his stuff and went home. Came to work the next morning like everything was normal. But then after work, he came to pick me up. That was last night. He took me to his place and made me dinner."

Lucia's slow smile warmed my heart. "Oh boy. This is going to be a thing isn't it?"

"Do not get excited."

Why not? You're getting excited. What if this could be real? I shoved that thought down immediately.

"I don't know if this is gonna stick. Right now it's good sex. And good food. Two of my favorite things. And obviously you know what he looks like, so huge ego boost."

"You're being ridiculous. He's the lucky one. Okay, so he made you dinner and then you guys ..."

"Well, it's very hard to keep my hands off that man. I'll just say that."

"Oh boy, you guys are gonna fall in love. I can tell. I can feel it."

I wanted to be excited. But I knew Lucia didn't have all the details. Lucia didn't know why I kept myself at arms length from most men. Lucia didn't know why Jonas wouldn't be sticking around forever. Lucia didn't know my deep and dark hidden secrets. So all my best friend could see was the happiness and potential.

The problem was, on the course I was on, either I was going to get hurt or Jonas was. And Lucia and the rest of the team were going to get caught in the middle.

Jonas

I WAS NERVOUS.

You have no reason to be nervous. You've already slept with her. Twice. This is just a date.

Except this wasn't *just* a date. I liked her. *You've always liked her.* Well, mostly I had wanted to shake her and sleep with her. But liked her? Not exactly. I'd always respected the fuck out of her. She was strong. Sexy. Smart. Kept me on his toes, which was awesome and annoying all at the same time.

Yeah, I'd always liked her. But somehow, it felt like I needed to do this right. Because there were so many ways that this could go wrong. And I didn't want it to go wrong.

And now, everyone knew. *Mostly because you can't help but stare at her.* Yeah, that was it. Twice during our debriefing meeting this morning, I'd been so busy staring out the glass window at JJ walking by that Noah had to snap his fingers in front of my face. When I had snapped out of it, all the guys had been looking at me with shit-eating grins on their faces. Fuck them all. I didn't care.

Yeah you do. Because you know how this will affect everyone if this shit goes wrong.

This was true. But given that we were grown-ups we could probably manage it. *Who the hell are you kidding? You'll go back to fighting like cats and dogs and actually hate each other.* Fuck, I really hoped that didn't happen. Because I had a feeling I'd be thinking about tasting her for the rest of my damn life.

I knocked on her door and she opened it with a wide smile. "What is all this?"

"This," I spun around adjusting my jacket and deliberately showing off, "is your date for the evening. Go get changed. Something sexy and flirty. You look gorgeous in red."

She paled. What was that about? Then just as quickly, she shook her head and smiled slightly. I wasn't sure what I'd said that could cause that reaction. Maybe she was feeling a little bashful remembering wearing nothing but my red tie last night.

"And just where would I be going in this red, sexy, flirty dress?"

"Can't tell you that. It's a surprise. Come on, get changed. We're going to be late."

I loved that happy, surprised grin that flashed over her face. I wanted to put that grin there all the time. Fuck, I had it so bad. This was going to end in disaster if I wasn't careful.

Slow it down. Don't overwhelm her.

This was supposed to be easy, fun, not too serious. I had to repeat that over and over again until my brain started to remember.

When she came back out, she'd opted for red and black. Fine by me. She still looked amazing; the dress tied at her neck, leaving most of her back exposed. Which meant I could touch as much as I wanted.

"You look—wow."

She grinned. "Oh, this old thing?"

"Come on. Let's go before everyone notices we're all dressed up."

With a giggle, she followed me through the path of least resistance, which meant from her bedroom, through the kitchen, completely avoiding the living room, gym area, and conference room. We snuck out the door, but not before Oskar called out, "You two kids have fun now. Jonas, remember to bring her back at a reasonable hour. And if you two are gonna get up to extracurricular activities, please warn the rest of us so we can wear our earmuffs. I don't think Matthias has recovered after the other day."

I groaned. I was going to fucking kill the German.

But JJ didn't miss a beat. "You guys can go eat a bowl of dicks, you hear me?"

A bark of laughter choked out of me. "A bowl of dicks?"

She nodded "Yep, I'm going with it."

"Woman, you are ridiculous."

She danced into the elevator. "That's why you love me."

I knew she was kidding. She was being flippant. She did not mean that. *But it's not untrue.* Oh shit. I was tripping over the landmines of my feelings. Because I *was* falling for her. Even though I could see the collision coming. I didn't care.

Once we were in the car heading toward the Met, she turned to face me. "A car service? My, my, Jonas Castillo giving over control? I must ask what is happening here."

"You and I both know I give you control. But I figured this way we could have some fun, and be irresponsible and not have to worry about driving anywhere. So relax. We're on a date."

"I love how all our dates thus far consist of you telling me what we're going to be doing."

I shrugged. "I see no problem with this."

"Well, hold onto your britches because I will plan a date for you, and it's going to be something you don't expect."

"I look forward to it."

I took her to a show at the Met. And admittedly the show wasn't all pleasure. It was also to do a check-in on a client whose husband had been more paranoid as of late. She'd come into the office to ask for protection and the team set up surveillance on her. But last week she called asking them to call it off. The event at the Met was mostly a welfare check on a would-have-been client. But after that, everything was all JJ.

The Met was featuring a lesser-known opera. And it was short; only an exhibition to get everyone to buy tickets to the big show. And of course there was the party after. But we weren't staying for that.

Mrs. Elliot Anderson looked none too pleased to see me. But still, she was cordial and introduced me and JJ around. When I managed to get her alone for a moment, she said, "I told you; I made a mistake coming to Blake Security. I'm not in danger."

"I understand what you're saying. At the same time, I just

want to be sure. Sometimes people say things on the phone if they're being coerced. So we like to do a welfare check in an environment where you don't expect us. More difficult to lie this way. But you're fine?"

She nodded. "Yes, absolutely."

I could see the lines of tension around her mouth. This woman was *not* okay. But I was learning to maybe let go a little bit. Of course I'd send Dylan or Ryan to follow her and sit on her place. But I couldn't force her to want protection.

Once I was done with her, I found JJ chatting with an artist we'd met earlier near the bar. The guy was laughing, reaching out a hand and caressing JJ's arm. That had me frowning immediately. *Mine.* Yeah, that constant thought, that was gonna have to stop, too. She would not like being referred to as mine. Still, I had to maneuver her away from the handsy artist.

I strode right up to her, leaned down, and nuzzled her neck. "You ready to go sweetheart? I want to feed you."

She turned into me with a happy smile. "You said my favorite words." When she'd bid the guy goodbye and we were halfway to the door, she turned to me. "Don't think I don't know what you were doing."

"And don't think I won't stake my claim. I want you. He was trying to poach. I didn't appreciate it."

"So you peed all over me?"

Again, the unexpected laugh. "Seriously? I mean, if you're into that ..."

"Eww. I am not. But someone's feeling very territorial tonight."

"Of course I am. I'm here with the most beautiful woman in the room."

The rest of the night, I couldn't remember when I'd had this much fun. I took her dancing. A little salsa, a little merengue. We were overdressed, but man, was it fun. And true to my word, I kept her well fed. The classic Mediterranean place I'd taken her to had a Michelin starred chef. And JJ squealed when she saw where we were going.

"I've been trying to get a table here for a year."

"I aim to please."

After dinner, once we were headed back to the car, I slid an arm around her before leaning down to gently brush my lips over hers. "So princess, your place or mine?"

"Aren't you being a little presumptuous?"

I laughed. "Hell yes. And I promise you sweetheart, I'm a sure thing."

"In that case, I'm yours."

CHAPTER SIXTEEN

Jonas

"All right. Get your asses in gear. We have a lot to do today." Noah rubbed his hands together and the room quieted.

I, however, had my eyes on the man sitting on Noah's left. It wasn't unusual for us to have outsiders in the office, but considering who the guests were, we were all on edge. I could see it in the hard set of Oskar's shoulders and the tense lines around Matthias's mouth. Ryan and Dylan didn't know the history Noah and the others had with ORUS, but even they could tell something was up. It wasn't often we had Ian, the head of ORUS, sitting in on our meetings.

"First up, lets do a status check on our current clients. Jonas, how are things with Lindsey Meyers?"

While I went over the details of my last check-in with Lindsey, I kept one eye on the man who'd accompanied Ian. David. The guy was pretending to pay attention, but every so often, his eyes would slip to the windows leading out into the main office area.

What the hell was he looking at?

I coughed and turned discreetly, checking to see if Lucia was walking around or something. Hell, if the dude got caught checking out Lucia we wouldn't have to worry about a probationary period. Noah would take him out before he even got started.

"Also Rafe is coming in a little later."

"Excellent. We need all the help we can get. Ok, I'll turn the floor over to Ian. He and one of his best agents have been working on a case for the past few months that they need assistance with."

As Ian stood to speak, I kept my eyes on the man still sitting. What was it about the guy that rubbed me the wrong way? Maybe it was the shit-eating smirk on his face, like he knew something we didn't, or was just tolerating being here.

When Noah had told us about Ian's unusual request for us to assist on a case, I hadn't minced words. I didn't like the idea of getting into bed with ORUS, even if it was only temporary. Also, the agent assigned to this particular case, David West, code name *Chamaeleon*, had been a little too trigger happy back in the day, in Noah's opinion. Matthias hadn't said anything, but I definitely got the impression he didn't like the guy either. Still, considering how valuable it could be to have the head of ORUS owe us a favor, I couldn't blame Noah for taking the case.

"Thanks for the help, Noah. This is a time sensitive situation. We might need significant technical assistance on this one." Ian glanced over at Matthias, who didn't move.

Movement caught my eye again. David had shifted in his seat slightly and was staring out into the main living area. I barely heard Ian droning on about rebel strongholds in Colombia because my senses were tingling. Something was up with this David guy, and I was going to figure out what it was.

Noah dropped into the seat next to me. "What's your take on this?"

I was used to Noah asking for my read on all types of situations. Coming from law enforcement, I had the training to detect liars and the general gut instinct to tell when shit was about to get real. But I wasn't entirely sure what to tell my old friend. Ian was Ian, no surprise there. The real wild card was David West, who was only here to assist Ian. So why did the guy make me so anxious?

"What's the deal with that guy?" I inclined my head slightly in David's direction.

Noah snorted under his breath. "Your typical over-confident ORUS agent. I remember him. He was always hanging around me and Rafe, trying to one-up us. Not exactly a team player. I don't know why Ian brought him in on this."

"Is he always this twitchy? He acts like anything could set him off."

Noah's eyes narrowed as he took in David's rapt attention to something outside the room. Finally I turned again. Lucia stood right outside in full view, laughing at something. The room was soundproofed so we couldn't hear her, but it was pretty obvious what David was staring at.

"Motherfucker." Noah stood, his chair scraping back from the table loudly. Everyone stopped what they were doing and looked at him. I figured I had about two seconds to defuse the situation before Noah went nuclear.

"Gentlemen, we've just gotten word of an emergency situation. Apologies, but we're going to have to cut this short."

Without waiting for another word, Matthias stood and walked toward the door. Ryan and Dylan glanced around in confusion.

"This is time sensitive," Ian began.

Noah held up his hand. "Ian, why don't you and David come with me to my office? Jonas can handle this situation while we finish up."

I smirked. I wasn't sure how I was supposed to handle getting Lucia out of sight, but I'd have to think of something. Hell, maybe

I'd just tell her the truth. She knew better than anyone how jealous Noah could be. Luckily she loved him madly and put up with him and his crazy ways.

"That's fine." Ian looked confused but followed Noah's lead. David walked up right behind me. To my surprise, Noah stuck out his hand.

"David. It's been a long time. How long have you been back stateside?"

The other man winced slightly, and I looked down to where Noah had his hand locked in a vice grip. "About six months," David finally ground out.

Jesus. I needed to get us out of there before Noah decided to go all He-Man and challenge the guy to a duel or something.

"I'll start handling the emergency situation," I said.

Noah smiled gratefully. "Thank you. I'll call you when we're done."

Translation: Don't bring Lucia back here until this mother-fucker is gone.

"Got it, boss."

I walked out of the office and was immediately able to see what Lucia had been laughing at. JJ was in the kitchen, just out of view, holding up a picture of something on her phone. My heart sped up when I saw her.

"Hey baby. I didn't even know you were back yet. That didn't take long."

She shrugged. "I couldn't find anything. Shopping isn't as much fun without Lucia. So I figured I'd wait until you guys could watch the baby so we can go. I need her to tell me which tops make my boobs look the best."

"I can do that," I promised.

"Yeah, I bet you can."

Damn, this was fun. As much fun as our bickering had always been, it had partially been born of sexual frustration. How amazing was it to have this back and forth chemistry with a woman who satisfied me completely in every way? Jessica Jones was truly my perfect match.

It hit me like a lightning bolt. She was the one. My future. My destiny.

My wife.

I almost fell to my knees at the intensity of the thought. Marriage had always been something that I figured I'd avoid. It wasn't as if I'd had the best exposure to the institution, and truthfully, I'd never understood the point of a piece of paper when you could just live with whomever you wanted. It wasn't like it was the 1950s and you'd get run out of town for living in sin.

But in that moment, I got it. I understood Noah's obsession with having Lucia as his wife. I wanted the same things with JJ. I wanted her to be mine. To carry my name. To be filled with my child. I wanted us merged and blended in every way possible because I knew without a shadow of a doubt that I was meant to be with this woman forever.

"I can so do that," I mumbled, reeling from the life-altering thoughts going through my head. The entire landscape of my future had just realigned in the space of a heartbeat, but the rest of the world went on unaware.

JJ smiled at me gently. "Did you hear anything I just said?"

"No," I answered truthfully. "I was too busy wondering how I got so lucky that you're mine."

Jessica

I OPENED my mouth but no sound came out. Everything became background noise. Lucia telling us how sweet we were, the rumble of Noah's voice, and even the sound of my feet on the floor as I walked over to Jonas. None of it registered in light of the heart-stopping look on his face.

"I feel exactly the same way."

The way his eyes crinkled as he smiled made me so warm inside. It was amazing how making him happy could complete me. But over the last few weeks, I'd slowly discovered that the formula for my ultimate happiness lay in Jonas smiling at me exactly like that.

"I love you, Jonas."

His arms opened automatically and I cuddled into his embrace. I stood on tiptoe and pressed my lips to his. He swallowed the little whimper I made and cupped my cheek to hold me still as he devoured my lips.

This was home, coming into his arms and knowing that I'd always be welcome there. It was more than I'd ever dared to hope for, but here it was. Living proof that dreams could come true.

Then, right before my eyes, it all turned to dust.

Because standing right behind the living embodiment of my dreams, was the ghost of the man who'd once torn them all down.

"No. It's not possible. No. No. No."

With a cry, I spun on my heel and ran from the room, dropping my phone in the process. I heard a chorus of voices calling after me but I didn't stop. I couldn't stop. His face swam in my mind, and I ran faster. I had to get to safety.

Where the hell could I go? Then I noticed the door to Noah and Lucia's room was ajar. I pushed it open, my eyes sweeping the room. My gaze landed on the flat wall across from the door.

The panic room.

Noah had made me and Lucia practice the code over and over when I'd first moved in. He'd claimed that muscle memory would come through for us in an emergency even if we were too rattled to remember the code. As my fingers raced over the buttons, I promised to thank him later. The door slid open and I rushed inside. I didn't take another breath until the door slid closed behind me.

"Jesus, what the hell?" The muffled voice from outside the door made me whimper.

How had he found me? I went to the far corner of the small room and curled up in a ball on the floor. After so many years, just when I thought I was safe.

Haven't you learned by now? Nowhere is safe.

I covered my head with my arms and sobbed.

CHAPTER SEVENTEEN

Jonas

I ran my hands over my face. She was in the panic room? What the hell? It took a few minutes for my brain to start working amidst the adrenaline rush of chasing after her. I glanced behind me. Lucia had followed and stood hovering in the doorway.

"Where is she?" Lucia asked.

Her eyes darted around the room and she held a hand to her chest as she panted for breath. A second later, Noah appeared in the doorway next to her.

I pointed to the wall across from us. It took a few seconds before she got it. Lucia's eyes widened.

"She's in the panic room?" Her eyes followed the same path mine did to the blank panel on the wall.

"It appears so. What was going on before I saw you guys? Was she behaving strangely?"

Lucia rubbed her arms. "No. She was totally fine. I mean, she was bitching about not fitting into any of the clothes she liked. But that's the usual. Then she was talking about getting one of you guys to babysit Isabella so we could go shopping together. That's when you came out. This doesn't make any sense." Lucia bit her bottom lip. "She was totally fine. We were talking the whole time you guys were having your meeting. What changed?"

I walked up to the wall. "JJ. Baby, it's me. Are you okay?" I listened intently. Nothing. Then I heard a soft sob. "I'm coming in."

"No! Don't come in. Don't let him in!"

I glanced behind me at Lucia who looked just as perplexed as I felt.

"What is going on?"

Lucia shrugged. "I honestly have no idea. She was so happy to see you just a few minutes ago. I don't understand why she doesn't want to see you all of a sudden."

I flinched. What could I have done that scared her this badly? I mentally reviewed everything that had just happened. She'd looked so happy to see me and maybe I'd been a little aggressive with that kiss, but I'd just had a major epiphany.

Had I scared her off with my intensity?

JJ wasn't keen on the idea of forever any more than I'd once been. Maybe it had been too much, too soon? It was a blow to think that the idea of forever with me was enough to send JJ literally running from the room, but I knew her fears and her past. She'd had valid reasons not to trust and not to hope for more. But slowly, every day, I was going to show her what was possible. It was my new mission in life to teach her how to love without fear.

Hell, I'd be teaching myself along the way too. Because this shit was terrifying already.

I knocked on the door again. "JJ, baby you know this room is only for emergencies. I know you're mad at me but you don't need to hide in the panic room. I'm coming in now, okay?"

The only response was another round of heartrending cries. She sounded like she was barely breathing. I cursed. Her sobs tore at my heart. Had I really done this? But nothing else made sense.

Although she probably wanted privacy, I couldn't take it anymore. I typed in the code and when the door slid open, my heart broke all over again when I saw JJ curled up on the floor in the corner.

Then she raised her head, and my blood ran cold. JJ looked completely terrified and not entirely aware of where she was. This wasn't about her being angry at me. Something had happened. I'd seen this kind of thing before in some of our clients, especially the ones who'd been abused. Something would trigger a memory, and then they'd react like they were right back in their personal hell.

"Lucia, it's okay. I've got this. Go tell the others not to disturb us please."

"Of course." Lucia patted my arm before leaving with one last worried glance back at her friend.

I ducked my head to enter the room. It was about ten feet by ten feet and painted stark white. Not designed for comfort, for sure. JJ couldn't be comfortable all crunched up in a ball like that. I sat next to her and then scooted as close as I could without touching her.

"JJ, I'm so sorry. I don't know what I did to scare you but I'd never want to hurt you in a million years."

She turned suddenly and threw herself into my arms. Relieved that she wasn't running away from me anymore, I held her, allowing her to sob into my shoulder. It was about ten solid minutes before she quieted. The only way I knew she was still awake was the shaky gasps of her breathing.

"He was right there. Right there in front of me. I haven't seen him in so long."

Suddenly she bolted upright. "Oh my God. He's out there with Lucia! I have to warn her. I have to get her away from him."

"Whoa. Hold on baby. Warn Lucia about who?"

"David," she cried. "I have to warn her about David! What if he hurts her or the baby? I was so scared I just ran. What kind of friend am I?"

Holy fuck.

"JJ, are you saying you recognized David West? That you know him?"

I sat up straighter, the events of the last hour racing through my mind. David's intense concentration on something in the common area. He hadn't even seemed to care about what Ian was saying. I had thought he was looking at Lucia because she had been the one visible to me, but had he been looking at JJ the whole time? She wouldn't have been able to see him since we'd had the tint on the conference room windows turned on, preventing anyone from looking in.

She nodded miserably. "He's ... He's the one. Jonas, he's the one who hurt me. The guy I told you about."

"Son of a bitch." I pulled my phone from my pocket and sent a quick text to Noah and Matthias. Hopefully they could read it without tipping off David or Ian.

My phone rang a few seconds later.

"What the fuck is going on?"

"I guess that means they're already gone. Damn it!"

JJ flinched and I reined in my temper. I couldn't let my anger touch her. She'd had enough of violence and fear.

Noah's voice was tight. "You need to explain. Why should I have detained them?"

"Give me two seconds. I'm going to get JJ out of here first, and I'll come find you. Can you have Lucia meet us? I think JJ could use a friend right now."

I knew that Noah understood what I meant. While Lucia took care of JJ, Noah and I would come up with a plan to take care of that fucker David West.

Take care of him permanently.

———

Jessica

HE WAS CARRYING ME.

Under any other circumstances, I would have more than a few snarky things to say about Jonas carrying me around. But honestly, after my little crying fit, I wasn't entirely sure I even had the strength to stand. After he'd made arrangements with Noah over the phone, he'd wiped the tears from my face with the kind of gentleness I hadn't known he possessed, and then he'd scooped me up in his arms. I'd rested my head on his shoulder and let him carry me to my room.

I'd expected to feel ridiculous, letting a man cart me around like I didn't have two perfectly working legs of my own, but instead I'd felt cared for and protected.

The way David once made you feel. Look where that got you.

Because the thought brought back the vague sense of panic, I pushed it away. I wasn't going to think about that. Noah and the guys were handling it, and I trusted that they wouldn't let him anywhere near me. Now that the first rush of panic had passed, my brain could approach the problem in a rational way. I was no longer the scared, young teenage girl who hadn't had the will to stand up to David. I was a strong, independent woman who knew my own mind. He couldn't manipulate me if I didn't allow it.

Those days were over.

I curled up in bed, burying my face in the pillow. His scent enveloped me, surrounding me with a sense of safety and comfort. After my crying jag, I felt like a dishrag that had been wrung out to dry, but I took a deep breath. Despite being older and hopefully wiser, I could still acknowledge the pull the past had on me. It had been an emotional gut punch to see David in the flesh for the first time in so long. I'd reacted with the instinct of the scared girl I'd once been. But I was okay.

Everything was going to be okay.

Then I remembered that despite not being a scared kid anymore, I was still only human, and David was still violent and unpredictable. He'd been standing only a few feet from me and people that I cared about. What if he'd hurt Lucia? Saying that things were okay might be a bit of a stretch.

"JJ, can I come in?"

I sat up at the sound of Lucia's voice. My friend's head appeared in the doorway. I glanced around the room uncertainly.

"It's okay. You can come in." I waved her in and scooted over so Lucia could sit next to me on the bed.

We sat in uncomfortable silence for a few moments before Lucia spoke. "Jonas just told me that you knew that guy. That he hurt you."

My eyes filled with tears. I could only imagine what my friend must be thinking. I'd kept secrets, and those secrets had put Lucia and her family in danger. I hung my head.

"I'm sorry I never told you."

That seemed to break the distance between us. Lucia grabbed my hand.

"This isn't about hurt feelings. I just want to make sure you're okay. You have the right to tell whomever you want about it. Or to never talk about it at all if that's what you want."

Relief that she wasn't angry flooded through me. I squeezed Lucia's hand. "I didn't want to talk about it. I just wanted to forget it happened."

Lucia paused. She looked uncomfortable. It wasn't often that we didn't know what to say to each other. We'd been friends so long that we were both used to speaking without a filter.

"You don't have to be careful with me, Lucia. I'm really okay, despite my little breakdown in there. We've never minced words with each other. Let's not start now."

Lucia smiled softly, but it was strained. "I'm just so sorry someone hurt you. And that I wasn't there to help out when it happened."

"You were there. You've always been there. I was the one who kept it a secret. I didn't know how to admit that I was in trouble."

Lucia stretched out on the bed next to me. It reminded me of when we were teenagers and would have sleepovers and stay up all night talking. Back then, we'd giggled all night about what our lives would one day be like. If we'd get married and have a husband and kids of our own. What it would be like to have a man who adored us and did all the wicked things we'd read about in my mom's romance novels.

But after Rafe died, things had changed for both of us. Lucia had lost her beloved brother and become a shell of her former self. I had lost my best friend, and I'd been desperate to feel … something. Rafe's death had been a blow to me too, for many reasons. Not just because of how it affected Lucia but because he'd been my first crush. It had been a shocking introduction to the concept of death to so suddenly lose the first man who'd ever made me feel like a woman.

Not that I'd ever told Lucia any of that.

"How did you meet him?"

I thought back. The moment would forever be emblazoned in my mind.

"He saved me, actually. There was this guy hassling me on the street. Wouldn't let me walk by. David just looked at the guy and he backed down. I thought it was so romantic back then, but looking back, I wonder if that wasn't my first warning sign. If criminals are afraid of you … "

"But there was no way you could have known that then," Lucia protested. "You've always been smart about guys. You were never the type to jump into things."

"Everything was so crazy then. With Rafe gone, everything

was different. And David was so nice to me at first. He made me feel special. He said he wanted to protect me."

Lucia sniffled. "How could I have not noticed that my best friend needed me? We were together all the time."

"Don't you dare blame yourself. You had enough to deal with grieving and taking care of Nonna. You just figured I was spending time with my boyfriend."

"A boyfriend who was hurting you." Lucia's voice sounded tortured.

"He always said that he'd never let me go. God, Lucia I believed him too. I never understood why he left me alone one day. It was so sudden, but all I could do was be grateful. Then I felt so guilty because more than likely the only reason he left me alone was because he'd found someone else to torment."

"That isn't your fault. He's the sick bastard, and Noah and the guys are going to kick his ass when they find him."

I closed my eyes. I didn't want the guys to go after him. At one time, maybe that would have been what I craved. Revenge. But now all I wanted was for everyone to be safe. For things to go back to normal. To have that perfect life I'd started to believe was possible.

"I love Jonas so much," I whispered.

"I know you do. He loves you the same way, I can tell." Lucia's eyes shone with glee. "You have to know how thrilled I am to see you guys together. He's the type of guy you deserve, JJ. A good guy."

But as we drifted off to sleep together, I couldn't help but wonder if that was really the kind of guy I deserved.

CHAPTER EIGHTEEN

Jonas

"I will fucking kill him."

It turned out that expression, 'seeing red,' was a legit real thing. I had never been so angry in my fucking life. I marched right past Oskar and Matthias, past the gym and straight for the weapons room. Noah was hot on my heels.

"Jonas, whatever's going on man, back down."

I spun around. "Back down? Are you out of your fucking mind? That asshole is a psychopath." I wasn't sure how much to say to Noah. But with Lucia in with JJ, Noah was going to know anyway. And we had a real fucking security problem now.

Noah frowned. "Dude, tell me what the fuck is going on. I've only ever seen you like this once. Talk me through it."

Matthias had been right behind Noah. And Oskar had followed them. Rafe lingered somewhere in the doorway, somehow still separate from the main group.

"Ian's bodyguard. Chamaeleon? That animal used to stalk JJ. He—hurt her."

Noah frowned. "What?"

Matthias got his time-to-start-killing-people face going. Rafe stood straighter and cracked his neck, wearing the expression I'd come to recognize as his kicking-ass face. Oskar was the only one who stayed calm, leaning against the wall. But when he spoke, his voice was quiet and deadly. I had learned that when pushed, Oskar could be far more dangerous than any of us. And that included Rafe.

"Explain, Jonas," the German said quietly.

"I guess they used to date. That's when it started. He beat her. Stalked her. Made her feel weak." They would know the whole story eventually when JJ decided to tell it. Right now I gave them the bare bones minimum.

Noah crossed his arms. "I'll give Ian a call."

"No, you won't give Ian a call. I don't want to give that asshole any knowledge that I'm coming for him."

"Not without me," Matthias said.

Rafe just nodded his head. He was always down for an ass whooping.

Noah shook his head. "No. No one's going in for an ass kicking. We need the full story first."

I was listening, but kept moving, focused on getting armed. Pistols. Yes. Extra magazines. Obviously. Then for shits and giggles I grabbed one of the shotguns, too. What I needed was a rocket launcher. Yes, I could blow up anything with a rocket launcher. I knew we had one in here somewhere. Where had Noah put that?

"Jonas, talk to me."

I stopped and turned around. "That's personal stuff for JJ to tell you. All you need to know is that asshole is not a good dude. He hurt her. From what she told me, he's been gone for a long time. So if he's back now, that means she's in trouble. The last few days she's been feeling like something was off. I bet you anything it's that jackoff."

Noah nodded. "Look, you know no matter what happens, I have your back. And we *all* have JJ's back." The guys all nodded. "But Chamaeleon is one of Ian's guys. This is no run-of-the-mill asshole we can pluck off the street, scare straight, and hand off to the cops. We need to be careful. So we'll talk to JJ, and we'll bide our time. Going in weapons hot like this is only going to get you or one of the other guys killed."

That took a little wind out of my sails. "I don't want anyone dying for me. I'll do this one alone."

I tried to brush past Noah, but he didn't budge even an inch. *Asshole.* I glared at Noah and he glared right back. " Jonas, I've told you this before. You want to fight, we'll fight. You want to work off some steam, I'm your guy. But I'm not going to let you walk into your own death. If this guy's been stalking JJ this long, he's not going to fight fair."

"Neither am I."

"Yeah, but there's a difference between you and that guy. At the core," Noah thumped me on the chest just over the heart, "you're a human being. You don't kill for fun or for sport. On the job, you rarely fire your weapon. That guy, he's a born and bred killer. That's what he is. If he's dumb enough to hurt someone like JJ, that means he's the lowest of the low. He will kill you and anyone who gets in his way for nothing. And I'm not losing any of my guys. We're going to do this smart, do you hear me? Because JJ is going to need you."

Motherfucker.

Noah fought dirty. *Because, he was right.* JJ would need me. She needed me now. If I ran off after this asshole, she would be all alone tonight. She deserved better than that. My shoulders sagged, and I let one of the pistols fall to my side.

Gingerly, Matthias came forward and took it from my hands. He ensured the safety was on, and removed all the ammunition.

Piece by piece, they took all the guns from me. Even my personal piece. Noah took that one.

When I growled at him, Noah held up both hands. "Sorry man. You'll get this back in the morning when you're more level headed, you hear me?"

Yeah, maybe he had a point. This way, I couldn't wake up in the middle of the night with a penchant for murder. That wouldn't be good for JJ.

"I hear you. But just so we're clear, that asshole dies, right?"

Matthias and Rafe nodded immediately. The thought of killing didn't turn their stomachs. What surprised me was that Oskar and Noah nodded as well. Noah had never taken to the life of an assassin very well. It had always eaten at him a little. And Oskar hadn't been an assassin like the other three. But when it came to protecting women and children, he erred on the side of killing the assholes and asking questions later.

"Yeah, okay. I'm gonna go see JJ."

Noah clapped me on the back. "I think that's a good idea. You'll do her more good being with her than going off half-cocked."

***

Jessica

THERE WAS a knock at the door and I lifted my head to find Jonas in the doorway. "Hey you."

His voice was soft, but I could sense the turmoil in him. He nearly vibrated with it. "How you feeling?"

"Tired. Raw. Like I scraped the scab off of a healing wound with a dull rusty blade."

He smirked. "You've always had a way of painting a picture. You got room in there for one more?"

I nodded and scooted over, alarmed at how much I needed

him. When Jonas reached the bed, he gently tucked my hair behind my ear, and then stripped off his own clothes.

Unmistakable heat flashed between my thighs, and I couldn't help a smile. After sliding under the covers, Jonas tucked me against him so we spooned with his hand cupping my breast.

"Jonas, what—"

"I'm going to hold you, if that's okay. You know how much I want you." He dragged in a sharp breath when I wiggled my ass against his thick erection. "Hell, you can feel it." His cock twitched against my ass. He clearly wanted me, but all he did was continue to hold me. "I need to hold you more than I need to make love to you. If that's okay."

I nodded then whispered, "Thank you for today."

Jonas kissed my ear softly. "You have nothing to thank me for. I'm not going anywhere."

It was in the cocoon of his arms that I was finally able to fall asleep.

Hours later, with streaks of moonlight casting shadows into my room, I moaned into Jonas's chest. I was awake enough to know I was having either the very best of dreams or one hell of a wakeup call. Jonas kissed me as his thumb and forefinger rolled one of my nipples. Sighing into the caress, I let myself relax into the kiss. His expert tongue caressed and teased mine into playing.

God, I relished what he could do to my body. The way he made me pliant. He never rushed me, even when I wanted to hurry. He always took his time with everything, even kissing, like we had all the time in the world. Like his erection wasn't straining.

I loved kissing him. His lips were so soft and skilled, and his tongue—every time he licked into my mouth, it made me shiver. When his hand dipped between my thighs, I parted them to ease his way. Skilled fingers stroked my cleft, teasing, driving me crazy. I arched my back trying to angle my hips into his hand.

Jonas slid a finger inside me as his thumb caressed my clit

and I cried out and sank my fingers into his hair. He grunted in satisfaction as my hips bucked, then he sucked on my tongue in time with his fingers sliding into my slick center. His heavy erection continued to press into my thigh and I moaned. I would never get over what he could do to my body. I'd never been so carnal, so aroused, so willing to give myself completely to anyone.

With a groan, he pulled back from the kiss and I mewled as I tried to follow his lips. His gaze scorched me. Dark and fiery, he stared from under hooded lids. "Jesus, what are you doing to me?"

My constricted throat made it impossible to speak, so I responded the only way I knew how—by arching my hips into his hand again.

He muttered a soft curse, and squeezed his eyes shut. As his fingers strummed me to the edge of orgasm, he chewed on his bottom lip. When he increased the pace of his questing fingers, I held tight onto his shoulders. I rotated my hips around and around until he swore again and rubbed his thumb directly over my clit.

My orgasm ripped through me, laying waste to every nerve and cell. Unable to think, I threw my head back giving myself over fully to the sensation.

"Holy fuck, you are so beautiful when you come."

I smiled up at him, expecting him to go for a condom, but instead, he burrowed under the covers. His hands parting my thighs had me tensing. "Jonas, I–"

He tugged the sheet down and lifted his head. After he crawled back up my body, he turned my chin firmly so I was looking at him. His gaze burned hot, the desire etched on his face was unmistakable. "Do you trust me?"

I nodded. "Of course."

"Good. Now I'm going to erase every memory of that asshole from your body. I will erase every memory of any other man before me. Tasting you is one of the highlights of my day."

"I-uh..." Wow. "In that case, who am I to stand between a man and his mission."

"There's my girl." His smile was lopsided. "Look at us sharing control."

He slid back down my body, placing kisses across my chest and belly as he went. When he reached my hips, he nibbled at the flesh on my pelvic bone, then scooted still lower.

Dusting feather light kisses on my inner thighs, he paused when he got to my cleft. "So pretty. And so soft." His first stroke of my slick center had me clenching my hands into the sheets. Oh God. He lapped at me, kissing and exploring with his tongue. He took his time, as he did with everything else. He seemed in no hurry. When his tongue circled the throbbing bundle of nerves, I flew apart in his hands again. But he didn't let up. He kept stroking. Kept lapping.

It wasn't until he slid a finger into my moist sheath again that I lost all my inhibitions. Forgot everything I'd been afraid of. Forgot the shadows that had been chasing me and gave myself over. If he was intent on killing me with ecstasy, then who the hell was I to argue?

Finally relaxing, I let my thighs fall apart and he moaned, parting my folds and dipping the tip of his finger into my center. My third orgasm rolled through me, chasing the tail of the previous one. He didn't let up until I lay limp.

He drew himself back up my body, pausing to nip at my hips again, then to suckle my breasts.

When he made it to my lips, he said, "I'm going to make that a new daily habit."

I shivered. He could do that to me any time he wanted. "God, yes."

He shifted against my parting thighs with his. And I moaned when the tip of his erection nudged my cleft.

He squeezed his eyes shut tight as he entered me inch by inch.

I met him halfway by raising my hips. His jaw stayed tight until he was seated all the way inside. He made love to me sweetly. Kissing me, holding me to him and looking into my eyes. "You're mine. And I am yours."

In that moment, the fear fell away. This was the perfect moment, the one I'd always looked for. This was the kind of love and acceptance I'd been seeking all my life. "I know." Blissful abandon started in my toes and cascaded through my body. I held onto him tight and muttered how much I loved him as the orgasm took over all my conscious and subconscious thought.

As my body held him inside, he whispered in my ear, "I am so lucky." With two more deep strokes, his whole body shook with release.

CHAPTER NINETEEN

Jonas

"You know you can't save the day every day, right?"

I looked up from my post at the floor-to-ceiling windows. I'd left a sleeping JJ to think this shit through. Besides, if I'd stayed, I'd have made love to her again. Marked her as mine ... again. I hated that someone had hurt her, had bruised that beautiful body.

Noah braced his arms in the doorjamb and studied me.

"Yeah, I know."

"Trust me. Above all else, I understand the run-in-and-kill-it compulsion when the woman you love is in danger."

"I know that, Noah. I just can't help it. I want to be out there. *To find him.*"

"I know. And I get it. But first of all, that's not you. You are the law-and-order guy; the justice guy. He's a prick and very likely deserves to go home in a body bag. But you know why I can't let you go off all renegade. This is not a Rambo movie."

"I just need to fix this for her. She's afraid, and there is nothing I can do. Do you have any idea what that feels like?"

Noah glared. "Have we met?"

I shook my head. "Yeah, I know. I know you know. I just—" I sagged against the window. "Is it supposed to fucking feel like this?"

"You mean that feeling of being totally out of control, when the only person you ever cared about this deeply is the one person you don't know how to protect?"

"Yeah. That feeling."

"It's called love."

"I mean, this is JJ. She's brash, and bold, and doesn't need anyone. On any given Sunday she's telling this lot over here, a den of killers, to go suck a bowl of dicks. More often than not she doesn't listen, she does not temper her emotions, and fucking hell is that woman loud."

Noah grinned. "Yeah, we've heard."

I glared at him. "You know, we all had to endure you and Lucia attempting to sneak around but doing a shit job of it. So JJ likes to scream." I shrugged. "I'm not going to stop the woman."

Noah put up his hands. "I'm not saying you should. It's just, well, we have a sleeping baby most of the time."

I rolled my eyes. "Shut the fuck up."

Noah chuckled low. "Yeah, I hear you. Look, we're a team. We do things together. We go in together, always. That is how we stay alive. That is how we keep JJ alive. JJ, Lucia, Isabella, each other. Not one of us gets to go off on our own. We've all seen how poorly that ends up."

"I love her," I whispered, finally giving myself permission to say the words. Some of the tension coiled tightly in the center of my chest eased. I did love her. All I wanted was her. Safe. That was it. Even if our shit didn't work out, and God, I hoped it did, I still just wanted her happiness most of all.

Then keep her alive.

Noah smirked. "Yeah, I was wondering when you were going to get around to figuring that out."

I chuckled. "Did everyone in this office think we were going to get together?"

Noah snorted a laugh. "What? You didn't think so? Because I could pretty much see where this was heading the moment you first laid eyes on her. You were completely gob smacked, standing there with your mouth open, catching flies and shit." His chuckle deepened. "I will never forget it. JJ strolled right up to you and said—"

I didn't even let him finish before quoting JJ myself. *"Yeah, I get this reaction a lot."* I shook my head. "She was so full of herself. Seriously. I just wanted to shake her. And kiss her. Which irritated me even more."

Noah's shoulders shook with mirth. "I know, man. She's a handful. And she deserves someone as good as you. So for once in your life, listen to me. We will get this asshole. But we will do it together, and we will do it smart. No one is going to touch her. This is our family and we protect what's ours. We'll figure out what's going on with ORUS and we'll get retribution for JJ. But first, we watch them. We study what they're doing. We keep this shit methodical. Then we move."

I nodded. "Then we kill the bastard."

Noah nodded. "Yeah, that too."

———

Jessica

EVERY SINGLE MAN in the penthouse was in total kill mode. Now, while some of that was kind of hot, I didn't want this kind of fuss just for me. This had not been my intention.

But what are you gonna do? Tell them not to protect you?

These guys, however frustrating they were at times, were my family. Which meant they would protect me with their lives. Not that I wanted that, but I knew them well enough to know that they would not listen.

"You guys, thank you for rallying the troops and all that. Especially since I have a penchant for telling you to go suck on a bowl of dicks. I appreciate it."

Matthias shook his head. "Don't mention it, love. We're family. We stick together."

His words were soft but he was nearly as scary as Rafe with the look he had in his eye. I didn't have all the details, but I knew that Matthias, Rafe, and Noah were not your garden-variety security folks. First clue were those tats that they sported on the backs of their necks and their wrists. They were all different, but extremely similar. To the casual observer, they were just a clustering of dots. Maybe freckles? But Lucia had told me once they were tattoos and refused to say anything else.

Truth be told, I had a feeling that I didn't really want to know. Although, I really *did* want to know. But these were the kind of secrets I had a feeling would get someone killed. So I kept my mouth shut.

Regardless, Noah was the least scary of the crew. He was mostly charming and happy-go-lucky. Unless it came to Lucia, and then the man went insane. He would do anything to protect her.

Rafe, by contrast, was serious. *All the time* serious. He rarely joked. The smiles were few, unless he was holding Isabella. Or talking to Lucia or Nonna. He had a few smiles for me too, but he didn't say much.

I had a feeling his seriousness had everything to do with whatever the hell had caused him to fake his own death. Again, it was one of those things that no one talked about. I was personally just happy to have Rafe back in our lives. And happy to see my friend get her brother back.

Rafe had tried to kill Noah and the other guys at Blake Security last year, so pretty much no one talked about that time. Except Oskar. Oskar brought it up as often as possible. Always poking and needling Rafe. I was secretly terrified that a proper fight would break out one of these days.

And then there was Matthias. Yes, he could be scary. Especially when he looked like this. But mostly, he was sweet ... as sweet as a British, tattooed, hacker-type could be. As far as I knew, he didn't do as much of the personal security work. He was more on the tech side. Whenever he did do security though, he got this look on his face. Like he'd beat anyone who even considered getting in his way. And when he looked like that, it was scary shit. He looked almost as lethal as Rafe did.

I wasn't an idiot though. All three of them were lethal. I just didn't want to ask if they had any practical experience.

"Thanks for saying that Matthias. You guys are the best family a girl could ask for. But seriously, this whole place has a Debbie Downer mood on it. You guys should go out. I get it; Jonas will be my bodyguard."

Oskar snorted. "Yeah, we all know how he guards your body."

I flipped him off. "Seriously, though. Noah, take Lucia out of here. She's worried. It's not good for Isabella. You guys go with Rafe. Jonas and I will stay and babysit."

To my surprise, Jonas nodded his agreement, even though Isabella was known for just smacking him in the face whenever he held her. She did it with such glee and a giggle, like it was her favorite activity. And she also had a penchant for vomiting on him. But still, he volunteered for babysitting duty.

"JJ's right. You guys go out. We'll stay here. Keep an eye on things."

Noah shook his head. "No one's going anywhere. We're all staying here until we get the lay of the land."

Matthias threw up his hands. "I swear to God, you lot act like a bunch of old biddies. I have eyes on Chamaeleon. JJ is safe. No one is going to let him near her. Why don't the lot of you go out? Lucia, you call the nanny. I'll stay and keep eyes on things. And that way, JJ, you get out too. Jonas, if I have to look at your dour face for another minute, I'm likely to stab you in the chest. So all of you go. Leave the baby with me. It's not like I don't know how to change little love's diapers by now."

I giggled. No one was sure what it was about Matthias. But every single time someone handed him the baby, Isabella gave him a nice warm diaper. So he had a lot of practice changing her by now.

Oskar tsked from the corner. "Does you wanting us out of here have anything to do with your crush on Katie the babysitter?"

Poor Matthias. A flush crept up his neck even as he glowered at Oskar. "Shut it."

Of course that just made Oskar laugh harder.

Lucia stepped forward and put her arm around me. "What do you think? Can you try and forget about things for a night and let us cheer you up? We'll have Noah and Jonas and Oskar, and I assume we'll be taking Ryan and Dylan as well. Rafe begged off, said he needed to crash. We'll have a night out. Most of the gang."

I slid Jonas a look, and he nodded.

"I don't know. I just feel like you guys will be all worried and tense, and I don't want anyone to feel like that."

Lucia just gave me a tight squeeze. "Come on. We're going out. Go get some sexy heels on and make these men buy us drinks and chocolate desserts, and maybe even makeup. You know how Oskar just loves spending an hour in Sephora while I look for just the right shade of lipstick."

From the corner Oskar moaned. "Please don't. Anything but that."

I grinned. "I'm having fun already. Okay. If you guys are sure."

Jonas came over and kissed me on the forehead. "Go get

changed. We'll work out some security protocols. We'll go have some fun and attack the problem in the morning, okay?"

I nodded. When I gazed up at him my heart squeezed. "I love you. You know that."

His smile was slow and confident. "Oh I know. You've been in love with me for ages." He nodded sagely as I rolled my eyes. "Which suits me fine since I knew I wanted you from the first moment you opened that sassy mouth of yours. So let's go out. We deserve to have some fun."

"You got it. I have just the backless dress and fuck me shoes for this occasion."

He groaned low. "I swear, you're trying to kill me."

I grinned up at him, feeling light for the first time since David showed up. "What a way to go."

CHAPTER TWENTY

Jonas

I am a truly lucky man, I thought to myself as I watched JJ make her way around the dance floor. When she noticed me watching her, her eyes heated and she sent me a sultry wink. I shifted in my seat, chuckling softly at the power she held over me. The woman could tempt a monk to sin with nothing more than a look.

Earlier that evening, she'd made a comment after shopping with Lucia about being all dressed up with no place to go. She'd been joking, but the words had cut through me like a knife. No matter what was going on, I never wanted JJ to feel I was keeping her locked up, away from the world. It was always going to be a challenge to temper my need to protect her and keep her safe, with her need to be free. But that was love, wasn't it? Balancing your own needs with the one you cared for. Giving up certain things to gain something far more precious?

It was astounding what I was willing to give up if it meant days and nights with JJ by my side.

She caught my eye from across the room, and immediately her lips curled up into a soft, secret smile. I loved that smile. It always seemed like she was plotting something or up to some mischief. Which wasn't ever far from reality. She was dancing with Lucia and both women were dressed to impress with silky gowns that enhanced their curves and had the power to make a man forget his own name. As I glanced over at Noah, I knew my friend felt the same way. We had found the dream.

"They're teasing us," I mumbled.

Lucia had her eyes closed and was swinging her hips, in a world all her own, probably unaware that her husband was on the verge of knocking the heads off all the men currently ogling her. JJ, on the other hand, was completely aware that she was driving me crazy, and she loved it. The little vixen watched me through hooded eyes as she danced, then executed a shimmy that almost made me come in my pants.

I reached beneath the table and discreetly adjusted myself, thankful that the long tablecloth gave me some privacy. It was bad enough that I had Oskar and the rest of the guys ribbing me about how whipped I was already. The last thing I needed was to give them more ammunition. Not that I really cared.

Besides, they were just jealous. I could understand. If I had to watch someone else with JJ, I would be jealous as all hell, too. Just the thought made me grind my teeth.

I cursed when I noticed a guy sidling closer to the girls. Then the man turned and met my gaze. My eyes must have communicated my intentions because the other man suddenly turned and walked the other way.

I chuckled. I wasn't fooling myself that I was that powerful. No doubt it was Noah, Oskar, Ryan and Dylan also glaring at him that did the trick. I was lucky to have a crew that loved her almost as much as I did.

"It's been a long time since we went out like this," Noah commented. "It's good to get out. I'm surprised Lucia hasn't said something before."

"There's been so much going on. But things are finally settling down now. It's time we start living our lives. Hell, maybe JJ and I will have a few babies so Isabella has someone to play with."

Noah chuckled. "Look at you, all domestic and shit. I would have never thought I'd see the day you were playing house with a woman."

I sat back in my chair, the idea settling in my mind like it had always been there. It would have scared the hell out of me a year ago to talk this way, but then I glanced over at JJ again and it just felt ... right. She was mine and there wasn't a single doubt in my mind about that. The thought of being with her forever wasn't scary at all. Hell, I never knew what the crazy woman would do next, so it wasn't like I'd ever be bored.

"She's worth it."

Noah clapped me on the back. "That she is. She's a handful though, so kudos to you for being man enough to handle her."

"I'm sure he doesn't mind handling her at all," Ryan commented with a little grin. He dodged the punch I threw his way easily. "No disrespect intended. It's just awfully hard to be around couples who can't keep their hands off each other. I thought Noah and Lucia were bad. I know you guys thought you were keeping it on the down-low when you started hooking up, but you guys are the worst secret shaggers known to mankind."

Oskar snorted. "At least they kept it to his office."

I winced. "Geez. A guy gets caught with his pants down in the hallway one time..."

"Twice," Dylan corrected. "And you tried to play it off like you just happened to lose your trousers on the way to the bathroom."

"Pretty sure it was more than that," Oskar said. "There was the time when we ordered Chinese and then that Saturday morning when they woke up Isabella. Then the time when they sneaked off in the middle of movie night. It was a Star Wars marathon, too. Some people have no appreciation."

"Wasn't there a laundry room incident?" Ryan added.

"Okay! I get it." I ignored their laughter. "You'd better not say anything to JJ about this. I don't want you goons embarrassing her."

Suddenly JJ plopped down in the seat next to me, bringing the fresh sunshine scent that was uniquely her own. "Tell JJ what?"

"About how much you and Casanova here are boning in the office," Oskar drawled.

I groaned and dropped my face into my hands. If he wasn't built like a brick wall, Oskar wouldn't get away with half of the shit he said and did. I could only hope JJ wouldn't get offended or think I was talking about our sex life behind her back. But before I could even respond, JJ slid a hand into my lap, perilously close to my dick.

"Well, maybe if you could lay the pipe like he does, you'd be getting some in the office, too!"

The guys all dissolved into laughter at the stunned look on Oskar's face. I knew my mouth was hanging open but couldn't seem to gain control of it until JJ patted my cheek.

"Everything okay, Casanova?" Her eyes sparkled as she teased me.

I turned so my lips brushed over her forehead. "Perfect. Everything is perfect. And so are you. I love that smart mouth of yours."

"And so do we," Ryan chimed in, still laughing. "Anyone that can put Oskar in his place has my vote."

Lucia was snuggled into Noah's lap, and the rest of the guys looked relaxed and happy. At least as relaxed as any of them ever were. But it was a good reminder that no matter how much we went through, we'd always have each other's backs. Blake Security was my family and I was grateful for it.

"Let's go home. Maybe we can bone in the laundry room again. The smell of detergent turns me on now."

JJ covered my mouth with her hand. "You are a sick, sick man."

"Oh, that's going too far?" I asked incredulously.

The entire group was in great spirits as Noah paid the check and we walked out to the parking garage. I opened the door for JJ, and she hopped up in the cab of the SUV. A loud yawn burst from her lips and she giggled.

"Damn. I used to tease Lucia about not being able to hang. All this boning with you has worn me clean out," she teased.

I leaned into the interior of the vehicle to kiss her. "I'll put you to bed as soon as we get home, Miss Jones."

"Promise?" The erotic gleam in her eyes had me rounding the vehicle much faster than usual to get to the driver's side.

———

Jessica

I WATCHED as the lights and familiar buildings of Manhattan rushed by. I was tired, it was true, but more than that, I was content. As much fun as it had been to take a night out for dinner and dancing, I was excited to be at home with my man.

My man.

I smiled to myself at the private glee the thought of Jonas always brought to me. After so many years believing that being alone was the only way to be independent, it was a bit of a shock to discover that not only did I enjoy sharing my life with a man, but I was coming to need him. Jonas had proven himself and his intentions. No matter what went down, I trusted him to be there for me with no questions. After what had happened with David ...

I shivered. I couldn't pretend that it didn't worry me to know that he was still out there. It was a bit of a mind fuck actually, to have this mental image of him walking around New York, able to show up and scare me at any moment. But I was assured that Noah and the guys were on it, and with Matthias tracking him, it wouldn't be long until he was located.

The whole time I'd dated him I thought he was a bouncer at a Manhattan nightclub. They had told me that he was an ORUS agent, so he knew how to hide, but even an agent could only remain underground for so long. Once he poked his head out of whatever hellhole he was hiding in, they'd have him. And I doubted they'd be turning him over to the authorities.

"What are you thinking about over there?" Jonas asked. He couldn't keep his eyes on my face since he was driving, but I could still see his worry in the crinkle of his brow, even in profile.

I definitely couldn't tell him my thoughts. We'd made a pact to be honest with each other and I took that seriously, but there were some things that would only bring him torment. Telling him that I was worried about David would only make him feel guilty that he hadn't been able to protect me. No matter how many times I'd told him it was ridiculous, he carried guilt over that.

Apparently Jonas thought he was superhuman and could foresee the future. But I knew the truth, which was that sometimes life was a bitch and just threw curveballs to keep you hopping. It wasn't anyone's fault; it was just the way of things. I didn't want him beating himself up over my past mistakes coming back to haunt me.

He'd shared more about his mother, his memories, and his greatest regrets. I had listened, comforted and cried more than a few tears over the fate of a gentle woman who'd wanted nothing more than to be loved. Jonas would always have a certain sense of responsibility to protect the women in his life because of his past. I knew that and accepted it, even when his overprotectiveness drove me up the wall.

"JJ. Everything okay?" Jonas glanced at me again.

I cleared my throat. "I'm fine. Just thinking about everything that's happened."

At his scowl, I reached over and squeezed the hand that wasn't on the steering wheel. "I know you guys are taking care of things. But I can't wait until it's all over. I don't want any of you getting hurt because of me."

Jonas picked up my hand and brought it to his mouth. The brush of his lips over my skin brought to mind a litany of erotic images. Scenes I knew we'd be acting out as soon as we got back home.

"There's only one person who's going to get hurt in this scenario. And that's David West. Or whatever his real name is."

I sat back abruptly. His real name. It shouldn't have been such a shock to hear the name he'd been using was an alias, but somehow it was. How strange that a man who'd had such a profound effect on my life and my distrust of men, probably wasn't even who I thought he was.

Sensing my distress, Jonas pasted on a smile that didn't quite reach his eyes. "I shouldn't have said anything. We've got this. Okay?"

We rode the rest of the way back to Blake Security in silence, each lost in our own thoughts. By the time we pulled into the underground garage, Noah and Lucia were already out of their vehicle waiting for us. Lu had already lost most of the baby weight and now just looked like a curvy pinup due to her new motherhood-enhanced chest. We'd been shopping earlier, and every one of the tops and dresses Lucia had chosen displayed quite a bit of that chest.

I smiled at the thought. Lucia had been waiting her whole life to have cleavage. I could hardly fault her for flaunting it now, although if the look on Noah's face was any indication, he wasn't enjoying the thought of anyone else seeing it.

Lucia put her arm through mine and hugged me close. Her eyes were slightly glassy. After abstaining from alcohol since getting pregnant with Isabella, she'd lost the little bit of alcohol tolerance she'd once had.

"I had so much fun tonight," I told her. "And I can tell you did, too."

Lucia grinned. "Yes, I did. After eating that delicious meal and not worrying about the calories and having a glass of wine, I'm going upstairs to rock my hubby's world!"

There was a snort of laughter from behind us. I turned just in time to see Noah smack Oskar on the back of the head.

"Well, before we lose you, do you mind if I come with you to check on Isabella? I need my baby fix."

Playtime with my favorite almost-niece was one of my favorite things. She'd been down for bed before we left so I hadn't had a chance to play with her. It hadn't escaped my notice that Jonas adored Isabella as well. Every time I saw him holding the baby, my imagination went crazy with images of him holding our child.

I placed a hand on my stomach. It was almost too much to imagine. Being with Jonas forever. Having his baby. A sudden sense of unease swept through me, making me shiver. It seemed like too much to hope for. Like I was tempting fate.

"Of course. Izzy loves you." Lucia presented her face and held still for the retinal scanner and we moved to the back to wait for the rest of the guys to get on the elevator. Once we arrived at the penthouse, we all went our separate ways with a chorus of *good nights* sounding behind us.

"I'm just going to kiss Isabella good night," I said.

Jonas smiled. "I'll come with you. This is good practice for us. For one day."

Even though it mirrored my earlier thoughts, it was a thrill to hear him say it. I grabbed his hand and dragged him behind me. Noah and Lucia trailed behind.

"It's so quiet in here. Usually Matthias would stick his head out to say hi or something."

Jonas shrugged. "He's been in a mood lately. Probably just doesn't feel up to making conversation."

I wasn't so sure about that. Matthias had been plenty chatty before we left, all smiles for the babysitter. Katie was a sweet girl, working her way through college toward a degree in sociology. Not who I'd have expected to ring Matthias's bells, but whatever. I was happy for him. Everyone should be in love.

Well, just look at me, I thought. *A regular Hallmark card.*

I turned the doorknob to the nursery and took a deep breath of the soft baby powder scent that perfumed the air no matter the time of day. It was almost midnight, so I hoped the baby would be sleeping soundly and wouldn't even notice us. The curtains were drawn, so the room was dark save for the small princess nightlight near the bed.

I tiptoed forward, stopping next to the crib. The room was decorated in all the frilly, lacy things that Lucia loved. It was like a Disney cartoon threw up in there. But for safety reasons, there were never any pillows or blankets in the crib itself. Noah had been even worse than Lucia in drilling the safety rules into all of our heads. Blankets, pillows and sheets were a suffocation hazard for infants.

Which was why I was puzzled to see that the baby was swaddled heavily in blankets.

"Lucia, did you tell Katie to swaddle the baby?" Immediately I reached into the crib to pick up Isabella. I wasn't sure why Katie would have done that when she knew the rules better than any of us. Noah had chosen carefully from a list of potential babysitters and they all had been experienced in childcare and CPR certified.

Lucia moved to my side. "No, of course not."

"Well, she did. I don't know what she was thinking." I pulled back the first layer of the blanket. When the baby's face was revealed, my blood instantly turned to ice.

"Oh my God."

I turned around. Lucia, Jonas, and Noah watched in confusion. Later, I'd wonder how I'd kept breathing when my heart had stopped beating.

"What's wrong?" Lucia asked. Then she saw the baby's face.

And screamed.

"Isabella? Where is Isabella?"

She snatched at the doll in my arms, examining it as if it would magically transform into her beloved daughter.

Tears spilled from my eyes as I scanned the room frantically. Noah already had his phone to his ear barking out orders. Jonas approached slowly, before putting his hand gently on my shoulders.

"I don't understand what's happened. Where's Isabella? Why would Katie put a doll in her crib?"

His eyes were heartbreakingly kind as he pulled me into his embrace. I let out a soft moan as I took my first deep breath in what felt like ages.

"She wouldn't," Jonas said quietly. "Oskar just called. He found Matthias in the living room unresponsive. Katie's gone. And so is Isabella."

I pulled back slightly. "Why would she do this? Money?"

"I don't know the answer to that, but we are going to find her. You can believe that."

Lucia's wails sounded from behind us, and my heart broke for my friend. That someone could hurt an innocent child ... It was chilling.

The babydoll lay on the ground at our feet, forgotten. I picked it up, mainly to make sure Lucia didn't have to lay eyes on it again. It was a standard doll, with a small wisp of dark hair on top and big blue eyes. However, someone had painted the lips a bright crimson red. I touched the lips and my fingers came away smeared with lipstick.

I've always loved you in red.

The memory slammed into me as crisp and clear as if it had just happened. David loved for me to wear lip color but he had particularly loved it when I wore red lipstick.

I turned to Jonas, clutching the macabre doll to my chest. "He was never really gone, was he?"

Jonas pulled me close and kissed the top of my head. "Who, sweetheart?"

"David," I murmured.

"We've had all our contacts watching out for Chamaeleon. You don't need to worry. You're safe," he promised.

But I had gotten the message. Loud and clear. I wasn't safe and I never had been.

And neither were the people I loved.

PART 2

CHAPTER TWENTY-ONE

Jessica

Numb terror.

That's all I felt. I was so angry and worried and sick I couldn't even move, breathe, or speak. Someone had taken Isabella right from our home. "This is all my fault. It had to have been David."

Jonas rubbed my back in slow circles. "This has nothing to do with you. This has to do with us. All of us. They want a war, they've got one."

I turned into Jonas's arms and my gaze flickered up to his. "I wish it was that simple. You don't understand. This is what he does. He terrorizes everyone around you so that you're completely alone. So that no one will want to be with you. So that you're a pariah. I wish I could say he's the kind of man who wouldn't hurt a baby just to fuck with me. But he would."

Jonas held me tight. "We're not going to let that happen. I promise. We're going to get Isabella back."

A sob racked my body. What was I supposed to do? How was I supposed to fix this? I had brought pain to my friends. Into my family. Once my parents moved away to Florida to be closer to their friends, I had no one else. These guys were the only family I had. And because of me, Noah and Lucia's baby was gone.

From the couch Matthias groaned, and Noah ran to him. "Kid?" Noah shook him hard and slapped his face. "Kid, wake up."

Matthias groaned some more, and even in his sluggish, obviously drugged state, he managed to defend against some of Noah's assaults. I was pretty sure I would've just lain there like a rag.

When Noah slapped him again, Matthias caught his arm, cranked it under his own, and then raised his other hand to hit him in the face. But then he blinked rapidly and realized who he was about to hit and released Noah.

"Blimey. Pretty sure the fucking twat drugged me. What the fuck?" He tried to sit up, but Noah shoved him back down.

"Easy. We don't know what she gave you yet. Doc's on his way to take your blood and will rush some lab results."

Matthias shook him off. "I'm all right. Just a fucking bitch of a headache."

Then he let out a slew of curses I could only assume came from a lifetime rolling about the streets of London. When he pushed himself into a sitting position, Lucia went to him and kneeled in front of him, holding his hands.

"Matthias, do you remember anything? Anything at all? They took Isabella."

Matthias's brows snapped down and he stared at Lucia hard. "The baby? Fucking cunt took the baby?"

His gaze darted to Noah whose expression was grim and his jaw set. But he nodded. "Yeah, they took the babysitter too."

Matthias shook his head, and then groaned loudly as he cradled it gently with both hands. "Nah, mate, no one took her. She brought me a drink. Said she made tea. Fucking Earl Grey. I was downed because I wanted a spot of tea. That is so fucking bullshit."

Lucia shook her head. "But I vetted Katie. *You* vetted Katie. We all did."

It was true. The nanny had been interviewed by every single member of Blake Security. They'd dug through her background, her past boyfriends, any roommates she had. They'd gone over her financial records. That babysitter pretty much had top-secret clearance at this point with all the background checks she'd had.

"I know." Matthias said. "But it was her. No one else could've accessed or bypassed the biometric scanner or the alarms. Unless those were on when you guys came in."

Next to me, Jonas stiffened. "No. No alarms. Our phones didn't go off either. Nothing."

Matthias cursed again. "Yeah. It was Katie then because no one else could have gotten in here."

"Kid, you feeling up to it? We need to access the security feed to see what happened, and you're the only one who can do that quickly," Noah said.

"Fuck. You've been waiting for me to wake up? We're losing time." He pushed to his feet and swayed, and Noah shoved him back down into a sitting position. "You stay here. Oskar, run and bring the kid his laptop."

I had never seen the German run so fast. But he was back in less than a minute and handed the laptop to Matthias. Matthias's fingers tapped over the keyboard at such a fast rate I could barely see the individual strokes he was making.

"Yeah, mate. Here she is; bloody cunt is in the kitchen making the tea." He turned the laptop around, but when we all couldn't see it he made another few quick taps, and the security footage appeared on the television set. He pointed. "Yeah, there she is, putting whatever it is in the tea. I was working on something. But Isabella refused to sleep, so I had her one-handed, you know. Like you do sometimes, Noah, so that she can see outward and play a little, and then she falls asleep."

Noah's lips twitched, and he blinked back tears. "Yeah, I know."

Matthias sniffed too. "Fuck mate. I'm so fucking sorry. I'm such a fucking idiot. I took the tea. I drank it. Didn't taste any different, didn't smell any different."

Noah shook his head. "This isn't on you. This is on her. We just need to see the rest of the video."

Matthias fast-forwarded the video to show what happened when his head started to nod back. Katie took the baby, and then she made one call. "Yes. He's out." She was silent for a beat, and then her gaze darted to Matthias and back to the baby. "I don't think I can do that. If that's what you want to happen, you'll have to come and do it yourself. Because I won't. I told you that already."

"Is there any way we can track who she was talking to?" Jonas asked.

Matthias frowned. "I might be able to hack her phone. Pinpoint her location. Read her text messages. But without the actual physical phone, it will be next to impossible to determine who she called. I'm fucking sorry. This is on me."

I stepped out of the comfort of Jonas's arms. "No Matthias. I've already taken the blame. It's because of me that all of you are in this position. He wants me. That's why he took her. Because he knows it would hurt me to see all of you hurting. Matthias this wasn't your fault. We'll find Katie. If anyone can do it, you can."

Lucia nodded. "JJ's right. You would be the one who could find her."

"I'll do my best. Again, I'm so fucking sorry."

"Don't be sorry. This wasn't you. Just find her," Noah said.

Lucia stood and turned to me. "Look, I know you blame yourself, JJ. I actually blame myself for leaving. I know Noah's gonna rip himself apart. And Matthias, you're killing yourself because you drank tea. None of us are to blame. The person to blame is this Chamaeleon character. He and Katie. We blame them. And now we all have to band together and bring my daughter home."

Noah wrapped his arms around her. "Lucia's right. We are a family. We won't crumble. And together, we're going to find my daughter. Even if it means taking the fight straight to ORUS. We will get her back."

Matthias tried to stand again but thought better of it. "That's just the thing you guys. I'm not entirely sure ORUS is behind this."

———

Jonas

CALM, I had to stay fucking calm. I dragged in a deep breath in hopes that one breath would keep me from wanting to pull something apart. I was going to kill that fucker. I was going to take my time. And I was going to enjoy it.

There's plenty of time for killing him later.

We had to catch him first. And as much as I wanted to kill the asshole right now, my priority was JJ. I could almost feel her shaking as she stood next to me.

"Babe, want to take Lucia into the kitchen? Make her some tea, see what you can do to help her. I'll talk to Matthias and see what we can seam together about the sequence of events, okay?"

The JJ I knew would argue about why she needed to be in the room with us when we were discussing things and vowing to kill the fucker herself. But that part of her was in shock. Instead, she simply nodded, went to her best friend, took her hand, and led her through the expansive living area to the back hallway and into the kitchen.

I could only stare after her as she left the room. Would this be the thing that broke her? How the hell did I help her fix this?

She'll be okay. She's strong. Right now, someone else needs your support.

I turned my attention to Noah and winced when I saw the fear in his eyes. His lips were thin, his gaze bleak. What hell he must be going through right now. I stepped toward my friend, but Noah jutted out his chin.

"Let's get to work. Matthias, are you able to get into our backup security feed?"

From the couch, the kid nodded and tried to get himself up. The kid was too weak though, so Oskar and Rafe helped him to his feet. He was so unsteady, they half-dragged him into the hallway and back into his domain. Once they had him seated in his usual post, he sagged into his seat. I had to give the kid credit, because as shitty as he must feel, he was still ready to work.

"All right lads, I know it's an easy thing to jump to conclusions about who's responsible for this, but I've had eyes on Chamaeleon since the other day. He hasn't moved. Not once, in or out, at least according to my feeds. I've also had eyes on ORUS headquarters just in case he found a way around my protocols. It's easy to assume it's him. But," he shook his head. "According to my research, the guy's agoraphobic or something. He hasn't left his flat."

Noah rubbed the stubble on his jaw. "How many exits are there in that building?"

"There are four. I have cameras on all of them."

I wracked my brain. "This guy is good at hiding. I mean that's pretty much what they trained him for. We have to be missing something."

Matthias shook his head. "No. His door hasn't even opened. Two days, and he's been holed up in that flat. Unless he sprouted wings and flew."

I scowled. "I mean, that's possible, right?"

"I appreciate the confidence in the skill set, Jonas, but even ORUS agents can't fly."

"No, but they can rappel and shit, right Rafe?"

Lucia's brother nodded. "That's a possibility. I've done it. But as a means of getting in and out of a building, it's risky. Someone is bound to see you. But if the building has a basement or connects to a tunnel, it's a good way in and out."

Noah spoke, his voice low and gravelly. Like every word was painfully wrenched out of him. "Matthias, start looking at building plans of what was there before this apartment complex. Then start looking for any connection between David West and Katie. Anything at all. In the meantime, I'll send Dylan to her apartment. Though it's doubtful she's there, he might find something that leads us to her. And let's have Ryan start canvasing her known haunts. Everywhere she's been known to go. I want her credit card numbers. I want her phone number. Hell, I want her library card number. Anything that can help find my daughter."

Matthias and Dylan gave him curt nods.

"Noah," the kid swallowed hard. "Really fucking sorry."

Noah visibly shook. "This isn't on you. This is on that woman and Chamaeleon. All we can do is what we all do best."

I studied Noah and wondered if he, Matthias, and Rafe would be coming out of assassin retirement to handle this guy. And if they were coming out of retirement did that mean that Katie was fair game too?

Noah hadn't ever given me full details of what he'd done for ORUS, but I'd been able to piece together enough. The three of them, they had killed before.

A lot.

The part of me that still believed in law and order bristled at that. But I knew better than anyone there were times when extreme measures were called for. This was one of those times.

And if there was killing to be done for the bastard who took Isabella, well then so be it.

"Matthias, walk us through what happened from the moment we left. Just one more time. Show us everything," Noah said.

I turned my attention to Noah. "Listen, I know you're going to tell me no. But why don't you let me handle this? Because right now you're too raw, and you're in shock. You and I both know you're not at your best right now. Not to mention the cops will be here any second. You're about to have your hands full. Let me do this."

Noah's shake of the head was automatic. "She's my daughter. *I'll* do this."

"You can't do *this* and deal with the cops. Go." Even as I spoke, the buzzer indicated someone was downstairs. "See, the police are already here. You deal with them and the official channels. Maybe this *is* a simple case of the babysitter going crazy. If it is, we'll find her in no time. If it isn't, the kid will work with the team. We have it under control."

Noah looked like he was going to refuse again. But when Dylan poked his head into the computer room and nodded at him, indicating the cops were there, he really had no choice. When he finally nodded, I could see the sag in his body. He was giving up the fight.

When Noah shuffled out of the room to deal with the police, I turned my attention back to Matthias and Rafe and assumed command. Rafe might be back in the fold, but I had the most seniority on this team.

"Okay, it's just us." To Matthias, I said, "How are you holding up?"

The kid flattened his lips. "Yeah, mate, I'm good. Now let's catch this cunt."

CHAPTER TWENTY-TWO

Jessica

I stood at the periphery of the room, watching as everyone moved with purpose. Noah was on the warpath, his phone to his ear while simultaneously looking over Matthias's shoulder. Jonas and Oskar were conferring about something in somber tones across the room, both with expressions of grave worry.

It reminded me of the way things were the previous year when Lucia had been the one in hot water. Noah would have probably locked her in the penthouse back then if he could have gotten away with it. They'd still been fighting the inevitable back then, but I was sure she wouldn't have minded being locked away with Noah too much.

My eyes swung to where Lucia was sitting alone on the couch. We had gone into the kitchen to make tea, but once we'd come back, the tea sat on the side table, forgotten as she stared into space. Every few moments, her fingers would twitch as if searching for the baby that should have been in her arms.

I shuddered. I wanted to go to her, hug her and tell her it

would all be okay. That was what I should have been doing as her best friend. But I couldn't seem to get my feet to move.

What right did I have to comfort her? It was my fault her daughter was missing.

"It's not your fault." Jonas's voice interrupted my thoughts.

I nodded because I knew that was what he expected, not because I agreed.

Jonas swore softly when I met his gaze. "You're crying. Come here, baby."

I walked into his embrace and buried my face into his shirt. He smelled like amber, something slightly smoky, and... home. I wasn't sure when it had happened exactly, but Jonas had become my safe place.

"It's rare that you cry," Jonas whispered. "I don't like it. I wish I could take the pain away."

I smiled tremulously. "No one can take this away. Not until Isabella is back where she belongs."

Inside, my mind was a muddle of guilt, confusion, and anger. What was David doing? It was like looking at a puzzle that had half the pieces missing. In the beginning, I'd assumed this whole thing was about showing me he was still around and could show up whenever he wanted. It was about control. David had always been so jealous and controlling, terrorizing me as I went about my life fit the profile of his previous methods perfectly.

But this? Taking an innocent child? This was something else entirely.

"We're pulling up security and traffic cams in the area to see if we can catch where Katie was going or if she met up with anyone." Jonas glanced over his shoulder to where Matthias was talking to Noah. "There's nowhere she can hide in this city. Noah has too many contacts."

I closed my eyes. "She's not the one I'm worried about."

Jonas sighed. "You still think it was Chamaeleon."

I shrugged. There was no use insisting when the evidence seemed so flimsy. It was more a gut feeling than anything else.

The whole time we'd been dating, he was careful to keep his abuse private. He'd only hit me places where no one would see the bruises. He'd been jealous of my attention to other men, but he'd played the affable, easygoing boyfriend in public, only to show his rage as soon as we were behind closed doors.

There had been only one occasion where he'd lost his temper where anyone else could see. He'd been careful to keep our dynamic away from other people, so why would he suddenly target Lucia's baby? I'd never even introduced him to Lucia back then. My friend had been mourning her brother's death and hadn't been going out much at all.

"JJ, look at me. You are not to blame here."

"He's right. You should listen to him." Lucia's voice came from behind Jonas. We both turned to look at her.

Lucia's gray eyes were shadowed and slightly red from unshed tears. It hurt me just to look at her.

As usual, Jonas could sense my emotions. He pulled me closer and kissed my forehead. "Lucia loves you. We all do. Remember that. I'll leave you two to talk."

I watched as he hugged Lucia before walking over to join Noah and Matthias. When I looked back to Lucia, my friend watched me with knowing eyes.

"You can't fool me, Jessica Jones. We've known each other too long for that."

The use of my full name pulled a reluctant smile from me. Lucia only pulled out the big guns when she was serious.

"I'm not trying to fool you. I'm just ashamed."

"Why would you be ashamed? You've been nothing but a loving, protective godmother to Isabella. And I have no doubt that if you'd been here when it happened you'd have kicked that babysitter's ass. But you weren't here, and neither was I. Blaming ourselves for not being here doesn't get my daughter back. I don't need you to distance yourself because you feel guilty. I need my best friend to hold my hand so I don't lose my mind."

I held open my arms immediately. Lucia practically threw herself forward, holding on to me like a lifeline. I had been keeping myself so busy with guilt and second thoughts that I hadn't realized I was also punishing Lucia.

"I'm so sorry. I didn't think you'd want to look at me knowing that I might have brought this danger on us."

Lucia wiped her eyes with the back of her hand. "Even if it is this Chamaeleon guy, do you think I blame you for the actions of that psycho? You're my sister, JJ. I couldn't love you any more if we were blood."

I blew out a breath as my own eyes welled with tears. "Oh hell, now you've got me crying too."

After a few minutes hugging it out, Lucia grabbed my hand and led me to the couch. I curled up on one side while Lucia took the other and we turned so our feet met in the middle. This was how we'd always sat together, starting from when we were teenagers. The familiar pose was a bit of comfort in the middle of chaos.

Lucia glanced behind us where the guys were talking. "Noah is going crazy. If I thought he was over protective where I'm concerned, he's way worse with Isabella. Whoever took her might as well pick out their gravestone." Her voice wavered slightly at the end.

I held out a hand and squeezed when Lucia took it. I could hear what my friend was pointedly not saying. Her deepest fear. That even though Noah would tear the city apart to find their daughter, there was no guarantee Isabella would still be alive by the time he found her.

"Matthias can find anyone. I'm sure he can find whoever did this."

Lucia's eyes swung over to mine. "You really think David would do this to get back at you? It seems so strange. It would make more sense if Izzy were your baby."

"Maybe not. I'm probably wrong, and it's some random person that Noah and the guys helped put in jail in the past or something."

I closed my eyes and wished with my whole heart that could be true. Because if it was David, it meant his obsession with me was even bigger than I could have ever known. It also meant they wouldn't find Isabella until he wanted them to.

After all, David had never lacked patience. He'd waited over seven years to come back and take his revenge.

———

THE NEXT FEW days were some of the longest of my life. Noah didn't appear to have slept the entire time and neither had Lucia, if I took a guess. Every night she went into her room, but she came out the next day with the bags under her eyes deeper and darker.

Not that I didn't understand. I'd brought work home with me but it hadn't taken my mind off things a bit. My sleep had been filled with nightmares of David holding the baby just out of reach and drawing on my face with lipstick. I woke in a cold sweat after that one.

One morning while sitting at the kitchen counter, I heard a commotion coming from down the hall. Noise was a part of life when living with so many men, but this was different. I abandoned my coffee cup and walked toward the sound. It was coming from Matthias's room.

I hadn't been in his room many times, but I remembered that it was taken up by a lot of screens and there were always a bunch of laptops lying around. As I got closer, I slowed my steps so the guys wouldn't hear me.

"I can't believe you found him."

That sounded like Jonas's voice. I inched a little closer. We'd all avoided speaking about the search for the missing babysitter in front of Lucia, so I'd only gotten a few updates from Jonas.

"It wasn't easy, mate. He laid a convincing trail to make it look like he lived in that other apartment. It would have taken way longer to find him if he hadn't gotten cocky and sent a message. He's definitely one of us."

One of us? What did that mean? I shook my head. Lucia had hinted about Noah, Matthias, and Rafe sharing some sort of shady background, but I didn't know too much about it. Did that mean that David knew them? Maybe Jonas was right and this really wasn't about me. The sound of Matthias's laugh brought me back to the present conversation.

"Bloody wanker. He actually thought he could proxy off some server in Russia for his emails to throw me off his scent. Like I'm some amateur."

Jonas's deep laugh came next. "Not sure what the fuck you just said, but I assume that means you know where he is?"

"Yeah, he's still in New York. Fucker got an apartment in the East Village on 10th. Not sure why he's still hanging around if he doesn't want to be caught."

My mind immediately started spinning. I put a hand over my mouth, sure that I'd scream or cry or something and give away that I was listening. But there was only one reason David would hang around New York instead of hiding out.

Me.

"Look, I think it's best if we keep this quiet for now. The girls are already on edge. So let's not mention anything until we know more." Jonas's voice brought me out of my daze.

It was just like him to want to spare us more pain. I thought of Lucia and her haunted eyes. I didn't want my friend to get her hopes up only to have them dashed either. Which was why I knew what I needed to do.

I slipped down the hallway, holding my breath until I reached my room. Jonas always seemed to have a sixth sense about when I was up to something, so I could only hope to make it out of the penthouse without arousing any suspicion. But I couldn't just sit here wasting time if there was a chance I could find David and end this.

You don't even know exactly where he is.

I ignored the completely reasonable doubts rushing through my brain. It was true that I didn't know exactly where David was but if I knew the street, there was a good chance I could find him if I walked around. I knew him. I knew how his twisted mind worked.

What he wanted was to break me down, scare me, and prove his dominance. That he could show up whenever he wanted and there was nothing I could do. It would be just like him to hang out a sign saying 'come find me JJ' just to fuck with my mind. As Matthias had pointed out, he was clearly hanging around for a reason.

Maybe if I gave him what he wanted, then he would give Isabella back and leave my friends out of this.

All I could do was pray that he hadn't hurt Isabella. Because if he had hurt my goddaughter, I was prepared to rain down whatever vengeance I could, even if I died trying.

Once I reached my room, I changed from my lounge clothes into jeans and a T-shirt. I avoided my own eyes in the mirror as I brushed out my hair and pulled it back into a high ponytail, the same way I'd worn it back when I'd been with David all those years ago. My stomach clenched, disgusted at the idea of dressing to please him, but I reminded myself that this was for Isabella. I could do anything, even flirt with a psycho, if it meant my best friend's daughter got to come home safe.

My fingers hesitated over my favorite red lipstick. It wasn't the same color I'd worn as a teenager, but it was pretty damn close. Before I could overthink it, I swiped the crimson shade over my lips. Then I grabbed my handbag and walked out into the hallway.

No one was in the hallway, a small blessing, so I didn't waste any time going directly to the elevator and riding it down to the garage level. My heart pounded furiously the entire time as I walked to my car, sure that at any moment Matthias would come running after me. The guy never seemed to sleep and had surveillance out the ass, so I could only pray that he was still distracted talking to Jonas. I didn't breathe normally until I pulled out of the garage and onto the street.

Then my heart started pounding for an entirely different reason. Every mile I covered was taking me closer to the source of all my nightmares. My personal boogeyman.

And I was placing myself right in his clutches.

I blanked my mind, clearing out all thoughts of how foolish this was, and focused on driving. When I saw an open meter I took it, even though I was still five blocks away. Walking would give me time to calm down and also the chance to scope out the neighborhood.

I was familiar with the East Village, of course, as any long time resident of the city would be. It really wasn't the kind of place I'd expect David to settle. He'd always been obsessed with having and being the best. I wouldn't expect him to like the punk, modern vibe of this diverse neighborhood. The David I knew would have wanted to find the most expensive, exclusive place possible in the city.

A guy selling T-shirts tried to get my attention, and I shook my head with a smile. Any other day I'd probably have bought one just to help the kid out. But today I had a mission. When I finally reached 10th Street, my nerves were strung so tight I felt one deep breath away from snapping in two. My eyes roamed both sides of the street, waiting. I wasn't sure exactly what I was looking for, only that I'd know it when I saw it.

Then my eyes landed on a shop across the street. The awning over the door had the store name in faded cursive.

Chameleon.

I stopped in my tracks, ignoring the muttered curses from the people around me. That was it. It had to be. It was spelled differently than the code name he used but the coincidence was too much. My hands tightened into fists. He thought he was really cute living above a store with his code name. This whole thing was one big joke to him.

I wasn't sure how long I stood there before I finally sprang into motion. Traffic was heavy, which made it even easier to dodge around the cars and taxis to get to the other side. Once there, I glared at the awning as if it could give me the answers I needed. Then as if I'd summoned him, he was there.

"David," I breathed.

To my surprise, he didn't seem alarmed that I was there. It was almost like he'd been expecting me.

"Jessica. There you are."

He smiled at me, as if I'd only gone out for coffee and he was welcoming me back home.

And I knew then that I'd made a terrible mistake.

CHAPTER TWENTY-THREE

Jonas

After discussing some options with Matthias, I headed straight for JJ's room and knocked. "JJ? You there?" When she didn't respond, I opened the door and stuck my head in.

It was empty.

All day I had been dying to get to her. Sure, I had only been gone for three hours, but she had been unusually quiet through text message. Normally, she would have at least butt-dialed me by now.

I backtracked and found Matthias still sitting in front of his laptop. "Hey, have you seen my girlfriend?"

Matthias shook his head. "No, mate. But from the camera, I can see her purse isn't on the hook by the door. Maybe she went out for some air. Maybe heading back to the office? Do you want me to check her phone?"

Part of me wanted to tell him no, that I trusted JJ. I didn't want to confine her to a prison much like her old psycho ex had done. That's what I told myself. But the words were out of my mouth before I thought about them.

"Yeah, would you?"

Matthias whirled his chair around. "You got it." In seconds, he frowned. "She's in the East Village. On 10th and—" suddenly Matthias dropped his head and kept shaking it. "For the love of Christ, is that woman mad?"

I did not like the sound of that. "What do you mean?"

When Matthias looked at me, his eyes were bleak. "I don't want you to panic, but it looks like she's headed straight for West's place."

Ice doused my veins. "What the fuck? Who let her out of the house?"

Matthias put up his hands. "Easy, mate. It's not like this is a prison. You and JJ both said you didn't want that for her. If that's what you wanted, I would've merrily locked her in her room, and she would've cussed me the fuck out. You know how she is. You know how she gets. You said you didn't want that. Which is fine by me, but we've all got to get on the same page. Either she's under protective custody, or she has freedom to move. But right now, how about we all just get down there and get her before she does something stupid."

I shook my head. "No. I'm going. Do me a favor and alert Noah and the others. I might need backup."

Matthias nodded even as he jammed his ear comm unit in.

I was out the door in a flash, just barely remembering to grab my keys for the SUV before running down to the garage. The elevator was too slow. I preferred the stairs, so at least I could physically do something.

The next ten minutes were an exercise in reckless driving. I navigated the streets like a complete maniac. Luckily, GPS and a proprietary software Matthias used directed me around all the traffic. And thankfully, I could park fucking anywhere.

"Come on, come on, come on."

The last thing on earth I wanted to be was too late. Too late to stop her; too late to help her. When I saw her, I skidded the car to a stop right in front of a hydrant. Fuck, they could tow me if they liked. This was more important.

In my ear, Matthias's voice rang clear. "Noah's on his way. Rafe too."

"Do me a favor and tell them to hurry."

As I approached, I saw that JJ was talking to someone. Right in front of the door of — oh fuck. Yeah that was West, and JJ was reading him the fucking riot act.

To his credit, the guy was taking it and just insolently leaning against the doorframe. As JJ went all extra-JJ on him, her cursing was inventive. Her arms were gesticulating wildly. She was at desperation-level angry and I picked up the pace, jogging to reach them. Before I could do anything, Chamaeleon pulled her close.

Mother Fucker. He held her so tight, JJ's arms and legs flailed.

I sprinted, my gun out of its holster and raised. "Let her go, asshole."

Over JJ's shoulder, the son of a bitch smirked. "As you wish. She came to me man. If you don't know how to keep your woman happy, don't put that on me."

Then he shoved JJ away from him so hard that she fell on her ass. Then the bastard turned and went back inside.

What I wanted to do was run in right after him. But JJ was my main concern. She was shaking, and had curled herself into a little ball, rocking backward and forward.

"Baby. Are you okay? Look at me. Tell me you're okay. I need to hear the words."

She nodded and said, "I'm okay. I... I'm so sorry. I know I shouldn't have come. But I couldn't sit around anymore and just wait. I overheard Matthias say he was here, and I thought if I just saw him and gave him what he wanted, he'd let Isabella go. But instead, he said he didn't know what I was talking about and called me crazy. And then I lost it. I know he's been watching me. I accused him and he said I was making it up and..."

Tears streamed down her face, and I bent down to my haunches and wrapped my arms around her. All I could do was hold her in the middle of the sidewalk with pedestrians streaming around us. I created a cocoon around her so that she was unaware of anyone else but me.

When Rafe and Noah showed up, I shook my head and inclined it toward the door. "He's in there."

Rafe patted himself down, doing an automatic weapons check, and headed straight for the door. But Noah clamped a hand on his shoulder. "No. I'm gonna tell you the same thing I told him." He inclined his head toward me. "We can't go in weapons hot. He's a private citizen, and that's his residence. The FBI's handling that angle. Besides, we don't know what booby-traps he's got set up. And I don't want us barging in there and him hurting my fucking daughter."

Noah's voice wavered, and a jolt of pain sliced my heart in two. My woman and my best friend were in the most unimaginable pain, and there was nothing I could do about it. What if I'd just taken a shot? I could've just taken the guy out.

But then we would have decreased our chances of finding Isabella.

In my arms, JJ started to shake, and all I could do was hold her tighter. I knew how terrified she was. I completely understood it because I was terrified as well. The difference was, I knew exactly what to do about it.

When I got my hands on David West, I was going to throw out all my opinions about due process and kill the fucker with my bare hands.

My hands shook as I clipped JJ into her seat. "Are you sure you're okay?"

She nodded. "Fine. I don't know what I was thinking. I just—if he hurts Isabella — I don't know what I'll do."

"We'll get her back." I tucked her hair behind her ear. "But not by you going off half-cocked."

She smirked, and I knew that the old JJ was in there somewhere. "You said cock."

"And sooner or later I can show you mine. But first, let's get you home. Okay? Lucia's got enough on her mind without worrying that something is going to happen to you too."

She flushed and ducked her head. "I didn't mean to make anyone worry. I just — I just thought I could—"

"Thought you could trade yourself for the baby?"

JJ brought her head up and her eyes were grave. "She's a baby. She's never done anything to anyone. And all he wants is me. I could do that. I could do that for my friend. I could get her baby back."

I took her shaking hands in mine and dropped my forehead to hers. "Yeah, but at what cost? What would I do without you? What would Lucia do without you? Noah, Matthias, Oskar, Ryan, Dylan? All of us. You're family. And no one's sacrificing themselves. We fight. We don't give up. And you walking into that asshole's lair, volunteering yourself and not telling anyone where you're going... that's a sacrifice. We're not doing that. Besides, I will attest that you are no virgin. Not after what I've done to you." I winked. "Only fighters in our camp. Do you understand?"

She nodded but didn't answer.

I slammed her door shut and tried to calm my temper while I walked around to the driver's side. Jesus Christ. Had I ever been so fucking scared in my life? That maniac could have taken her.

He could have killed her on the street, and we'd still be no closer to finding Isabella, and JJ would be gone. That woman was the most infuriating, stubborn, love of my life, and I'd almost lost her. Shit.

Before opening the driver's side door, I took a calming breath and then spoke into my comm unit. "All secure. She's in the car, we're heading back."

"You got it." Even Matthias sounded calmer. And he was almost always calm and efficient. Why couldn't JJ see how much we all cared about her? Why couldn't she understand that if she was lost, none of us would survive?

I climbed under the wheel and patted her knee. "You ready to go home?"

She nodded, but her eyes were still distant. I understood. It was that feeling of being completely impotent; of knowing that you needed to do something, but having no idea what to do. Yeah, I knew that feeling all too well.

I wove effortlessly into the traffic downtown, ready to make a turn and head back up to the penthouse when Matthias's voice was crisp and clipped in my ear.

"*All hands. All hands.* Chamaeleon spotted leaving his apartment. He's wearing a baby carrier and what looks like a baby. Headed east on 14th Street. All hands, I repeat all hands."

I tapped my comm. "*Roger*. Turning around."

Noah's voice came over the comm unit clearly. "Rafe and I are closer."

Next to me, JJ stiffened. "What's happening?"

I whipped the car around in an illegal U-turn and headed back in the direction we'd come. "Chamaeleon left his place. Wearing a baby carrier."

I could see the shock on her face as she whispered, "I knew it."

I had nothing to say. She had known it. She'd gone there to get the baby back and I'd stopped her.

No. You stopped her from getting herself killed.

"I know. We're going to get her back." I said, but the words sounded empty to my own ears. How else was I supposed to soothe her? Traffic came to a complete standstill, and I cursed before making an illegal U-turn, swerving to avoid collision with the honking cars and taxis.

As we approached 16th Street, Noah raced by us and we followed in hot pursuit.

"Matthias, where is he now?"

"He's turning left on Liberty Street. Zuccotti Park. No cars. Only pedestrians, you're gonna have to get out and run."

I glanced at JJ. "What are the chances if I park the car and asked you to sit here, that you'll listen?"

"Probably about as high as you letting me cut off your dick and carry it around in my purse."

"Fair enough. In that case, keep up. Be aware. Don't let him catch you."

"What's happening?" She had already unfastened her seatbelt.

"He's turned left up ahead."

Noah's heavy breathing came through the comm unit. "Giving chase. Rafe is headed around to cut him off."

I pulled up to a fire hydrant, not caring about the illegality, and jumped out of the car. JJ yelled, "I'm right behind you."

I needed to find Isabella and keep JJ safe. I knew how these guys thought, at least according to Noah's snippets. This could be a trap, and I wasn't letting JJ out of my sight. Eventually, I gave up and took her hand, dragging her along behind me.

To her credit, she followed quickly, didn't ask too many questions, and ran like there was some kind of sample sale.

We caught up to Noah, who was spinning around in circles. "Matthias? Where the fuck did he go?"

"He cut across the grass. To your right. Blue baseball hat."

Sure enough, we saw him, wearing a baseball cap and the baby carrier.

Noah had his gun out of the holster in a second, but I had to remind him, "Noah, there are civilians."

"You don't think I have a head shot?"

"I think you do, but things happen all the time. And this could be some kind of trap. So put the gun away, and run your ass off."

JJ was panting hard, but she kept up as we ran. When we got close to Chamaeleon, he stopped and turned right before the pond in the park. He took the baby out of the carrier and held her over the Koi pond.

Noah screamed. "Don't. She's a baby. She's done nothing to you."

The fucker smirked. "I don't give a fuck. It's not her I care about. It's her." His gaze locked on JJ, and I could feel her stiffen beside me.

JJ ran forward. "You can have me." I tried to grab her hand, but it was too sweaty and slipped out of my grasp. "I'll come with you. Just put Isabella down. I'll come with you. Whatever you want. Just leave the baby alone."

"No. Not like this. Not while your friends have shooters aimed at me. You'll come with me eventually. You and I are going to be together, but I'd rather us have our conversation without an audience. So you can come after me or you can save the baby." And then he tossed Isabella into the pond.

"No!" JJ screamed as she and Noah both ran straight for the baby.

One of us needed to go after Chamaeleon. I tapped my comm. "Rafe. He's headed West. Through the park. You go after him. We have Isabella."

Noah was in the pond faster than any of us, lifting his legs and wading through the water until he reached the baby. Then he screamed so loud and so low that Jonas was pretty sure the earth shook.

"Noah. Noah, is she alive?"

My friend lifted his head, the anguish drawing all his features down. "No." He shook his head. "It's not even her. It's another doll. But this one is fucking animated."

I cursed under my breath "Son of a bitch."

CHAPTER TWENTY-FOUR

Jonas

I had never felt more helpless in my life. Watching JJ break down, falling to her knees right in the middle of the pond, took me to a dark place. One I wasn't sure I could crawl back from. I'd been down this road before, watching a woman I loved being terrorized and broken down, piece by piece.

But fuck that. I'd be damned if I'd just watch as JJ slowly lost everything that made up her ballsy, flat-out, fearless self. Maybe that was what gave me the idea to approach Noah with the most insane idea ever.

Once the team had returned to the penthouse, I pulled Rafe and Noah aside and floated my idea. I was met with are-you-fucking-kidding-me glares.

"You want us to go to the head of ORUS and ask for his help apprehending one of his own agents?" Noah shook his head, like he wasn't sure he'd heard correctly.

"I know it sounds crazy," I muttered.

Noah glared at me. "It doesn't just sound crazy. It is crazy.

Normally I'd approach Ian with an offer, maybe some information he needed in exchange for a favor. But this is one of his guys; an active ORUS agent."

Everything my friend was saying made sense. Hell it made perfect sense not to walk right into the fucking lion's den and announce your presence, but I was done sitting around and waiting for that fucker West to make a move. So far David had been the one calling the shots, arranging us all where he wanted us like chess pieces on a board. We needed to turn things around, pull him out of hiding on our terms.

Noah made a frustrated sound. "Even if he believes us when we have no proof, there's no guarantee that he'd help us. Ian is better than most, that's why we installed him as the head of ORUS. Better the enemy you know, right? But I'm not sure I trust him that much. We could be walking right into a trap. For all we know, this is exactly what Chamaeleon wants us to do."

"I don't think so," I said softly. My mind flashed back to the way West had looked at JJ. It hadn't been calculated at all. He'd been wearing an expression of utter obsession, one that made my skin crawl even as I remembered it.

"You didn't see the way he was looking at her. He wants JJ, and he's willing to do whatever is necessary to get to her. I seriously doubt Ian wants a loose cannon like that out there possibly putting ORUS at risk. He might not want to help us, but if he can rein West in, he might help us inadvertently."

Noah stood, his face a blank mask. He left the room and returned a couple of minutes later with Matthias and Oskar.

"This is the deal. Jonas thinks we should get Ian involved."

Matthias opened his mouth to protest but Noah held up a hand.

"Believe me, I know. But he has some good points. Ian might be the only one who can actually control West, and we think that might give us the opening we need to figure out where he's keeping Isabella."

No one spoke for a few moments, and I knew they were all thinking the same thing. It might help us, or it might piss David off. And if that were the case, who knew how he'd react?

Matthias acted as a voice of reason. "Maybe we shouldn't—"

"This is the only thing we can do," Noah cut him off. "The longer he has her, the less likely it is that she'll still be alive when we find her. This has to work."

Rafe's voice was calm but deadly. "You know me. I'm behind you all the way."

For the next hour, we discussed strategy and armed ourselves to the teeth from the armory room. Ryan and Dylan were going to stay behind to protect the women, something JJ would likely give us an earful about later. She hated it when we went off leaving the "little women" behind, but I wasn't sure how she wanted us to handle it. I didn't want to shut her out, but I for damn sure wasn't going to bring her into a dangerous situation.

I'd noticed Noah had been taking more time to reassure Lucia lately, telling her what he was doing before leaving, which was unlike him. I smiled thinking of how stoic and unbending my friend had been before finally admitting his longtime feelings for Lucia.

We took three separate vehicles with Rafe on his own, Matthias and Oskar in one of the vans we used for surveillance, and Noah and me in the SUV. When we left New York, I glanced over at Noah.

"He's meeting us at the X." The X was the location that ORUS used for mission prep. They never ever discussed details of black ops in their shiny office uptown. The X's location changed monthly.

I knew better than to ask too many questions. It had been

years before Noah had confided in me about his past with the borderline-legal, government-sanctioned, shadow organization known as ORUS. I'd figured out on my own that Matthias had been in, too, and with the things Noah had mentioned about Rafe, I was pretty sure Lucia's older brother was also a former agent.

It made sense given the timeline of when Noah said he'd come into the DeMarco's lives. Plus, the way Rafe fought indicated he was either an ORUS agent or former special ops. The dude had beaten the hell out of Matthias and Oskar and had almost blinded me. I rubbed my eyes absently at the memory.

Not that I was still bitter or anything.

This month, the X was an abandoned dock. When we pulled up, Noah parked and got out immediately. I followed, my eyes scanning the surroundings. Rafe appeared silently at my side. Matthias and Oskar climbed out of the van.

"There's no one stationed to the East or the South."

I nodded once just as Rafe appeared.

"Looks clear. Let's get this shit over with." Rafe's hand hovered close to the piece in his waistband.

We climbed over the metal guardrail and made our way down closer to the water. Ian stood next to a trashcan where a fire burned. Anyone looking would see nothing more than a random bum warming himself by a fire. Not the head of a secretive and lethal organization. Maybe that was part of the lesson we all had to learn, not to judge too easily because nothing was truly as it appeared.

Noah stood next to Ian, stretching his hands out to the heat of the fire. Ian didn't acknowledge him in any way.

"One of your dogs is off his leash," Noah finally said.

Ian grunted. "My dogs don't have leashes, they have microchips. If there's a problem, I'll take care of it. Not sure why that warrants a trip to this shithole so I can freeze my ass off."

"It warrants a hell of a lot when my daughter's life is at stake. You brought a predator into my home, and now I need you to help take him down."

Ian froze and then turned slowly to look at Noah. "Chamaeleon?" The word was barely a whisper, but Noah nodded curtly. "Why would you think it was him? He's been overseas for years and just got back. If he was after you, why would he wait this long?"

"It's not me he's after. It's a friend. Isabella just got caught in the crossfire."

Ian glanced behind him at me and the others, then barked out a laugh. "Well, you certainly came with a show of force."

"This is my daughter, Ian. I need your help. I made you Orion because I thought you'd be different."

Ian scoffed. "Like that was some favor. Might as well have painted a permanent target on my back."

"Don't fuck with me, Ian!" Noah's outburst took us all by surprise, Oskar shifting restlessly while Matthias clenched his fists.

I wanted to put a hand on Noah's shoulder, but under the circumstances, my friend was likely to bite it off. The only one who didn't move was Rafe. He just stood staring at Ian with the blank visage of a man who had no trouble killing to get what he wanted.

I shook my head. It was Rafe's niece at stake, after all. The dude was a stone-cold killer, but the only people he ever looked at with love were the grandmother who'd raised him, Lucia, and the mischievous baby girl who'd brought us all so much joy.

Chamaeleon had no idea what he'd started. Things had escalated from a skirmish to a full-scale nuclear war the moment he'd taken Isabella.

Ian finally spoke when it seemed we'd settled a bit.

"I'll handle this. He's still in contact so I can have someone bring him in. Alive."

Noah let out an anguished sound that hit me right in the chest. It was the sound of a man who was close to losing it. We needed to get out of there before he did something to make Ian take back his tentative offer to help.

"Let's go. Maybe one of the boys has something by now."

Noah nodded silently, but his pain hung in the air between us, so thick it was choking us all. We turned to leave, but before we got more than a few feet, Ian's voice floated from behind us.

"I'll handle him this time, Leo. But if you ever come at me like this again, be prepared for your funeral."

Noah turned and nailed the other man with a dark stare. In that moment, I realized I was seeing the true Noah, the killer ORUS had trained him to be underneath the civilized mask he wore every day.

"If anything happens to my daughter, *we'll all be dead.* Because that's the only way I'm not getting her back."

———

Jessica

I ROLLED over and buried my face in the pillowcase. Even after a hot shower and wrapping myself in one of Jonas's shirts and a huge robe, I still couldn't seem to get warm. This was a different type of cold, the kind that got into your bones and made you feel like you were being punished.

Maybe I am.

I pulled the covers up to my chin and tried to sleep, only because I'd promised Jonas that I would. A tear slipped over the bridge of my nose to dampen the pillow. I bit my lip to make sure I wasn't making any noise. The last thing I wanted was to raise Lucia's suspicions even more.

Noah had asked us not to tell Lucia what had happened. We'd only told her that I had gone to confront him and that he'd pushed me. Even though I didn't agree with Noah's decision to keep Lucia in the dark, a small, secret part of me was thankful. I wasn't sure I could bear to look my best friend in the eye and admit that I didn't think David was going to give Isabella back.

I shivered remembering the satisfied look in his eyes when he'd seen me standing outside. He was getting off on this, on the power to draw me to him against my will. It was terrifying and humiliating, but I'd have gladly borne all of that if it brought Izzy back.

There was a quick knock on the door before Lucia stuck her head in. I sat up, wiping my tears on the sleeve of my robe.

"Hey, you can come in. I'm not sleeping anyway."

Lucia shut the door behind her. I moved over so she could sit on the edge of the bed.

"I wanted to check on you and see if you were really okay, not just pretending so Jonas wouldn't worry." Lucia's gray eyes roamed over me as if looking for bruises.

It only made my stomach churn harder. Lucia was so loving and nurturing, we'd always joked that she would have all the babies and I could just be the crazy aunt who sneaked them candy and told them inappropriate stories about men once they were older.

What would happen to Lucia if we couldn't rescue Isabella? It would destroy her. It was the worst thing in the world to see destruction coming on the horizon when you were locked in place and could do nothing to stop it.

"I'm okay. Physically."

Lucia pushed her hair back. "That's not what I asked."

I sucked in a tremulous breath. "He's insane, Lucia. I don't know what to do. He was enjoying it, denying everything and watching me lose it. I don't know what he'll do next, but I am terrified. I bet Noah is wishing you'd never met me."

"We can't give up. I have to believe that there's a purpose to all of this." Lucia lay down next to me and grabbed my hand. "And Noah loves you like a sister, just like I do. Everyone here loves you. I'll have to keep telling you that until you finally believe it."

"If you don't mind, Lucia, I'll take over from here."

Jonas's deep voice cut through the room, startling us both. Lucia squeezed my hand before getting up. She patted Jonas on the arm on the way out.

"Hey," I said finally, not sure what else to say. Part of me was afraid to ask exactly where he'd been. I wasn't sure I could take any more bad news today.

"Hey," Jonas whispered back before lying down next to me. He rolled over so our lips were only a few inches apart. "You should listen to your friend, you know. Everyone here loves you. You're not just someone they put up with to make Lucia happy. They adore you in your own right."

I closed my eyes, mortified that he could zero in on my insecurities so easily. It was impossible to hold any resentment toward Lucia, even though she was the delicately beautiful, feminine ideal that I had never quite been able to meet. Lucia was all sweetness and light while I was all gunpowder and hot sauce. There were definitely times when I'd felt people only tolerated me because I was friends with Lucia.

"I love them, too. That's why this is so hard. Being here is putting them all at risk. It's selfish of me to stay. I should just run away, somewhere David will never find me."

Jonas grabbed me so suddenly I squeaked. In the next few seconds, I found myself pressed beneath two hundred pounds of pissed-off but completely aroused male. He flexed his hips, driving his hard cock between my legs. I moaned at the contact, the pressure hitting right where I ached.

"First of all, you aren't going *anywhere*." He kissed me on the neck, sucking right over my pulse. "Second of all, if you run, I'll follow you. There's nothing I wouldn't do for you, Jessica Jones."

One minute I was staring into his eyes, the next I was wrapped around him, my legs twined with his and my arms clamped around his neck. He was what I needed, that port in the storm that made me feel safe.

I held on to him for dear life, kissing every bit of skin within reach. Maybe I could merge into him and lose this desperate feeling of isolation. Jonas seemed to understand what I wanted because he kissed me for long moments, tangling our tongues together while holding me closer, one of his big hands tucked under my ass, holding me in place for the slow, rolling movement of his hips.

"I've got you, baby," he whispered.

I moaned when he bit my lip gently. I clutched at him, trying to get his shirt off. Jonas chuckled as he moved back slightly so I could tug at the cotton. "Take it easy, baby. I'm not going anywhere."

But I didn't want to take it easy. I wanted it fast and hard, wanted to feel him everywhere. Anything to cover the feeling David's eyes had painted on my skin.

"Faster, Jonas. Please."

He raised his head, and whatever he saw in my eyes made him move. One arm reached behind him, and he yanked the shirt off in one smooth motion. I was on him immediately running my hands greedily over the golden brown skin revealed. He moaned low in his throat when I slid down and sucked at his nipples.

"Christ, you're trying to kill me."

I was lost in the sight, sensation and feel of his skin against my mouth. He tasted slightly salty and uniquely masculine. I tugged and yanked until I finally got my robe off. Suddenly he flipped me over, his weight covering my back, pressing me into the mattress.

"Hold on, angel. I know what you need."

He grabbed my hands and pushed them over my head. I struggled slightly at first, but a gentle kiss to my cheek made me relax. Just like that, I melted, completely safe in his embrace. He was going to take me, comfort me, pleasure me, and all I had to do was trust it.

Trust him.

"I need you, Jonas." The admission felt like swallowing rocks. I wondered if I'd ever felt safe enough to admit that I needed anyone before.

"I know you do, baby girl. I'm going to take care of you."

I reared up off the bed when his fingers made contact with the edge of my panties. Every touch, every brush of his lips against mine felt like live wires. My skin was starving for his touch.

"Jesus, you're soaked for me already." His voice was husky with desire and purely masculine appreciation.

Normally, I would have made a smart comment, but my breath was stolen at the first thrust of his fingers. I cried out, remembering at the last minute that the others might be able to hear us and biting my lip.

His mouth covered mine, sucking gently at the lip I'd abused. I let out a greedy sound as I ran my hands over his muscles. All the guys were in great shape, it was a prerequisite for their line of work, but none of them could compare to Jonas in my opinion. He was built on the slimmer side but his workout regime had packed his frame with muscle. I loved the feeling of him pressing into me.

He tugged at the edge of my shirt and I held my arms over my head so he could pull it off. Jonas groaned at the sight of me in nothing but my panties. I lifted my hips so I could pull the panties down my legs, my eyes taking in his every motion as he struggled to get out of his boots and jeans. He hadn't worn any underwear so as soon as he tugged his jeans down, his cock bobbed out, thick and ready. I leaned forward and sucked on the tip.

"Christ. JJ, you can't do that. I won't last, baby" he warned.

I smiled around him, reveling in his erotic curse as I hummed against his skin. His fingers tangled in my hair and I moaned again, incredibly turned on by the sharp tug at my roots. When I looked up at him, Jonas was watching with slitted eyes, taking in the sight of my lips wrapped around his swollen cock.

Something in my eyes must have set him off, because he tugged gently and then pushed me back on the bed. I started to protest but then lost my train of thought at the first touch of his skin against mine. His skin was so warm, and I wanted to feel it all over me. But Jonas had other ideas, nuzzling my breast before sucking my tight nipple between his lips. He alternated between my breasts until I thought I'd scream, and then I did cry out when he entered me a moment later, his thick cock stretching me to the limit.

"Oh my god." I bit him on the shoulder, and his hiss of surprise mingled with my harsh breathing.

It was all I could do to hang on, clutching his shoulders as he rolled his hips. As he tunneled deeper, I felt like we were melting into each other. That was what I wanted, to be overtaken and overpowered. To know that Jonas was in control and wouldn't let anything bad happen.

I needed to believe that.

"I'm not going to let anything happen to you, baby. Believe that. You mean too much to me." Jonas pushed the hair off my face and the motion was so tender it brought tears to my eyes. "I love you, JJ."

"I love you, too. So much."

I shuddered as waves of pleasure spread through me like lightning bolts. It was a struggle to keep my eyes open, but I didn't want to miss a thing. Jonas didn't disappoint me either, his face tightening a few moments later as he fought his own release.

"Come with me, baby."

As soon as he said the words, I let go, flying into a storm of light and sensation. His hands tightened under my bottom, and I heard his sexy-as-hell growl as he let go. The last thing I heard before I drifted off was Jonas telling me to rest and that I was safe with him.

CHAPTER TWENTY-FIVE

Jonas

My fucking eyes hurt. The throbbing had started behind my orbital bone as soon as we came back from the damn park yesterday. That motherfucker had played us. All of us.

West had known he was under surveillance the whole time. He knew exactly where the cameras were, he knew exactly what moves we would make. Because they were moves that *he* would make. Because West and Noah had been trained by the same people. And so Blake Security had come up against a dead-end.

I still couldn't imagine the kind of pain that Noah was going through—to think that he had his child and then to have that hope ripped away from him, knowing the man who had done it had gotten away with it.

I had begged Noah to take some time off, but he wasn't having it. He said other people needed us too. But really, I could see Noah fraying at the edges. Lucia was practically catatonic. Matthias was still blaming himself. And JJ, well she was basically a shell of herself.

I had no idea how to help except to be there.

So I camped out at the penthouse, but I needed fresh clothes and a fucking moment to think. Because right now my best friend wasn't thinking clearly, and the woman I loved was blaming herself for everything. I needed a little separation to figure out what the fuck to do and then I'd go right back. Right back into the fray and support the people I loved most the best way I knew how.

I parked my car in the garage and took the private elevator up, the tension rolling in my shoulders. Jesus, all I needed was a shower, and a good night's sleep. The problem was sleep was hard to come by at the moment, for all of us. Because every time anyone closed their eyes, all they thought about was Isabella and if she was okay. The good news was the nanny had seemed anti-murder, so very likely the baby was still alive.

Yeah, because that's a small favor.

I would still thank God for it, because after that bullshit meeting with Ian, we didn't have much else.

When the elevator doors opened, the hairs on the back of my neck stood at attention. Something was wrong.

I had my gun out of my holster and in my palm without even blinking. The closer I got to the apartment, the more my body gave me that *heebie-geebie, creepy-crawly* feeling. Something was definitely off. I walked to my apartment cautiously, and studied the door for any hints of a break in. But there weren't any. Not even scratches on the doorknob to indicate someone had attempted to pick it.

Cautiously I stood to the side and tried to turn the knob. It gave way easily. Oh fuck. The door was unlocked. And I'd most definitely locked it after the last time I was here.

Plus, my alarm system didn't go off. The moment that door opened, my phone should've chimed. But it didn't. Someone had disarmed it.

For the love of fuck.

Cautiously, I stepped in, and cleared the main foyer and then the kitchen.

Even though the hairs on my arms were now standing at attention, I had a feeling that the apartment was empty. And then I walked into the living room.

No. No. No. No. No. No.

Blood. Everywhere. "Oh Jesus. Jesus Christ." My hand slapped for the lights on the wall. In the middle of my living room Katie was sprawled in a pool of her own blood. Oh God. And there was a baby carrier turned away from me.

My heart hammered, and my mouth went dry. Oh God. No. Not Isabella. Please. God no.

I ran over to the carrier and found Isabella seated in the center. Her mouth was partially open, tongue out, and she was sucking merrily on it as if it was a nipple. Oh thank fuck, she was asleep. *She's alive.*

My phone was out in a second, dialing number one on the speed dial. Noah answered before it even finished ringing. "What's wrong?"

"Katie's dead. She's at my apartment. Isabella's alive. I have her."

"Motherfucker. Are you sure the apartment's empty?"

Fuck. I'd been so worried about Isabella I hadn't finished clearing. I quickly turned on my security feed then manually cleared the two bedrooms, the bathroom, the pantry, and the closets.

"No one's here. Isabella's asleep. The nanny is dead, Noah. There is blood —" And then I heard the sirens and saw the flashing lights outside. "Noah. The police are already here."

"Don't say anything. I'll have the lawyer at the station to bail you out before you even get there."

"Noah, he was here. He did this on purpose. I'm not leaving the baby here on her own. Otherwise I'd –"

"Thank you, Jonas. Oskar and I are on our way."

I had no choice, I wasn't leaving Isabella here. Not without her parents, not without someone who would at least look after her until they could get here.

The police came right to my apartment with guns raised. As if they knew exactly where I would be and what they would find.

I set Isabella down gently and raised my hands. "I'm on the job. I work for Blake Security."

One of the officers that had barged in first had to turn quickly and take a deep breath at the sight of the room. Yeah, welcome to the shit show. There was a lot of blood. The other officers yelled at me to get my hands in the air and I complied.

"Like I said, my identification is in my right breast pocket. I work for Blake Security. We're a security firm. I have a license for concealed carry. I came in and found her like this along with the baby. The baby's fine. Her parents are Noah and Lucia Blake. They've been notified of where to find her."

"You didn't call an ambulance first?"

"I knew right away she was dead. You know the pool of blood is kind of a major indicator."

"Oh, you're a smart ass then?" The officer wrenched my arm behind my back, and I cursed.

"No, I'm not being a smart ass. I'm just giving you the necessary information so you can do your job."

"We'll tell you what we need from you. You have the right to remain silent."

I was going to exercise that right. At least now Lucia and Noah had their daughter back safe. That was all that mattered.

As they perp-walked me out of the building, some of my neighbors scuttled back into their apartments, shocked and frowning. Right now I didn't give a shit what happened to me. I knew to keep my mouth shut, but as they tugged me out to the car through the small crowd forming with their ubiquitous cell phones trained on me, I saw the man I was looking for across the street.

For a second I forgot myself and struggled against the cuffs. But the cops were on me with swiftness and shoved me back in the car. All I could do was stare at David West as I was driven away.

I didn't know how, and I didn't know when, but I was going to kill that fucker.

———

Jessica

I HAD BEEN SO USED to seeing Jonas when I left my office that I didn't even realize it wasn't him driving until I pulled open the door. "Hey, any news? Oh—"

Oskar gave me a small smile. "Sorry, just my pretty face. No ridiculously expensive threads today."

"Is Jonas busy today? Have we heard anything about Isabella?"

Oskar's face turned serious. "Yeah, there's been a development."

"Tell me." I got into the passenger seat and clicked on my seatbelt. "Do we know where David is? Do we have a sighting of Isabella?"

"We not only have a sighting of Isabella, we have her. She's at the hospital right now with Noah and Lucia, getting checked out."

My heart exploded with joy. "Oh my God." I doubled over in the seat, clutching my hands on my knees, as a wave of nausea rolled through me. "Did that bastard hurt her?"

Oskar shook his head. "Didn't look like it. She'd been fed and taken care of. We think he gave her something to sedate her, but other than that she's probably going to be okay."

"Oh my God. I've been so worried. Where did they find her? Did he—"

Oskar cut me off. "I don't have any other answers. All I know is that *we* have her, and it looks like she's gonna be okay."

I nodded, the relief chasing away some of the nausea, but the spike of adrenaline made my hands shake. "Okay. Thank God. So what now, did we kill David?"

He shook his head. "Fucker wasn't there."

I slid him a glance. "Oskar, if you want to keep your balls intact, I suggest you start telling me everything from the beginning. If we have Isabella back, why do you look even more German and stoic than before? And where the hell is Jonas?"

His lips thinned again. "JJ. I'm sorry. When Jonas got home this afternoon, he found Katie dead in his living room in a pool of blood. Isabella was there in her carrier, unharmed. But the police arrested Jonas."

I stared at him in shock. "Arrested him? And you couldn't fucking lead with that? I swear to God I'm going to rip someone a new one. He works for a security company, for the love of Christ — Take me to the police station right now. I'm going to get him out of there."

Oskar held up his hand. "Look, I know. I know this is upsetting. I was instructed to take you back to the penthouse."

I raised a brow. "The hell you will. You're gonna take those brawny shoulders of yours and you're going to drive me straight to the police station because I am going to get him out. If you don't, your nuts will be your dinner tonight."

"Jesus, woman. No need to threaten my balls. Listen, we have the lawyer on it okay? He's going to get a bail hearing. Normally, it wouldn't happen until tomorrow, but he's making it happen tonight. The lawyer's on it. There's not much you can do."

"I swear before God, I will fill your bed full of dildos that vibrate if you do not get me to Jonas this instant."

Oskar's eyes widened. "Seriously, woman, what is wrong with you? How do you even come up with shit that diabolical?"

"Don't be such a prude Oskar, you might like a dildo."

He surprised me when he gave me a wolfish grin. It

completely transformed his face, making him seem carefree and roguish and showing off the full brightness of his handsome features. Jesus Christ, it was a good thing the guy barely smiled.

"Oh, I know what to do with a dildo and a woman. It can help enhance the experience in so many ways. But a bed full of them? You're just being cruel now. My bed's empty, so what am I going to do with a dildo?"

JJ grinned. "Well, I have a few ideas. They involve shoving them where the —"

Oskar shook his head. "You know what, keep that to yourself. My instructions are to take you home, so that's where we're going."

"And I swear to God if you do not take me to Jonas right now, I will cut off your balls in your sleep."

"You think I'm going let you close to my balls?"

She sat back and crossed her arms, smiling beatifically. "Well, you do like those cookies I make. All I have to do is drug one of them, and then you'll pretty much let anyone do anything."

His mouth fell open, and he stared at her. "Jesus. Fine. There's no need to get nasty. I'll take you to him. But let me call it in to Matthias first. Then maybe he can send Dylan to meet us so that at least you'll be protected. Don't forget, West is still out there, and he wants you. Jonas won't forgive any of us if anything happens to you."

"Well, Jonas is just going to have to deal. Because this time, I'm going to be there for him."

"I swear to God. You women might be more trouble than you're worth."

"Said every man ever, but still all you boys keep coming to the yard don't you?"

"Ain't that the truth?"

CHAPTER TWENTY-SIX

Jonas

I didn't exactly know how to walk with my JJ blanket. The moment I'd been released on bond, JJ had attached herself to my side and refused to let me go.

Not that I was angry about that at all. All I wanted to do was hold onto her tight. Right about now I might never let go of her. My lawyer had already notified me that Isabella was fine and that she was just at the hospital getting checked out. So at least that weight was off my mind.

And JJ was with me. So as far as I was concerned, all was right with the world. The only thing left hanging was the question of how many ways we could kill David West.

The moment the elevator doors to the penthouse opened, I was enveloped by a simultaneous feeling of security and chaos. The whole crew was in attendance. Dylan, Ryan, Matthias, Oskar. Rafe was on a job, but he'd be in later.

Even the team doctor was there. Noah had probably called him just in case I needed anything for shock. Which was ridiculous because I was fine. Though, I couldn't deny I'd been more than a little alarmed at the possibility of spending the night in jail. The thought of running into anyone I'd helped put away years ago made me a little twitchy.

Everyone gave me the awkward man hugs, and then from the back room I heard a baby cry. My heart stuttered for a moment.

Lucia came out from around the back hallway, with Isabella in her arms. "Someone heard her godfather was home, so she insisted on seeing you."

My gaze went straight to hers. "Is she okay?"

Lucia nodded and nuzzled her daughter's cheek. "Yeah. She's perfectly fine. It seems like she wants to be held by her godfather."

JJ released me, and I missed her warmth immediately. But when Lucia placed a squirming Isabella in my arms, I had to fight back the stinging in my eyes. "Hello, Angel. We had quite a fright looking for you. I'm so glad you're okay."

Isabella reached up with a tiny fist, and I was pretty sure I was about to get hit in the nose again. But then she opened her little hand and patted me gently on the cheek as if to say, *It's okay. I'm fine. You worry too much.* And then she made a series of very loud baby sounds. As if she was really trying to have a conversation with me.

Unfortunately, I didn't speak a word of baby, so I held her and rocked her instead, whispering little cooing sounds. After a moment she scrunched her face and kicked her little feet before letting out a wail.

Lucia giggled. "She's hungry. I think they were feeding her formula. She probably didn't like it, so I need to go and feed her real quick if that's okay."

I nodded. "Of course." I gave the baby back to Lucia and lifted my gaze to find Noah leaning against the wall.

"You good, Noah?"

He wiped at his eyes with the back of his hand. "Yeah. I'm

good. She's home. So, I'm trying to be grateful for that and calm my murdering instinct."

"I have the same instinct," I said.

JJ tugged on my hand. "Can we not talk about murder for just a minute? Okay? We just got him home."

Everyone followed us into the living room, the men taking their usual spots; which meant Oskar and Matthias on opposing sides of the main couch, fighting over the remote control; Ryan, as usual, by the door looking for his fastest possible exit and Dylan, as he was the youngest and wanting to prove himself the most, taking his ever-watchful post at the window. Even though he knew no one could get up here.

Not anymore, anyway.

Anyone who wanted to try would have to bypass biometrics and a series of security checkpoints below. It was no cakewalk getting up into this penthouse now. But still, he watched the street.

JJ sat on the softer couch by the window, and I followed, wrapping my arm around her. I couldn't help but feel grateful to be home with her by my side. Noah leaned against the wall, watching us all with his arms crossed.

"When Rafe gets back from watch, we need to figure out a plan," I said, breaking the silence.

Matthias nodded from the couch. "I vote to kill him. Fuck Orion, mate. He's known this whole time where that wanker was and who he is. He's known that West was stalking JJ. He needs to be put down like a rabid dog."

I nodded in agreement. "I wanted to kill him days ago. But you guys stopped me."

Matthias shook his head. "Rafe and I were down for it. Look at him," he inclined his head at Noah. "He was the one who said we couldn't kill him."

Noah nodded. "I know what I said. And I stand by my decision then. Because that was the information we had at the time. But now we have new information, so I'm all down for the plan of killing the asshole."

JJ raised a hand. "You guys know I'm still here right? And you're just casually talking about killing people?"

Matthias flushed a little, but he asked, "You don't want us to kill him?"

Beside me, JJ stiffened. "No. Are you insane?"

I stared at her. "You don't want us to kill him?"

She shook her head. "No. Of course not." She turned to face me. "I want to do it myself. I want to get close enough to him to stab him in the nuts and keep stabbing him until he dies."

A thick silence fell over the room with every single one of the guys wincing.

I shuddered. "Wow, okay. A for enthusiasm. But we're not letting you anywhere near him. He's dangerous."

"So am I. He tried to hurt me. Then he took my best friend's baby. And then he sent my man to jail. So pardon me if I want a little bit of payback."

I shook my head, pulling her closer. "You really do know how to pick them sweetheart. Your ex is one sick fuck. Good thing I am too."

"So you'll let me kill him?"

Noah vetoed this from the wall. "No. No reason you should have all the fun, JJ. We're going to come up with a plan that we can all agree to. And then Chamaeleon is going to stop breathing. Posthaste."

Jessica

THE BOTTOM HAD FALLEN out of my world. David had planned a fresh kind of hell for all of us, and we'd all fallen right into his trap.

I had to fight the rage I felt every time I thought about how he'd managed to put a man like Jonas in jail. We were lucky we'd gotten him out so quickly.

Jonas was strong. And he was tough. To hang with this gang, he was clearly a fighter. Maybe he was even capable of being a killer. But he was just, and he wouldn't go looking for a fight. He wouldn't put someone down just to prove that he was the biggest, baddest guy on the block or whatever the hell they called it in prison. And if he was unwilling to kill for his own survival, that refusal would get him killed. Especially once everyone found out he was a former cop.

Even though I'd known the team had it covered, I'd been scared. For those forty-five minutes I'd been at the police station waiting for him to be released, I'd been terrified.

The lawyer on retainer had been waiting at the station before Jonas had even been brought in. And he had the time-stamped footage of Jonas leaving Blake security, proving that he couldn't have killed that girl.

We'd been out in forty-five minutes. And just in case that hadn't done the trick, Matthias had been on standby to hack whatever system the police used and pretty much make Jonas disappear from existence. Matthias had a new name and new identity ready to go for him if it had come to that. But that would have meant Jonas would have to disappear for a while.

Which was fine by me, as long as Matthias made me one, too. Because there was no way Jonas was going anywhere without me. *Fact.*

But it hadn't come to that. The police didn't have enough to hold him, but since Katie had died in his apartment, he was still a person of interest. But I knew they wouldn't find any evidence and he would be exonerated.

Given the timeline on Katie's body and how long she'd been dead, he was lucky that he'd been held up at the office for so long where there were security cameras everywhere. Which was all well and good, but then the police started asking questions about why someone would kill a girl in his apartment and why they'd leave a kidnapped baby there.

The less we said about David West the better. The last thing we wanted was the police looking too closely at our lives.

I smiled as I watched Oskar reach out to hold Isabella. The baby clutched onto Lucia koala-style, but eventually transferred to Oskar. And wonder of wonders, Isabella gave Oskar a wide smile. Right before — *oh no.*

The baby hiccupped and let out a torrent of vomit all over Oskar's face. I used my hand to cover my mouth before ducking out of the room to laugh.

I was laughing. Actual, *real* laughter. Poor Oskar. Poor Isabella. Poor thing probably had to burp. Who knew what kind of food Katie and that maniac had been giving her? The doctor said she was fine, but that baby was about to get spoiled rotten.

"How did I know I would find you out here laughing?"

I turned to face Jonas and leaned against the wall. "Because that shit was funny. Did you see the look on Oskar's face?"

"Why are you laughing at Oskar's woes and misfortune?"

"I'm not. But that was funny. She knows he's too uptight."

His lips twitched. He was clearly fighting a smile and working hard on his stern face. I could see right through it. Eventually the chuckle broke through.

"Yeah you're right. That shit was hilarious."

From the living room, we could hear Oskar cursing softly in German. It was funny, his German accent always became thicker when he was irritated or pissed off. But irritated or not, he used hushed tones for Isabella.

"No, my darling. We talked about you saving spit up for your Uncle Rafe. He's the one who's truly deserving." Then he muttered under his breath. "Noah, your offspring is fucking with me."

The best part was every single man in that room, Noah, Rafe, Matthias, Ryan, and Dylan all muttered, "*Language.*"

As if we all weren't bad about it ourselves. Everyone was aware that Isabella was going to grow soon, which meant the usual sailor talk would have to be curbed. The crazy thing was I was worse than any of us. As Isabella's godmother I took it as my personal mantle to teach that girl how to curse properly.

I had already resigned myself to being the cause for Isabella's first appropriate use of the word fuck. Hey, we all had our cross to bear.

I slid my hand into Jonas's. "Are you sure you're okay?" I shook my head. "I can't imagine the scene you had to walk into today or how terrifying it must have been to face the possibility of jail."

He nodded. "I'm fine. I promise. Believe me, I've seen worse. Plus it was only jail, not prison. I had our lawyer. They processed me in, asked a couple of questions and watched the security footage then they processed me out. That's it. Nothing bad happened to me."

I nodded even as I held my breath and tried to hold back the sting of tears. I'd been terrified when Oskar had broken the news and worried about what could happen to him in there.

"I just —" I sniffed. "I was worried."

He pulled me close and kissed my forehead. "Aww, come on now. I'm too pretty to be someone's jailhouse bitch."

I whacked him on the arm. "I'm being serious. You don't know David. He's crazy."

Jonas gently traced his fingers over my lips. "What I want to do right now is focus on you. I want to take your hand, lead you back into your room, strip these clothes off and sink into you. How does that sound for a plan?"

Well then, that was one way to shut me up. Because the moment he said the word sink, my core clenched and the hum of electricity danced on my skin. It had only been hours since I'd seen him, but I'd missed him.

It had been a long day. And with everything that had happened, I needed him. Now.

Jonas took my hand and tugged me behind him. Once in the bedroom, he closed the door behind us and reached for me. But I knew what he was up to, and I wasn't going to be distracted.

I pushed him back by the shoulders. "No. You got arrested today. David could have killed you."

Jonas licked his bottom lip as he narrowed his gaze at me. I knew that look. It was all intensity and lust and need. "I know you were scared today. A part of me was scared, too. But I know my team. There is always a way out. Trust that no matter what, I'm not going down without a fight. You can't control the world around you, baby."

My lip quivered. "Right now, I need control. I need to remind myself that you're alive, and that you're here, and that I didn't almost lose you today."

His gaze softened, and he leaned back against the door. "Okay. In that case, I'm all yours. Do your worst."

And I had every intention of it. "Stay there. Do not move. Do you understand?"

The grin he gave me was all cocky. But he nodded. "Yes, ma'am."

Hastily I tugged my blouse out of my skirt, unbuttoned the tiny row of buttons then shrugged it off my shoulders. Jonas's gaze homed in, and he turned that laser focus to my breasts. With every movement, jostle, and wiggle, he licked his lips.

"I know what you're looking at. You're only torturing yourself. It's gonna be a long night. Ready?"

"Woman, I just got out of the joint. My patience can only take so much before I jump you."

"Well in that case, I better get down to business." I slipped out of my skirt, leaving only my stockings and my shoes on. When I stepped over to him, he groaned low.

I began working on his shirt, my bare hands tracing the planes of his chest, and he hissed. "Woman, you're killing me."

"That's the plan. To show you what you've been missing all day. Teach you not to get arrested next time."

His chuckle was low as I slid his shirt off his shoulders, and pressed a kiss to his nipple. "Yeah, I don't really have much to do with that. See, what happened was—"

"Hush. I'm busy."

Jonas cleared his throat and then laid his head back against the door. "Yeah, I can see that.

When his shirt dropped to the floor with barely a sound, I kissed across his fine pecs, and then shifted down to kiss each of his ribs and over his abs, sinking lower onto my knees.

"Oh God. JJ. Jessica —"

"Sssh. Woman at work here. Try to focus."

"Fuck, I am focused. You're all I'm focused on. I just —"

I was in no mood to listen to him. I just unbuckled his pants and smirked at the designer belt buckle and the dark wash of the $300 jeans. Jesus Christ, the man loved clothes more than I did. Even his boxers were designer. But of course they would be, because this, my big man, this was Jonas. All of him.

Once free, his cock bobbed in front of my face, fully erect, completely at attention, and begging for mercy. "My, my, someone has been missing me."

"I've just been to prison," he muttered through clenched teeth.

I chuckled. "I thought it was only jail?"

Jonas groaned when I teased my nails over the skin of his balls. "I need to get conjugal visits. JJ – fuck." He panted as I stroked him up and down gently, teasing the head then stroking down and cupping his balls.

"What were you saying?"

"Jessica, I need —"

But he was done talking when I leaned forward and wrapped my lips around his dick. He stopped talking altogether. All that came from him were a series of moans and groans, as I worked him over with my tongue and my lips, and occasionally very gently with my teeth.

He dug his hands into my hair, and I relished every moment. The possession of it, the visceral nature of it. He was tugging on my hair. He was here. He was safe. He was *mine*.

He tried to pull me back, but I wasn't having it and instead took him deeper, forcing the back of my throat to relax and defer to him.

"Oh my God, JJ," he growled. "I'm going to come."

Instead of drawing back like he wanted, I planted my hands on his hips and dug my nails into the top muscle of his ass and took him deeper.

His muscles tensed and bunched as he held me in place, and finally, he let go. When I eased back, Jonas's harsh pants tore out of his chest as he stared down at me. "Woman, Jesus."

"See, you like it when I'm in charge." I rose to my feet, intending to take my time with my stockings. He probably needed a minute, and in that time, I could grab a shower — before I knew what was happening, Jonas had me flat on my back in the bed.

He didn't bother removing my thong, but instead shoved the flimsy fabric aside and sank into me deep as he kissed me.

I gasped. "Jonas."

"You didn't think we were done did you? After all, I've just come home from prison. And I'm in my woman's bed. We're going to be here a while. So you might as well go ahead and get used to the size of me inside you."

I was so down for that.

It didn't take long. Two deep strokes, a quick flick of his thumb over my clit, his tongue sliding over mine, and I was flying.

I jumped with him into the abyss of bliss, finally letting go of the fear and the worry and the panic from today. He was home, he was safe, he was mine. And I was never letting go.

CHAPTER TWENTY-SEVEN

Jonas

Over the next few days, I tried to catch up on paperwork. Noah didn't want me out in the field, so I'd done as much at the penthouse as possible, burying myself in reports that I'd been too lazy to file last month. I figured if I was busy, I wouldn't have time to dwell on the ongoing investigation into Isabella's kidnapping and Katie's murder.

But despite all my efforts, there was only so much paperwork I could do. And when I got JJ from work each day, it took all the energy I had to keep a smile on my face for her sake.

Not that it fooled her. JJ was just as on-edge as I was. And I spent each night staring at the ceiling as every detail of both cases scrolled through my mind.

There was something I was missing, and I was desperate to find it. JJ hadn't been sleeping any better. She tried to be quiet so I wouldn't know she was awake, but her breathing gave her away. My baby didn't know it, but she actually snored most of the time. A little tidbit I was saving to tell her at just the right time.

"You know, you could have taken a little time off."

Oskar's voice came from over my shoulder. I turned to look at him. His usually stoic expression was twisted with worry.

I sighed. The guys I worked with might be stone cold killers, but inside, they were all a bunch of gossipy, little old ladies. If I wasn't careful, they'd stage an intervention and force me to talk about my feelings.

"I'm fine. Like I told Noah this morning and Matthias this afternoon, I'm fine."

A woman going into the restroom we were guarding glanced at me in alarm. I pasted on a benign smile, and she glanced away quickly. Great. Now I was scaring the public.

"I'm just saying, no one would think less of you for needing a little time after everything that's happened." Oskar's eyes scanned all the people walking up and down the hallway.

We were on the security detail for Sharla Winters, a B-list actress in town to do press for an upcoming movie. Normally I avoided these sorts of details like the plague, but I'd taken the job at JJ's urging. It turned out my girl was a fan of Sharla's sorority house movies. Unfortunately, Sharla was nothing like the spunky, smart heroine of the movie series and was instead a spoiled brat who'd made this security detail unnecessarily difficult.

And besides, it was a job.

I couldn't allow Chamaeleon to run the show anymore. I'd spent the past few nights reassuring JJ that everything would be fine, and I was determined to keep that promise. My girl wanted everyone to believe she was hard as nails, but she'd been deeply affected by Isabella's kidnapping. I knew she still carried guilt over it and a deep-seated worry that David wasn't done screwing around with her loved ones.

I didn't think it was over either, not that I'd share that thought with her. JJ needed to feel safe and protected, something I suspected she hadn't felt in a long time. That motherfucker had stolen her sense of safety, and I was determined to be the one who restored it.

No matter what I had to do.

"She's been in there for a long time," Oskar muttered.

I glanced at my watch and realized it had been almost ten minutes since Sharla had entered the restroom. Oskar had done a sweep before she went in but it was still odd. In this line of work, you learned to trust your instincts, and mine were ringing big time.

"I'm going in," Oskar growled, clearly feeling the same way.

I sharpened my gaze on all of the people walking by. Only two women had entered after Sharla, both on the list of attendees at the event that we'd previously vetted.

But that doesn't mean someone wasn't in there already.

I cursed, more certain as the minutes passed that something was wrong. Suddenly there was a loud shout and a crash against the door.

"Oskar!" I pushed against the bathroom door but there was something blocking it.

I pushed harder and managed to squeeze through the opening in the door. Oskar was on the ground right inside the door, writhing in pain. As much as I wanted to stop and check on my friend, protocol dictated that I secure the area first.

I drew my weapon and swept past the small sitting area and into the actual restroom. One of the faucets was running, and the small window over the last stall was open.

"Fuck! How the hell did we miss that?"

I would have sworn there were no windows or doors leading out of this restroom when we'd done our earlier walkthrough of the building.

In the last stall, I also found Sharla standing on the toilet looking terrified. "Is it safe to come out? Oskar told me to hide in here."

I nodded and then immediately raced back to the sitting area at the mention of Oskar. My friend was red in the face and didn't look to be breathing.

"Sharla, call 911!"

I dropped to the ground and put my fingers on Oskar's pulse. Steady but getting fainter.

"Tell them I'm starting CPR," I called over my shoulder, hoping like hell that Sharla would follow directions for once.

I started chest compressions, then pinched Oskar's nostrils, tipped his chin up, and started breathing for him. After a moment I listened, and when I didn't hear breathing, started chest compressions again. Just when I was about to pinch his nostrils again, Oskar leaned to the side and coughed violently. One of his huge arms swung out and swatted me so hard I fell over.

"God damn, if you wanted to kiss me that bad, all you had to do was ask."

I was so relieved I could only laugh. "That's what I get for trying to save your life, asshole."

Oskar struggled to sit up. "Where is she? That crazy bitch hit me with a taser!"

I shook my head. "Whoever she was, she's gone. When I came in, the window was open, the window that wasn't there when we did our sweep earlier, and you were on the ground."

Sharla appeared at my shoulder. "Why would someone attack him though? That chick didn't even look at me. What kind of deranged fan is that?"

I had to refrain from rolling my eyes. Sharla seemed disappointed that her "fan" hadn't attempted to hurt her. God, I was done protecting the Hollywood set. Completely self-absorbed, all of them.

"She has a point," Oskar rasped, one hand pressed to his chest. "If Sharla was the target, why didn't she attack once I was down?"

My mind spinning, I stood and walked back into the restroom.

The magic window still hung open, and the sound of traffic and voices floated in. As I got closer, I could see where the drywall had been ripped away to reveal the glass beneath. Whoever had planned this had done their research and had known that window was there. Someone with that level of precision wouldn't allow a prime opportunity to attack pass them by.

Which meant they'd gotten to their intended target.

"Sharla wasn't who they were after."

Jessica

AFTER COMING IN FROM WORK, I waved absently over my shoulder at Matthias, who had picked me up.

"Hey, JJ! How were things today?" Lucia came out of her room, Isabella bundled in her arms.

The sight of my goddaughter snuggled safely in my friend's arms brought a lump to my throat.

I smiled brightly. "Great! I think we're catching up finally." I backed up toward my room. Desperation clawed up from my throat, making me feel like I was on the verge of screaming. "I'm just going to go drop my stuff off."

Lucia watched me with knowing eyes. "Okay. I made lasagna for dinner. I'll save you a plate."

I smiled my thanks and hurried into my room. I closed the door and for the first time all day, allowed the smile on my face to drop.

"Oh thank god," I whispered, resting my head against the door. The cool wood against my skin grounded me and calmed the raging surge of emotions bubbling just beneath the surface.

It was harder than I'd expected to keep it together and pretend to be fine. Especially with both Jonas and Lucia watching me like a hawk. A few saucy comments had fooled Matthias, and he'd pretty much left me alone during the day, even though I'd been aware of him in the corner of my office typing furiously on his laptop. But Matthias was a quiet sort himself and didn't expect, or want, conversation.

Fooling those closest to me was another story. Each night, I spent some time with Lucia and had even held Isabella a few times. But it was getting harder and harder to make small talk and pretend to be relaxed when inside I was shredding into a million pieces.

How could everyone else be so calm when at this very moment, David was out there, probably watching and plotting his next move? How could they breathe knowing he could attack at any moment?

They don't know him like I do, that's why.

I shuddered, thoughts of David making me instantly wish for a shower. My hands tightened around the straps of my handbag. It was relatively new, a white and red striped tote bag that I'd loved as soon as I saw it. Had David been watching even then? Perhaps followed me around the store as I'd contemplated between the available bags? I had no idea how long he'd been watching and waiting to make his move.

Would I ever feel safe again?

Overcome, I slung the bag across the room. It skittered over the bed before falling over the other side with a thump. Enraged, I yanked at the bracelets on my arm and threw those, too. Part of me wanted to strip everything away, as if ridding myself of the pretty clothes David had always loved to see me in could purge him from my life. I tore at my blouse, buttons popping off and landing on the floor, before pushing my skirt down. Tears streamed down my face as I stumbled while trying to get the skirt down my legs.

"Get it off. Get it off," I mumbled, frantic to be free. Hands settled on my arms, and I shrieked in surprise. "Don't touch me! Stay away from me."

"Whoa, baby! It's me."

Jonas's voice penetrated through the fog of panic, but I was too far gone to stop. I pulled at my bra, shuddering when strong arms wrapped around me tight, holding me in place.

"Stop, baby girl. You're scratching yourself. Just hold on."

I struggled weakly in his arms before all at once, my energy drained and I collapsed against his chest. I let out a ragged breath, wrapping my legs around his waist as he carried me over to the bed. When I felt the mattress beneath me, I curled up in a ball. After a moment, I opened one eye and watched as Jonas shed his clothes too.

"Scoot over, I'm coming in."

His husky voice brought a smile to my face. I had to give it to him, no matter how strangely I behaved, Jonas just rolled with it. The man had the patience of a saint, but how long could that last? Especially when he realized that I hadn't been completely honest with him. It was only after staring at him that I saw the strain on his face, the lines around his eyes and mouth that no one else would probably notice.

Something was wrong.

"What happened?"

Jonas turned his head toward me. His heavy sigh carried a wealth of meaning. "Someone came after Oskar today with a taser. They didn't go after the client at all."

He didn't say anything else, but I could read the worry in his voice. This wasn't just a random thing. Just as I'd suspected, David had decided how to extract his pound of flesh.

Through the people I cared about.

"He's never going to stop, is he?" I whispered.

Strong fingers gripped my chin and forced me to hold still. I kept my eyes squeezed shut for a minute but I couldn't hide from this forever. When I opened them, Jonas was watching me with the gentlest look in his eyes.

"It's not your fault." He leaned forward and pressed a soft kiss to my forehead. "He's going to make a mistake eventually. Then we'll take him out."

I didn't bother asking what he meant by that. Over time, I'd clued in to the alternative methods Noah and his whole crew employed when dealing with the various scumbags they encountered. Once upon a time, I'd have been bothered by it. Before I knew how many people in this world didn't play by the rules. Now if given the opportunity, I would take David out myself.

"You're only saying that because you don't know him. You don't know what he's capable of and how deep this obsession runs."

"So tell me," Jonas countered, his eyes holding mine. "Tell me whatever it is you're so afraid will change things."

Of course he'd known all along that I was holding back. How silly that I'd ever thought I could fool him. For so long, I'd kept Jonas at a distance with harsh words, but that was probably because I'd sensed that once I let him in, there would be no more secrets. I was going to have to reveal every layer of my shame for everyone to dissect and judge.

Maybe it was time. It was my sins coming home to roost. And if I had to bare my soul to clean the slate, that would be my penance.

"Okay. I'll tell you everything. But it has to be all at once. I can't retell it multiple times. I just don't have it in me."

His hand was still tangled in my hair, rubbing a gentle circle. I closed my eyes and savored his touch. After this story came out, there wouldn't be any more soft kisses or comfort from Jonas. I'd be lucky if I had a place to stay.

"I'll tell the others. We'll call a meeting so you can tell everyone at once. Once it's out there, maybe we can end this."

I nodded. "We can end this."

It would be the end of everything. On impulse, I sprang forward, plastering myself to him, locking our lips together and running my fingers through his hair. Jonas groaned deep in his throat, his hands automatically gripping my ass, kneading and caressing. I shuddered, licking into his mouth before biting his bottom lip hard.

"Jesus, you're killing me."

If we had more time, I'd have pulled him into the bed and had my way with him one more time. But now that I'd made the decision, it was time to follow through before I lost my nerve. So I sat back and took a deep breath. Jonas watched me carefully before pulling out his phone. As I watched him typing out a message, I put my hand on his.

"Tell them Rafe needs to be there, too."

Jonas frowned. "Why does he need to be there?"

"He just does. This involves him, too."

Jonas's brow furrowed and he held my eyes for a moment before nodding sharply.

CHAPTER TWENTY-EIGHT

Jonas

"Okay, we're all here now. JJ, this is your show."

I knew I sounded like an asshole, but ever since those words had left JJ's lips, *this involves him too*, I'd been on edge. I glanced at Rafe from the corner of my eye. When I'd texted Noah with the request for a group meeting, including Rafe, I wasn't the only one who thought it strange.

Rafe worked with us, but it was relatively recent. He did the jobs Noah assigned without complaint, and there was no denying he was a lethal bastard, but he usually wasn't included when we discussed company business of any kind. Not that Rafe seemed to care. I didn't get the impression the man enjoyed spending time around other people, anyway. The only ones who brought out any sign of humanity in him were his little sister and his grandmother.

Speaking of, Lucia seemed to sense the strange tension in the room as well because she hadn't left Rafe's side since he'd arrived. Rafe put an arm around her, and she leaned into him.

"Yes, I did ask for this meeting." JJ glanced at me and smiled tremulously.

I smiled back, rewarded when the haunted look in her eyes receded slightly.

"I need to tell you about how I met David."

Noah leaned forward. "Back when you and Lucia were teenagers."

"Yes. It was right after..." she glanced over at Rafe, "you know."

Rafe stood up straighter. "You met him right after I disappeared?"

JJ nodded. "He saved me from this guy who was hassling me on the street. At the time, it seemed so romantic. Like he was protecting me. We started dating soon after that."

She fell silent, and I reached over to hold her hand. There was obviously more to this story than boy meets girl, boy becomes stalker. JJ had been tense ever since she'd asked me to call this meeting, and her request to see Rafe had definitely put me on edge, too.

I wasn't too proud to admit that I didn't want that guy anywhere near my girl. I wasn't normally the jealous type, but Rafe could probably trigger that instinct in any guy. Hell, I wasn't too proud to admit that I couldn't best the guy in a fight, either. The only one who might have a shot was Noah, and that was because Rafe had trained him for years.

"David was really nice to me at first. He took me out and listened while I told him about everything going on in my life. Rafe had just died and everything was crazy."

Lucia sniffled. "I can't believe I didn't know anything about this."

JJ walked over to Lucia. "You were grieving. And I didn't want to say anything that would make it worse. David was an outsider, so I could talk to him without bringing up any bad memories. Or at least, that's what I thought. I was trying to be there for you and Nonna, but it was a lot to process for a teenage girl. I had never known someone who'd died before. Especially not someone..."

She glanced over at Rafe and swallowed. "Not someone I loved."

I blinked. When I looked over at Rafe, I saw that the other man was also frozen in place.

"What?" I asked what everyone in the room was thinking.

JJ put a hand to her cheek, which was slowly turning pink. "I had a crush on Rafe."

She said it so softly that I could barely hear her. But I knew Noah had heard because of his soft intake of breath.

"Oh shit," Oskar muttered.

"Anyway," JJ continued loudly, "David listened to me, and he told me about losing his father years before. We bonded and before long, I was spending more and more time with him. Too much time. He didn't want me to hang out with anyone else. If I wanted to go see Lucia, he would follow me and wait outside. He'd walk me to and from school and if I was even a minute late, he'd accuse me of staying behind to flirt with the boys in my class. It started to feel like I was in prison."

Rafe and Noah exchanged glances and Rafe said, "That's straight out of the ORUS playbook. Establish a rapport with the target and then isolate them. Do you think this was Orion checking up? Maybe he suspected that I was still around and was using JJ to confirm?"

"It's possible," Noah admitted. "Although it would have been more likely that he'd go after Lucia."

"I don't think that's what he was after," JJ said slowly. "David asked a lot of questions about Rafe, but not like he doubted his death."

Rafe narrowed his eyes. "What kind of questions?"

JJ instantly blushed bright red. "Just what kind of stuff you liked. Whether I saw you a lot when I visited Lucia. Then other things." She fidgeted with the edge of her shirt.

Lucia put her arm around her. "It's okay."

JJ kept her eyes on the floor as she continued. "He wanted to know if I'd ever kissed Rafe. He was obsessed. If I ever brought his name up, it enraged David. He knew how I felt about him and wanted to prove he was the better choice. Any time a guy looked at me on the street, David would try to fight him. Like he wanted to prove how strong he was. Then he started asking me to call him Rafe. When we... you know."

Everyone shifted uncomfortably. Noah looked like he'd rather be anywhere else but somehow got it together to ask what was necessary.

"He wanted you to call him Rafe's name during sex."

"Um, yeah. Uh huh." JJ put a hand over her heart and rubbed. "He started getting rougher with me and I got scared enough to leave. But he was waiting for me after school the next day. That was the first time he hit me."

Lucia pulled her close. "And I wasn't there for you. I'm so sorry."

JJ leaned her head against Lucia's shoulder. "It wasn't your fault."

"But still, you went through this all alone."

JJ swiped at her eyes. "I was afraid to tell anyone. He controlled what I wore and where I went, and he made sure I knew there was no escape. He said if I ever left him again, he would hurt my mom. He couldn't get to Lucia since Noah was always around, but I still worried that he'd try something. I figured he was going to eventually kill me. Nothing I did seemed to satisfy him. Then all of a sudden, he was just gone."

Noah narrowed his eyes. "That must have been when Orion sent him overseas. Do you think he found out what was going on?"

Rafe shrugged. "It's possible. ORUS agents aren't supposed to form any attachments. If Orion caught wind that Chamaeleon had a girlfriend, especially one connected to me, he'd have squashed that shit quickly."

"But why bring him back?" Jonas wondered.

"Ian didn't know about any of this. He wasn't in charge back then, remember? It's been almost seven years," Noah mused. "Even if all this was documented somewhere, no one would think a relationship he had with a teenager years ago would be a threat anymore."

Rafe put his hands on his head. "I'm going to kill that fucker."

"Get in line," I growled.

I flexed the fingers that had been clenched in a fist for the past ten minutes. I'd thought there was nothing worse than hearing about how my woman had fantasized about Rafe, but hearing how she'd feared for her life with nowhere to turn was even worse.

Not that I hadn't been motivated to find the fucker before, but now I wanted to find him and cause him pain. David West was going to know the same terror he'd put JJ through for months.

———

Jessica

I HAD REACHED the limits of my endurance. I pulled away from Lucia, squeezing her arm gently. There was going to be a long gab session in our future, I was sure. Lucia was still digesting everything she'd heard today, but I had no doubt I was going to be in for it later. It was a huge secret I'd kept from her for years.

"We'll talk later, okay?"

Lucia nodded. "There's plenty of time for that. Right now, I think you have one very patient man to explain a few things to. And for what it's worth, he really loves you."

My eyes met Jonas's over Lucia's shoulder. He watched me with a burning intensity that under any other circumstances, I would have thought was desire. But then his eyes swung over to where Rafe stood, and the spark shifted into something closer to rage.

Uh-oh.

"Yeah, I think maybe Jonas and I need to have a chat."

More like, I needed to get to Jonas before he started something with Rafe. I'd heard from Lucia what had happened the last time Rafe had fought the guys. He'd singlehandedly managed to injure half the team. The last thing I wanted was anyone fighting over me.

Rafe ducked out of the room and by the time I looked for Jonas again, he was gone. My pulse sped up as I glanced around. Oskar was across the room talking to Matthias. Noah stood behind them, waiting for Lucia. Ryan and Dylan had left already.

Oh shit.

"I'll see you later." I hugged Lucia again and then walked out into the entryway. Rafe and Jonas stood glaring at each other. It brought to mind two lions facing off in the wild. No one spoke or turned when I approached.

I stepped in between them and took Jonas's hand. "Can I talk to you for a second?"

A beat later, his eyes met mine. His nostrils flared briefly, but he nodded. "Yeah. I'll be there in a second."

"Right now, actually."

I tugged on his hand, not even acknowledging Rafe. If I so much as glanced in his direction, the tentative cease fire between the two would probably go up in smoke. I mentally rolled my eyes. Juggling the egos of all these alpha males was like tap dancing around dynamite.

It took a few tugs, but Jonas finally allowed me to pull him back into the living room. All I could hope for was that Rafe would leave, otherwise I'd have to worry about the two men getting into it all night. Although I doubted Rafe really wanted to stick around.

It had been beyond humiliating to have to say those things in front of him and everyone else. Embarrassment flared again. The poor man was probably going to ask Lucia to start coming to him when he wanted to see his sister.

The living room was empty, everyone having gone back to their various rooms.

"So, I figured maybe we should talk."

Jonas shrugged. "We don't need to talk. You were right that hearing the whole story helped. David's behavior has been erratic and unpredictable this whole time, but understanding what makes him tick will only help us."

My mouth fell open. He was talking like this was any other standard case and the only thing he was concerned with was chasing down a target. Of all the reactions I'd expected him to have, this wasn't one of them. It couldn't have been fun to hear his girlfriend admit to fantasizing about one of his coworkers during sex. Especially a co-worker who'd once hurt him so badly.

"I hope it does help," I said finally, at a loss as to what else to say. If he didn't want to talk about all the embarrassing stuff I'd said, then I definitely wasn't going to bring it up.

"Okay, so maybe we should just stay in and take it easy tonight. We can watch something on Netflix, and I'll make us some sandwiches," I suggested.

Jonas nodded. "Sure. We can make some popcorn and chill."

We were interrupted by Noah, and I stepped back to allow the men to talk. Jonas gestured for me to wait and followed Noah from the room, so I figured I'd get started preparing our little picnic.

I'd been stressing ever since I'd asked him to call for the meeting, sure that once it was over, Jonas would be annoyed with me. Not because of what happened years ago, but because I'd kept it from them all. Also, he was a typical guy, competitive and slightly possessive. Not enough to be a problem, but I knew he didn't like the idea of sharing any part of me. It would only be natural for him to wonder if any of my earlier feelings had survived my teenage crush.

Especially now that Rafe was back in my life. But all I felt for him was a brotherly affection, similar to how I'd viewed him before my crush took hold. Lucia was thrilled beyond reason to have her brother back, and I was so happy for her and Nonna. But his reappearance hadn't changed my feelings at all. Jonas was the only man I wanted.

After having my trust shattered by David, it had taken a long time before I'd felt ready to be vulnerable with a man again. I couldn't have done that with anyone but Jonas. No one else had been willing to spar with me and endure the barbs to get to the real Jessica beneath the attitude.

"I'll have turkey on mine," Jonas appeared at my elbow. His forehead was crinkled the way it always was when he was worried about something.

I glanced behind him. Noah stood at the edge of the kitchen watching us. I couldn't decode the expression on his face, but he glanced at Jonas one more time before he turned to leave.

"Is everything okay with Noah?" I finally asked.

Jonas grimaced. "Noah needs to mind his own business."

Whoa. I wasn't going there. I was under no impression that the guys always agreed. Noah was their boss and he wasn't exactly a tactful guy. But I'd never heard Jonas say even one negative word about his friend and boss before today.

Before I pushed him to the edge.

Wordlessly, I reached for the sliced turkey, making sandwiches for us both. Jonas worked quietly beside me, putting the food on a tray and then putting some popcorn in the microwave. I opened the refrigerator and pulled out a coke for him and a Dr. Pepper for myself.

Jonas's eyes landed on the sodas as I put them on the tray. "Dr. Pepper," he murmured.

I stilled. "Yeah. It's my favorite. I've been drinking it since I was a teenager."

His eyes flared. "Rafe drinks Dr. Pepper. It's the only soda I've ever seen him drink."

My heart sank. I thought back to when I was a young girl, watching Rafe mainline Dr. Pepper like it was water. I'd started drinking it too, thinking maybe he'd notice that I liked the same thing he did.

How had I forgotten that?

CHAPTER TWENTY-NINE

Jessica

I licked my lips nervously as I turned to face Jonas. "Look it's not like—"

His voice, as icy as steel, cut me off. "Be quiet."

Gone was his usual smug smile or cocky smirk. I could see the muscles of his jaw working as he clenched his teeth together. Holding my hand tight, Jonas turned down the hall and stalked into one of the bedrooms, kicking the door shut behind us.

"Jonas, that was a really long time ago. I don't have a thing for Rafe now. You have to understand that."

Jonas said nothing, just narrowed his gaze at the mention of Rafe's name. He backed me up and with a few short strides, he laid me on the bed, following me down.

With a muffled growl, he scooted me up toward the headboard then dragged me over him so I straddled his lap. Easing up his grip on my hair, he gently massaged my scalp until I was nearly limp and pliant in his arms. I could feel his anger coursing through him, but at the same time I knew I could trust him. Knew that he wouldn't hurt me.

When he brought my head down for a kiss, I couldn't help but moan. His tongue slid over mine easily and I whimpered. Jonas nipped at my bottom lip before sucking on it gently. My lips tingled, the pleasure flowing white hot through me, and I wondered if I might be able to come just from his kisses. And if not, the delicious rub of his cock against my sensitive flesh would do the trick.

One of his big hands gripped my ass, gently rocking me into him as he devoured my mouth. With every rock of our hips together, we both made this satisfied, muffled *mmph* sound. As if that was exactly what hit the spot, what we both needed.

Holy hell. I was close and so far all he'd done was kiss me. But it was more than that. The tension between us was so thick, winding tighter around us with each moment.

I wasn't an idiot. I knew there was still a lot of underlying tension with Rafe. After all, Rafe had tried to kill him before. But I'd had no idea that he would respond like this. Any feelings I'd ever had for Rafe were a schoolgirl crush. That crush didn't come anywhere close to what we shared. Not even close. But how the hell did I drive that message home?

At that moment, he was acting like a caveman with a need to mark me... not that I minded. I trusted him. He wasn't going to hurt me. I just didn't want him thinking that any part of me wanted anyone else.

Jonas tore his lips off of mine, panting as his gaze bore into my eyes. With a muffled curse, he flipped us so that he lay on top of me, his hips fitting in that space I made just for him between my thighs.

"You are the most beautiful woman I've ever laid my eyes on. And you're mine. If you're gonna tell anyone to sit and spin it'll be me. Is that clear?"

I nodded as I reached for him, making this little mewling

sound in the back of my throat. Was that really me? Sounding needy and desperate? "Okay, Jonas. Just—"

But it was like he couldn't hear me. Against my skin, he whispered, "Did you know how many times I used to dream about touching you? About all the ways I could make you scream my name?"

"Jonas—"

He kissed behind my ear as he rocked his cock against my heat. "I used to spend a lot of time in the shower every morning and night thinking about you. About how you'd taste, how your breasts would look soaped up. About how bad I wanted to lick you everywhere. And when I'd take my own cock into my hand, I'd pretend it was you sliding your fingers over me, making me feel good. I'd pretend you were squeezing just how I like, bringing me to my knees. I'd pretend you were slick, and wet, and ready for me, begging me to make love to you. And every time I came, it was your name I'd call."

He nipped at my skin and I arched my back. My brain offered up the mental image of him stroking his thick erection, squeezing tight as he pulled the skin taut and groaned out my name.

"D-do you always use my name when you're touching yourself?"

Jonas rocked his hips into me as he kissed the column of my throat. "Yes. Most of the time I imagine you're there, touching me. Wrapping those gorgeous lips of yours around me. Sucking me as you blink up at me, adoringly. And while I'm sliding into your mouth, I'm telling you all the dirty things I'm going to do to you."

Dirty talk—I was a fan.

If this was what happened every time Jonas got pissed off, maybe I'd have to push his buttons more often. Everything he said to me just made me wetter, especially when he coupled it with rubbing his cock just over my clit.

"What kind of dirty things?"

He pulled back a little so he could look at me. A slow, devilish smile played across his lips. "Judging by the curiosity in your voice, you want me to tell you every dirty detail, don't you? You want me talking to you all dirty, telling you how I'm going to work my way backwards with you."

Oh God, so close, the tingles spread over my skin and I arched into him, begging him silently for more friction. "Yes, Jonas."

"You want me to tell you how you suck my cock so good, taking me deep, using your tongue against me, making me beg."

"Mmmm." More. I needed more.

"Then just as I'm about to explode, I pull out before you can make me come and I slide my cock bare inside your hot little pussy. Inch by inch, you cling onto me, milking me, begging me to come."

I wondered why the idea of him making love to me without a condom sounded so hot. I'd always used condoms. But with Jonas, the idea took root and flourished. What would it feel like?

"Then you fuck me so good with your slick wet, heat, and I make you come over and over again."

Oh hell yes. I wanted that with him. More than I'd ever wanted anything in my life.

"But I won't be done, sweetheart. As you already know my rule is ladies first. Then second. And then if I'm lucky, maybe third before I come. But I still won't be done with you. Because you need to know I am the only one who can make you come like that."

He shifted and slid off of me to make quick work of my shoes, tossing them over his shoulders. They landed with thuds somewhere by the door. He was impatient with my dress, yanking and tugging quickly until it was somewhere in a corner.

He took his time watching me, paying particular attention to my breasts. When he leaned back over me, he reached behind me and unsnapped my bra one-handed. The motion was so quick, I had to laugh.

"I see you've had some practice with that."

Jonas smirked as he leaned back over me. "Only a little." He kissed me again before sliding his lips to my jaw, his hands rising up to lock with mine.

I rocked my hips upward and reached for him, sliding my fingers through his hair. "Please hurry."

"I'll get there when I get there." He said with a harsh chuckle. "But not before I remind you of who's in your bed. Of who exactly it is that loves you. Who is about to be inside you."

He grazed along the column of my throat even as his hips rocked into mine, pressing gently. Teasing me with the ridge of his erection.

I bit my lip. "Fuck. I know who's about to be inside me. Your name starts with a J right?"

He chuckled even as he smacked my ass. "Naughty thing. So you know, after we make love, I'm going to use my fingers, I'll slide them inside you and over your skin. I'll find your G-spot and touch it just right. Just enough to make you come again. I know you'll be sensitive, but it's going to feel so good."

He sped up his movements, his hips rolling into mine. I rose to meet him, arching my back, begging him to rub me where I needed. His lips skimmed over my skin, across my collarbone to my breast. His words alone were driving me crazy. But coupled with his lips, his hands intertwined with mine, I was ready to explode.

"I want to make love to every inch of you. Especially these. But tonight, when I'm done stroking you with my fingers, I'm going to taste you. I'll put my mouth on you and lick you until you melt." When his lips reached the top swell of my breasts, he moaned. "Jesus, you are so pretty. So full, so soft."

His lips brushed my nipple ever so slightly. The motion sent a spear of need directly to my core. Next he used just his teeth, raking gently, careful to keep his full weight off of me. His teeth felt so good and I wondered if it was possible to die from anticipation.

When he laved my distended nipple with his tongue and then wrapped his lips around me, I held on for my life. With tug after deep tug, he sucked on me.

It didn't take much, I was so tightly wound. But it was the secondary pleasure when he teased my other nipple with his thumb that sent me over the edge. I came hard and fast, my whole body shaking.

"Jonas. Oh my God."

He pulled back with a satisfied grin. "That's one." His clothes went quickly and he took far less care with them than he'd taken with mine, except when he snagged a condom out of his wallet. The only other time he slowed was when he worked my panties down my legs.

He hooked his thumbs into the elastic and ripped. I gasped. When Jonas licked his lips as I placed my sex directly in front of him, I felt powerful. Jonas kissed down my thighs and my calves to my feet before tossing what was left of the flimsy garment over his head.

He ripped open the condom and slid it on before settling between my thighs. "Look at me, JJ."

As if I could look anywhere else. Even though I felt like a limp noodle, I still wanted more.

One hand teasing the hair at his nape, the other tracing his pecs, I canted my hips up. "Jonas, more."

His voice might have been teasing, but I could see the tension in him as his arms shook. He was having a hard time with control.

Would talking to him drive him as crazy as it drove me? He lined his erection up with my opening and I whispered, "I want to know what this feels like bare. Just you and me, nothing between us. Do you think you'll like that?"

He stared down at me, lips slightly parted. "What?"

"It would be a first. I want to know what it feels like to have you come inside me."

With a curse, he wasted no time and rocked into me in one deep stroke, my name on his tongue. He cursed low and deep, a long drawn out *"Fuuuuck."*

Jonas slid in and retreated, adjusting our position so I sat on his lap. Oh yes, he hit so deep like this. Our motions were a frenzy of skin, lips and hands. There wasn't a part of him he didn't touch me with. Body and soul.

My second orgasm was stronger than the first, but with a slow build. Once the fire took hold, there was no stopping it and I exploded in his arms, a scream tearing out of my chest.

Jonas was right behind me. His hips bucked as he came, and he gripped me my tightly as his muscles corded and his teeth clenched. I wrapped my arms around him, holding tight. He was mine. *And I was his.*

———

Jonas

I WAS ACTING like a jealous prick. I knew it, but I didn't give two shits right at the moment. I had spent half the night making sure she knew she was mine. It had been part seduction, part distraction, part branding.

With everything I'd been through lately, I should let her rest. But then my brain would remind me that she used to fantasize about Rafe, and then I'd need to brand her all over again.

You're acting like a moron. You love her. And she loves you.

You can protect her. But that didn't make the gnawing annoyance and fear in my gut dissipate.

She wiggled in her sleep, and I groaned as her bare ass slid over my dick.

Why couldn't I get enough of her? More importantly why was I acting like such a crazy man?

Because I've never loved anyone before. Not like this anyway. It was more than just her schoolgirl crush on Rafe. The whole David West situation was gnawing at me. I hated that that psychopath had ever been near her let alone put hands on her. I wanted to erase that memory from her mind as well.

All I wanted to do was wrap my arms around her and keep her safe. I wanted to fuck her too... *again.* And again. But I liked just holding her, watching the play of early morning sunlight on her hair.

I listened to her breathing. *Sap.* How in the world was her breathing sexy? Easy. Everything about her was sexy.

She rotated her hips again, and I slid my hands down the flat of her belly to the juncture of her thighs. Even sleepy, she slid them open for me, welcoming my touch. She was so responsive. When I slid my fingers through her smooth lips, we both gasped. Me at how soft she was; her at my penetration. I whispered against her nape, her soft curls tickling my nose.

"Touching you is an addiction now."

"Good."

I nipped her neck as I slid another finger into her, penetrating deeper, my fingers growing slicker. She hooked her leg over mine and slid her hands behind her to wind into my hair. Fuck, I loved it when she tugged a little. She was so hot. So ready.

I removed my fingers and she whimpered, but then I slid them over her lips. And when she tentatively licked them, I almost came. Staring at her pink tongue, I slid my cock along her slit, fighting the urge to sink into her deep. But her words from yesterday rang in my skull and I just had to feel her.

When she sucked my fingers into her mouth, I cursed. "Shit, Jessica. I could explode just from watching you."

She released me and turned slightly, meeting my gaze directly. "I want you to."

My smile spread slowly and I kissed her lightly. Her taste on my lips was enough to have the base of my spine tingling. So close. So damn close.

My cock twitched against her folds. She scooted her hips back, sliding her slick pussy over my length. My already tenuous control snapped then, and I firmly hooked her leg over mine, sliding in to the hilt.

God, that was good.

"Jessica..." Her name tripped reverently off my tongue. She was so tight and so warm around me that I lost another piece of myself.

And as I took us both slowly over the edge of ecstasy, I knew I was never going to let anyone hurt her.

CHAPTER THIRTY

Jonas

When I woke again, I felt like roadkill. I groaned and rolled over, pressing a hand to my forehead that was currently splitting and felt like it was partially detached from the rest of my body.

Damn, getting old was hell. I used to be able to engage in an all-night sexathon without waking feeling used up and dried out. Obviously, not any longer. And if the soft whimpers coming from the other side of the bed were any indication, JJ wasn't feeling much better than I was.

"Oh god, is it morning already? I have to go to work!" JJ screeched.

I clapped my hands over my ears. "No, you don't. It's Saturday."

She sighed in relief and dropped her head back down to the pillow. It occurred to me that I wasn't actually sure *what* day it was, but it was worth the lie if it kept her from screaming in my ear. Considering how much she worked, I figured she had to have some sick days coming, even if it was a workday.

What time was it? It took me a while to gather the energy to sit up, but once I did, I instantly regretted it.

That was it. I was buying a new head. This one was officially broken. Not that I regretted anything. All I had to do was think about how hot, open, and responsive JJ had been last night, and I was hard as a rock. I hadn't even thought my dick was capable of filling again after putting in five impressive performances.

I smiled in satisfaction. I might be tired, but I still had it, damn it.

"Did everybody hear me screaming last night?" JJ asked, almost as if she could hear my thoughts.

Her voice was small, and it instantly wiped away the prior satisfaction I had been feeling. Yes, I'd wanted to brand her as mine and yes, I'd wanted the whole world to know it. But in the midst of my alpha-male posturing, I'd lost sight of how it would make JJ feel to have her best friend and the guys she had to see everyday hearing her scream her head off.

Way to go, asshole. You just embarrassed her when you're supposed to be showing her why she belongs with you.

"I'm sure everyone was asleep," I lied.

"Right. Everyone slept through me screeching like a banshee and moaning your name. God!"

JJ pressed the pillow to her face and fell back to the bed dramatically. Despite everything, I found myself smiling at her antics. This was what I'd dreamed of, sharing this intimate time with her when her hair wasn't done and we both had creases in our faces from the pillowcases. I loved that I knew what she looked like when she woke up and the husky timbre of her voice when she was fresh from dreaming. No one else got to see her like that.

"I'm not going out there. I'll just stay here."

I chuckled. "All day?"

"Yes. All day. I can have food delivered. Hopefully, Adriana will let me work remotely from now on."

It took a lot of cajoling and some sneakily placed kisses, but I was finally able to convince JJ to leave the sanctuary of the covers and venture out for breakfast. We'd both burned a lot of calories the night before. Plus, I figured we might as well get the good-natured ribbing coming from Noah and the guys over with.

When JJ realized it was going to be the same teasing they were used to, she'd get over her shyness. Hell, she'd probably tell them to stop being pervs and listening. JJ was a ball buster, and I loved her that way.

"I'm so hungry," JJ moaned as we walked down the hallway after a hot shower. "I hope Oskar hasn't eaten all the bacon."

Before I could answer, we rounded the corner into the kitchen and stopped in our tracks. Dylan stood in the kitchen pouring a cup of coffee, but everyone else was sitting around the long oak table in the dining area.

Including Rafe.

"Good morning!" Lucia called. "I saved you some pancakes and bacon."

JJ smiled gratefully at her friend, but I could already see the pink inching up her cheeks. She rarely blushed, and most of the times I'd seen her do it had been over the last few days.

Because of Rafe. She blushed for that bastard.

"Thank you. We're both starving." I turned to Lucia, determined to ignore the other side of the room. Until I heard a round of masculine laughter and my eyes were pulled over again.

Rafe smirked.

"I bet. Yo, we get it. She's yours and you're the only one who can make her scream your name. But I don't think they heard her in New Jersey."

JJ blushed bright red and dropped the plate of food she was holding on the counter with a clatter. "I'm not hungry."

"*Rafe!*" Lucia yelled.

Rafe looked slightly chagrined. "Come on blondie, I was just joking," he yelled after JJ's retreating form.

A few seconds later, a door in the hallway closed firmly.

I was across the room before I had a chance to think, and only Oskar stepping in my way stopped my momentum. "Fuck you, man. What are you even doing here?"

"I work here, remember? And my sister lives here." Rafe drawled lazily, as if the entire situation amused him.

That only infuriated me more. The bastard acted like everything was a joke. Especially considering how long he'd been gone from his sister's life. He thought he could flit in and out of his family's life with no consequences? I didn't even know the whole story, but I was furious about Rafe's actions on Lucia's behalf. She'd mourned her brother for years.

"Your sister living here didn't seem to influence your decisions at any other time in your life," I pointed out.

Like a black cloud had just passed, the temperature in the room dropped a few degrees.

Rafe stood slowly. "You don't know what the fuck you're talking about."

"Why don't you come over here and tell me then," I sneered.

Rafe laughed. "I think we all remember what happened the last time we fought. *Can you see me now?*"

I growled and tried to push past Oskar. My eyes had fully recovered from whatever Rafe had thrown at me last year, but just the memory of that shit hurt. Months of built-up frustration were about to be released all at once. We'd accepted Rafe because Noah asked us to, but there was only so much a man could take. Even if I died in the attempt, it might be worth it to wipe the smug smile off that asshole's face temporarily.

"Okay, settle down children. The real enemy is out there." Noah appeared from somewhere, and a huge hand landed on my chest, keeping me immobile. He leaned closer to whisper in my ear. "Take a break. Calm down. I've got this."

I clenched my teeth before turning and stalking down the hall. I trusted Noah a hell of a lot. We'd walked through fire together, literally, and there was no one else I'd rather have covering my back. But Noah had sure as hell better handle it.

Because if he didn't, I would.

Jessica

IT WAS a wonder I didn't trip and fall as I ran blindly down the hallway, so angry I could barely see straight. I was also awash with a raging flush of embarrassment. Bursting through the door to my room, I kicked it shut behind me.

"Ugh! I just..."

Not sure what to do with the rage, I turned in circles before finally running and diving onto the bed. My scream was muffled by the pillow. It still wasn't enough so I rolled and wrapped the bed linens around me. I couldn't see or hear anything right now because if it was any of those guys' stupid faces, I was seriously going to punch someone.

There was a quiet knock and then a minute later, another one. I figured if I ignored the world long enough, everyone would go away. I heard the door open and then shut quietly. I sighed softly, my warm breath pooling beneath the comforter, thick and stifling. It was tempting to stay under the covers all day but knowing Jonas, he'd snatch the covers off anyway. He liked to face things head on.

Normally that was something I liked also. It was a bit of rub to discover that I could hide my head in the sand with the best of them. But after everything that had happened, my sensitive underbelly was exposed, and I was getting a little tired of taking hits.

"You might as well stop hiding. It's just me."

Surprised at the sound of Lucia's voice, I whipped the covers back. She stood at the end of the bed holding a plate of pancakes and a mug.

"If that's coffee, I'll promise you my firstborn."

My friend's easy laughter comforted me and drawn to the warmth, I finally sat up. I accepted the plate and then moved until my back hit the headboard. The first mouthful of steaming hot pancake drizzled with butter made me moan.

"Okay, I forgive you."

Lucia's gray eyes rounded. "Forgive me? For what?"

"For having such an asshole for a brother," I grumbled.

"Well, that part isn't my fault. Nonna always said he was exactly like my dad. So I guess he's to blame."

At the thought of Lucia's deceased parents, I instantly felt ashamed. "Sorry. I guess Rafe isn't the only one who doesn't think before speaking."

"It's fine. He was completely out of line. I yelled at him, but I can go yell some more if it makes you feel better."

After a few more mouthfuls of pancake and several bracing sips of coffee, I finally felt human. "I appreciate you coming to check on me and bringing food."

"Of course." Lucia winked. "What are best friends for? I wasn't going to let you suffer back here alone. I wouldn't have stuck around to take shit from the guys either."

"Jonas had me half convinced that no one heard us. That everyone was asleep."

"Um... nobody got any sleep last night, I'm sure." Lucia covered her mouth but I could still see her shoulders shaking. "That man of yours sure likes to put on a show."

I rolled my eyes. "He's just marking his territory. It couldn't be any more blatant if he'd raised his leg and peed on me."

Lucia was laughing so hard tears pooled in her eyes. "Now that's a visual. The two of you are perfect for each other."

I squeezed my eyes closed. "It's just so embarrassing."

Lucia immediately stopped laughing and moved closer. "Oh honey, no. I know the guys were teasing, but it's all in good fun. You know that, right?"

"I was talking about the whole thing with Rafe."

I kept my eyes closed. It was way too weird to be talking about my former crush on Lucia's brother. But my eyes popped open at Lucia's soft chuckle.

"Seriously, JJ? You thought I didn't know? I'm your best friend, and you think I couldn't tell how you felt?"

In hindsight, it was a little ridiculous to think that I'd been so stealthy with my secret. I should have known that Lucia would pick up on my crush. After all, no one knew me better. Not even my own mother, who had tried hard to relate to me but could never quite understand her brash, aggressive daughter.

My mom was very reserved and soft-spoken. My father had been too busy working to spend much time with me. I had spent my teenage years sure my parents would have been much happier with a more docile, sweet type of daughter. It was only at Lucia's house that I'd felt accepted.

"You always were the only person who really got me."

Lucia glanced at me from the corner of her eye. "But not anymore. Because of Jonas?"

After a brief pause, I admitted in a soft voice, "Yeah. Because of Jonas."

It felt like a risk even saying it aloud, as if stating it would tempt fate to take it away.

"But now I wonder if being so isolated has caused some of this. Maybe if I'd trusted you more, I would have told you about

David before this. Stupid pride might have put Izzy in danger. Because if I'd talked about all this earlier, the guys would have known about David and would have been prepared when he walked in. If they'd known what he was capable of, they never would have let this happen."

Lucia patted my leg. "You can't blame yourself. It probably wouldn't have even mattered. David or Chamaeleon or whatever his name is, knows how to hide. He's ORUS. These guys are trained in how to hide."

Curious, I narrowed my eyes. "How do you know all that?"

"Noah probably wasn't supposed to tell me any of that but it's lonely for them, having no one to confide in. But that's part of how ORUS turns them into weapons. They strip them of everything that makes them human. Relationships, friendships, ability to show emotion. These guys are trained to become a blank slate that the government or whoever can use as weapons. When they're in, no one knows who they really are or anything about them. It's like they don't exist."

I thought back to all those nights when David had talked to me. He hadn't behaved anything like Lucia described. In fact, I'd gotten the sense that he was hungry to tell me about himself. It wasn't unusual for him to describe his childhood, his friends, and the things he wanted for the future, right down to the furniture he planned to build for the dream home he wanted to buy for me.

I sat up suddenly. "It's like they don't exist? But he existed with me. He *loved* to talk to me."

Lucia looked thoughtful. "For someone like him, with no family or friends, I could see how appealing it would be to have someone to confide in. Maybe he thought it was safe because you were so young and had no idea who he really was?"

The more I thought about it, the more it made sense. David definitely hadn't been holding back with me. Even though I'd been young, even at the time I'd been aware that his obsession with me wasn't natural. His happiness had seemed to hinge on impressing me and having me see him as the best and the strongest. Nothing could enrage him faster than any hint I might prefer someone else.

Especially Rafe.

"I think he really was telling me the truth about himself. Stuff that he never thought anyone would find out about, which means he's not as hidden as he thinks. Because we already have everything we need to find him."

I turned to Lucia with a triumphant smile. "Me."

CHAPTER THIRTY-ONE

Jonas

If that stupid asshole didn't wipe that smirk off his face, I was going to wipe it off for him.

Several seats away, Rafe lounged back in one of the conference chairs mirroring my stance. We glared at each other over Ryan, Dylan, and Noah. Matthias sat closer to the window in front of the monitors. I was pretty sure Noah had arranged the seating this way on purpose so that the two of us couldn't go at it again.

A part of me knew I was being irrational. Any kind of feelings JJ might have had for Rafe were over.

Done. Finito.

She was in love with me. And I was in love with her.

Still, the idea that she'd ever wanted that muscle bound asshole at any point in her life made my skin itch. It made me twitchy as fuck and infused me with the desire to hit something. Namely that jackass's face. That sensation wasn't eased any by the smug grin Rafe flashed every time he looked at me. I could practically hear the asshole taunting me. *Oh yeah, she wanted all of this.*

Let it go. It's not important.

The real enemy was out there. The asshole who'd actually tried to hurt JJ. But that was all easier said than done. The whole situation made me want to leave the conference room, drag JJ back to her bedroom, and make her scream my name again, over and over and over.

That can be arranged. And it could be. But then my insecurity would be showing. And I was not going to be insecure about that asshole.

Yeah, I was still smarting from the fight a little over a year ago. The one where Rafe had almost blinded me, and nearly killed both Matthias and Oskar. We'd all lived to tell the tale, and now Rafe was part of the fold. All one big happy family. Except we weren't. Well sort of. But Rafe was still an outlier, and I didn't trust him.

Yeah, you do.

Because when it came to his sister, the guy would give his life. Almost did. The real question was if that courtesy extended to the rest of us. Rafe had been more than willing to kill us a year ago.

I forced myself to roll my shoulders and relax. Rafe caught the movement and his brow lifted as a smile teased his lips.

In response, my hands curled into fists.

Noah slanted the two of us a glance. "Are you two fucking focused? Rafe, sit the fuck up. And Jonas, either quit pouting or go get your girlfriend and go screw her somewhere other than here. You guys work out your shit on your own time then come back when you feel more up to it."

Fuck. Had Noah just scolded my ass?

Didn't you deserve it?

Shit, deserved or not, I didn't fucking like it. But Noah had a point. Rafe might be a supreme asshole but we had bigger fish to fry, and I was letting my personal shit get in the way of things.

"I'll take you up on that later. Right now we have work to do."

"I'm glad you agree with me." Noah rolled his eyes and turned his attention back to the team. "Okay, so like I was saying, from the information that Ian gave us, these are his likely locations. Personally I like this one. It's a mission he's most likely to accept. Lots of exits. Never locked in. As far as we know, as far as Ian has told us, he hasn't checked in. I think —" the conference room doors opened, and all the men lifted their heads to find JJ and Lucia strolling in.

My gaze pinned to my woman immediately, my eyes raking over her, and I couldn't help but think about everything I'd done to her last night. All the ways I'd made her scream.

She's mine. Just get over it already.

I needed to, but the shit was eating at me. When her gaze met mine, all her skin turned pink. And it made me want to smile. Yes, she maybe was a little embarrassed, but she hadn't been worried about a damn thing last night. Maybe I'd take Noah up on the idea of taking her to a hotel. She could scream all she wanted there without any embarrassment whatsoever.

The image of her spread out over a hotel bed with my mouth planted on her pussy took over. I shook my head to clear my mind. Now was not the time. I was already going to have a helluva time explaining to the guys why I wouldn't be able to stand up after this damn meeting.

Noah frowned. "JJ? Sweetheart? What are you two doing here?"

I watched as JJ shifted her weight, and when Lucia spoke up, I could see the worry etched across her face. She was never one to back down, but this whole situation with David, or Chamaeleon, was clearly affecting her more than she let on.

"JJ has something she thinks might help," Lucia said, breaking the silence in the room.

I couldn't help but feel a surge of protectiveness towards her. JJ was always strong and confident around me, but seeing her like this, vulnerable and uncertain, made me want to take her in my arms and shield her from everything.

JJ cleared her throat before speaking. "So, Lucia and I were just trying to run through any information that I might have on him. Where he might go, anyone he might call. I think it's safe to say that anyone I might've met when we were together was probably a front; fake names, business associates. I will never know who they really were. But the one thing he was really obsessed about was family."

She paused, her eyes flickering towards me briefly before continuing. "He kept talking about us, you know, getting married one day and having kids and moving to a split level home in Bliss, Connecticut. And not just like pie-in-the-sky, oh-one-day kind of dreams. I mean he would pull up houses on real estate websites and pick out specific homes. I don't know, but maybe after all this time he would've finally found a house like that. So maybe if Matthias did a search on homes that were owned by someone with an identity that couldn't be traced back more than the last couple of years, maybe we could find him that way."

Noah shook his head. "JJ, that's good but all his activity suggests that he's been here in the city all this time. You're here. You're the object of his obsession. Yeah, he might have wanted to buy you a house back then, but now it doesn't make sense. He doesn't have you. That idea of happy families and all that shit doesn't apply. You're with someone else."

I couldn't help but grin at that, knowing that I was the one she was with and I couldn't resist the urge to reach out and take her hand in mine. JJ looked at me with a small smile, and I squeezed her hand reassuringly.

"I... I know. I just mean when I say he was obsessed, I mean like really obsessed. He wanted everything he thought Rafe had. And I'm telling you, this means something. I can't even believe I didn't think about it until now," JJ said, her voice laced with frustration.

Matthias spoke up, "It won't hurt to have a look. Could take a minute though."

JJ nodded, looking relieved that someone was taking her seriously. "Yeah. Okay. I just wanted to make sure I let you guys know."

But Lucia wasn't done. "No, JJ. Don't move. JJ's brought you valuable intel. As obsessed as this guy was with her, with the idea of them having this perfect life, you guys need to take this seriously."

Both Rafe and Noah shifted uncomfortably under Lucia's intense gaze.

Yeah, she had that effect on the two of them. Funny thing was that JJ usually had them all by the balls with her take-no-prisoners look, but Lucia was pretty damn good at it too when she wanted something.

"Matthias, you're going to look into it now. Today. You guys can play secret government kill squad all you want, but at the very least, look into this. It took JJ a lot of guts to walk in here."

JJ's eyes met mine, and I winked at her. She tucked her chin up and inhaled a deep breath. "Yeah, cool, when I was a teenager I had a crush on Rafe. No big deal. And caveman over here thought it would be a real good idea to brand me last night. Which you all heard, so fair enough. It's not like this entire office hasn't seen Noah and Lucia going at it, which by the way, eww you guys. Seriously, keep it behind closed doors."

Noah just grinned and had a self-satisfied smile on his face.

JJ continued. "The sooner we all get past this, the better for everyone. Look, I know it might be a long shot but, I really think this might be something. And I'm not leaving the room without your word that you're going to look into it."

Matthias nodded from the foot of the table. "I've already got a search running."

She nodded. "Well, in that case, I'm going, gentlemen."

Lucia paused, giving each of us a stern face. "If a single one of you brings up yesterday to her, I'll kill you myself. And this one," she pointed at Noah, "Won't be able to save you." Then she stormed out after her friend.

I wondered if that applied to me too, but at this point, I knew better than to mess with Lucia. All I wanted was my JJ back. The feisty version of her, who didn't take shit from anyone. I wanted to catch this asshole so that she could finally move on with her life and see that she had someone who loved her right in front of her. Someone she would never have to be afraid of.

After JJ and Lucia left the room, Noah shook his head. "Well then. Matthias make sure you get that information to everyone immediately if anything pops. In the meantime, we keep with our current plan. Find any hiding holes he's got. And that takes all men on this team. No matter our differences, right?"

I might not like Rafe, and maybe one day we would eventually bury our hatchet, but for JJ, I would do anything. Anything to see that smile on her face again.

So I nodded slowly. "You'll get no problems and no arguments from me."

Noah nodded at me and turned his gaze to Rafe. "What about you, big brother? You going to keep poking at my boy?"

Rafe tossed his hands up. "As long as he doesn't poke at me, we're good."

I rolled my eyes. That was about as close to a truce as we were going to get. For now.

First, we had a chameleon to find.

Jessica

"SEE, that's the key. I told you there was nothing to be embarrassed about."

I stared at Lucia, my mouth slightly open. "Are you serious right now? I mean, I'm not shy, but every single one of those guys pretty much heard Jonas um—"

Lucia grinned. "Staking his claim?" she offered helpfully.

I nodded. "Yes, staking his claim. It's humiliating."

Lucia put her hand on her head. "Humiliating how? You don't want anyone to know about you and Jonas?"

I wrinkled my nose. "Don't be ridiculous. I don't care who knows. I want to shout it from the rooftops."

"Okay, so you shouted it from your bed. What's the problem?"

"I don't know. It was more about how that whole thing unfolded. I mean, it's embarrassing, okay? This is me, love-em-and-leave-em JJ. I had a stupid crush, and made a bad decision about a man, and the next thing I know, everyone is all up in my business."

Lucia sighed. "Honey, you have been my best friend since we were kids and we met in Mr. Patterson's class. You think I don't know that you're mostly bravado and hard exterior with a soft, warm, gooey center? What's crazy is you thinking *they* don't know that about you."

I scowled. "I'm tough."

"No one is disputing that, honey. But most of us see that show for what it is, a suit you put on every day. One that keeps you protected. One that keeps you *safe*. As your best friend, I personally like the suit. I think it's fun. But guess what, we all love the woman inside. The one who's warm, and sweet. The one who buys Earl Grey tea for Matthias just to give him a taste of home. And you know he doesn't drink coffee. You're the one who on her way home buys those German cakes for Oskar and leaves them on his desk. And you never ever say that it's you, but we all know.

It's like how you remember Noah's birthday and always try to get him something appropriate. You used to do that for Rafe too when we were kids, remember? You'd always get him some silly little gift. And you've always been there for me. You listened to me when my parents were gone, when Rafe was gone. You are always a rock, and you're always the one guaranteed to make me laugh. To let me see that there is a fun side to life.

So, we all love you and we see the real you. We love the sass, we love the mouth. It's part of the fun. But there's also the you underneath it all that we see and love. So you know what? No one cares about how you had a crush on Rafe. It's not like we didn't know, I told you that already. Rafe knew. Noah knew. *Everyone* knew. So what if the rest of the guys know?"

I sighed. "It's just, ugh, I don't like being vulnerable."

Lucia grinned. "No one does, that's why it's called being vulnerable."

My goddaughter took that opportunity to wake up from her nap and screeched the house down. Isabella was never a fan of waking up alone.

"I guess the princess summons me. I'll be right back." Lucia ran to get the baby, who likely needed to be changed or fed, or a combination of both.

I went into the kitchen and pulled the fridge open, determined to go for the red velvet cake in the back that Noah had brought from Nonna's. When I pulled out the cake, I almost jumped a mile and splattered cake all over my face when I found Rafe leaning against the doorway.

"'Sup, JJ?"

My face went hot. And no doubt I was bright crimson at this point. *Fantastic.*

"Hey Rafe. Want a slice?"

He shook his head. "But if you have a spare fork, I'll take a bite."

I pulled open the cutlery drawer and pulled out two forks. I handed one over to him, before digging into the cake and shoving a fat piece of delicious goodness into my mouth.

Oh God. Yes. Sugar and icing were just the balm my bruised ego needed.

Rafe took a bite and actually moaned. "Jesus Christ. That's one thing I missed, you know? Nonna's cooking. And her baking. Pretty much everything actually."

I sighed. "You know, we never even talked about what it must have been like for you. I mean I'm the best friend, so I guess I've always been on the outside looking in at that whole situation."

Rafe shook his head. "We didn't see you that way. You were part of the family. Sure sometimes I thought you were my sister's annoying best friend. But you were a fixture in Nonna's house. You were one of the people I missed."

"Yeah, I guess everyone's heard how I missed you, so there's that."

He chuckled low. "You really think I didn't know?"

"Shit, I guess I wasn't real subtle."

He nodded. "Pretty much. I mean you used to stare at me a lot. And admittedly, I caught you and Lucia practicing kissing on your hands once. You referred to your hand as Rafe. That was a pretty clear sign."

I covered my face with my hands. "Oh. My. God. That's almost worse than last night."

He grinned. "Yeah. Don't worry about it. I thought it was cute. Besides, have you seen me? I'm pretty hot."

I snorted. "I was 13. Cut me some slack."

His chuckle was low and deep. "I'll cut you some slack when you cut yourself some. It's no big deal, JJ." He cleared his throat "I —I do owe you an apology though."

I took another forkful of cake. "For what?"

"For never saying I'm sorry to you. Like I said, you were like family to me. My annoying-little-sister kind of family, but family nonetheless, and I never said I was sorry for the years of pain you went through as a result of my decision."

I forced myself to swallow the piece of cake around the sudden onset of sawdust in my mouth. "You don't owe me an apology. I made my decision about David on my own. That had nothing to do with you."

"I don't know. I feel a little responsible. If I'd been there, I would've steered you away from him. I would've seen him for what he was. It was my job to protect you."

"Stop. It wasn't your job to protect me. *I* made a bad choice. And I suffered the consequences. The good news is, now I won't make choices like that anymore."

He nodded. "All the same though. I'd personally like to kick that guy's ass for you. You were a good kid, and I did love you. I *do* love you. Not the way that Jonas does. And I'm pretty sure he's probably going to want to kill me for saying it."

I giggled. "Yeah. He's still kinda mad at you for everything that happened last year."

Rafe rolled his eyes. "You try to kill a guy *one* time. I swear, it was a misunderstanding."

I grinned. "That was one hell of a misunderstanding. Are you guys ever going to tell me who exactly it is that you work for or what you do, or did, or whatever?"

He studied me for a moment his expression impassive. "Lucia told you?"

"Not much. I sort of guessed that you guys were more than just a security company, but she hasn't really said explicitly. So I let my imagination run wild. And my imagination is very, very good."

He nodded. "Well, yeah, I guess we don't exactly keep a lot of things super-secret."

"So this isn't the part where you tell me now that I know that you have to kill me?"

"Nope. Right now my job is to protect you. You, Lucia, Nonna, Noah, and by extension these idiots." He shrugged. "You're all family. That's how it goes. For what it's worth, that was good intel that you brought into the conference room. I know it can't have been easy to walk in there after — after last night."

She shrugged. "Well, talking to Lucia helped me remember his level of obsession. You know what's funny? I didn't even realize it then, but I probably fed into his obsession. Every time I would talk to him about how much I missed you or how much it hurt Lucia not having you there, he would ask me to talk about you and told me it was therapy, that it would help me feel better. And like an idiot, I played into that."

Rafe took another bite. "You're not an idiot. You trusted the wrong guy, yes, but you did nothing wrong there. You were being open and kind and trying to move on with your life after the bullshit I put you guys through."

"Yeah, still feels like I should've seen something. But he was everything I thought I wanted, you know? Like the perfect kind of guy. And then I saw it was something much more dangerous, something darker than that. I didn't understand it. Now I see how much he hated you. You were the one he really wanted to hurt."

"Well, the good news is he's not gonna get the chance. We're going after him before he even comes anywhere near us. You're safe now."

For the first time in my life, I actually believed that. Between Jonas, Noah, Rafe, and everyone else, I knew that I was safe here. Safer than anywhere else in the world.

"You know, he was obsessed with me. But not as much as he was obsessed with *you*. A part of me feels like the only reason he was ever so fixated on me was because of you in the first place. I keep thinking if I make myself bait or something, that would bring him running, but I don't think so anymore. I think *you're* the one he wants. I think he'd do anything to get a shot at you."

Rafe stood straight. And then he studied me for a long moment. "You know, JJ, you might be absolutely right about that."

CHAPTER THIRTY-TWO

Jonas

Rafe's voice broke through the darkness, interrupting my thoughts. "You still got your panties in a twist, or are you ready to work?"

We were hiding under cover of bushes, waiting for the signal from Matthias and Noah. The only light we had was from the moon, and we had our night-vision goggles at the ready in case things got messy. It had been fifteen minutes of tense silence. Neither of us wanting to give way.

"My panties aren't in a twist. It would be a shame to do that to Italian silk," I replied, trying to keep the mood light.

Rafe chuckled. "Fair enough."

I knew what was coming next. "Since we're here and all, I guess now's a good time to ask if you're sure about this," I mumbled.

Rafe's jaw tensed. But he kept his voice steady. "Yes. Besides, no one's supposed to get hurt today. I'm only playing assassin again. It's not for real."

I couldn't help but bring up the past. "You know, you, Noah, and Matthias all get that same look on your face whenever you talk about what you used to do."

Rafe narrowed his gaze and did another sweep through his binoculars. "Yeah. ORUS changed every single one of us. That's the problem when you do that kind of job when you still have a soul. There are plenty of guys in there who have no soul." He shrugged. "Who knows, maybe now it's the kind of organization it was supposed to be in the first place. Only taking out the worst of the worst, cleaning up the trash. But, I still don't trust them. It's hard to say."

"You regret bringing Noah in?"

Rafe didn't even look at me as he answered. "Every fucking day. I mean it wasn't like I brought him in myself you know. That was Ian. The kid saved Ian's life so that was that. Ian thought he was saving him. The problem was Ian didn't see the toll it was taking. And I had to train him, or he'd get killed. So I regret him being in that life, but I'm glad I taught him to be the best he could be. It kept him alive. And you can't get out if you're dead, right?"

I nodded in agreement. "Yeah, that's one way of looking at it."

After a long moment, Rafe asked, "So, we cool on the JJ thing?"

I clenched my jaw. "Yeah. We're fine. As long as you get that she's mine."

Rafe chuckled. "Man, what the fuck is it with you guys when you fall in love? All caveman and shit. Me Tarzan, she Jane. I swear you and Noah are ridiculous. I mean, you're too pretty to be a caveman anyway. You're too Metro."

I shook my head. "There is nothing wrong with a little manscaping and decent clothes. You might try something other than basic black all the time."

Rafe frowned. "What's wrong with black? It goes with every-thing. And helps, you know, when you're trying to kill people. They can't see you coming."

I had to hold back a chuckle. "Seriously? I'm beginning to doubt your sanity."

"What? I'm just being honest."

"All I'm saying is it wouldn't hurt you to put a little effort into it. You know mix it up, change your fabrics."

"Look, I'm just going to leave the pretty-boy antics to you and Noah."

"Oskar sees nothing wrong with a blazer every now and again."

"Yeah, you realize you're talking about the accountant, right?"

I considered that. "Yeah, you have a point there."

We'd sat in relative silence for several more minutes when Rafe frowned and grumbled. "Something's wrong."

I shifted slightly. My arm was falling asleep in my current position. "Why do you say that?"

Rafe shook his head. "It's quiet. Almost too quiet. We haven't had a single person walking a dog or turning off their porch lights. It's like the whole neighborhood's dead."

I frowned. "Please don't say the word dead."

Rafe pressed his comm unit. "Matthias, can you verify we have movement in the house? And while you're at it check the other two neighboring houses. The street's too quiet."

Matthias's voice came back in the comm unit. "I still see heat sigs. There's a body upstairs, master bedroom. So target is there. Still alive as far as I can tell. Other houses, everyone's snug in bed."

As soon as Rafe voiced his suspicion, I felt a nagging sense that something was off. I couldn't quite put my finger on it, but my gut was telling me that we weren't in the right place.

I pressed my comm unit and asked, "Are we sure this is the location Ian identified? Something doesn't feel right. And I'm not some superspy with heightened senses."

Rafe chuckled beside me. "You'll do okay. Cop senses aren't too shabby either."

"I'm serious. We've been here for over an hour. Either he's a no-show or he found another way in that we don't know about."

Noah's voice crackled through the comm unit. "Roger. Alpha unit, move into the house. Secure the target if necessary. But you're right, something's off. Beta team, fall back to their flanks and watch their six."

Despite the stiffness in our bodies from lying in position for so long, Rafe and I sprang into action, quickly crossing the street and ducking for cover. We communicated through sign language and hand gestures as we approached the side door of the house. Once inside, we cleared each room in succession, but an eerie silence hung over the house. It was too quiet. And when I spoke into the comm unit, my voice was tight with tension.

"Matthias, we have a problem. The house is too cold."

Noah's voice was urgent. "Get to the target now."

With our guns drawn, Rafe led the way, and I watched his back as we made our way towards the master bedroom. But then I heard Rafe's cursing, and when he spoke into his comm unit, his anger was palpable. "We have a fucking problem. Target's goddamn dead."

Matthias's voice crackled through the comm unit. "What the fuck do you mean he's dead, mate?"

"I'm talking ashes to ashes. Time to baste the formaldehyde turkey."

"That's not fucking possible. I'm showing your heat signatures and his."

I glanced over my shoulder. Rafe was right. The guy was too still in the bed. Not moving.

"Yeah, Rafe's not lying. The guy's not moving."

Matthias cursed on the other line. "Then why do I see a fucking heat signature?"

Rafe sighed. "The son-of-a-bitch used a warming blanket. Temperature's currently set to one hundred degrees. And he's tucked in tight, like a cocoon. Hate to say it, but he's fucking cooking in here."

On the other end of the line, Noah swore. "Fucking Ian. We've been played."

———

RAFE and I carried the body out of the house into the back yard where we at least had some cover. Noah and Matthias met with us within a minute.

"The people in the houses next door, they're all dead." Noah muttered. "*No one* was supposed to die."

I stared at him. "We're not dealing with someone sane are we? He not only took out our target, he took out innocent civilians."

"Jonas, you think I don't know that? You think I don't feel the pressure?"

Rafe stepped between the two of us. "Never thought that I'd be doing this, but we need to focus. We need to identify the people in the houses next door, identify the target for confirmation, and get the fuck out."

In our comm units, the alarm sound blared. Rafe glanced at Matthias. "What is that?"

"Proximity alarms. We have incoming."

Rafe and I immediately put on our night-vision goggles.

"I've got three guys coming from the south."

Rafe drew his gun. "I see two coming from the east.

Matthias and Noah went on red alert. What we didn't account for, was the basement door bursting open, and two men running out.

All four of us backed up against each other to face our opponents. Our guns had silencers, and we each had extra ammo. But this was not the kind of fight we wanted. None of this was supposed to happen. *You're a cop*. Ex-cop.

In situations like this, I'd call for fucking backup. *Well your backup's here. Do what you gotta do.* I knew that some people were going to end up dead. I just prayed it was none of my team. I turned toward the two guys that had barged out of the basement, Rafe chuckled before sheathing his gun back in his holster.

"What the fuck are you doing, Rafe?"

The guy must have completely lost it because he laughed. "It's time to have some fun."

A swift glance around told me that Matthias had also put away his gun. Instead, he had out knives. *Knives at a goddamn gunfight.* I knew what happened to people who carried knives. They fucking got shot.

Noah was the only one who was acting sane. He at least had out his gun, scratch that, two. Okay then, so it was like that.

In the span of a second, I wasn't paying attention to what was happening with my friends. I was fighting for my life. I squeezed off a bullet, hitting one of the guys in the upper thigh, but the asshole didn't even go down. Instead he just kept on coming.

"What the fuck?"

Somewhere near my right, Rafe called out, "Body Armor. That's why the guns are useless unless you can fire a kill shot at a moving target."

Well fuck me. Before I knew what was happening the shorter guy on the right lunged at me and knocked me over. The air whooshed out of my lungs as the asshole pressed all his weight on top of me.

From beneath, I defended against the blows. The taller slimmer one on the left had jumped onto Noah.

Noah had fired a kill shot for one of the guys coming from the south, but the other was still coming. And now I had more company. I had to get the fuck up off the ground. Somewhere above my head to the left, I heard the slicing of knives, metal on metal, and a series of grunts, kicks, and curses.

All I could do was block the blows and try to survive. But then the guy on me made one fatal mistake. He eased back, to reach for a weapon maybe? But he didn't know that I had Jujutsu training.

I loved nothing more than to grapple if I could get a leg in. I wedged my knee between my body and the guy's chest then shoved back. The guy flew backwards, and I was on my feet in a second.

Then it was a matter of hand to hand. The good news was this guy was not as good as Rafe. Oh, he had been trained. Really, really fucking well-trained. Like assassin trained.

I took a left cross to the jaw and staggered. Then the guy moved forward, grabbing me by the shoulders and delivering a series of knees. *Motherfucker*. The pain spread through my chest as my ribs took a pounding. But on the last knee kick, I grabbed him under the thigh, and unsettled him enough to knock him on his back.

And then it was on. I pounced on him, raining blows on his face. The guy reached underneath himself and I heard the *shhhht* sound of metal being unsheathed.

A knife.

I leaned back in the nick of time to avoid a slice of the knife across my jugular, but the damn thing caught my arm. *Son of a bitch.*

I grabbed the guy's hand and dropped several elbows on his face. But even though the guy's eye was glued shut now with blood, he still tried to work his legs out from under me.

I pinned one of his arms with a knee, which essentially put my dick right in the guy's face. "Hey man, maybe you like balls in the face, but now would be a good fucking time to stop moving."

The asshole beneath me still tried to come at me with a knife, raising his arm, and I had to duck and weave and grapple for that free arm. When I grabbed it, it was a battle of wills and a battle of strength. The guy tried to turn the knife around on me, but I didn't let go. No, then it would be lights out. Party over. And then what the fuck would happen to JJ?

JJ. Fuck. Just thinking about her gave me the extra boost of strength I needed. And with all my might, I turned the guy's wrist, shoving the knife down into his neck. It took several seconds, but eventually he stopped moving.

Don't stay still. On your feet. There's more of them than there are us. When I turned, I found that one of the guys that had come from the south was already dead. Another one was down. One guy was limping and reaching for his gun. I went right for him. Stepping on his hand before bending down, grabbing the gun, and twisting his hand until I heard it crack.

The guy made a muffled moan, but tried to twist around and grab my ankle. "Stop fucking with me or I will kill you." But he still reached for the weapon.

What the hell was wrong with these guys? None of them seemed to want to live. I had no choice. One shot to the head. Without even thinking about it I dropped the guy's arm and turned to face my friends.

Matthias had one down on the ground, they were wrestling with one of the knives, but then Matthias head butted him and made sure that knife sliced home and implanted in his neck. Then the kid was up on his feet in no time. His face was covered in blood, and his hands were up, both knives gripped by the handles, ready to slice and fight.

Noah delivered a kick to the skull of the guy he had been fighting with. But the guy refused to go down. He came at him with fists and knees, but Noah dodged and avoided them all. He delivered a couple of good knee strikes before a very nice elbow to left hook combination. The guy staggered back and delivered his own elbow, ringing Noah's bell. Before Noah could rebound, there was a *pffft* sound and the guy sagged to the ground. Noah whirled around, hands up.

Rafe just shrugged. "You were playing with your food. You want a work out, I'll give you one."

Noah nodded. "Thanks. Fucking lost my gun."

I handed a gun to him. "This it?"

"Yeah. Those assholes had me pinned down and took it off me."

Rafe gave him a wry grin. "Not the first time I saved you in a firefight."

Noah clocked him on the arm. "Probably not the last." Then he checked in on each of the rest of us. "Kid? You good?"

Matthias, who still had knives at the ready and was breathing hard and heavy standing over the carcass of the man he'd carved up, didn't respond at first.

Under normal circumstances, I would have described Matthias as a good kid. Loved his nerdy T-shirts, and the super-hero movies. Given the way some of the female clients smiled at him shyly, women didn't think he was too hard on the eyes. And there was a somewhat innocent quality about him. Women tended to want to take care of him.

Hell, they all looked at him as some kind of little brother.

But at that moment, with his knives in his hands and pure, visceral hate and anger radiating over his body and his face, I knew the truth. Matthias was all killer. This was who he was underneath the carefully crafted exterior. Peel back one layer of the onion, and it was clear the kid was no one to fuck with.

Matthias didn't move.

Noah's voice was soothing. Quiet almost. "Why don't you go ahead and put your knives away, and step back. Head back to the communications van. Call our cleanup crew. I want IDs on all these guys. Preferably before we head over to deal with Ian."

Fuck, we weren't done. "You think he sent them?" I asked.

"Not sure. But he knew exactly where we would be tonight,

which means either he told someone, or we were set up. Either way, he's gonna have to answer some questions about it."

Rafe went over to Matthias. He didn't touch him though. "Kid, did you hear Noah? He needs you to get the ball rolling. The time for killing is done. Back away."

Matthias just blinked back at him. There was a gleam in his eyes, like he wanted to go toe-to-toe with Rafe. Like he was desperate for a rematch of what had gone down a little over a year ago.

Rafe adjusted his footing. "Matthias. Stand down." He was on the balls of his feet, hands up in what looked like a defensive posture, but I recognized it as the fight stance for krav maga.

Noah's voice took an edge as well. "Kid, comms. Call in Delaney."

That seemed to shake him out of it. And he blinked several times. When he saw the position of his knives, he sheathed them and met Rafe's gaze. "Sorry." When he turned, he nodded at Noah. "I'm good."

Noah visibly relaxed. "Yeah, I know. Get on, we'll bring all the bodies out. Photograph them, so at least you can have them cataloged. It'll make the cleaner's job easier."

As Rafe and Noah headed to the house on the left, I stared after Matthias. Just how dangerous was the kid? I didn't have time to ask those questions though, because we needed to clean up and then find out if Ian had set us the fuck up.

CHAPTER THIRTY-THREE

Jonas

I still couldn't believe that Noah was letting me take point. And, well, I did feel like sort of a badass with my own personal kill squad behind me. When we bypassed Ian's security easily, in through the front door, we found the new leader of ORUS in his kitchen, two guns pointed in our direction and a grenade on his countertop.

"Wow, dramatic aren't you? You can put the guns away. A grenade? Jesus." I slid a glance to Noah. "Is every single one of you a prima donna? We just came to talk."

I turned my attention back to Ian, who hadn't lowered his guns at all. The guy's right eye twitched when he saw Rafe and Matthias come in behind me and Noah.

"What do you want?"

I palmed my own weapon. "Look Ian, we're just here to talk. About that little death squad you sent for us?"

"Death squad?"

I nodded as I rounded the counter. "Yeah, the team of seven you sent after us, after you told us that everything was all set and we could set the trap and spring it for your boy Chamaeleon. David. Jesus, do all of you have code-names?"

From behind me, Rafe chuckled. "Yeah. You wish you were cool enough."

I shook my head. "I'll stick with Jonas Castillo if you don't mind. Has a nicer ring to it. So anyway, Chamaeleon left us a few little presents. Dead presents. I swear, your boy's like a rabid fucking dog. He killed the target. Dead. He killed innocent civilians in the two neighboring homes."

Ian's brows snapped down as he glared at Noah. "What?"

"Don't look at Noah, look at me. I'm the one who's fucking pissed off. I'm the one who's trying to protect the woman I love. So you're going to start talking, you're going to call off the kill squad that's on its way here to protect you right now, and then we're going to have a conversation about your boy David West."

Ian lowered his guns and carefully picked up the grenade, opened the drawer underneath the counter, and placed it back inside. Then slowly, he pulled the phone out of his back pocket. He tapped in a few numbers, and put it to his ear. I could only assume that someone on the other end had answered when he started speaking. "Code 754312. Orion. Condor has flown." He hung up then. "It wasn't a trap. I didn't set you up."

Noah shrugged. "Ian. You and I go way back. In some ways, I have you to thank for the life that I have. But you need to stop fucking lying. Why are you covering for him?"

"I'm not covering. I did everything as we discussed. I let it slip that we were letting Rafe back in the fold. I simply discussed it with him as we talked about who the target might be. After that, it was up to him to get information. And it looks like he did."

Noah leaned against the countertop. "Yeah, he got there before us. He set up the whole goddamn house. Turned the temperature down, had warming blankets on the guy so that we'd think we had a live body inside. And then, I don't know what kind of armor you guys have now, but he was able to conceal the watch-dogs he had in the basement."

Ian sighed. "Temperature in the house very cold?"

Matthias nodded. "Yeah, fucking frigid, mate."

Ian nodded. "We have these new thermo-suits. They serve a dual purpose. Keep your body temperature nice and even, while showing nothing on the exterior. So if you have heat sensors like you guys clearly did, they won't pick it up. And they also act as excellent bulletproofing. Better than Kevlar. Lighter, faster. Recently, we had body disposal for a couple of agents we lost, and their suits came up as unlogged."

Noah threw up his arms. "And you think now is the best time to fucking tell us?"

"How the fuck was I supposed to know? I inherited this goddamn problem; an inheritance by the way, that you perpetrated."

"Like you got the poor end of the deal? Fancy house, more money than you know what to do with, and your own personal kill squad."

Ian shook his head. "You know that's not me. I've never been in this for the power. You know why I do this."

I slid a glance at Noah. "You mean there are reasons to become a homicidal assassin?"

"Can it, Castillo," Rafe muttered.

I turned on Rafe. "Really? We can just roll up in here to your leader and I don't get to ask questions?"

Ian sighed. "Not about my personal life, no. But listen, I know that Chamaeleon is a problem. He was a problem for the Orion before me."

I had to take control of the conversation again. If I left it to Noah and Rafe, we'd all be standing around in a circle jerk for another hour. And if I left it to Matthias, every one of us would be dead. Eventually, Noah and I would have to talk about the kid.

Because there was something dangerous lurking just underneath the surface with him.

"Okay, look. Start talking, Ian."

"Fine. David West, also known as Chamaeleon, has been an agent since maybe a year before Noah came on board. Brash, uncontrollable, obsessive. Rafe, he looked up to you. He wanted to be you, maybe. When you were taken out of play, he became even more obsessed with your life. Started following around your sister, your grandmother, your sister's friend."

I advanced on him, grabbing him by the lapels. "You fucking knew?"

With a series of practiced moves, Ian had himself free. But I wasn't going to let up and advanced on him again.

In a flash, Rafe had me in a choke hold. "Easy does it, let the man talk." Rafe easily restrained me until I forced myself to relax. Then I was released.

"I didn't personally know. It was only after I went through the employee files that I found the notes. He was obsessed. And that was his MO. There'd been a girl before he became ORUS. He hurt her, killed her. Evidence points to an accident, but still."

"Jesus Christ," I swore.

Ian frowned as he leaned back against the sink. "My predecessor saw skills that could be honed. But, his obsessive personality was a problem. DeMarco, he knew that Orion regarded you as one of his best agents. Considering how young you were and how quickly you rose, he saw you as the one to emulate."

Rafe clenched his jaw. "My record is nothing to be emulated."

Ian narrowed his gaze but made no comment about Rafe and his record.

"After you were gone, Orion was worried about the blowback. West was too obsessed, wanted to be in every aspect of your life, DeMarco. When Orion found out he wasn't just following but had inserted himself into your family, he was taken out of play and sent on an overseas, long-term mission. Five years. After I became Orion, I was doing an assessment on all the agents and discovered he was still active. DeMarco, your personal files are buried. But West must have had access to them after your death. It's possible he knows you even better than Noah does."

"You want to tell me why you didn't take him out?" Noah asked.

"I'm still digging through all the information and cleaning house with my agents. Most of them are true to the cause, patriots. There are some that were either forcibly removed, or let go. I should have done the same with West. But until now, he was an unknown."

I could only stare at him and then back at Noah and Rafe. "So all of you are telling me you had all this information at your finger-tips, in essence, and no one did a thing?"

Ian shook his head. "I didn't know. When I brought him back in play to assess him to see if he'd be fit for duty, I had no idea. All I knew was that the work he'd done overseas was solid. I didn't know I'd be triggering his obsession again. We all learned that the hard way. Let me bring him in. I have men at the ready to do it."

I shook my head. "Fuck no. Like we trust your men."

Noah agreed with me. "No. We'll use our guys."

"Look, I want him gone just as much as you do. I've authorized shoot to kill orders on him."

Normally that should've triggered my old cop genes. But this time it didn't. West had already proven that he was a psychopath. And that he was not above taking a baby, or her nanny, or killing an innocent victim. He had to be put down.

I turned my attention back to Ian. "So what's our plan?"

"I've narrowed down a few possible locations. The best places to flush him out."

I nodded. "Fine. Then let's get to work."

———

"SO LET ME UNDERSTAND, you guys are going to go back out there and search out all of his favorite hiding spots, after he sprang a trap for you and sent men to kill you?"

I cupped my hands over JJ's cheeks and traced my thumb over her bottom lip. "We're going to be fine. I came home to you after the last time, didn't I?"

"Beaten and bloody. You promised me you would be safe."

I did love it when her temper was up. But I didn't want her to worry. "I know what I said. It was unexpected. But we're not going in blind. We'll have ORUS backing us, we'll be fine."

"I don't believe that. You need better backup."

I chuckled bitterly. "There's no such thing. The kind of situations that Noah has gotten people out of... they have connections like you wouldn't believe."

She glanced up at me curiously. "You mentioned that once before, that Noah got you out of trouble but I wasn't sure if I should ask."

"You can ask me anything you want, you know that." I took a deep breath. "I was in a bad place. There was a woman."

JJ glanced at me from the corner of her eye. "Isn't there always?"

My arm tightened around her waist. "It wasn't like that. Emma needed help. We'd responded to domestic calls there before but she always declined to press charges. She wasn't an immigrant, like my mom, but she reminded me of her. The police didn't take her seriously because her husband was a wealthy local business-man, lots of friends in high places. He really didn't appreciate some small time cop sticking his nose where it didn't belong."

Her hand caressed the side of my face. "You were trying to help her, weren't you?"

"Yeah. Convinced her to press charges. Then the next thing I knew, I was being arrested for assault. It was my word against his about what happened. I was going to go down for sure, he was friends with the Chief of Police and plenty of judges. Emma was the only one who could testify that I hadn't raised a hand against her but in the end, she sided with her husband. After everything I'd done to try to help her, it wasn't enough. I still don't know how Noah got me out of that one but the next thing I knew, I was being released from jail and told by the chief that my resignation had been accepted. I was too shaken to ask many questions."

JJ pulled me close, resting her head against my chest. It was exactly what I needed right then, the warmth of her embrace permeating the chill thoughts of the past always brought.

"It wasn't your fault, Jonas. You did everything you could. Sometimes, even when you do all you can, it just doesn't work out."

"Exactly," I stated, leaning back so I could look her in the eye. "Which is why I don't want you anywhere near this. Noah has called in help from some friends. Rafe has called in help from the feds. It'll be okay. And the team, we're together on this."

"Okay, fine, I hear you. But I still think I should come with you. We all know I make really good bait."

I tugged her against me. "You understand I lost years off my life watching you stroll right up to that asshole and proceed to start screaming at him, right? I am not strong enough to do that again, so no can do."

JJ shoved at me and I released her. "What's that supposed to mean? I can take care of myself you know."

"Sweetheart, I know. I believe in you. I do. But, all I want to do is keep you safe. You are my heart and my love, and more than once I've had to watch you face complete terror at this guy's hands. I can't do that again. I don't know what I would do if I lost you."

"Well I don't know what I would do if I lost you. I mean, what am I supposed to do without you? I had never planned on falling in love, and now I am. *You* did that to me."

I chuckled. "Well, sweetheart, you're right about that. And if you stop yelling at me, I can do it again."

"Are you serious right now?"

I held up my hands. "Well, it's true, I am irresistible. And I turned my charm on you. So I mean obviously you would fall in love."

She poked me in the chest. "This is not funny. I'm not used to loving someone."

I laughed. "You love people all the time. You just don't want them to know that you love them. Only difference is now I *know*."

"Yeah, but don't go getting all smug about it."

"Me, smug? Never. Now, why don't you help me get out of this battle gear, and you can kiss my boo-boos and admonish me for all the reasons you're mad at me."

"Sex is not going to solve this. I want to help. I want to do *something*. Anything. Let me ride in the van or whatever it is. I can run the communications."

"JJ."

She huffed and held her shoulders stiff.

"*Jessica.*"

The use of her name had her body softening a little bit, and I was willing to use whatever I could to get in her good graces.

"Sweetheart, I love you. But I can't let you do this. And if you try, I really will lock you inside this penthouse."

"You are welcome to try. See how well that works out for you. I swear to God you'll be missing a nut in no time."

My lips tipped into a smile. "There are more pleasurable things you can do with my nuts."

"You keep talking, jackass, and no one's going near your nuts for a very long time."

I grinned. God, I loved her sassy mouth.

"Yes, I hear you. But, that's really biting off that perfect pussy to spite your own libido. You're not going to cut me off because you need me too much. I bring you all the good orgasms."

She still whacked at me. "So what? I'm sure if I found Lucia's giant toy, it would get the job done too."

"Oh, you wound me." I placed a hand over my chest. "Don't be mad at me. I'm just trying to keep you safe. That's the only thing that matters to me right now and for the rest of my life. Keeping you safe and loving you. Two main directives, that's all I've got."

She harrumphed. "You know, you're not supposed to be so sweet."

"I've always been sweet. You were just too busy sniping at me to notice."

She narrowed those beautiful eyes at me. "Between me and you, who was doing the sniping?"

I nipped along her neck. Why did she always smell so good? "I think we know the answer to that."

She groaned and her breath caught. "You. I'm an angel. Ask anyone."

I laughed as I nuzzled her throat. "Yes, maybe an angel of torment. Now come on, I need you to kiss my boo-boos. And I'll sweeten the deal. I'll match you kiss for kiss. Right now I need the woman I love. I need to hold her, need to touch her soft skin, I need her to touch me. What do you say?"

"Well, when you put it like that how could I say no?"

CHAPTER THIRTY-FOUR

Jessica

I knew what he was trying to do. Distract me. Seduce me with those kisses that always made me forget my own name so I wouldn't be thinking about the possibility of him being hurt, or worse, dealing with the nightmare of my past.

"Are you trying to seduce me into dropping this subject?"

He looked me right in the eye. "Yes. Because I don't want you worrying about any of this shit. I'm going to fix it for you."

Even though I knew he was trying to do something good, something positive for me, I was done sitting back and letting others be in control. There had been a time I'd wanted that, when I was young and lonely and grieving. But I'd also like to think that I'd learned from my mistakes. Having a man want to control things for me had never ended well.

"You're trying to look out for me, I get it." I put my palm gently against his cheek. "But having someone take care of things for me isn't what I want. I've had a man want to take care of everything before. You've seen how that ended up."

Jonas rested his forehead against mine. "I would never treat you like that. My impulse to take care of you doesn't stem from possession. It's just caring. I want to make your life easier and make you happy. Most of all, I want you to be safe."

I nodded. I already knew that in my heart, but it helped to hear it stated. Being with David had damaged my confidence in my own judgment and decision making. But sometimes when things in life were shitty, all you could do was grab onto anything good. And this was good.

Being with Jonas was explosive and intense but also sweet and comforting. If you'd asked me just a few months ago if I thought this kind of happiness and trust was possible, I would have flat out denied it.

I've become a believer, I thought as I gazed into his eyes.

His love had made me a believer.

"Kiss me, Jonas. Make me forget all this craziness and all this fear. Let's have one more night where it's just us."

Jonas watched me with knowing eyes then smiled that gentle lilt of his lips that I loved. "It's not going to be just one night, baby. Something this good is meant to be."

Despite his words, he pulled me close and covered my lips with his. I could taste the saltiness of my tears mingling with his distinctive flavor but didn't stop. Instead, I held him closer. If I'd learned anything over the course of my life, it was that right now was all I had. Each moment was to be savored, and there was so much to taste and touch and hold.

"You're so strong," I whispered. My cheeks warmed when our eyes met. "I love everything about you."

"Stop. You're going to make me blush."

I nuzzled the strong pecs that I loved to rest my head against. His sharp intake of breath when my lips skimmed over his nipple thrilled me. With one hand he reached over his head and yanked his shirt off. Immediately my hands were out, caressing the silken skin and pressing against the hard muscle beneath.

"I love your hair and those big blue eyes. Nothing in the world affects me like seeing those eyes watching me. You make me stand taller, JJ."

Determined not to spend any more time worrying, I tugged at his belt. The hard length pressing against the front of his jeans was practically pointing at me already. Maybe once I had him in my hand, I could forget all the bad things lurking in the background and just enjoy this precious connection we'd forged together.

"Hey, it's all going to be okay." I covered his hand with mine and together we slid the zipper of his jeans down. He stood briefly to push them off, almost tripping as he rushed to remove his boots.

I laughed and then followed his lead, our eyes never leaving each other as articles of clothing flew around us, landing in piles on the floor. We came together on the bed in a pile of naked skin, seeking mouths, and greedy hands.

Jonas let out a deep moan when my hands landed on his ass and squeezed.

"Damn, you don't play fair."

I bit his ear. "No, I don't. You know what I want."

He reached over to the nightstand and pulled out a condom. "A guy tries to have some finesse and no one appreciates it."

I helped him put the condom on, pushing it down his length with gentle strokes. "Oh I appreciate all of your finesse."

He clenched his teeth. "You really don't play fair. Your hands feel amazing on me."

Suddenly he turned us so that I was straddling him. Turnabout was fair play, and I found myself hovering right over his hard cock, the length brushing against my clit every time I breathed.

"Ride me, baby. Show me how much you want it."

Hearing him ask for it was so arousing. I loved how we could say anything to each other.

"That's what you want?" I teased, lowering myself to rock back and forth against him. His hands landed on my hips and I gasped as the tip of his cock slipped in.

Teasing him had become my own personal torture. So I decided I'd earned my satisfaction. Placing my hands firmly on his chest, I bore down, taking him all the way in. My muscles clamped down on him immediately, the erotic drag through my tight muscles making me shiver.

"Every time," Jonas gritted out. "You fucking destroy me. Every single time."

I panted as I worked my hips, every thrust hitting right in the perfect spot. All the while his hands roamed my skin, making my senses sing and spreading the tingling sensations all over.

"God, Jonas. I feel you everywhere."

His eyes glittered with satisfaction. "That's what I want. I want you to feel how much I love you so you'll always know."

And I could feel it, with every movement of his hips and every brush of his fingertips. Love was dripping all over us, and I wanted to roll in it until it was a permanent stain on my skin.

"I do feel it," I gasped.

Then it was all too much, and the orgasm that had been building all along broke over me like a tidal wave. I slapped a hand over my mouth, trying to keep from screaming, but Jonas leaned up and swallowed the sound with his lips.

And as I broke apart, he put me back together with every touch.

———

Jonas

I CALLED on all the strength I had to hang on through her orgasm. It was captivating to watch JJ when she was so vulnerable, a view that I was privileged to witness. And one I hoped I'd see multiple times before we were through.

It took a few minutes before she opened her eyes again. Her hair was flying all around her head, and her gorgeous blue eyes were glassy.

"You didn't..." she looked down at me in confusion.

I pulled her forward until she collapsed on my chest. "Oh you didn't think I was going to let you off that easily, did you? I plan on keeping you up all night."

Her soft laugh puffed warm across my chest. "You're going to kill me! I can barely catch my breath."

I flipped us, ignoring her squeal. I was going to get so much shit for this from the guys, but I didn't care.

JJ covered her eyes with her hands. "Did everyone hear me scream again? Tell me that was quiet."

Even though I'd just been having a similar thought, I wasn't going to bullshit her. She was too smart for that anyway.

"Probably. But who cares? Hell, let them listen. Maybe they'll pick up a few pointers."

JJ giggled, her eyes shining. "I'll be sure to mention that to Oskar tomorrow morning."

That got a chuckle out of me, too. "This whole situation is crazy but honestly, I'm grateful that we all ended up here. There's no one else I'd want watching my back in this situation."

She sobered instantly. "I know. Maybe that's how I need to look at things. That I'm exactly where I'm meant to be." Her fingers trailed through my hair and I could have purred like a cat at the feeling.

"You're meant to be with me. I knew that the first time I heard that smart mouth."

"Like yours is any better." JJ opened her mouth to say something else, but the words dissolved into a soft sigh as I kissed her on the breastbone.

"What was that?" I asked innocently. Then I trailed my lips over the dents of her ribs and licked gently over her belly button.

I felt JJ's fingers tangling in my hair and holding me against her. I grumbled in appreciation as her legs fell open. One large hand on her abdomen held her still as I licked her clit delicately.

"Oh!" JJ shuddered so hard she almost dislodged my hand.

I fucking loved pleasuring her this way, surrounded by her warm, sugary, female scent and hearing her helpless little cries. There was no greater feeling of sexual mastery than to have my woman melting beneath my tongue and so lost in pleasure that she screamed my name.

I worked her faster, flicking her clit with the exact rhythm I knew would take her up quickly. Then just when she was about to fall over the edge, I throttled back, licking all around and kissing her mound gently. She let out a soft sound of disgruntlement but was soon whimpering again when I attacked her clit. I took her even higher and closer this time before backing off again.

Her fingers clenched in my hair so hard I saw stars. "What are you doing?"

"Easy, baby. It'll be even better if you work for it." I nipped at her belly and she moaned.

"I don't want to work for it. This is torture."

"Erotic torture." I pushed a finger gently through the clenching muscles that were hungrily looking for something to grasp.

Her head fell back again. "Yes, just like that."

"I'm going to give you what you need. I'll always give you what you need," I whispered, seeing how my soft words stoked her desire even higher. She nodded frantically as I continued whispering to her, and I saw the exact moment when she lost control.

And I loved watching the only woman I'd ever truly loved.

JJ came down slowly, blinking sleepily at him. "You are entirely too good at that."

I grinned. "You definitely know how to make a guy feel good. But it's no hardship licking that sweet pussy, baby. I plan on making a meal of you every chance I can. So get used to screaming."

JJ covered her eyes with her hands but it didn't hide her red cheeks. "You know, Lucia said we're perfect for each other. She's totally right. Because I didn't think anyone had a mouth as filthy as mine!"

I grabbed another condom, cursing softly when I saw there was only one left. From now on, I was buying those things in bulk. I needed the lifetime supply because I was for damn sure going to be making love to her for at least that long.

The image of me as a randy eighty year old still chasing after JJ to squeeze her ass made me smile.

"You love me filthy."

JJ's satisfied smile was almost as good as an orgasm.

"You bet your ass I do."

CHAPTER THIRTY-FIVE

Jonas

The next few days we existed in a state of deliberate avoidance. JJ was busy pretending that we weren't plotting a dangerous mission to find her ex. I pretended that the entire situation wasn't happening and made it a point to shower JJ with affection, reassurance and plenty of nights distracting her with sex so good that I didn't think she gave a damn who heard her screaming.

But like all good things, it had to come to an end. JJ chewed her thumbnail next to me as we watched Noah kissing Lucia goodbye.

"We're going to get this asshole, and then I'll be home before you wake up. Okay?" Noah stroked her face and looked into her eyes so intimately that I was embarrassed to watch.

JJ turned to face me. "I think this is a mistake."

I kept my face placid. This was a conversation we'd had many times over the past few days. Maybe she thought if she kept saying it, we'd change our approach. But we were following intel Matthias had found. JJ was upset that we were going in the opposite direction of Bliss, where she was pretty sure David would be hiding out. We'd already sent someone to check it out, but there was nothing there except a quiet town with friendly inhabitants.

"I know, baby. And I am going to look forward to saying 'I told you so' tomorrow morning."

"Wake me when you get in. I don't care how late it is," she insisted.

I wasn't fooling myself that she would get any sleep anyway. More than likely she and Lucia would stay up, binge watch some shows on Netflix, and pretend they weren't both dying inside wondering if their men were okay. I understood because I understood how JJ worked. And I loved that she cared about me enough to worry, even if I hated to put her through this.

"Okay. I'll wake you."

"I still really think that you or Noah should have gone to Bliss to check things out. You guys are going in the complete opposite direction."

I nodded. "I know. But the trail is hotter where we're going. You know how good Matthias is at this stuff. He wouldn't lead us astray. This is our best chance to end this."

JJ sighed. "That's what I want. For this to be over and for things to go back to the way they used to be."

Lucia's voice interrupted from behind us. "You mean when I was running from a stalker and almost got kidnapped?"

JJ turned and accepted a hug from her friend. "I guess there's no normal for us, huh?"

"Probably not. But that's okay. I'll settle for safe and happy. Normal is boring."

Noah approached just then. I could tell he was also armed to the teeth. Oskar appeared behind him with his grim face on. Dylan and Rafe stood at the doorway to the room but didn't enter. A few seconds later, Matthias appeared from down the hallway where his room was, dressed in all black and looking as lethal as I had ever seen him.

"I guess it's time," JJ muttered. She turned and hugged me tightly. Her softness pressed against my jacket, bumping against all the weapons underneath.

The thought of her pressing against all that metal sent a cold chill through me. What if this was the last time I'd ever get to hold her like this? My heart started racing, and I sucked in a desperate breath. I wished and prayed to a God I wasn't even sure I believed in before finally releasing her. Her arms slid from around my waist slowly. She didn't seem any more excited about letting go than I was, but at the same time, I didn't want to leave her worried or upset.

This was going to be tricky enough as it was, even with a whole team going up against David. The thought of her being upset would only distract me. We all needed to be on our A-game tonight.

"Give me a kiss for luck," I whispered.

She leaned up to kiss me. Maybe she could read the worry in my eyes because she pasted on a smile and said, "Okay, I think Lucia and I are going to have a movie marathon."

Noah nodded at her appreciatively before kissing Lucia again. "That sounds good. Dylan will be watching over Nonna, just in case. Ryan will be here if you need anything."

"You mean he got stuck being our babysitter," Lucia teased.

Noah only smiled before motioning to the other guys. They all fell in line behind him as they left the room. Lucia grabbed JJ's hand and squeezed hard.

I turned back and walked up to her. "I just want you to know that we're not giving up. Even if this trail goes cold, we'll go check out Bliss. But no matter what, we'll get him. Okay?"

She nodded. "Okay. I trust you."

I kissed her quickly and then ran out after the others.

———

Jessica

AS SOON AS the door closed behind Jonas, Lucia let go of my hand. She turned to me with a gleam in her eye.

"We aren't really trusting them to do this, are we?"

I snorted. "Hell no. I just have no idea what to do yet. But we're definitely not going to sit here and watch movies like good little womenfolk, or whatever."

Lucia snickered. "Good. I was starting to get worried about you. Things are going to be tricky with Delaney here."

We both turned surreptitiously to look at Ryan. He was moving around the kitchen making a sandwich. When he felt both of our eyes on him, he paused and raised his eyebrows in question.

I waved prettily. "This is going to be a problem," I muttered out of the side of my mouth. "He might be younger, but all of these guys are paranoid as hell. It won't be easy to get around him."

Lucia hummed in agreement. "I know. But I think I have an idea. I just need to make a call."

While Lucia went to her room, I figured it would make the most sense to proceed as if the movie marathon was actually going to take place. I gathered several throw blankets and brought them to the couch then queued up Netflix to a show that I'd never seen before. When Ryan looked up again, I walked to the kitchen.

"Do you want to share some popcorn with us?"

Ryan nodded. "Sure. What are you guys going to watch?"

Lucia came into the room with Isabella balanced on her hip. "Weren't we going to watch that breastfeeding documentary, JJ?" The innocent look on her face didn't waver as Ryan's expression changed to one of horror.

"Oh, no. That's okay. I'll let you two have some girl time." He snatched up his sandwich and left the kitchen.

A few seconds later, a door closed down the hallway. I burst into laughter. "You seriously just scarred the poor boy for life."

Lucia grinned. "Desperate times. If our plan is going to work, we need him off kilter."

"Plan? We have a plan now?"

"We do. Nonna is coming over to watch the baby and then we are going to go check out Bliss, Connecticut."

"Uh oh. When I said I wanted to do something, I didn't mean something that would put you in danger." I didn't want to lead my friend into trouble. I didn't want to think about Lucia exposed to David's special brand of crazy.

"Not me, but you'll put yourself in danger?" Lucia demanded. "No way. We've been friends a long time. If you wanted to keep me away from trouble, well I have to tell you, that ship sailed the day we met. And I wouldn't have it any other way."

I shook my head. "Noah is going to kill us. What am I saying? Jonas will too. That's if we can even get out of here. Ryan might allow Nonna to take the baby since Dylan is covering her. But there's no way he's going to let us walk out of here without him. Which means we're not getting anywhere near Bliss tonight."

Just then there was a knock on the door. Ryan came from the back immediately. If he was surprised to see us standing around talking instead of watching movies the way he'd expected, he didn't show it. After confirming who it was, he opened the door to a beaming Nonna.

"There's my bambina!" Nonna walked forward with her arms outstretched. Isabella let out a full belly laugh and tried to throw herself out of her mother's arms.

I closed the door and then smiled at the older woman. Nonna had all of the men at Blake Security wrapped around her little finger. Or maybe mesmerized by the delicious homemade Italian food she brought over all the time.

"Ryan, I brought tiramisu. Dylan is bringing it up. I know how much you love it."

Ryan practically melted into a puddle of drool. "Tiramisu? I do love it. Thank you so much, Mrs. DeMarco."

Nonna rewarded him with a sweet smile. "I told you to call me Nonna."

Ryan nodded. "Yes, ma'am."

Dylan appeared then carrying an aluminum pan, and Ryan followed him to the kitchen. As soon as the men were out of hearing range, Nonna looked at us sternly.

"I expect you two to be careful. And watchful. I wouldn't help you if I didn't believe you would be."

"Yes, ma'am." I replied instinctively. No matter how old we got, Nonna DeMarco would always be the boss of us. "What is the plan, if you guys don't mind me asking?"

Lucia leaned forward. "Nonna brought the cake to distract Ryan. Now that we're all in the same place, Dylan will leave since he was technically supposed to be off duty tonight. Once he's gone, we'll trick Ryan into going into the panic room and then lock him in there."

I winced. "Damn, he's going to get in so much trouble."

Lucia looked uncomfortable, too. "I know. But I won't let Noah fire him. I don't care what I have to do."

Nonna raised her eyebrows. "That's enough about that, young lady."

We all chuckled together.

"Ok, so we just have to wait for Dylan and Ryan to come up with the idea of Dylan going home on their own. They aren't going to do it if we suggest it."

Nonna smiled slyly. "Don't worry about that. I took care of it."

"What do you mean you took care of it?" Lucia asked suspiciously.

We all froze at the sound of footsteps. Dylan and Ryan appeared. Ryan was holding a paper bowl filled with tiramisu and eating it noisily.

"Well, if you don't mind, I think I'll take off. Nonna fed me a really big dinner and I'm exhausted. Since she's planning to spend the night here so the girls can watch movies, we both don't need to be here, right?"

Ryan nodded, never taking his eyes off his cake. "Go on. You were supposed to be off anyway. Noah won't care. Matthias upgraded the security here, so once I turn the external alarms on, this place is safer than the Pentagon."

Dylan waved at us. "I'll see you ladies tomorrow then."

"Good night, dear!" Nonna called out. When she finally looked at Lucia and me and saw the looks on our faces, she huffed. "What? I may be old but I know how to knock a man out. His stomach. I stuffed that boy so full of gnocchi it'll be a wonder if he doesn't fall asleep before he makes it down the stairwell."

I was impressed. "Way to go, Nonna!"

Lucia glanced behind us. "One down, one to go."

To make our story more believable, we moved into the living room and turned on our Netflix show. Nonna bounced the baby on her lap and after an hour, I thought I'd lose my mind. What were we doing? Ryan had shown no sign of relaxing, I'd seen him upright typing on one of Matthias's spare computers when I'd gone to the bathroom.

Then Nonna stood and handed the baby to Lucia. "Young man! Yoo-hoo!"

Lucia and I exchanged confused looks but didn't move from our perch on the couch. Whatever Nonna was up to, we definitely weren't getting in her way.

"Yes, ma'am." Ryan appeared in the doorway to the room.

"I need your help carrying out the surprise present I brought for my granddaughter." Nonna marched down the hall, Ryan following.

Lucia leaned over. "She had Dylan bring in some big box

when they came. But I'm not sure what that has to do with her plan."

A few moments later, there was a loud "Hey!" and then the sound of something crashing.

"What was that?" Lucia gasped. We both stood and rushed down the hallway toward Noah and Lucia's room.

I gaped at the scene. Nonna stood next to the panic room holding one of Lucia's fancy stilettos. A loud bang on the other side of the panic room door startled us all. Ryan's words were muffled, but it was easy to tell he was cursing up a storm in there.

"Oh, he is really upset with me," Nonna murmured.

"How did you get him in there?" Lucia asked.

Nonna looked satisfied with herself. "I asked him to lift that big box. While his back was turned, I opened the panic room and then pushed him in. I disabled the lock pad with this!" she held up Lucia's shoe.

Suddenly she narrowed her eyes at us. "Now, before you go anywhere, you girls are taking weapons, right?"

I glanced behind me to see the keypad to the panic room was cracked. I looked back to Nonna with new eyes. "Wow. Remind me to never get on your bad side."

Nonna ambled over and patted my cheek. "There's no bad side for you, *cara*. You're family."

CHAPTER THIRTY-SIX

Jonas

It felt like it took forever to get there.

At least that was how it seemed to me. Noah took the lead as usual, so Matthias, Oskar, and I rode along. Rafe was right behind us, driving a second Jeep in case we needed alternate transportation out of there.

I didn't like to think of anything going wrong, but after years of tactical training, it was second nature to prepare for the worst. Because no matter what, we were going home.

"Okay, so once we're there, Rafe goes in first. We'll hang back while he scouts. Once we have confirmation that Chamaeleon is there, we go in hot. This shit ends tonight," Noah growled.

Matthias spoke up from the back. "All indications point to him crashing with an old friend in the Bronx. He tried to cover his tracks, but several people in the neighborhood were able to ID him."

I blew out a breath. "Good. This shit needs to end. Then we can go home."

Once we got closer, Rafe's Jeep split off and went down a

different street. Noah pulled around until he found a quiet street where we could park. Once he cut the engine, it was still as a tomb.

"Well, hell. Somebody say something," Oskar finally drawled.

Noah cracked a smile. "You'd think I employed a bunch of kids. Shut the hell up so we can focus."

Oskar held up his hands. "Just trying to lighten the mood a bit."

Another few minutes went by in silence before Noah's phone beeped. "Yeah. What do you mean?"

I rubbed my forehead, calling on all my strength not to snatch the phone from Noah's hand.

"No one's there?" Noah turned in his seat to stare at Matthias incredulously.

The kid paled slightly. "But I was so sure." He pulled out a laptop from somewhere and started typing frantically. "No, no, no. This morning when I checked, there was a lease on file at this building for Ernest Fairway."

I squinted, trying to remember. "Ernest is the guy David met while overseas, right?"

Matthias continued typing like a man possessed. "Yes. But now I see nothing in the landlord's system to indicate Fairway ever lived here at all."

I slammed a fist into the dash. "Motherfucker! He's slipped right under our noses again. I promised JJ we'd get this sonofabitch. I promised her she'd be safe."

Noah's voice was soft, the kind you'd use to approach a wounded animal. "And you will. Jonas, listen to me. You will keep her safe. We all will."

Oskar's big beefy hand landed on my shoulder. "You know we've got your back."

I did know that. But at the moment that was poor consolation since the man terrorizing my woman was still out there and apparently about five steps ahead of us all the time.

How the hell was I supposed to keep JJ safe when I wasn't entirely sure I could outsmart someone like David West? The dude was obsessed and diabolical, a bad combination. Not to mention, he had unlimited time to carry out his plans. None of us knew how long he'd been plotting this.

All we knew for sure was that West was obsessed with Rafe's life. And that ultimate obsession had also encompassed JJ. If he'd gone through the trouble to leave clues to lead us here, there must have been a reason.

"I need to call JJ. Make sure she's okay." I pulled my phone out and dialed her number. Every ring that went unanswered only ratcheted my fear higher.

"Nothing?" Noah asked. His brow furrowed and he pulled out his own phone.

I watched as he finally hung up. "Lucia didn't answer either?"

"No. But they're probably just watching television and can't hear the phone. You know how Lucia likes to talk through every movie. Send Delaney a text. I'm sure they're fine."

I blew out a breath. "Okay, first let's figure out where we went wrong tonight. Because I really don't want to go home with nothing."

Matthias saluted me. "On it. This might not be the right place, but we'll figure it out. He can't hide forever."

I wasn't worried about Chamaeleon hiding forever because that didn't fit in with his goal. I was worried about him hiding long enough for JJ to relax her guard.

And then taking her away.

———

Jessica

I PEERED over the steering wheel and tried to follow the directions Lucia called out.

"No, left here. And then down this street and one more right."

It was dark and there weren't that many streetlights. My churning stomach combined with the absolute certainty that this was a really bad idea made it pretty difficult to navigate.

"This is it!" Lucia put her phone in her lap. "This is Rafe's old house."

I didn't park at the house, but instead kept driving and then circled around. We parked farther down the street. The house was an adorable little rambler. Exactly the kind of place that David had always talked about owning.

"Maybe we should call the guys," I finally said.

"Oh they already called," Lucia admitted.

"Wait, what? When?"

"While you were driving. I hit 'ignore' on both of our phones."

I shook my head. "I'm surprised they haven't sent out a search party for us." Then I winced. "They probably think we're okay since Ryan was with us."

Lucia sighed. "I do feel really bad about that part. But we had to do this. I'm not about to sit back while some psycho torments my best friend. And the guys didn't even listen when you told them about David wanting to live in Connecticut."

I knew she was right. If we'd left it up to the guys, we'd likely have missed any chance of nailing David before he moved to a new location. But we had to be careful about this. We'd just sneak up and take a look, enough to get hard proof he was there. Then we'd run like hell and call in the guys.

I was a strong, independent woman. But that didn't mean I was willing to put myself in danger to prove it. The guys had way more experience with this kind of thing. Lucia and I could restrict ourselves to the surveillance portion of the security business.

"Okay, did you bring the binoculars?"

"Yes! I did. These are some new, heat sensing binoculars that Noah was really excited about. I also grabbed this!" Lucia held up the gun she'd taken from the weapons room.

I held up a hand. "Okay, let's save that for hopefully never. This is not going to be some kind of female James Bond -Charlie's Angels situation. We are going to spy on him, but I don't plan on getting anywhere close to David ever again."

"Of course. I just brought it because... well, you never know. Rafe taught me that." Lucia put the gun back and handed me one of the heat sensing binoculars.

I trained it on the house down the street. Nothing.

"Are they supposed to light up or do something?"

Lucia put her pair to her face. "I'm not sure. I hate to say it, but we probably need to be closer."

I gulped. "Okay, let's get out. Leave the car open so we can run back and jump inside quickly if we need to. But we'll walk up the street and see if we can detect anyone inside. If no one is there, we might be doing all of this for nothing."

Lucia took off her seatbelt. "I don't think it's for nothing. At least we're checking out a valid lead. If he's not here, it gives Matthias one less place to focus on."

We left the car unlocked and closed the doors as quietly as possible. It was a bright night, the moon shining directly overhead, making up for the lack of streetlights. The house in question only had one light on up front, and there were no cars in the driveway.

"What if he drives up while we're walking by?" Lucia whispered.

I had just had a similar thought. "Keep an eye out behind us. If you see anyone driving up, we can knock on one of these other doors and pretend we're lost or something."

Luckily no one drove up or down the street as we were walking. I raised my binoculars and pointed them at the house. I pulled the binoculars down with a frown.

"Are these supposed to do something? I don't see anything."

Lucia shrugged. "I think you're supposed to see things change color when they detect heat."

"Well, if that's true then no one is here. I don't see anything."

"Oh, dang. I really want to get some proof so we can get the guys to take this seriously. I wasn't expecting to actually see him or anything, but a sign would be nice," Lucia complained.

I couldn't help but laugh at that. "A sign that says *super secret psycho man's hideout?*"

"Yes. Exactly like that," Lucia added.

I wasn't sure what came over me but before I knew it I was marching toward the house. No one was there, I'd already seen that. So it wasn't that big of a deal to get closer and look inside. Maybe we'd see something that could prove David was there if we took a quick look. But I was tired of waiting and worrying about when he'd pop up. This might be my only chance to outsmart him.

"JJ, what are you doing?" Lucia whispered frantically as she followed me around to the back of the house.

"He used to always say he'd hide his keys under a planter," I muttered. Then just like I'd conjured it, I saw it. A huge planter right by the back door. I lifted it and took out the small silver key underneath.

"You aren't going–"

"Inside. Yes, I am," I stated before Lucia could even finish. "For once we're ahead in this twisted game, and I'm not going to let this opportunity pass me by. You can wait in the car if you want."

Lucia punched my arm. "I'm not leaving you. I'll keep a lookout while you search the place. Plus, I brought this. Just in case, remember?" She held up the gun.

I blew out a breath. "Okay, let's do this."

I opened the back door with the key and then paused, listening. It was quiet and still. We moved through the house quickly, not wasting any time. Lucia posted herself by the back window while I searched the front room. There were piles of mail on the side table addressed to Charlie Townsend.

Another alias? Then I lifted the cushions of the couch to see if he'd hidden anything there.

A soft sound behind me made me freeze in place. But when I turned, nothing was there.

"Lucia!" I hissed into the shadows.

Then one of the shadows moved and formed a familiar shape.

"David," I breathed.

CHAPTER THIRTY-SEVEN

Jonas

"Jesus, Ryan, what the hell is up?"

"What the hell is up is that I've been calling you the last two hours. Reception in here sucks."

I sighed and pinched the bridge of my nose. "Sorry we went radio silent. "What's up? Is everyone okay?"

"No, everyone is not okay. The girls, they fucking locked me in the panic room."

I shook my head. "Wait a sec, let me conference Rafe in."

After pushing a few buttons, Rafe answered with a grumbled "What?"

I put the phone on speaker so everyone in the car could hear. "Okay, Delaney repeat that."

"They locked me in the panic room. Lucia, and JJ. And Nonna. The old lady helped!"

Next to me, Noah sat up straight. "What did Nonna do? Where the hell is Isabella?"

Ryan's exasperation was clear on the other end of the line. "That's what I'm trying to tell you. Lucia had the old woman come over to spend time with the baby. Since they were all in one place, Dylan went home. Next thing I know, Nonna asked me to carry something in your room for her. I went in to help her, and before I knew it, she'd shoved me in the panic room and did something to the lock so I can't reset it. I'm locked in here. Fucking battery's dying to boot."

I stared at the phone and then lifted my gaze to Noah. "You know, I wish I could say I was surprised, but I'm sure this was Lucia and JJ's idea."

Noah chuckled. "You might be surprised. Nonna is a pistol. Hey Rafe, any idea what your grandmother is up too?"

Rafe's voice grumbled over the line. "No idea. But we need to find those girls. Isabella is safe. Nonna would never risk her safety. So we just have to find the girls."

Oskar shook Matthias awake. The kid jerked, and his right hand immediately went to palm one of his blades. "Easy, kid. Need your hacking skills not your slicing skills."

Matthias blinked for several seconds as if trying to orient himself before he nodded. "Yep, on it." He pulled out his laptop. "What am I looking for?"

"You're looking for Lucia and JJ."

Matthias frowned. "I was out for all of five minutes. What the hell happened to them now?"

I shook my head. "I don't think something happened to them, I think they happened to Delaney. For some reason they wanted out of the penthouse. So they locked him in the panic room."

A slow grin spread over Matthias's lips. "No shit?"

Noah chuckled even as he made a left turn. "No shit. Can you track down the girls? I just hope both of them haven't forgotten everything I've ever said about safety and have left their damn phones on."

"Even if they have, Lucia has likely forgotten about the tracker you stuck in her purse. So we can find them that way."

I blinked my eyes in amazement. "Noah, you're still tracking Lucia even after she found out last year?"

Noah didn't look the slightest bit sheepish. "Well, I wasn't. And then that idiot took my baby. So I turned the tracking back on."

I chuckled. "Man, I hope we find them. Because I want to see the look Lucia gives you when she finds out that you're still tracking her movements."

"Man, shut up. You worry about your woman, and I'll worry about mine."

"Yeah, if only that was the way it worked. Because the moment you start yelling at yours for pulling a stunt this stupid, mine's gonna jump on the bandwagon and start chewing your ass out."

Noah grumbled. "Yeah, you're right about that."

Matthias pulled up their location and cursed softly under his breath. "I have them. Neither one of you is gonna like where they are."

"Out with it, Matthias," I prompted.

"Bliss, Connecticut. Looks like they've gone hunting on their own."

Rafe cursed. "They've gone to my old house."

Matthias nodded. "I guess JJ got fed up with us not looking into it."

I took the laptop out of the kid's hand and stared at the monitor. "Oh, for the love of Christ."

Lucia and JJ had gone after Chamaeleon on their own.

Jessica

"I KNEW you'd come back. I bought this house for you."

I backed away. "David. You don't want to do this."

"Do what? Have you? You are mine. I was sent away for a while. But, I'm back now. And there's no reason we can't be together."

I frantically searched for a weapon. Something. Anything. Lucia had the gun. I hadn't wanted anything to do with it. So all I had was a nail file in my back pocket as part of the lock picking kit we'd brought. Such a dumb idea.

What made us think we could be in and out and he wouldn't notice? What the hell had I been thinking?

You were thinking about keeping Jonas safe.

You are Jessica freaking Jones. You are smart. Think your way through this. He wants you. He's not going to hurt you.

Lucia was protected because she had her gun. Which meant I just had to keep him talking until Lucia could shoot him. Yeah, okay that was a plan. Maybe not the most thought-out one I'd ever had, but hey, in a pinch it wasn't bad.

Maybe not, but I did have my phone. And one thing I was good at was texting with my eyes closed. I put my hands behind my back even as I stepped backward trying to keep him talking.

"David, listen to me. We don't want to do this. You and I, we don't work. You weren't happy with me anyway. I never made you happy."

"I decide what makes me happy. And it's not about happiness. I own you."

I hoped I'd managed to unlock my phone and had found the app properly by memory. Lucia was the last person I'd texted, so she should get the message.

Send help.

He's got me in the kitchen.

"Why did you have to do it? Hook up with that guy? He's weak. He's not as strong as I am."

"He's stronger than you are. He's a better man. He's kinder, and I love him. And he's better in bed."

Okay, maybe that was going too far, but the truth was the truth.

David lunged for me, and I scooted out of the way. But I wasn't fast enough, and he managed to grab me by the wrist, hauling me up against him. Then he grabbed the front of my dress and lifted me easily off the ground.

"You were always such a lying whore. You know I'm the best you've ever had or ever will have again. I am Rafe fucking DeMarco."

I blinked at him. Jesus, he'd lost it. Having me call him Rafe during sex was twisted enough, but he really believed that he was Rafe. That was —sick.

Yeah, any way I looked at this, we had arrived at cray-cray town.

"You are going to live here, and you're going to be my wife. We are going to raise children in this house. Just like the life you always wanted with me. We're going to live in the house I grew up in. I'm going to have the one thing that he couldn't have."

"You've got it wrong. I didn't love Rafe. He was a crush. This obsession you have, you can't see the truth. Rafe and me... we were never a thing. Your obsession with him, it's why you sought me out. Lucia was too broken. But I was the perfect target. I know this isn't about me. This is about Rafe."

"No, no, no, no." He pressed me up against the wall, and I tried to struggle out of his grip. "I am Rafe. We are going to have children in this house. Two of them, and we're going to name them Rafe Jr. and Lucia."

"You're a sick bastard."

"I'll be as sick as you want. Is that what you're into now? You know I bugged Castillo's apartment, right? You like being controlled. I know that much. You like being told what to do, you like being dominated, you like having control stripped away."

"You're an asshole of the lowest order. I hate everything about you."

He bared his teeth, and I could see the fury written all over his face. He banged me against the wall, and pain ricocheted through my skull, making my teeth ache.

Somewhere in the back of my mind, the self-preservationist part of my brain told me to be quiet.

To stop talking.

To not make it any worse.

But I couldn't help it.

"You realize you're a little-dick motherfucker right? Shit, I have balls bigger than yours. The fact that you have to scare and terrorize a woman to make her be with you makes you pathetic. It makes you sad."

Again he banged me against the wall.

Fuck that hurt.

Then I saw a flicker from the dining room. I could only hope, I could only pray that it was help. So I kept him distracted.

"Do you know that every time we had sex, I used to imagine it was Rafe? I mean I didn't know what sex could be, and all I really wanted was that loved feeling, but I hated having sex with you. Every single time, it was awful. God knew I never once, not once, had an orgasm. And you know what? All Jonas has to do is look at me, and orgasm is imminent. You could never do that. Because you're half the man he is. Hell, you want to borrow my brass balls for a second?"

He lifted me again, ready to bang my head into the wall. But then his grip eased on the front of my dress, and my feet hit the ground.

David sagged, and Lucia stood over him holding a metal pipe. "That's for taking my baby."

I met her gaze. "Oh my God. I cannot believe you did that. Although, that's what I call laying pipe."

Lucia stared at the metal in her hand, her lips twitching with a hint of a smile. "I think he's been living in the basement. It's where I found this. There's only one room with anything in it. I couldn't figure how to get the safety off the damn gun, so I had to get closer. I'm sorry. Are you okay?"

She reached for me, and I winced. "I am. Now let's get out of here."

But as I stumbled over his body heading for the dining room and the front door, David grabbed Lucia's ankle. "You're not going anywhere."

Lucia went sprawling, and so did the pipe and the gun. "JJ, take those. Run."

The hell I was running without my best friend. I picked up the gun and checked the safety. It was jammed. With all my might, I pushed up to release it and heard the click. Then I aimed.

God, the last thing on Earth I wanted to do was hit Lucia. And Lucia was putting up one hell of a fight. Elbows, knees, biting, scratching. There was blood everywhere. But when David had her pinned down with his hand on her throat, I didn't even think. I just fired.

The loud crack reverberated throughout the room. But I didn't stop there.

I remembered every single time he'd ever lifted his hand to hit me, every single time he'd ever held me down and ignored my protests about how I didn't want to sleep with him.

I remembered every single time I'd been made to cower, every single time he'd deliberately hurt me, and I fired again.

Crack.

I thought about all the things he'd said to me about how I was pathetic and sad, and the times he'd told me that I wasn't beautiful.

Crack.

I'd fired a bullet into his chest, one in his shoulder, and another in his neck, but the rage was still in his eyes as he continued to choke my best friend.

Terror shook my body as I spoke. "I only came here to tell you to stop. This has to end. You don't have to die today."

He sneered at me then stared down at Lucia. And Lucia just gasped for breath.

"I will never stop."

I knew he wasn't lying, that every word out of his mouth was the truth. Then with calm in my heart, I released another bullet that hit him right between the eyes.

CHAPTER THIRTY-EIGHT

Jonas

I was frantic. It baffled me that anything got done over the next hour because my brain felt like it had been through a blender. JJ was out there, possibly in danger, and I was too far away to help.

"Can't we go any faster?" I barked at Noah, who was currently driving the car practically at warp speed.

The look he shot me would have turned a lesser man to stone. As it was, I felt my balls shrivel a few sizes.

"I know where your head is at, brother," Noah said in a deceptively calm voice. "My woman is out there, too. You know I'm going as fast as I can without this Jeep growing wings."

I took a deep breath and then another. Attacking the people on my side wasn't helping the situation. Plus, I knew how we all felt about JJ and Lucia. Those women were special to each of us in different ways. There was no other team more invested in bringing them home safely. But still, they didn't have their entire lives wrapped up in this outcome.

Well, Noah did.

But the others, they had no idea. Until you felt that way

about someone, you couldn't understand how their safety and happiness was the key to everything being all right in your world.

"There's a chance we're panicking for nothing," Noah continued. "Lucia wouldn't put them in direct danger, not after all of the safety lectures she's gotten from me. If anything, they're probably just driving around that area looking for clues."

"Maybe," I hedged. But in my heart, I knew that if my JJ was out there, she wasn't hiding in the car. Crazy woman that she was, she wouldn't approach with caution, she'd charge straight into trouble and tell everyone there to go to hell.

Jesus.

"What the hell were they thinking?" I muttered.

"I hate to be the voice of reason," Matthias began. "But they were probably pissed that we didn't act on the information JJ offered right away."

I roared, "Well, why the hell didn't we?"

My heart felt like it was bouncing around in my chest like it wanted out. Everything was out of control and I wasn't sure exactly what I was supposed to be doing. All I knew was that whatever I did might not be enough. Because I knew what kind of trouble Jessica Jones was capable of getting into.

Oskar's meaty hand landed on my shoulder, probably the only thing strong enough to keep me from launching out of the seat. "We've always done the best we could with the information we had at the time," he said. "It didn't seem likely that Chamaeleon would be hiding out playing house in some sleepy little Connecticut town. But seeing how crafty this dude is, maybe that's why it makes sense. He's always doing what we don't expect."

"And information changes," Matthias interjected. "Because when I searched before, there was nothing to indicate that Chamaeleon was there. But I just got the utilities records back, and Rafe's old house is drawing more power than it should considering that the owners are out of the country."

I swiveled in my seat. "Shouldn't there be no power if no one is currently living there?"

"There's always a residual amount drawn as long as the power is connected. But there are spikes here at night, which definitely indicate that someone is using it. Could be squatters but..." Matthias shrugged.

"But you don't think so?" I pressed.

"With this new information, the fact that the other hideout is empty, and his obsession with Rafe, I don't think so. I think he's been there for a while, plotting."

"And JJ tried to tell us." I rubbed a hand over my face. If I couldn't get to her in time, I would never forgive myself. She'd tried to tell us. She'd trusted us to protect her.

No, she trusted *me* to protect her. And I let her down.

"What the hell are we walking into?" I asked.

"It could be anything. Maybe we've taken him off guard and this will be a quick, in-and-out, take-him-out operation," Oskar answered.

"Or?" I was almost afraid to ask about the other option. Because I had a gut feeling that the "or" included JJ and Lucia putting themselves in danger. Or was not something I was prepared to face.

Apparently Oskar felt the same way. "Let's hope 'or' doesn't happen. We need to find this dude and fast. Before he realizes that JJ and Lucia are looking for him."

Noah slowed as we exited the highway and entered the small town of Bliss. From what I knew, there wasn't a whole lot to the place. Small country ramblers, a few mom and pop stores, and a whole lot of fields. Not the kind of place where you'd expect a psychotic, ex-secret agent with a weird bro-crush to reside.

"We're going to proceed with the same amount of caution

we'd use under any other circumstances," Noah stated, giving me a pointed look. "Going in with guns blazing could backfire if he's got the girls."

Rationally, I knew he was right. But it didn't quell the urge to palm two guns and bust through the door in a blaze of glory.

"We'll be tight," Oskar assured Noah. "I just texted Rafe to approach from behind as usual. Then we can go in the front and fan out in teams of two."

We all checked our gear as Noah parked down the block. In addition to all the guns, we were all fitted with in-ear comms. From a distance, the house in question was dark and looked completely unassuming. I signaled to Noah that I would fall behind as we approached, the only sound the barely detectable whisper of our boots over the grass.

"Front door is locked." Oskar's soft murmur came over the comms.

A few seconds later, we heard Rafe confirm that the back door was open.

Noah pointed at Matthias and Oskar to remain at the front and then headed for the back, with me following right behind. There were no lights on, but we all had excellent night vision. I could easily make out the shape of Noah right in front of me, and then once we turned a corner in the house, Rafe ahead of him.

Suddenly, we heard movement to our right, and we all swung our weapons in that direction.

"Hands up!" Rafe commanded.

There were screams, and I immediately recognized JJ's voice.

"JJ?" I asked, hoping that she was safe.

"Oh my god! It's you!" JJ dropped what she was holding. "I'm so glad you're here. We didn't know what to do!"

I heard Noah's voice over the comms letting Oskar and Matthias know it was safe to come in. But the only thing I could focus on was what JJ had been holding. As soon as she stepped back, I could see what it was.

David West's arm.

"Holy shit. Is that–" Rafe stared incredulously.

"David? Yes, he's dead. I shot him." JJ huffed. "We were trying to figure out how to get him out of here."

"I thought we could wheel him out in this suitcase," Lucia continued, gesturing to an oversize brown suitcase next to her. "But it turns out he's way heavier than he looks. So it's a good thing you guys are here. This part sucks."

Rafe burst into laughter and glanced over at Noah. "This is what you've done to my sister? I raised a perfect angel, and now she's hiding dead bodies?"

Noah snickered. "She's a DeMarco. What the hell do you expect?"

"Um, hello?" Lucia screeched. "Dead guy at two o'clock. Are you guys going to help us get rid of this or what? Because I need to get home and feed the baby. Nonna will be expecting to hear from us soon."

JJ grinned. "That's right. And I'm sure she'll want to know her plan went off perfectly."

"Her plan?" Rafe repeated.

"Of course. Nonna is quite the mastermind." JJ seemed to take great pleasure in watching our shocked expressions. "Men always think they have the women in their lives figured out. Well, no one is ever going to put me in a box."

Mindful of the dead body on the floor, I pulled her closer and kissed her forehead. There wasn't a single doubt in my mind that JJ would be just as gutsy as Nonna in her older years. More than anything, I hoped to be causing trouble right beside her.

"Take me home, please," she whispered.

"You got it, baby." I pulled her close. "After this stunt you'll be lucky if I ever let you out of the bed again. At least I know you're safe there."

JJ smiled and her thoughts were telegraphed as if she said them aloud.

If I thought she would be safe in bed, I was kidding myself. She would cause just as much trouble in the bedroom as she did everywhere else.

———

Matthias

I WATCHED EVERYONE LEAVE. JJ was being unusually docile as she allowed Jonas to lead her out the door. I overheard something about never letting her out of bed again, which I ignored. No more mental images of those two were needed.

Some of the things I'd overheard lately could never be forgotten. It was a wonder I could look anybody I lived with in the face these days.

Speaking of PDA, my boss was currently trying to be stern with his wife, while Lucia was pretending to listen. The smile on her face pretty much said 'I'll play nice for a while but in the end, I do what I want.'

As sweet as she was, Lucia was surprisingly headstrong. Oh, she'd keep a smile on her face the whole time, but no man controlled her. It was one of the things I had always liked about her.

A woman like that would fight by your side through anything.

"Sorry to put you on cleanup duty, Matthias."

Noah actually did look apologetic, not something he did often. But it was no real secret that Noah and the others tried to shield me from anything too grim.

I cringed. I hated that anyone knew so much about me, about

the things I'd done. It was weird knowing that they were all watching, expecting me to go off the rails if I was exposed to anything too dark.

I didn't need to be coddled. I pulled my weight. Always had. Probably more than my fair share.

"It's all good, guv. You know I can handle things."

Noah smiled at the slang term for boss. He'd always found the British way of speaking amusing. I loved to remind him that Yankee slang was just as strange.

"Good. Call me as soon as the ORUS man comes through." Noah saluted as he led Lucia out.

I didn't let out a breath until the door closed behind them. Then I turned to survey the grim scene left behind in the house. With my training, I could see exactly how things had played out.

Chamaeleon on the ground, maybe on his knees? JJ must have been standing over him to get that angle. I knelt slightly to examine the bullet wound in the former David West's forehead.

Dimly, I was aware that this was a little twisted. Some of the most cold-blooded agents I'd worked with had been a little squeamish about getting close to the dead, but it had never bothered me. Hell, the hard part was over at that point. It was actually rather fascinating, how someone could be alive in this world one second and then gone the next.

I supposed it was a by-product of seeing so much death in my life that it fascinated me so.

Once I heard the Jeep pull away, I pulled out my phone to wait. Once Noah made contact with the head of ORUS, they'd be sending a cleaner out. It wasn't exactly glamorous work, but someone needed to be here to oversee things and make sure nothing was missed. We couldn't afford any aspect of ORUS's fuckup to blow back on us later.

The girls presence added another layer of complication to things, because they didn't have the training not to leave forensic evidence behind. After the grim work was done, I would go over every inch of the place until there was no sign that JJ or Lucia had been there.

That anyone had been there.

I killed an hour playing a puzzle game on my phone before I got the message from Noah that ORUS was sending someone. Another hour went by before I heard someone at the front door. Reflex had my gun in my hand before I could even blink. The man who stepped through the door was unfamiliar but completely recognizable. Hair shorn close, non-descript clothes, blank eyes.

I figured I was probably just as predictable.

"You're the cleaner?"

The man nodded once and turned his arm slowly to reveal his wrist. The small pattern of dots revealed were similar to the ones that I still sported, as did Noah and Rafe. The symbol of a grim brotherhood.

"Good. Let's get started. There's a lot of blood and I want a completely clean sweep of this place."

The other man nodded. "This is going to take a while."

I pushed up my sleeves, ready to get to work. I didn't mind if it took all night if it meant JJ and Lucia were protected. It was some-thing I could give back to the people who had become my family.

They thought I was standoffish and distant, but if they only knew where I'd started... Emotionally, I had given them the very best I was capable of giving.

Whatever was left of my heart was theirs, even if they didn't know it.

CHAPTER THIRTY-NINE

Jessica

As soon as we arrived home and stepped off the elevator, Jonas wrapped his arms around me. "Jesus Christ do you know how happy I am to have you home safe? I was too terrified to believe it in the car. But with you home, it's more real now."

I snuggled into Jonas's embrace. "Let me guess, you're not letting me out of your sight for a while?"

"Woman, can you really blame me? I mean you girls fucking locked Ryan in the panic room."

"Well, it's not like he was gonna let us go willingly. He would've called you and you would've talked us out of it and said you had it handled. But you had the wrong location. None of you were listening."

"Okay, okay I hear you. Next time let's have a code word for when I'm being an idiot and not listening and you're about to do something stupid to get my attention."

"It wasn't *completely* stupid. We had a weapon."

Jonas shuddered. I could feel the shiver run through his body.

"I hate to think of what would have happened if he'd have

gotten a hold of it. If Lucia hadn't been there. All these horrible things were running through my head a million times today. Do you understand that?"

I nodded. "Yeah, I understand. And I'm sorry."

"I know. Listen, let's do first things first."

I cocked my head. "Seriously, you want to have sex now?"

He stared at me for a long moment. And then chuckled. "Yes, actually. But that's not what I meant."

Behind us, there was a giggle. Noah had his arms wrapped around Lucia and lifted his gaze and met Jonas's. "Listen, I need to have a conversation with my wife about her antics today. We'll need about an hour. Make sure Nonna's okay with the baby, and get Delaney out of the panic room would you? Matthias reset it already but he said you'd have to enter the code from the outside to get him out."

"Yeah, Delaney. That was actually my first stop."

Noah blinked at us like he was crazy. "Yeah, okay. But uh, Lucia is my first stop."

Lucia rolled her eyes and swatted him on the arm before following her husband as he tugged her down the hall into his office. I would've loved for that to be my first stop. But honestly, I was still reeling and shaking, and didn't know what I felt or how I should be feeling.

All I felt right now was numb and hollow. And God, I just wanted to collapse. I'd killed a man today. Shot him dead. Several times.

But he was going to kill Lucia if you hadn't.

I might act tough, but that shell I put up for the world to see, didn't mean I didn't care. It didn't mean I wasn't affected by things.

Jonas pulled me close. "Let's get you in the shower, I'll deal with Delaney. Then I'll call Oskar and Dylan and have them escort Nonna home."

I shook my head. "No. I need to let out Ryan. I feel like we owe him one."

Jonas studied me carefully. "Are you okay?"

"Yes. No. I have no idea."

Jonas nodded. "I know it couldn't have been easy doing what you did today. I know how terrifying it must have been."

"That's just the thing, Jonas. When I saw him hurting my friend, I didn't even think twice. I might have emptied the whole clip into him at the end there. I just kept shooting."

"You reacted to save your friend. That's what you're supposed to do."

"I know. But I also reacted to save myself."

"That is a good thing. Because for once, you thought about survival. I'm proud of you."

He took my hand and pulled me down the hall into Noah and Lucia's room until we stood in front of the panic room. Then he carefully pushed the combo into the cracked keypad.

When the door unlatched, Delaney was hanging by his hands in the doorjamb, looking pissed and ready to kill someone. "Are you fucking serious right now? We will never speak of this again, do you understand?"

I opened my mouth to apologize. I really meant to. But instead, what came out was, "What's the matter Delaney afraid of the dark? Or are you pissed off that three little women outsmarted you?"

Delaney opened his mouth and then snapped it shut. "I was *worried* because I was on Isabella duty. I don't think having two men on her and Nonna is enough."

I winced. "I am sorry. But I knew you would've stopped us."

"Damn straight I would've stopped you. You could've been killed. You could've gotten Lucia killed. And then Noah would have killed us all."

I nodded. "I know it was stupid. But I had to do something. I'm so sorry that you got caught up in it."

It took him several beats, but then he nodded.

Within fifteen minutes, Dylan and Oskar were back with Nonna and Isabella. Nonna, for her role in all this, acted as if everything was fine. She just smiled and gave me a kiss on the cheek.

"Oh, JJ. There you are. We had a lovely walk out in the park, didn't we boys?"

Both Dylan and Oskar looked a little worse for wear. As if Nonna'd had them running for their lives. I would have to ask her later exactly what she'd done to them.

Either way, everyone looked safe and happy.

Isabella must have known she was home though, because the moment the stroller came to a stop she let out a tiny wail, which of course drew her parents out of the office. Both of them had bed hair and Lucia had that satisfied, smug look on her face that screamed 'Hey, I just had sex with my husband.'

"Oh my, sweetheart. Mama's here."

With Isabella in Lucia's arms, I let my head drop to Jonas's shoulder for just a moment. Lucia had saved my life today.

And you saved hers.

"Can a godmother get a kiss too? I know you're hungry little one. But I just want one little baby kiss." I kissed my goddaughter and was never more grateful for the family that I had.

Noah inclined his head for the guys to follow him to the conference room. "Hey guys, let's get this over with and call Ian."

Jonas followed, but he grumbled. "I can't believe we're still going to deal with that guy."

Noah was philosophical about it. "Look, we're not necessarily going to be friends, but we don't need to be enemies. Besides, now he owes us. And I've a feeling with this bunch we'll be collecting on that favor sometime soon."

———

Matthias

I HAD to get the hell out of the penthouse. Away from all the happy couples. It was too much. I left without a word, but Oskar saw me going.

When the German gave me a quizzical glance, I just ignored him. After everything that had happened in the last couple of days, I was still feeling raw. The monster inside me was too close to the surface, and I needed to take the beast out for a walk away from the people I cared about.

I needed to put my past to bed.

Something happened to me at that house. The moment my hands had grasped those blades, I'd started to enjoy the fight. It was one thing to go hand-to-hand combat, it was another thing to actually use my weapon of choice.

Knives were personal. And I'd enjoyed it a little too much. Now stuffing the monster back inside was a little more difficult to do. Especially since he'd been out to play in spectacular fashion.

I followed the directions to the letter. I took the train downtown to the meet point, across the street from Club Throb. In the small neighborhood park I took the bench facing the club and waited silently for the rest of my party to show up.

There was no running away now.

I felt more than heard when the bench behind me was occupied. "I told you your past was coming for you. But it's here. I've had a sighting."

I sighed. "Do they know where to find me?"

"Not sure. But given that your boss is so tight with Orion, it might only be a matter of time. They knew where to start looking. So I'm not sure how much time you've got."

"Well, if they come looking, they're going to find trouble."

"Are you going to tell them?"

That was something I'd thought about long and hard. What did I tell Noah?

I'd never really disclosed all of my past, just given him bits and pieces that were enough to form his own version of the story. Although what Noah knew already was the stuff of nightmares.

But real life was so much worse. Bad enough to keep the devil himself awake.

Before I'd come into ORUS, I'd been barely human. A real-life Dr. Jekyll and Mr. Hyde. Orion had flipped a switch inside me that made everything go from terrible to monstrous.

"I'm not telling them anything. It's my mess. My past. I want to protect them as long as I can."

"Matthias, if your old family is looking for you, then you probably need to warn Leo at the very least."

"Not going to happen."

"Mate, if you're not gonna warn them, there's not much I can do to help you."

I ground my teeth. "If anyone comes knocking at my door, they're not going to be happy about it."

"If you ever need me…"

"I won't."

We sat in silence for a while, watching the movements of the club-goers across the street with a growing sense of unease. My past was catching up to me, and there was nowhere left to run.

The other man finally looked over. "I feel like I need to do something. I owe you my life."

I stood, already done with the conversation. "You've done enough. Debt is paid. You come knocking on my door again, and I'm going to assume that you're with them. And we both know what I do to enemies."

CHAPTER FORTY

Jessica

"I need you to put this on."

I leaned against the SUV and stared at Jonas. "You know I'm not into bondage."

His smile was wolfish. "Now, let's not tell lies. You're in for a little blindfold fun, and you liked it when I restrained you that one time."

I flushed. Which, considering the things we'd done together, was slightly ridiculous. "Okay, you might have a point there. But I'm still not wearing a blindfold."

"Come on, it's a surprise. I thought you loved surprises."

I let my gaze slide down the straining cotton of his T-shirt, down his taut, chiseled abs, and then to his belt. I very deliberately gave him a devious smile. "I like surprises."

He groaned and then planted his hands on either side of my shoulders, barricading me against the SUV.

"Woman, we just made it out of the penthouse. I would actually like to go forward with the surprise. But if you keep looking at me like that, we won't leave. I'll drag you back upstairs to our room, and do all sorts of naughty things to you. And then our surprise will be delayed. We'll probably get there at night, and you won't be able to see it properly."

"You say that like it's a bad thing. Besides, maybe I'll distract you and you'll forget all about this surprise that requires me to wear a blindfold."

He bent and nuzzled my neck, and I could feel myself melting. He was too good at that.

Far too good.

Matter of fact, if he kept that up, I would pretty much give him anything he wanted.

Oh, the possibilities.

"I will not be persuaded by kisses."

"Come on. I'm just asking to give you a surprise. Let me give you something. You trust me don't you?"

His lips curled against my skin. I could do this. Give him a little leeway and let him think he had the upper hand. Because, let's face it, we both knew I had the upper hand.

I had the boobs. And the ass. Boobs and ass trumped everything when it came to men and women.

"Okay," I said finally. "You can blindfold me."

He immediately pulled back and flashed a boyish grin. "Really? That was way too easy. I anticipated a lot more convincing. You know, driving you to the brink of orgasm, refusing to let you come until you said you'd let me blindfold you, and then keeping you on the verge of coming until we got to your surprise."

I narrowed my gaze at him. He knew what he was doing. His words alone were enough to make me hot. "I've been teaching you too much."

"Hey, I'm still trying to pay you back for that little trip to Vegas a month ago."

I had to smile at that. I had worked with the guys to secure a private jet so we could spend a couple of nights in Vegas. On the plane ride there, I'd handcuffed him to his seat and then given him a private lap dance and tortured him until he pretty much begged me to come.

"You know what? You enjoyed every moment of that."

His gaze narrowed, and the flash of heat was instant. God I really did want to drag him upstairs. Fine, so maybe I was just as susceptible to distraction as he was.

"Maybe."

"Maybe I take you upstairs and remind you."

He shook his head. "Too late now. You've already agreed to let me blindfold you. Turn around."

"You want my hands on the car. Are you going to arrest me officer?"

As I turned around, he groaned low. "You are pretty much playing to every single dirty fantasy I've ever had about arresting a hot woman."

"You want to play cops and robbers?" I added a seductive note to my voice. Behind me Jonas just chuckled as he delicately placed the blindfold over my eyes and tied a knot securely at the back of my head.

When I blinked, I realized I could still see some light. So not total darkness. Besides, he was right. I might fight him on things like this, but when it came down to it, I trusted him. I knew that he would never hurt me. And he would annihilate anyone else who tried. He'd already proven that.

"Naughty robbers get spankings, JJ."

"Oh, you're scaring me now, Officer Castillo," she said.

His voice was low and husky with just a hint of bite. "That's Detective Castillo to you."

I giggled "Oh, so sorry, *Detective* Castillo. What is it that you want me to do?" I deliberately swung my hips, rubbing my ass against his erection.

"Fuck, JJ. We're on the street. If you don't stop that, you'll be face down in the backseat of the SUV, and I'll be dragging those shorts over that sassy ass of yours. So behave." With that he swatted my bottom.

"Damn it, Jonas."

His chuckle was low and seductive as he took my hand and gingerly led me around the car then settled me in the passenger seat.

"Behave."

Once he was in the driver's seat I turned to him. "Just where are we going? Am I even dressed appropriately for this adventure?"

"Not to worry. I had Lucia pack your bag."

I frowned. "Lucia? She helped you with this?"

Jonas laughed and his voice washed over me like warm chocolate. "Yep. Everyone did, even your ball buster of a boss. You have a whole week off from work."

"What? You really can't do that. I have things I need to —"

Jonas squeezed my hand. "I know you have things you need to do. But we're taking one week. Just us. Besides, don't you want me all to yourself? Imagine the things you could do to me with a blindfold and handcuffs?"

I opened my mouth then snapped it shut. "You do have a point."

"Somehow I thought you'd see it my way," he chuckled.

Wherever he was taking me, it took forever to get there. We were in the car a solid hour and a half. Of course it was Jonas, so it wasn't like we had nothing to talk about.

We made a list of movies to see over the next few months, where to take Isabella for our next outing. Easy stuff. The kind of stuff I never thought I'd be able to share with anyone. But I had it now. And my life was downright perfect. I couldn't have asked for anything better.

Of course, there was a part of me that was still afraid I didn't deserve this.

That I didn't deserve *him*.

No. Stop it. No more self-defeating thoughts. You deserve all the happiness in the world.

I had to get used to believing it. With Jonas by my side, I was almost there.

He finally pulled the car over and squeezed my hand. "We're here, baby."

"Can I remove this now?"

"Was it that terrible? I mean, I've never brought anyone to my secret lair where I plan to chain you up and never let you go. But thanks for coming willingly."

I laughed. "As long as you promise to have your way with me every second of the day, I probably won't complain too much."

His chuckle was low as he reached over and undid the knot. "That can be arranged."

When the blindfold was off I blinked, trying to let my eyes adjust to the light. When I looked out the window, all I saw was green. We were in the woods. In front of us was a large rustic-looking cabin.

"Where are we?"

Jonas gave me a grin. "Somewhere no one will bother us. They don't have cell reception out here. Not to worry," he pulled a black bag from the backseat. "I have satellite phones in case of emergency. Out here, it's just you and me. For a whole week."

Oh wow, he'd done this for me. Except, *the woods?*

I wasn't really a rustic kind of girl. I was more *glamping* than camping. But still, I did love the sweetness of the gesture. He wanted uninterrupted time with me. And we were going to get it. For a whole week.

With no cell phone.

Or TMZ.

But I would survive it. Because I had Jonas, and honestly, we could be as naked as we wanted anywhere we wanted. So that was definitely a bonus.

"This is beautiful. You didn't have to do this."

"Yes. I did. Everything has been kind of a blur since we got together. I wanted to slow down, so I can show you how much I love you."

And how the hell was I supposed to not completely fall in love with him all over again?

Jonas climbed out of the car, speeding around to my side to open the door for me. "Come on. Let's have a look inside."

"Do you want to grab the bags first?"

He shook his head. "Nope. I've had a hard on since we left the city. So if you don't mind, I want to make love first. And then I can get the bags."

He practically dragged me to the front door of the cabin before unlocking it. I had no choice but to follow behind. When he opened the door, I gasped in surprise.

While the outside and the surroundings were completely rustic and secluded, the inside was utterly modern. Rustic-cabin modern, with glass, granite and stone.

"Oh my God."

Jonas chuckled. "Woman, you think I don't know you? You'll still be able to catch up on all your shows. I'll even marathon watch *The Bachelorette* with you. But if you tell Oskar that I enjoy it, I may have to kill you."

I laughed, doing a little happy swirl as my boots clicked on the hardwood floor. "Jonas. It's gorgeous."

"You like it?"

I nodded. "I was a little worried that you were going to have me chopping wood and stuff, but this is — *Oh my God* look at the fireplace."

"Yep. I had the whole place remodeled around the fireplace."

I whirled around to meet his gaze. "What do you mean you had this place remodeled?"

"Oh you know, when I knew I couldn't stop touching you, I figured we might need a place to get away. So I started having my contractor bring it up to your standards."

I rapidly swiped tears away. "You did this for me?"

He nodded. "Of course. I would do anything for you. I love you."

The warmth that spread through my chest was uncontainable. I'd never been this happy in my life.

"Well, Mr. Castillo, I would like to show you my gratitude. But first, we need that blindfold."

———

I LOVED the fireplace so much that after a full tour, Jonas insisted we spend the day curled up on the couch in front of it. He'd brought along sandwiches and a bottle of wine, so we snuggled before a crackling fire, eating and just relaxing.

To anyone else, it might not seem like a huge deal but to me, this was the culmination of a lifelong dream. Something I'd always hoped for but never dared to dream could be possible for a mouthy blonde from Queens.

Contentment.

"What are you thinking about?" Jonas murmured, nuzzling my cheek. "I've gone to a lot of trouble to put a smile on your face and I don't want anything ruining that."

I reached up to caress his face. His beard was just starting to grow in so he had that sexy scruff I absolutely loved. He was so handsome, my guy.

"You. This. How I never thought this would happen to me," I answered finally.

"What? Having your own house?" Jonas raised his eyebrows.

"You're smart and driven, JJ. I know that you would have been a homeowner eventually if you wanted to be."

I sat up slightly. "No, not that part. I mean, yes, the house was part of the dream. But not the most important part. It was about this," I gestured between us. "I had this whole picture in my head of what my dream life would be."

"Tell me," Jonas whispered.

I closed my eyes. "I used to imagine living in a cute little house in a quiet community. Where all the neighbors know each other and say hello while getting their mail or pruning the rosebushes. I would have a big kitchen and could cook those crazy huge meals like Nonna DeMarco always does and invite lots of people. Especially the ones with no family of their own."

"That sounds beautiful, baby. Why would you think you couldn't have those things?"

I leaned forward and kissed him. "Because I haven't gotten to the most important part yet. My favorite part of the dream was when I'd imagine who I was coming home to. A man who was strong, funny, and not afraid to call me out on my shit. The kind of man that I respected and loved. Someone I loved so much that I wanted my children to be just like him. A perfect blend of the two of us."

A slow smile took over Jonas's face. "Children, huh? So there were children in this dream? How many are we talking?"

I chuckled. "A few. Honestly, it didn't even matter. I just wanted someone to love. Whether it's one, two, or even six, I'd be happy."

"Six?" Jonas repeated with alarm.

I had to chuckle at the look on his face. "I'm just saying. However many I had, I would count myself as lucky. I never wanted to admit it, but I've always wanted to be a mom. And I would be a good mom. I wouldn't try to force my kids to be more like me. I would love them exactly as they are."

He grinned. "You would be a great mom. I have no doubts. Fierce and willing to shoot and stuff in a suitcase anyone who threatened them."

I laughed. "You're never going to let that go are you?"

"Never. I've never been so damn mad and so damn proud at the same time." He glanced over at me with a sly smile. "So, this perfect life you used to imagine, is that still what you want?"

I leaned back and stared into the flames. "Yes," I whispered. "More than anything."

Jonas carefully slipped his arm out from beneath my head and then knelt on the carpet at my feet. "Good. Because I want to be that guy in your dream. The one you come home to every day, the one who makes you smile, and the one who loves you forever. I want to have those six kids and wave at our neighbors together."

I could barely speak. "Oh my god. Jonas!"

He wiped away a tear from my cheek. "I've finally taken you off guard, I see. I plan to do that a lot for the next fifty years."

I threw my arms around his neck. "You did! I can't believe you want that. Are you sure you're ready to take me on?"

Then his hand came from behind his back holding a ring, a simple round diamond on a gold band.

I gasped. "You have a ring? I thought you were just saying someday."

"No. I'm saying right now. Let's get married and raise hell together. I can't wait to get our life together started." He sobered, his expression more serious than any I'd ever seen him wear. "I want to give you everything, Jessica Jones. Especially my last name. Will you marry me?"

"Yes!" I squealed and pulled him close. He kissed me softly, and I knew I'd never been happier than this. But of course, I couldn't resist messing with him a little.

"But about this last name business, how about you take my last name? This is a new millennium after all."

He threw his head back and laughed. "We can hyphenate both of our names, Miss Ballbuster. How does that sound?"

I grabbed him by the front of his shirt and kissed him.

"It sounds like a dream."

———

THANK you for reading *Broken Ties*. Did you miss Noah & Lucia's story?

The last thing I promised my best friend was to protect his little sister. But Lucia DeMarco hates me. And if she discovers what I've been hiding, I'll lose her forever. Start reading Broken Trust!

NEED MORE BLAKE SECURITY? Find out what bonus material is available at malonesquared.com/brokentrust

ABOUT THE AUTHORS

M. MALONE is a RITA® Award winner and a NYT & USA Today Bestselling author of completely inappropriate romantic comedy. She lives with her husband and their two sons in the picturesque mountains of Northern Virginia even though she is afraid of insects, birds, butterflies and other humans.

She also holds a Master's degree in Business from a prestigious college that would no doubt be scandalized at how she's using her expensive education. **mmalonebooks.com**

USA Today Bestselling Author, **NANA MALONE**'s love of all things romance and adventure started with a tattered romantic suspense she borrowed from her cousin on a sultry summer afternoon in Ghana at a precocious thirteen. She's been in love with kick butt heroines ever since.

With her overactive imagination, and channeling her inner Buffy, it was only a matter a time before she created her own characters. Waiting for her chance at a job as a ninja assassin, Nana, meantime works out her drama, passion and sass with fictional characters every bit as sassy and kick butt as she thinks she is. **nanamalone.com**

One More Chance

Want to read one of my romantic comedies for free?

Join my VIP list at mmalonebooks.com

<u>**Royals United**</u>

Royal Tease

Teasing the Princess

<u>**Royal Elite**</u>

The Heiress Duet

Protecting the Heiress

Tempting the Heiress

The Prince Duet

Return of the Prince

To Love a Prince

The Bodyguard Duet

Bodyguard to the Billionaire

The Billionaire's Secret

<u>**London Royals**</u>

London Royal Duet

London Royal

London Soul

Playboy Royal Duet

Royal Playboy

Playboy's Heart

London Lords

<u>***See No Evil***</u>

Big Ben

The Benefactor

For Her Benefit

<u>***Hear No Evil***</u>

East End

East Bound

Fall of East

To Catch a Thief

<u>***Speak No Evil***</u>

London Bridge

Bridge of Lies

Broken Bridge

The Donovans Series

<u>*Come Home Again (Nate & Delilah)*</u>

<u>*Love Reality (Ryan & Mia)*</u>

<u>*Race For Love (Derek & Kisima)*</u>

<u>*Love in Plain Sight (Dylan and Serafina)*</u>

<u>*Eye of the Beholder – (Logan & Jezzie)*</u>

<u>*Love Struck (Zephyr & Malia)*</u>

London Billionaires Standalones

Mr. Trouble (Jarred & Kinsley)

Mr. Big (Zach & Emma)

Mr. Dirty(Nathan & Sophie)

The Player

Bryce

Dax

Echo

Fox

Ransom

Gage

The In Stilettos Series

Sexy in Stilettos (Alec & Jaya)

Sultry in Stilettos (Beckett & Ricca)

Sassy in Stilettos (Caleb & Micha)

Strollers & Stilettos (Alec & Jaya & Alexa)

Seductive in Stilettos (Shane & Tristia)

Stunning in Stilettos (Bryan & Kyra)

~~~

In Stilettos Spin off

Tempting in Stilettos (Serena & Tyson)

Teasing in Stilettos (Cara & Tate)

Tantalizing in Stilettos (Jaggar & Griffin)

Love Match Series

*Game Set Match (Jason & Izzy)

Mismatch (Eli & Jessica)
~~~

Don't want to miss a single release?

Sign up at http://nanamaloneromance.net

www.ingramcontent.com/pod-product-compliance
Lightning Source LLC
Chambersburg PA
CBHW031303210726
48287CB00005B/1401